Queen of the Cephalopods

ROGER WYSE

Roger Wyse (signature)

YELLOW BOOK ROAD PUBLICATIONS

A Yellow Book Road Book
Copyright © 2000 by Roger Wyse

All rights reserved. This book, in whole or in part, may not be reproduced or transmitted in any form or by any means, electronic or mechanical, including photocopying, recording, PDF format, or by any information storage system, without the express written consent of the Publisher. For information, contact the publisher at YellowBookRoad.com. Or send e-mail to books@yellowbookroad.com.

The Yellow Book Road worldwide website address is www.YellowBookRoad.com.

Sale of this book without a front cover may be unauthorized. If this book is coverless, it may have been reported to the publisher as "unsold or destroyed" and neither the author nor the publisher have received payment for it.

Printed in the United States of America
Published simultaneously worldwide
November, 2000

ISBN: 0-9706132-0-2

*For Patricia and Joseph,
Ed, Joe and Sherry*

Queen of the Cephalopods

Prologue

She lay in a corner of the cave, adhering to a large rock.

Four arms were curled under her, exiting the rear of her mantle, stretching out unevenly along the ocean bottom. Four more were folded haphazardly in front—arms that could cradle her offspring in a loving embrace or pop the head off a man like a cork off a champagne bottle, if need be.

Behind the arms was a head, a monstrously large, balloon-shaped head. But it was not filled with helium or air. It was not filled with water, save the millions of molecules filtering through the gills. Instead it was filled with the supple intelligence of a unique species, a missing link between cephalopod cousins.

Together, the head and arms created a massive continent of cephalopod flesh that could fill the cave, or dissolve into the corner, if need be.

But there was no need for that now.

She rested on the rock, watching, waiting, wondering when the white cylindrical stalks above her head would release their inhabitants.

Like the argonaut, the female offspring of her species would be 20 to 50 times larger than the males. And like the octopods, they would show no vestiges of the exoskeleton encasing the head. They had lost the argonaut helmet but gained its size—and then some.

Unlike her cousins, though, she would live to see her offspring, and she would live to have more. There would be just one or two females at birth; the others would be males. And unlike her cousins—or any other cephalopods she knew—the offspring would not disperse. They would form a colony around her.

A colony whose sole purpose would be to protect, feed, and defend the queen.

As she contemplated these things, her eyes were mere yellow slits shading the sun filtering in. Time for sleep. In her world, night was day. Day was night. Unlike the world of men.

Mostly she avoided man, for she knew that man was evil, man was bad. A recent encounter with a female diver, though, had led her to question her beliefs.

But she did not wish to think of man right now, and she did not wish to sleep, despite having been up all day. There was too much to do. So she changed into colors more suitable for her work. A dazzling array of chromatophores fired instantaneously, causing a sea-change of color across her mottled skin.

She moved slowly from the rock in a tangled, but oddly coordinated movement of arms. She preferred to move slowly for nature had not endowed her with great speed. When in danger, though, she would point her head and jettison away by sending great streams of water through her funnel. But there was no need for that now.

Her break was over. It was time to get back to work.

One

SHE WAS BRIGHTLY dressed that evening—not in an evening dress, but dressed nonetheless—in pink with white pinstripes lining the breadth of her fifty-foot arms and ten-foot wide mantle. In a long tunnel adorned with white stalks hung like crystal chandeliers, she was busy at work. Her forearms were tidying the floor, while above, her middle arms were cleaning the stalks, bathing them in streams of water bubbles blown from her funnel.

As the bubbles rushed by, she observed with great satisfaction the dizzying pace of life and limb. With her rear arms, she surveyed the next bunch of white stalks, staying one step ahead of the cleaning operation. Delicately, two small, armtip probes checked the condition of the gelatinous ovals contained within the stalks and moved on to the next site. Grateful that many arms make light work, she moved a few more times and then exited the tunnel into a large cave.

This was her home. She had searched long and hard to find it. She knew every inch of it, and every inch was used, including the ceilings and floors, the nooks and crannies.

The entrance was narrow, about several arms wide. At first it had been a struggle for her to get in, but after a while she had learned the proper twists and turns to get in and out rather quickly, as if she were some undersea carnival contortionist.

Inside the cave, there was room for a good deal of movement. At one end was a high ledge that was the doorstep to a giant cavity stretching deep into the rock. Shells of every imaginable shape and size were stacked within along with the exoskeletons of her crustacean prey. At the other end was her dinner table. Consisting of a large, angular rock with a smooth plateau at its center, it was never set but was always ready for meals. Strewn all around the rock were bits and pieces of crab shells, lobster shells, and other scraps.

At the back of the cave was the tunnel, which split into two long and winding branches leading to the open sea. She returned there for a moment to inspect her work, marveling at the hundreds of white stalks suspended from the ceiling, gently swaying in the warm ocean current. They appeared to be in fine shape, and she was satisfied with their progress.

By now, the daylight water had dimmed a few shades darker; it was nearly dusk. She had toiled for too long. She was tired and hungry. And not a single crab had wandered in to investigate the chemical enticements she was secreting or the tasty bits of vegetation she was cultivating. It had been many days and nothing had worked. She would have to go out and look for food, though she felt uneasy about doing so. Before leaving, she peered behind a small rock in the corner, blew a stream of water from her funnel, and slipped out through the entrance of her cavernous home.

Outside she looked for sharks, and seeing none, moved her huge but nimble body along the ocean floor in a coordinated movement of seemingly tangled arms to propel her along.

Soon she heard the sounds of a boat. This concerned her, but she did not retreat to the safety of her home. From time to time, boats cruised these waters unaware of her, and there was no reason to believe that this time would be any different.

Two

Captain Gregory looked out from the bow of his boat to the jut of land ahead called No Man's Land, a series of rock formations about 50 miles off the coast of Maine. It had been a long trip. The usually reliable Sea Horse had lost power, and they had been delayed most of the day. Now that they were under way again, Captain Gregory was eager to check his traps. He had a feeling that he would catch something and when he had that feeling, he was seldom wrong.

Today's quarry was a member of the mollusk family, though not just any mollusk. Starfish, cuttlefish, squid, clams—none of these would do. Captain Gregory hoped to catch a rare species of octopus, a female, preferably, and its eggs, commodities that would fetch tremendous prices in the Asian fish markets. He'd check the traps first, then search the moss-green rocks, the labyrinthine caves, and the sea floor. Then he'd search for the eggs, cave by cave, rock by rock, cranny by cranny, if need be.

Captain Gregory was no stranger to this kind of search, or any other. He was captivated by it. He was inspired by it. He thrived on it. His whole life had been a series of treasure hunts—first to command a submarine, next to find a kindred spirit, and then to net the perfect catch.

A commission in the Navy had seemed all but certain, but had proven to be elusive. He had graduated from the Naval academy with honors. He had taken on the most difficult and demanding tours of duty. He had played the game the way it was supposed to be played and had risen through the ranks. Then at the pinnacle of his career, he'd been promoted to captain, only to have his submarine mothballed before she ever put out to sea.

While the Navy had proven fickle, so too, had his luck with women. And this, more than anything else was at the root of his restlessness. The only woman who'd ever understood, ever known, ever loved him, was a marine artist from Veracruz. Maria Alvarez understood his dreams. She knew his disappointments. And she loved him for the man he was, not the man he could have been.

It was as if she could read his mind, or rather, paint his mind. Her paintings were lovingly caressed with splashes of turquoise on white canvas, like waves upon the sand. There were grand murals of humpback whales in the dimly lit ocean nudging their calves up for their first breath. Millions of thimble jellyfish congregating en masse in a water color fresco. And in oil, a whale shark floating like a great clump of speckled seaweed in a vast ocean.

On holiday in her home town, they'd been scuba diving in the Sea of Cortez. She'd been looking for a new subject. He'd been trying his hand at spear fishing. When the fishermen's boats arrived, they had not been too concerned. After all, it was a popular fishing spot. What they didn't know was that the fishermen were jigging for squid—big squid.

When the first Humboldt had come, Captain Gregory had motioned to Maria to get back to the boat. He knew that they could be unpredictable. But Maria wanted to take pictures. She'd found her new subject. Several clicks later, she'd found its companion.

Several boats had begun trolling above them and Captain Gregory had noticed something flash near the surface. He went up to investigate and saw the spoonlike jigs spinning near the surface. He knew what that meant.

Sensing danger, he immediately dove to find Maria. But he was too late. By the time he had reached her, he had to turn away. She was already gone—enveloped in a salmon-colored cloud of arms, tentacles, and hooks. The squid were in a feeding frenzy. They were feeding on her, and they were feeding on each other.

For the moment, Captain Gregory had just drifted in the ocean currents, motionless, dumbfounded, suspended from reality. But soon his need to survive had reemerged, and he had headed back to the boat slowly.

Captain Gregory stared wistfully at the sea, recalling the major events of his life. His search for a kindred spirit like Maria had remained elusive; his ambition for a commission in the Navy, torpedoed. These two treasures were long buried at sea as far as he was concerned.

The only treasure left was the perfect catch. The one catch that would say that his life had been worth something. That he had achieved something noteworthy. That his efforts had not been in vain. This treasure was the only treasure worth fighting for now. And he had dedicated every fiber of his being to its pursuit.

As he looked ahead at the large rocks in the distance just taking shape in the early evening light, he felt a presence. The salt air, the sunset, the sea—these permeated his being as surely as water moved through his body by osmosis. But it was not the salt air he felt, though it invigorated him. It was not the awesome majesty of the sun setting in the sea, though its bright red glare dazzled him. No, it was the hope that today he might trap the perfect catch that filled his spirit like a brisk wind in a main sail. Somewhere in the depths, in the sea, was the perfect catch. And in the sea there was hope, promise, and the future—his future.

As the sea pitched and heaved in liquid rhythm, these thoughts kept bubbling to the surface. He took out his binoculars, straining to see the buoys in the distance. It was too early to make them out, though they appeared to be in the exact locations that he had left them. Not a good sign.

As Captain Gregory nervously drummed his fingers on the enormous brass wheel in front of him, Manuel came by with his logbook. "You want to go for a dive if we come up empty?" asked Captain Gregory, hoping Manuel would say yes, knowing he would say no. Manuel did not like deep-sea diving, plain and simple, but Captain Gregory did not relish the idea of diving with his other shiphand, Neil Cranston.

Manuel looked Captain Gregory in the eye, hesitating. "Sure Captain...all right...I guess," he said, shifting his feet. "If you want."

"All right then," said Captain Gregory, pleasantly surprised that Manuel agreed at all.

"But you said you had a feeling we'd catch something, Captain. So why chance it? It's getting late."

"Don't worry Manuel, you're only on the hook if we come up empty."

"Okay then, only if we come up empty," said Manuel as he headed down to the galley to get the meal ready for later on.

Captain Gregory sighed, frustrated by the thought of coming up empty-handed again. At one time, the Gulf of Maine had been teaming with marine life. There were spiny dogfish, sea bass, and Atlantic salmon. There were lobsters stepping lightly on the ocean floor, crabs making homes under every rock, and shrimp hiding in the sea grass. Lurking around rocky ledges and coastal shipwrecks were seven-foot wreckfishes. There were capelins by the thousands and anchovies by the millions.

As he gazed into the water, Captain Gregory could almost hear the two hundred pound sand tigers gulping air and expelling bubbles. He could almost touch the basking sharks filter-feeding on zooplankton while their huge tails swept the water in slow-moving swirls. And he could almost see the scads pushing pebbles into piles on the sea floor where they'd lay their eggs. But that was no more.

Now, the only bubbles were those that escaped from underwater vents. The only swirls were from the ghosts of fish that had come and gone. The only piles of pebbles were from those collected by the ocean currents.

Large and small, all of these species had been part of an ocean fabric torn, ripped apart, and thrown away by the enormous wastefulness of the commercial fleets.

Captain Gregory altered course somewhat and secured the wheel. He left the bridge and headed for the bow, looking over the side of the boat as it cut through the water. Schools of dolphins used to accompany them to No Man's Land, cutting, dodging, and criss-crossing in front of the bow. Lately, they too had abandoned the area. Now Captain Gregory stood alone, a stoic figure in the battle for survival occurring above and below the surface of the ocean. But he was afraid that both fish and fisherman alike were losing the battle. Things were getting so bad that Captain Gregory was unsure how much longer he would fish these waters.

As he stood in front of the bow, he took out his binoculars once more and looked at the buoys. This time he could see them clearly. They were in a straight row, undisturbed. Captain Gregory's heart sank. In a semi-trance, he gazed at the water world below, picturing a sea of cephalopods waiting to be harvested and wishing it were so. Suddenly, his thoughts were interrupted by a long shadow passing over him. Startled, Captain Gregory whirled around to see Neil "the eel" Cranston staring at him from above deck.

Tall, long-necked, thin-lipped, and rather serpentine, Cranston looked like an eel, a giant moray eel. Even his skin was somewhat oily, and his appetite like others in the order Apodes, was insatiable. Unlike his greener cousins, though, his appetite was for taking things—anything that wasn't his. Sometimes that meant mocking Captain Gregory to rob him of his dignity; sometimes that meant stealing tackle from the boat; and sometimes that meant destroying the ocean's precious resources, just for the fun of it. But Captain Gregory had seen enough to know that no matter what form it took, it never quite satisfied the eel's desire for ill-gotten gains.

Cranston cocked his head and extended his neck over the deck rail, as if to get a better look at the buoys in the distance. "You see anything, Captain?" he asked.

"Not a blasted thing," said Captain Gregory, who thought he detected a feint smile on Cranston's lips.

"Oh, that's too bad."

"Yea, I thought for sure one of them would have moved," said Captain Gregory, looking once more through the binoculars to be sure.

"Well, don't give up hope, Captain," said Cranston. "After all, there's fifteen of them down there."

Deep in thought, Captain Gregory did not respond as he studied the traps intently. A few moments later, it dawned on him what Cranston had said. He could feel the anger well up within him, like the buildup of fermented gases in a bottle of old wine left at sea for too long. "Now how did you know that there were fifteen? I never told you that."

Cranston's long neck retracted ever-so-slightly into the recesses of his shirt. "You mentioned it once before."

"I never once mentioned it," said Captain Gregory, the lines on his forehead wrinkling into a fearsome tangle. "Now I'm only going to ask you this one more time. How did you know that there were fifteen?"

Cranston waited, seemingly unruffled by the frontal assault that Captain Gregory was waging. With great suddenness he reextended his neck from the recesses of his shirt, smiled somewhat defiantly, and said, "I know because you used to have fifteen jars on board, and now they're gone. So naturally, I assumed that you set that many."

"I'll bet," said Captain Gregory under his breath, turning away from Cranston. He stared out to sea to calm himself down, but it didn't work. Instead his temper got the best of him and he said, "Now get your sorry ass down here and break up the ice."

Saying nothing, Cranston came down the steps to the bow and started to ready the coolers. He didn't have to say anything. There was a scowl on his face, poison darts in his eyes, and a vengeance in his hands hacking at the ice. Unfazed, Captain Gregory watched him like a sea hawk, all the while jingling his necklace made of the teeth of a rare species of octopus, Octopus Giganticus.

Captain Gregory was more knowledgeable about Octopus Giganticus than most of the experts in the field. At one time, the males of the species were exceedingly plentiful; but because they were small (two-foot arm spans), lived in colonies, and sometimes congregated like squid, they were easy to net and the population dwindled. For some unknown reason, not a single female specimen had ever been trapped or netted. Biologists theorized that at some point in the life cycle the males actually turned into females, like some amphibians, but the theory was never proven.

Captain Gregory knew better. He had fished these waters, dove among its inhabitants, and explored most of its innermost secrets. It was just a gut feeling, but he knew. There had to be females. The perfect catch was out there somewhere, and he was going to find her. He jingled his necklace again, wanting, waiting, wondering when he would find her.

Cranston looked up from the coolers and smiled coolly. "Where'd you get those teeth? They your baby teeth?"

Captain Gregory glared at Cranston. It wasn't that he minded Cranston poking fun at him. He had heard plenty of that in the Navy. It was just that Cranston had no respect for authority. That was reason enough to dislike Cranston, but there was another. He was mean. Instead of stabbing an octopus between the eyes or chopping its head off, he would torment the poor creature, jabbing at it, poking it. Then when he'd had enough, he would bite it between the eyes. Just for the fun of it. Captain Gregory had no tolerance for those who showed no mercy, and he had no patience for the eel, whom he had grown to dislike—no, detest. This would be the last time he hired that spineless excuse for a real fisherman.

Captain Gregory lit his pipe and jingled the teeth of his necklace again, making Cranston wait. "These are from the species Octopus Giganticus. Males used to be plentiful. And the females, well let's just say that they're unusual," he said, winking at Manuel, who came up from the galley.

"What do you mean?" asked Cranston.

Captain Gregory smiled as he lured him in. "She's unlike any other. They call her the red giant. Thirty foot arms and a head the size of a Volkswagen. I've heard tell of the red giant taking a small ship down with her. And of squeezing a man to death and then biting his head off."

"You're joking, old man, right?"

Captain Gregory's eyes glimmered like pale moonlight on dark water. "Oh, she's a tricky one all right, and downright nasty. You heard about the boat that was found on the rocks off No Man's Land last year, didn't 'ya?"

Cranston stopped icing the coolers and leaned forward. "Yea, what about it?"

"It was a beautiful mahogany trolley with a tall masthead, and a club-footed sail. Well, the mast was snapped in half like a twig. She ripped it from its foundation. And bit the sail off the mast and boom. Put a new pattern in the reef cringle. Pretty mangled, I'd say."

"Maybe we should rig the automatic harpoon."

Captain Gregory puffed on his pipe, savoring the moment. He looked Cranston in the eye, laughed loudly, and said, "Got 'ya." Manuel joined in the laughter, but Cranston did not. His face red with anger, he stabbed at the frozen block in the cooler, looking as if he'd like to put the captain on ice even more than a load of fish. Looking up, Captain Gregory realized that they had almost overrun their traps. He turned to Cranston. "We're even now. Go take your post."

Cranston headed toward the helm to take the wheel. They were too far to the starboard side, so he angrily spun the wheel to the left. The ship slowed down as it approached a series of buoys all in a long row.

"Look sharp now," Captain Gregory said to his shiphands. The ship slowed as they came upon the first buoy. He pulled up the first trap. The jar was empty. The boat moved forward, a bit too far to the left. "Not so fast, Cranston. Pull in starboard. I said STARBOARD!" yelled Captain Gregory.

"All right, sir," said Cranston, and then mumbled, "you old squidhead."

"I heard that," said Captain Gregory. "Now quit your horse-assin' around, Cranston." He pulled up the second trap. Nothing. They moved slowly to the next. Nothing again, except a highly agitated crab too small to keep. Captain Gregory scratched his head and ran his fingers along his chin. He was beginning to think that the water around No Man's Land wasn't good for fishing or prospecting anymore.

When the rest of the traps came up empty, Captain Gregory pounded his fist on the gunwale. "Oh, hell!" he shouted. "There's nothing left around here but a lousy crab." He looked up at Cranston, who smiled back. Captain Gregory furrowed his brow, eyeing him suspiciously. Maybe it was that low-down, slimy eel after all. If he ever found the eel stealing from him, he'd wring his long, ugly neck with his own bare hands.

But he was in no mood to tangle with him now; they had work to do. "Head to No Man's Land. We'll drop anchor there," he ordered.

Manuel froze momentarily, like a giant manatee in the path of an oncoming boat. Then he snapped out of it. "That place is bad luck, Captain."

Captain Gregory chuckled. "That was just a story, Manuel. There is no red giant. Although come to think of it, I did read about some researcher who claimed to have seen one."

"Red giant or not, that place is bad luck. You know the mast was broken on that woman's boat near there, and she was found floating nearby." Manuel reached into his pocket for some salt and threw it over his shoulder.

Captain Gregory ignored the ritual. He had seen it all before. "Just high winds, Manuel. Look if it bothers you, I'll take Cranston with me and you can stay on board. Go get the gear." This suited Captain Gregory just fine. He didn't trust Cranston, and it would be better to keep him in sight. Manuel was the only one he could trust, the only one who would not abandon ship when the going got rough.

SHE LAY THERE SILENTLY, BLENDING IN WITH the mottled patterns of the sea grass and sand below. A large, crusty old Maine lobster was stepping lightly toward its destiny, into a death bed of ever-shifting sand and sea grass that lay ahead. She was just about to wrap her arm around it when she heard the boat coming closer to her home. She paused and her colors changed instantaneously to sheet white, the first of her alarm states. She was concerned about her home, and more importantly, the white stalks hanging from the ceiling. Even more distressing was how long it would take to get back. So, although this was a particularly large lobster, she turned her head and pointed toward home. Sending a large stream of water through her funnel, she slowly jettisoned forward. The lobster was so surprised, it didn't know where to run, so it danced in place. Then, seeing the direction she was going in, it turned in the opposite direction and scuffled away as fast as it could.

She tried not to think about the boat as she swam home at full speed, but the thought kept creeping into her mind. Scuba divers. The very image of them sent shivers up her spineless body. It wasn't that she was afraid of the bubble-blowers themselves. It was their weapons. She had seen sharks shot with spear guns and blue tuna skewered on spears. She had seen the carcasses of juvenile whales with broken harpoons in their sides sinking to the bottom of the sea. She knew how that happened. But the thing that she feared most was the egg poachers and their pilfering little hands.

She was so distressed that she hardly noticed a pair of sharks swim by. They didn't matter. In the distance, she could hear the boat idling near her cave. She knew that boats always stopped for a reason. She envisioned the intruders in her home, and instantaneously, her giant, cauldron-like head began to boil under the pressure.

Three

Captain Gregory finished putting on his gear and motioned for Cranston to hurry up. They didn't have all day, maybe just another hour of daylight left. There was work to be done, and he was eager to do it.

After Manuel checked his gages, Captain Gregory tightened his straps, put in his mouthpiece, turned backwards, and went tank-first into the water. He surfaced momentarily, and Manuel handed him his spear gun and a sack. With all of his gear assembled, he submerged.

With a splash, Cranston soon joined him and they headed for the sea floor below. About a half mile from the boat, the floor dropped off about fifty feet or so, and they explored the sea shelf below. Several large schools converged along the shelf to peruse the lush vegetation for plankton, parasites, and other delicacies. The fish ignored the divers as they went about their business. The two men looked beneath the vegetation for hidden treasures, grabbing small clams and other delectables clinging to the shelf. Then they moved on to No Man's Land.

Captain Gregory looked at his watch and his depth gage. They were about 75 feet below the surface; it was getting late, and they had found hardly anything worth selling. He motioned to Cranston to split up and meet back at the point in twenty minutes. Cranston nodded and they headed in opposite directions, following the cragged lines of the rugged exterior of the cliff.

Captain Gregory swam for awhile, looking for an opening. He turned a corner, and the cliffside gave way to a rather small recess hidden from view by two staggered rock formations jutting out at an angle. Inside the recess, a small opening restricted the access to what was inside. At first, Captain Gregory dismissed it, because the opening appeared to be too small for him to get through with tanks. But he tried anyway, and much to his surprise, he was able to wiggle through. Once inside, Captain Gregory was astonished at what he saw. It was a huge underwater cave! A dim light was filtering in from the ceiling above, but it was not enough to see the chamber from wall to wall. So, he turned on his flashlight and looked around.

There was a large rock ahead to the left. A build-up of sand in the corner to the right. And a large collection of seashells on a ledge up above, all perfect homes for an octopus. Captain Gregory puzzled over this, because the octopus was usually a solitary creature, unlike some of its cousins. Then it came to him: what if the shells housed a colony of Octopi? Given the tremendous variation in physical and social characteristics of the octopus, virtually anything was possible. Captain Gregory swam up to the ledge and looked inside one of the shells. A small fish shot out, startling him. Quickly recovering, he picked up another. Nothing. And another. Nothing again. After sampling several more, he concluded that the shells had been abandoned.

Turning from the shelf, he shone his flashlight on the floor and saw another rock that had been obscured by its much bigger cousin.

Nearby were crab shells strewn everywhere. Obviously, the den of a cephalopod. Captain Gregory withdrew his knife and carefully lifted the rock, ready to plunge a knife between the eyes of the unsuspecting prey. But then he dropped the rock. His eyes grew wide, and his lips uncurled into a large smile. Behind the rock were three enormous ostrich-sized eggs presumably laid by an octopus or squid species he did not recognize, though he thought he knew them all. He quickly looked around as he gently placed the eggs in his sack.

He was just about to leave when he flashed the light in the corner of the cave by the small rock. The cave was not a single room after all! There was a long tunnel—a corridor—that went on and on like a great hallway of some underground castle. To Captain Gregory's amazement, hanging from the ceiling were stalk after stalk of white octopus eggs! Like the flower of the buddleia plant, there were bunches of at least a hundred or more. He swam into the hallway to investigate.

Looking closely, he saw layer upon layer of thousands of small eggs. It was tremendous! He had never seen anything like it. He began to breathe more quickly as the significance of the find struck him. He pointed his flashlight down the hallway and saw more bunches, perhaps seven sets in all. That would mean hundreds of thousands of eggs, maybe millions.

Captain Gregory scratched his chin. He couldn't possibly fit all of these eggs into his sack. He would have to come back, alone. This was his find, and the eel could not be trusted. For all he knew, Cranston might come back and clean out the cave before he could get to it. Besides, he found the cave. This was his boat, his fuel, his gear. He was paying his crew to help him—not to lay claim to his treasure. Let Cranston find his own. Manuel was a different story, however. Captain Gregory did not mind at all sharing some of the booty with his trusted hand.

All of these thoughts circled around Captain Gregory's mind like a whirlpool, and he decided that he must leave the cave at once so that Cranston would not find him there. He quickly gathered up his sack and headed for the opening to the cave.

All of a sudden, half way there, another realization hit him like a wave crashing at the shore. What if the three eggs were queens, and the rest were male drones, organized in the same way as bees or ants in the insect world? Outside of the insect world, he knew of no animal societies organized around a large queen. This could be a stupendous discovery.

If it were true, then there had to be thousands of cephalopods that were occupying the same cave. Or maybe one large one... And if it came back, he would have to kill it and then sell the meat in Tokyo. His contacts would pay a hefty price for such a rarity. But that would be like killing the goose that laid the golden egg. He would do that only if he had to kill it. *If he could kill it...*

This thought troubled him greatly. He swam more quickly, pumping his legs harder and harder. He looked at his oxygen gage. Running low. He had stayed in the cave longer than he had intended. What if she returned before he got out? If she were as big as he envisioned her, he might be in trouble.

He looked at his spear gun, and this calmed him a little. At least he had that. As he swam, he looked all around to make sure that she had not followed him from the hallway. Nowhere in sight. He kept swimming and swimming, and looking back. Too concerned with things astern, he ran into some vegetation at the mouth of the cave, entangling his spear gun. He wrestled with it, but it would not come loose.

Captain Gregory was nearly panting he was so excited. Collecting himself, he swam out of the entrance, ashamed that someone as experienced as he could lose both spear gun and composure. Before venturing out into open water, he peered out from the crags protecting the entrance. The occupant of the cave was nowhere in sight and neither was his shiphand.

He swam out from the rock formation and rounded the corner, bumping into Cranston, who was headed toward the cave. Captain Gregory nearly jumped out of his suit he was so startled, even more startled than a summer ago in the Great Barrier Reef when a Moray eel sprung from its lair to bite him. It took a second, but he quickly regained his composure once more, pointing to his gage, signaling that they should leave. As they headed toward the boat, Cranston motioned to him, asking if he had picked up anything. Captain Gregory motioned back, nothing much.

AS THE DIVERS ROUNDED THE CORNER AWAY from her, she slipped in the front entrance and went immediately to the tunnel. It seemed to take forever to navigate the cave as her front probes shot through the water. To the first bunch. Everything intact. To the next. That one was okay. To the next and through to the rest. All okay. She heaved a big sigh of relief, but just for a moment. Turning her attention to the rock, she crawled quickly from the tunnel back to the cave.

In the corner of the cave, she looked behind the rock. Her eyes grew wide. THEY WERE GONE!! ALL OF THEM!! She turned from sheet-white to full crimson red. Enraged, her entire body shuddered. The anger filled her from the tips of her tentacles to the top of her head until she felt as if she would explode. She could not recall a time when she was as consumed with fear, hatred, and utter rage, not even when she was attacked by a sperm whale, an encounter that ended with her wrapping a stranglehold around the whale's blowhole as it took her on the ride of her life.

Whirling around, she jettisoned to the front entrance and rushed out into the twilight water, leaving the safety of her home to *seek out* the poachers, something she would never had considered under ordinary circumstances. But these were not ordinary circumstances. They had her *babies*, her queen babies. And without them there would be no future generations; her colony would die off; and that would be the end, something that she could simply not abide under any circumstances.

Outside, she looked around the rock formations but didn't see them. Then she saw a light from around the corner. Sure enough, they were swimming toward the boat in the distance, with their flashlights on.

She jettisoned forward and in little time at all was upon them...

CAPTAIN GREGORY FELT A PRESENCE, A LARGE overpowering presence, and he turned around and saw her... She was magnificent... She was beautiful... She was fiendish!

He reached for his knife but was too late. An immense arm wrapped around his torso, just below the tanks, tying up both of his arms. He felt her terrible, slimy arm creep into his skin as the grip quickly tightened. He thrashed and twisted, trying to wriggle free, but it was no use. Another arm quickly wrapped around his thighs, and he could feel a tentacle adhere, squeeze the water and air out, and form a tight seal on his wetsuit. Another adhered, and another, and another, around both legs, until he was completely immobilized. He held onto the sack of eggs with his left hand, but it tingled as the blood stopped flowing to his fingers.

Another arm went up the nape of his neck, sending chills like shock waves through his body. It twisted around his neck, turning his head harder and harder. He dug his chin into the arm, but it would not release its grip. *She's going to break my neck.*

All of a sudden, the grip around his neck was released, and the tentacles making his flesh crawl withdrew. In an instant, he was whipsawed around, and he could see that she had

Cranston, also, in her iron grip. He was struggling without his spear gun, almost completely immobilized.

She drew them both in, slowly, as if to make them think about their fate before it happened. Captain Gregory wished he could somehow communicate with her, maybe to make a trade for the eggs that were in the sack he was still holding. As if she had read his mind, another arm reached down and gently tugged at the sack. But Captain Gregory would not let go, because he sensed that she *knew* what was in the sack. And as long as he had the eggs, he could buy time. She would not fight hard, for fear of smashing its contents. So he hoped.

He saw that Cranston was trying to reach for a knife strapped to his thigh. If only he could distract her, then perhaps Cranston could reach the knife. He turned his head and glared at her. Her eyes were huge saucers, and there was something both sad and monstrous about them. As he stared at her, he became aware of something else. He didn't know how he knew it, but by the way the red monster was looking at him, he just knew.

She was intelligent.

She tugged harder at the sack, and Captain Gregory held on. She pulled even harder until finally it jerked away from Captain Gregory's taut fingers, and an egg flew out into some sand nearby. She didn't notice the errant egg, instead pulling the bag quickly into her mantle for safety.

In that moment, Cranston got hold of his knife and thrust it into the fiendish creature's arm. She writhed in pain and, for an instant, loosened her grip, allowing him to break free. He swam away quickly and picked up his spear gun.

Captain Gregory was ecstatic. Hope, like a shot of adrenaline, coursed through his veins. Now they had a fighting chance...at least he had thought so until he saw Cranston pick up the egg and smile at him. In an instant, Captain Gregory knew that he had been betrayed. Even so, he was surprised at the depths to which his shiphand would sink for greed. But it wasn't the egg he was worried about now. It was his life.

He wished the monster had caught Cranston in the act, but she had not. She looked at him for a fleeting moment and then looked at Captain Gregory's sack, tightening her grip. Cranston swam back to the boat, and the monster, satisfied that she had what she wanted, let him go.

But she apparently had no intention of letting Captain Gregory go. She slowly reeled him in, staring at him with those hideous eyes that seemed to be studying him in minute detail as he drew closer. And closer. When he was within a few feet of her eyes, for the first time in his life he felt sorry that he had taken—no, stolen—the eggs in the first place. Suddenly, she relaxed her grip ever so slightly. Captain Gregory noted the coincidence and saw an opportunity. *Please let me go. I will protect you against the fishermen, and anyone else. If you just give me a second chance.*

She blinked, and her color changed back to a mottled brown before his eyes. It was incredible how she could do that, but Captain Gregory couldn't think about that now. It would have to wait. He had to get out, or there would be no second thoughts about this or anything else. He looked her in the eye. *Please. I will protect you, help you, do anything for you. If you would just let me go.*

She looked at him with what, for a moment, appeared to be pity. Then she rotated her mantle, exposing a giant beak with razor sharp jaws and a giant double-tooth. Captain Gregory gulped, fearing that the moment had arrived.

But miraculously, instead of being drawn into her mouth, he felt a rush of water. They swam slowly toward the cliffside, around the bend, and then to the two jagged points. Her grip did not tighten or loosen during the entire ride. In the turbulence, Captain Gregory could see little, but he sensed it: *She's keeping me alive for some reason.*

At the entrance to the cave, she pulled and he resisted, but to no avail. After several tie-ups, they squeezed through the entrance, swam slowly into the dimly lit cave, and paused by the large rock strewn with crustacean shells. At that moment, Captain Gregory knew the reason he had been brought to the cave: for dinner.

Again, she began to draw him closer and closer.

His skin began to crawl. He felt as if he was trapped inside an aquarium whose only occupant was a giant red octopus—and now him. He struggled to get free but it was no use. The more he thrashed, the more the grip tightened. Finally, all he could do was look straight ahead at her. Her long, milky-white underside. The thunderously large arms. The double rows of tentacles leading from the tips of the arms to a single point in the center of the mantle: her beak.

It opened wider and wider, exposing the giant double-tooth, rows of smaller teeth, and a large black hole that was undoubtedly the belly. This was it, the moment he had dreaded. Captain Gregory closed his eyes as his head was drawn into the cavity. The beak hung over him like a giant can opener, about to split his skull open like a can of V-8. He felt a sharp pain at the base of his neck, like a needle injecting anesthetic, and then a tremendous swelling sensation...until he felt nothing, except a mucous spray of some sort engulfing him like a mouthful of spit. And then he heard a loud sucking sound he did not recognize, and all of a sudden he tasted blood. And everything went pitch black, like a boat's lantern turning off in the middle of the night...

MANUEL HAD BEEN CHECKING HIS WATCH every few minutes. What was keeping them? His shipmates would have to return soon or they would be out of oxygen. They only had five, maybe ten, minutes left. Something was wrong; he could feel it. He turned the lantern on the water searching for them, but they were nowhere in sight. He began to panic.

Quickly, he opened a trunk and pulled out the spare wetsuit and scuba gear. If they didn't come back in the next couple of minutes, he would go in after them! He had just gotten on the wetsuit and flippers when he saw something coming to the surface. It was Cranston! Manuel was overjoyed at seeing his fellow shiphand, even though he didn't like him very much. Cranston's put-downs, petty thievery, and poisonous nature had long ago caused bad blood between them. For now, that didn't matter. Manuel felt so relieved that he could have kissed him, until he realized that the captain was not coming. As he helped Cranston into the boat, he asked, "Where's the captain?"

"He's met with a piece of bad luck, Manuel."

"What's wrong?" asked Manuel, trembling.

As cool as an Arctic icebreaker, Cranston said, "A red giant's got him and is going to have him for dinner. He's had it, and there's nothing we can do about it."

"I knew it. I'm going in after him."

"Are you crazy? That's suicide to go in after him now."

"I don't care. I'm going in. You stay here."

Cranston glared at Manuel. "Now wait a minute. Let's get something straight right now. I'm the new captain of this boat, and I give the orders. If you want to work for me, I could use a hand. *You* stay here."

Manuel could feel the hair rise on the back of his neck as he finished putting on his tanks and gear. "You ain't nothin'. And this ain't your boat. When the captain hears about this, he'll show you a thing or two."

Cranston shook his head as Manuel jumped into the water. "Go ahead, you stupid wetback. She's had the captain for dinner, and now she'll have you for dessert!" He laughed deliciously as he grabbed the egg from the sack. If ever there was a golden egg, this was it. It was pink with three white bands encircling the long end, and it felt like hardened jello. The gelatinous material had a translucent quality to it, and for a moment Cranston thought that he saw gold doubloons inside. He had to protect his prize possession but didn't know what to do with it. The coolers might damage the structures inside, making it worthless. He needed something to preserve the egg, not freeze it until it oozed.

As he searched for the proper container for the egg, he tried to decide whether or not to leave Manuel behind. He had never killed a man before, and this would be his first. After all, the captain didn't count; he just didn't help him when he had the chance. He felt certain, though, that leaving Manuel behind would count the same as killing him with his own hands.

This did not trouble him at all. Given the motive and the opportunity, he was confident that he would not hesitate to kill. No, what was troubling him was that Manuel was a good worker, and everyone knew cheap labor was hard to find. He would surely need help in his new enterprise. But could Manuel be trusted now that he had shown himself to be fiercely loyal to the captain? In fact, he might even steal the egg.

There would be no egg to steal, however, if he didn't preserve it, and soon. What he really needed was a jar of formaldehyde to put it in. So, he forgot about Manuel and headed for the Captain's Quarters to look there.

SHE PAUSED FOR A MOMENT AND LOOKED around as she held Captain Gregory's head in her mouth, the rest of him dangling helplessly, twitching occasionally. But she had yet to clamp down hard, and sever the head from the body. Nothing had changed, except that she was now preoccupied with examining the contents in the bag. One egg. Two eggs. And... She turned the bag upside down, emptying it furiously.

There was *ONE MISSING*! Her mottled brown mantle turned instantaneously to crimson red as she sent both probes up and down Captain Gregory's body searching for the egg, but she did not find it. Then she spit him out and pulled him in close to her like a mother nurturing a baby—or the thing that would help get her baby back. In an instant, they were at the front entrance of her home again.

She hesitated for a moment as she felt an enlargement and pressure inside. She knew that more eggs would be coming soon. They would not wait. Laying the eggs in the open currents would certainly be disastrous for the male drones. She didn't want to risk losing them, but she just had to get her baby daughter back even if that meant risking going to the dreaded boat. So she headed out again. This time, she knew where to go and what to do. First, go to the boat. Then entice the other one into the water using her captive as the bait!

She saw the glow of the lantern in the water in the distance and headed straight for the boat with Captain Gregory in tow. Great swirls rushed behind her as she sent tremendous streams of water jettisoning from her mantle. About a half mile or so from the boat, she saw a diver with a flashlight coming toward her. She stopped at the sea shelf and sought refuge among the sea brush along the ridge. Sure enough, it was him! She wouldn't have to go to the boat after all, and she breathed a sigh of relief. Being out of water, even an arm or two, was positively terrifying to her.

She quickly moved Captain Gregory forward, propping him up against some large rocks and wrapping two arms around him for support: the bait. But maybe the diver wouldn't see the bait. Then she had a brilliant idea. She took the flashlight from his waist band and struck it against a rock. It turned on! She placed it upright beside Captain Gregory and slipped behind the rocks, blending in effortlessly with her surroundings.

⊕ ⊕ ⊕

MANUEL SAW THE LIGHT AHEAD AND MOVED cautiously. He saw the captain sitting by the rocks but couldn't understand why since his oxygen was undoubtedly running out. Manuel concluded that the captain must be entangled in the brush or perhaps his leg was caught between the rocks. He approached cautiously. When he was within fifteen feet of the captain, he sensed another presence and turned around, but there was nothing there. As he turned back, Manuel was startled to see an armtip just inches from his face. The monster! Before he could react, the arm wrapped around his neck, and he scratched at it with both hands, frantically trying to loosen its grip. He felt sickened by the slimy quality of the skin, the pain of the suction grip, and the ferocity with which he was being whipsawed. Another arm shot around his legs, making it impossible to swim away. Slowly but surely the monster began to draw him in...

Closer and closer until he could see that the captain was also wrapped in its grip. He didn't appear to be moving, although it was hard to tell in the midst of the struggle. For a fleeting moment, Manuel wondered if the captain was knocked out or if the monster had already killed him. At any rate, he concluded that he would be joining him soon. He could see the monster now, illuminated by the flashlight and the red flare glow of its skin in the night water. Before pulling Manuel into its mantle, the monster paused, probing him for something, searching his hands, belt, and flippers. What was it looking for?

The monster drew Manuel in once more, rotating its mantle to expose a milky-white underside and a horrendous beak. *Please, don't eat me, monster*, Manuel cried inside as he struggled to get free. When he was within about ten feet of its beak, the mantle shifted quickly, and he was virtually eye to eye with the monster. It maneuvered around as if trying to get comfortable. Its color turned to a mottled brown. And it blinked several times. None of this meant anything to Manuel. Sheer terror registered on his face as the monster stared at him and the captain, as if trying to decide what to do.

Manuel screamed under water *"LET ME GO*!!... *PLEASE*!!", as if that would do any good. Moments later, without warning, it released him and the captain! Then it turned its head toward the sea cliffs and slowly jettisoned away with a tremendous blast of water bubbles.

As the monster faded from view, Manuel blessed himself three times. He was amazed that it had left so abruptly, but he did not question his good fortune. He quickly grabbed Captain Gregory by the arm and pulled, but the captain would not budge. In the strong currents that were generated by the powerful departure of the monster, Captain Gregory was entangled in the sea brush. Manuel struggled valiantly to free him but was unable. Hurriedly, he found a knife in the captain's belt and used it to hack away at the brush. It took about fifteen well-placed chops. Upon freeing the captain, he put an arm around his chest and slowly pulled him back to the boat.

AFTER PLACING THE EGG IN A JAR OF formaldehyde that he had found in the Captain's Quarters, Cranston closed up the coolers and prepared to leave. He was just beginning to hoist the anchor when, much to his surprise, Manuel surfaced with Captain Gregory in tow. "You're back! I can't believe it."

"Get a line quickly!" Manuel shouted.

He threw Manuel a line, and he quickly tied it around Captain Gregory.

Manuel secured himself to the ladder at the side of the boat. With Cranston pulling on the other end of the rope, Manuel struggled to hoist Captain Gregory into the boat.

Cranston craned his neck to see. "Is he still alive?"

"I don't know," said Manuel. "We can only hope."

FAR BELOW, IN A CAVE THAT SHE CALLED HOME in the sea cliffs, she picked up the rock, aerated the two eggs, and gently placed the rock back in front. Satisfied, she crept over to the corridor and began to lay more eggs...

Four

As she lay on the couch that morning, Jane's mind was a blank. She felt as if she were nothing more than an artist's idea, a starting point to be shaped, sculpted, and molded into a whole subject. But she was not made of sand, marble, or clay, but of living, breathing, flesh and blood. At least it felt like flesh and blood.

Yet the woman rummaging about the office for a pen, Dr. Royale, was unlike any artist she had ever known. Dr. Royale did not shape and mold Jane with her hands, nor did she draw her with pen and ink. Instead, she took notes to recreate the real Jane, growing back her old personality and reconstructing her mind on paper.

At least that's what Jane thought Dr. Royale was trying to do. Her methods were so unconventional, and Jane didn't know much about psychiatry, or amnesia for that matter. She only knew that she couldn't remember much of anything, and she wanted desperately to regain the memories—and whatever else—she had lost.

Jane stared at Dr. Royale, waiting for her to begin the usual onslaught of questions, questions she was sure would lead to the same place they had been for the past several months, nowhere. She looked around and marveled at how amazingly cluttered things were in the office space, and how amazingly uncluttered things were in the space inside her mind. That was the odd thing about amnesia. Her mind was completely uncluttered. In fact, it was a blank, and that was the problem.

At last Dr. Royale sat down on a chair next to Jane. "For the past few months we've talked about the things you can remember. This morning I'd like to take a different approach. Let's talk about the things you *can't* remember." Dr. Royale puffed on a cigarette, delighting as she always did in blowing a cloud of smoke in front of herself, as if it were a curtain between her and her patient, one from which either could make a quick retreat if necessary.

"But I don't understand. How can I talk about the things that I can't remember, if I can't remember them?" Jane closed her eyes and winced. She kept them closed for a minute trying to remember every detail of the room. There was the cherry wood walls, built-in bookshelves, a fireplace of imported sandstone, tiffany lamps, a large mahogany desk, mountains of paperwork in every imaginable nook and cranny, and of course, the obligatory couch, upon which she was reposing. She opened her eyes and looked around, noting with satisfaction that she had not missed a single detail. There was nothing wrong with her memory. She had the memory of a librarian; she just didn't have access to the archives.

"Start by identifying the things you can't remember. We've already talked about some of them, but that's all right. Start right from the beginning. That will take us to the edge of what you can and cannot remember." Dr. Royale rummaged through the folders scattered on top of her desk and found her notes. She leaned forward in anticipation.

Jane was curious about her files and could not resist the temptation to glance at the notes. It read: "First patient. Female. About 35. College educated. Sun-streaked hair, some wrinkles, lived near ocean. Shows some ill-effects from neck injury-head trauma. Awoke from three-month coma with no speech problems. Total amnesia." Dr. Royale quickly tilted the pad so that Jane couldn't see the rest of her notes.

"That's not fair," said Jane, upset about the notes she had seen—and the notes she hadn't. "You get to know what I'm thinking, but I never get to know what you're thinking."

Dr. Royale took another puff on her cigarette. "That's because I'm the doctor, and whether you like it or not, Jane, you're the patient. Now please begin."

Jane ran her fingers through her honey-blond hair and wished that she could join Dr. Royale. She had quit smoking before the accident. At least she thought that she had, but she wasn't sure about that or anything else that had happened before.

There were a number of things that she could not remember, but Jane held back for a moment just to show that she had some control over the situation. After all, she didn't have to reveal anything. She knew that the doctor just wanted to help, but she resented the invasion of her privacy.

Stronger than the resentment was the jealousy. Jane was jealous of Dr. Royale's auburn hair, which was bound in a bookwormish bun; her ocean blue eyes that appeared many fathoms deep; and the smooth landscape of her peach skin, which belied a very sleek figure dressed in a prude Victorian dress. Jane, who was a beautiful woman in her own right, thought that beautiful figures were wasted on women like Dr. Royale, who were obviously insecure about their femininity.

She took a deep breath. "Well, I can't remember my name of course. But Jane is all right with me. I've gotten used to it." She paused for a minute, trying to decide whether to continue. "Let's see, what else...I can't remember where I lived. That pretty much says it all. Now can we talk about something else?"

"No, please try to think of something else you can't remember."

Jane felt as if as if she were in a fishbowl, looking through a distorted lens at her past. "I can't remember what I did for a living. I can't even remember who my family is. I can't...I can't remember anything. But you already know that."

"I know, dear. But I know you can do it, if you just give it a try," said Dr. Royale, sprinkling kind words like fish food into the top of the fishbowl.

"Well, I can't think of anything else."

"You mean you won't," said Dr. Royale, determined to bring her to the surface.

"This is hard," said Jane, wincing.

Dr. Royale immediately softened. "I know it's hard. But please, go on."

Jane looked around the cluttered room. One thing was for sure, Dr. Royale was not a good housekeeper. Notepads and folders were strewn on the floor and on every available counter top. And the bookshelves were overflowing with books. At first, Jane couldn't quite put her finger on it, but there was something very strange about those shelves. Then she realized what it was. She knew every title on the shelves, as if she had picked them.

She mused at what the odds were of knowing the title of every book. Very strange indeed. But then, everything had seemed strange to her since she had awakened. She stared at one of the books, "Love Lost in a Dream", and became misty-eyed. "I can't remember my boyfriend, or my dreams, except one that I've been having over and over recently... and I can't remember the accident," she said.

Dr. Royale looked up from her notes, startled. "Whoa, hold on a second. Let's take these one at a time. Let's start with the boyfriend. When you say 'I can't remember my boyfriend', you mean you can't remember if you *had* a boyfriend or not, right?"

"Oh, I had one all right, and it's really bothering me that I don't know who he is, or where he is."

"Why didn't you tell me this before? This is fascinating." Dr. Royale puffed on her cigarette, burning it down to the filter.

Jane motioned to her to put it out. "You never asked."

Dr. Royale looked puzzled as she rifled through her notes. Pointing to one of the pages, she said, "No, Jane, in our second session I explicitly asked you if you could remember any loved ones, and you answered, 'No'."

Jane smiled, gleeful that she had regained a small measure of control over her situation. "That's right. You only asked me if I could remember any loved ones, not if I *had* one or not."

Dr. Royale was no longer puzzled. She was completely baffled. "But how do you *know* that you had a lover if you don't know his name or can't remember anything about him? Maybe you didn't have one at all."

In an instant, Jane turned from gleeful to glum. Dr. Royale was right. She didn't have any way of knowing, only feeling. Jane stared into Dr. Royale's eyes, hoping that something might be reflected back, something about who she was, what had happened, and what had become of her. Dr. Royale looked away, not allowing the patient to conduct her own nonverbal interrogation.

It was just as well. No images came to Jane, not a glimpse, a reflection, or even a distortion of her past. Propping herself up on the sofa, she said, "Look, I had one, all right? It's a feeling. I know that he is real. Isn't that enough?"

"Okay, I believe you. Tell me more."

Jane looked down at the floor, purposely avoiding Dr. Royale's eyes. Two could play at that game. "I don't want to talk about it anymore."

With her index finger, Dr. Royale gently raised Jane's chin, forcing her to look up. "It's important for you to get your feelings out on this subject, and for me to know," she said.

Jane squirmed a little. "What do you want from me? It's like you're trying to pry into my mind."

Dr. Royale smiled. "That's true, and I won't try to deny it. The mind is like a giant clam. Sometimes we have to pry it open to get to the pearls."

"Why, what difference does it make? I can't remember a thing about him. It only causes me pain," Jane said, becoming more agitated.

"But your pain may provide a breakthrough."

"You're looking at this from such a clinical point-of-view." Jane wiped a tear from her eye. "Doctor, do you know what it's like to love someone and then to lose them?" She stared at Dr. Royale, expecting—no, demanding—an answer.

Dr. Royale returned her gaze. "Yes," she replied softly, "I once lost a child."

Jane was completely stunned by this revelation. She sat up, looked around the room, and confirmed that there were no pictures of any family. For that reason, she had always assumed Dr. Royale was a single woman. But this bolt from the blue shed light on a whole new side of the doctor. "Oh, I'm very sorry."

"There's nothing that can be done about that. So, let's drop the subject, okay?" said Dr. Royale, slightly irritated.

Jane was incredulous. "How can you sit there and tell me that you lost a child, and then tell me to drop the subject, just like that?"

Dr. Royale turned red with agitation. "Jane, *you* are the patient, not *me*. Maybe some other time I'll tell you about that.

But for now, let's talk about you. Please continue. What else can't you remember about him?"

Feeling powerless again, Jane stared at the floor and paused for a few moments. If the good doctor wouldn't open up to her, she'd have to wait until Jane was good and ready. Finally she looked up and said, "Just about everything. I can't remember his face because I keep picturing him with a mask on. But even though I can't see him, I know that I love him very much. He is an angel."

"And this love that you speak of. What is it like?"

"You're joking, right?" Jane took note of the earnest look on Dr. Royale's face. "Well, *you've* been with a man before—you know."

"No, I haven't."

Jane looked at her quizzically. "But you said..." She snapped her fingers. "Oh I see, your child was adopted."

Dr. Royale said nothing but quickly jotted down a few notes on her pad. Jane wondered if she was trying out a few answers or just making her wait. "No, it's true; it was nothing conjugal," said Dr. Royale. "And I personally know several females who have done it that way."

"Why in the world would a beautiful woman like you want to adopt unless you couldn't have children?"

Dr. Royale squirmed a little. "I'm sorry, Jane, but you're getting too personal. I'll ask the questions, thank you."

"Oh, I forgot, you're the doctor. Well, Dr. Royale, let me help you out on this one. All a woman with your looks has to do is raise the hem line an inch, and you could go a mile with a man. You should try love the old-fashioned way. You might like it."

Dr. Royale leaned forward. "Well then, what about old-fashioned love? What is it really like to love someone, to really long for the opposite sex—a man."

"Oh, come on," said Jane, waiting for the obligatory wink, but it never came. If her jaw had not been hinged to her head, her mouth would have dropped to the floor. She leaned forward to see what Dr. Royale was writing so furiously in her notebook: "Subject was intimate with male. Beginning to open up. Recall is improving. Fascinating." That was all that she could get before Dr. Royale abruptly held the notebook to her chest, as if it guarded secrets to which Jane could not be privy.

"You know, I'm beginning to think you want to live vicariously through me," said Jane. "Instead of asking me, why don't you just go out and meet someone?"

"No, no, you don't understand," said Dr. Royale, waving her hands. "I want to help you remember him, so that I can help you *find* him."

"You'd do that for me?"

"Yes, I would."

Jane was touched. It was the first time in months that she and Dr. Royale had shared a moment of true friendship and trust together. She moved closer and put her hand on the doctor's. "You don't know what this means to me. Perhaps I can return the favor."

"What do you mean?"

"Dr. Royale, it's painfully obvious to me that you need a man. Maybe I can help you meet one."

Dr. Royale turned bright red with embarrassment. She fumbled for a cigarette and lit it, regaining her composure. "Okay let's end the morning session right here."

THAT AFTERNOON, JANE LOOKED AROUND THE room while Dr. Royale searched for a pen in a stack of files and folders, a search almost as futile as finding a needle in a haystack. The room was filled with diplomas, memorabilia, and vaguely familiar pictures of Dr. Royale. Jane couldn't quite put her finger on it but there was something odd about the diploma on the wall, which read:

> "The University of Johns Hopkins bestows upon Isabelle O. Royale the degree of Bachelor of Arts in Psychiatry"

As she turned away, Jane realized what was wrong with the diploma. It should have read "Johns Hopkins University"...She looked again and, to her astonishment, the diploma read correctly. Perhaps she was imagining things or maybe even hallucinating. She didn't know which. All she knew was that nothing had been right since the accident. After her head injury, she didn't feel that she could trust her own perceptions of the world around her.

After rummaging about, Dr. Royale found another pen and was ready to resume. "Let's pick up where we left off this morning. What else can't you remember? You said something about a dream?"

Jane could tell from the clinical tone of her voice that Dr. Royale was ready to get down to business again. Their brief rapprochement from that morning was over. To regain control over a situation in which she had no control, Jane felt compelled to make Dr. Royale wait for her next answer. She bent over to tie her shoelaces, and afterward she said, "I haven't been able to remember my dreams—until recently."

"When did this start? How many dreams can you remember? Are any about him?" asked Dr. Royale, bombarding Jane with questions like waves against a breaker.

"Since the session last week. I've been getting the same dream over and over again. But it's not about him."

"Please tell me about it anyway," said Dr. Royale, feverishly jotting notes in her yellow legal pad.

Jane took a deep breath. "I awake in the night, screaming..."

Dr. Royale looked up from her notes, her eyes wide open with surprise. "What?! What happens before then?"

"Well, it's not a question of then, really, because I don't know the sequence of events; it's more like a feeling, actually."

"Okay, then tell me about the feeling." Dr. Royale swiveled slightly in her chair, leaning forward.

"I feel cold. Like I'm going for a swim in the ocean."

"What ocean would that be?"

"It's the Atlantic, I think."

"Why do you say that?"

"I don't know."

"Perhaps you live there, or have some relatives on the Eastern seaboard?" Dr. Royale could see that she didn't know. "That's all right, continue please."

"I have goose bumps all over. I can't feel my legs. And my flesh feels like it's crawling, all tensed up. My limbs are restrained, something is gripping me tightly, and I'm being moved," Jane said, shivering.

Dr. Royale lit a cigarette. "Do you know where this is happening?"

"I don't know, but it's the nighttime, I'm sure, because I can't see a thing. It's pitch black and not a star in the sky."

"Perhaps you're unconscious."

"I know that I feel a numbness in my neck. And then a sharp pain, as if someone were stabbing me. And then I struggle for a few moments."

Dr. Royale puffed on her cigarette, waiting for Jane until she could wait no longer. "And then?"

Jane became agitated as she contemplated the next part of the dream. "I see circles. And then it comes into focus, and I realize that it's not circles. It's two eyes staring at me. And a face that I will never forget."

"Your boyfriend, maybe?"

"No, doctor, it's the face...of a serpent," said Jane, shuddering.

"A serpent?! What kind of serpent?" asked Dr. Royale, puffing away, blowing a cloud of smoke between them.

As the smoke cleared, Jane noted that Dr. Royale, too, was apparently frightened by the vision. The good doctor was as contradictory as night and day. She was a cold, calculating clinician on the one hand, and a warm, intuitive, empathetic on the other. Jane didn't know whether to like her or to hate her.

"I don't know. I can only see the face. Everything else seems murky." Jane leaned forward and motioned for Dr. Royale to hand her a cigarette. She didn't care whether she had kicked the habit or not; she needed something to calm her nerves.

Dr. Royale rummaged through her purse, pulled out a pack, and discovered that it was empty. "I'm sorry. I'm all out... Please tell me, what happens next?"

Jane paused, unable to speak as the emotion welled up in her. "And then I wake up screaming."

Dr. Royale looked at her with soft, kind eyes. "Why are you frightened?"

"Because the eyes are staring at me through a cloud of red. And I realize that the cloud of red is...my blood." Jane began to tremble. "You know, I think this dream has something to do with the accident."

Dr. Royale returned to the role of the clinical psychiatrist. She looked at Jane, studying her as if she were some animal in a cage. "According to my records there was no external blood from the head trauma that you suffered."

"So they tell me, but I still see red, that's all I can tell you."

"Perhaps a little blood in the eye."

"I wouldn't know. I don't remember the fall."

Dr. Royale looked up from her pad and then jotted down a few more notes. As she did, Jane peered at the notebook once again, trying to read the words which appeared upside down: "Flash retention of event. New synapses being formed to reach stored memory. Fascinating." The notes were curious. Jane didn't know exactly what to make of them, except that they were obviously about her amnesia.

As she wrote, Dr. Royale ran out of ink. She shook the pen but nothing came out. She shook it harder, and harder, until suddenly red ink sprayed from the point and landed all over Jane, who let out a loud, piercing scream.

Dr. Royale nearly jumped out of her chair. "Oh, my dear, I'm so sorry. I've really made a mess of things." She put her arm around her, trying to comfort her, but Jane was shaking and sobbing gently and would not respond.

"What's wrong, Jane? If it's the dress, I promise you, we'll buy you a new one."

"No, it's not that."

Dr. Royale reached for a remote and pressed a button. "Perhaps this will calm you. It's a therapeutic device I just had installed for my patients." The cupboard door raised on the wall to reveal a large aquarium, which was filled with small vegetation and a rough landscape, like a miniature sea floor. In the corner of the tank was a small plastic figure in scuba gear. From behind a rock in the opposite corner, a small octopus with unusual pomegranate markings crawled out.

Jane's eyes grew wide and her heart grew fearful as she stared at the tank. "That's it."

"What's it?"

Jane pointed at the octopus in the tank. "That's the serpent whose face I see." Then she pointed to the small figure. "And the angel whose face I cannot see." As if her trembling hands were the tremor before a large earthquake, suddenly Jane's whole body began to shake.

Dr. Royale put her arm around Jane again, who was surprised at the soothing effect this had. "There's nothing to be afraid of. It's just a small octopus, and the scuba diver is just a plastic figure that can be purchased in any pet store."

"It's Octopus Giganticus, I'm sure of it. It looks just like the one in my dream; the markings are the same, only the one in my dream is gigantic. That's what's so strange, because the species is actually quite small. That's always been the joke about the name. No one has ever seen a large specimen."

Spotting a pen on the floor, Dr. Royale picked it up and began to write furiously. "You know the name of the species? Then you must have been a biologist?!"

"Why yes. I think I was. In fact I'm sure of it." Jane's eyes lit up the room as if each was the first ray of sunshine piercing through a cloudy day. "Hey, wait a minute. *Now* I remember something about the accident...Yes, that's it," she said snapping her fingers. "I was swimming near No Man's Land and then suddenly I saw the octopus. It was huge...beautiful...graceful... and grotesque as it moved along the cliff there. All of a sudden, it turned a brilliant crimson, and I thought that it was alarmed at seeing me. So I didn't get too close for fear that I would startle it, or even cause it to attack. And then it seemed to be motioning to me, almost inviting me into its den. And I couldn't figure out why, but I was too scared to move forward. And then it disappeared behind two jagged rocks, and I felt another presence... I turned around and was so startled that I couldn't move as a great white shark swam by me, brushing against my arm. It turned around and headed back toward me, swimming very aggressively, and I knew that it was going to attack.

"For some reason I swam toward the cave; I guess because I figured the shark wouldn't follow me in there. As I swam, I sensed that the shark was closing in, and I wondered if I would make it. As I neared the entrance, I looked back, and the shark was about twenty feet away. Then I turned to maneuver through the opening and slammed into something—a jutting rock, I suppose—and was completely dazed from the impact.

After that, I don't remember a thing." Jane folded her arms, trying to calm herself. She took a drag from Dr. Royale's cigarette and gave it back. "You know, I can't figure out why I'm here. Why the great white didn't attack. Why I ended up here at the hospital. All I know is that a while later, or what seems to be a while later, I remember the sensation of rising, as if I was being pushed to the surface."

Dr. Royale leaned forward until she almost fell off the edge of her seat. She slid back onto her chair. "Your swim in the ocean; was it part of the dream or do you believe it actually happened?"

"Well, I'm pretty sure that it really happened. But I'm not sure how I was rescued. Nobody seems to know."

"That doesn't matter. The fact that you were rescued is what counts. I can tell you this: You were rescued or you wouldn't be here. While you were recovering from your head injuries you were in the trauma center, and then they moved you to the psychiatric wing of the hospital after you regained consciousness."

"Oh, I see. But don't you think that the rescue holds the key to my memories?"

Looking away, Dr. Royale tapped her notepad against her knee. "No. I'm quite sure it's the man in the scuba gear that we're looking for; he will unlock the door to most of your memories."

Jane smiled. "Dr. Royale, for the first time in a long time, I really feel that there is hope for me."

Dr. Royale placed her hand on Jane's for a moment. "Well that's just excellent. We've really made a breakthrough today. We now know that you were a marine biologist and that you had an intimate relationship with a man who is probably one as well. That'll be enough for today. I don't think I have enough pens to write down all of my observations." She clipped her notes to her notepad and put them on her desk, shoving a few items here and there to make room. As she did, a large pile of files fell to the floor.

Jane bent over to pick up the files and noticed that each had her name on it. "Doctor, I was just wondering, am I your first patient?"

Dr. Royale looked surprised. "Why yes, you were the first. But now there is another whom you will be meeting soon."

FIVE

---✦---

Captain Gregory had been at the hospital several weeks since the accident, slipping in and out of consciousness, in and out of the landscape of reality and dreams. By his reckoning, he had been operated for neurological injuries twice, to repair brain damage from the puncture wound at the base of his skull and to stop the bleeding. But Captain Gregory was a tough old salt, and it would take a lot more than a 100-foot-long giant octopus to stop him. The doctors weren't so sure, and perhaps, they reflected the same nagging feelings that Captain Gregory had about himself. There was the numbness in his head, the double vision, and the very strange visions, ones that he felt had to be a figment of his imagination, only he had never been one to hallucinate in the past.

Captain Gregory propped himself in bed and very gingerly rotated his legs over the side, being careful to lift his buttocks, which were still sore from a gash suffered during the accident. He looked at the Demerol dispenser on the stand by the bed rather wistfully and, with a quick jerk, pulled the IV attachment from his hand and applied light pressure. He was untethered now, freed from the plastic umbilical cord. While gripping the bed rail, he slowly slid off the end of the bed, touched the floor, and looked over at his private bath: first destination. Weak and unsteady, suffering from vertigo, he slowly walked into the bathroom and closed the door. Mission accomplished.

He looked in the mirror to survey the damage: there were bandages with dried blood stains on them; soon-to-be removed stitches on his buttocks; and dissolvable stitches where the shunt had just been removed from his head the day before. He peeked under the bandages on his head and saw that the wound was nearly healed. Good as new.

Reaching into the vanity drawer, he pulled out some scissors he had stolen from one of the nurses that morning. He cut the identification bracelet from his wrist and threw it in the waste basket. Freedom at last.

It was time to exercise that freedom. A quick check of the hospital room revealed nothing but hospital gowns. That was an advantage. Dressed as just another patient milling about the hospital, he could slip out the door unnoticed. He made up his mind. He would go, and as soon as possible.

He opened the door to the room, pausing for a moment before venturing out. As he looked both ways down the hallway, he was gripped by another bout of vertigo and was about to fall. Grabbing hold of a handrail on the wall, he regained his balance and stood there for a moment, stunned at his feebleness. Slowly, he walked back into his room, deciding to get some bed rest before going on his journey.

Propped in his hospital bed once again, Captain Gregory surveyed his surroundings, as if he were taking inventory of a Captain's Quarters. He shook his head; these quarters would never do. There was no table for laying out maps, no old-fashioned sextant, no shelves filled with nautical books, no bunk with fresh-water basin beside it, and no port-hole looking out on the seascape. Instead there was a small pull-out chair beside a rolling hospital bed with new-fangled controls, a small window looking out on a complex of buildings interconnected by walkways, and cabinets and shelves filled with all sorts of test equipment. In fact, this hospital was just as he had imagined it would be, and that was why he had to get out of there.

He stared alternately at various points on the ceiling and the wall, as if his eyes were spinning a fine web in the corner of the room, hoping to catch something—anything—that might interest him. The sound of rustling papers diverted his eyes to the door for a moment. Suddenly, the door sprung open. As it started to close, a foot with a delicate ankle bracelet was stuck in it, and a young woman, with folders, clipboard, and purse dangling from her arms, walked in. She was dressed that evening, not in a prude Victorian dress, but in a stylish plaid skirt that she seemed unaccustomed to wearing.

Captain Gregory stared long and hard. Though his first love had always been the sea, for the second time in his life he felt a powerful attraction to another great lady. When he saw her, it was as if the last wave at high tide had crashed against the rocks, dislodging a jagged old rock and drawing it slowly but surely out to sea. In his life, Captain Gregory had often felt like that jagged old rock. But this was an alluring new temptress, and he was drawn to her as powerfully as he was drawn to the sea.

Apparently, she felt the same sensation of sand and surf. She returned his gaze with one equally as powerful, and not knowing what to say, blurted out, "Well, hello there, handsome." She immediately cupped her hand over her mouth and glanced around to see if anyone was looking, or perhaps to see if someone else had said it. But there was no one else in the room.

Captain Gregory smiled. "Well, hello there yourself, beautiful," he said, shaking his head, amazed that he had returned the salvo. "You are quite beautiful, you know. Even a crusty old sea barnacle like me can see that."

Intrigued, she hesitated for an instant, trying to restrain herself, but to no avail. "What makes you say that?" she said, playfully wrapping a wave of luxuriant auburn hair around her index finger.

"Do you really want to know?" he said, not knowing what in the world had possessed him to offer his innermost feelings.

"Yes, I really want to know," she said, slowly gravitating toward him, as if drawn by an irresistible force.

Captain Gregory felt the irresistible force, too, and it seemed to be pulling him, bed and all, toward her. He didn't know which was happening, whether he was being pulled or she was being drawn, nor did he care. He only knew that the same attraction was bringing them together. That he had willingly succumbed to her charms. And that this beautiful woman—this beautiful, lovely woman—had sparked the romantic nobleman in him.

As she stood by his bed, he gazed into her royal blue eyes and was stunned by the words that came to him like never before. "Well, let me tell you missy. I've seen a lot of things in my life. I've seen the ruby sun dissolve into the sea at sunset. I've seen the rainbow stripes in the early mist of the morning. And I've seen the Northern lights dance and flicker on a sea of glass. But never, ever, have I seen anything as beautiful as you."

Dr. Royale blushed. "I think maybe you've been at sea too long—way too long."

"That may be true, but my eyes haven't failed me yet," said Captain Gregory, a bit confused. It was strange. She had reacted as if she was somehow less than worthy, as if she had never received such a compliment before. Yet this made her all the more charming, all the more alluring, all the more enchanting. "So what are you here for, anyway?" he asked, watching the wisps of her auburn hair moving elastically from side to side.

"I'm here to help you."

"Then you must be a doctor, or maybe a nurse. If you're a doctor, let me tell you, I'm as fit as a fiddle. And if you're a nurse, well, I've already had all my bandages changed."

Dr. Royale glanced at the Demerol dispenser and the IV dangling from it and then stared at Captain Gregory reproachfully. She attached a new needle to the line and then gently took Captain Gregory by the hand. "I'm neither," she said as she inserted the IV into a rather large vein on top of his hand.

With one prick of the needle, Dr. Royale deflated the passion that had been building. "Hey! I don't need that... And what do you mean, neither?!" said Captain Gregory, frowning.

"Let me introduce myself. I'm Dr. Royale, your psychiatrist."

"A shrink! What do I want with a shrink? I don't have a screw loose."

"Oh, so that's what you think we do, is it?" said Dr. Royale, smiling. "It's not just about restoring the proper mental equilibrium. You're obviously of sound mind, so you don't need that. But we do much more than that. We mend broken hearts and restore lost memories, to name a few things."

Captain Gregory was dumbfounded. This Dr. Royale was obviously off her rocker, like most shrinks, if she really believed she could do that. "Well, I've got news for you, missy. You missed the boat. My heart's already been broken, and there's nothing you can do about it."

Dr. Royale looked at him with hopeful eyes. "Well, you know captain, I've heard that love is a many-splendored thing."

"You sound like a Saturday morning matinee."

"I'm not sure what I sound like, or what I know. But I know one thing: Someday you will learn to love again. I feel it," she said, placing her hand on his.

"I doubt that," he said, removing his hand.

"Why is that?"

"Oh, what the hell, I might as well tell you. A long time ago, I was in love. But the woman I loved was killed by the Humboldts," he said, his face crinkling up in pain.

"Oh, I'm so sorry. But if you don't mind my asking, how?"

"If you must know, she was eaten by the Humboldts," he said, staring at the floor.

"Eaten by the Humboldts! The Humboldts are cannibals?!" asked Dr. Royale, disgusted.

"No, no, the Humboldts aren't human!! They're squid," said Captain Gregory, looking up and gesturing wildly. "You know, the big five-foot bullet-heads with eyes like saucers. Don't you know anything about the sea?" Captain Gregory winced. Whether it was the pain of his recent accident, or the pain of accidents long ago, he didn't know. Nor did he care. The pain was too great, and he punched the pain button several times.

"Oh, so that's what you call them. On the contrary, captain, I do know something about them. They're pugilistic, primitive, and prone to feeding frenzies. Will eat just about anything, including their own kind," said Dr. Royale matter-of-factly as she pushed her glasses high on her nose.

"Now how do you know about that?" asked Captain Gregory, intrigued.

Dr. Royale waved her finger like a pendulum. "Ah, ah, ah, Captain. I'll ask the questions, thank you. You answer them, please. Now, if you don't mind my asking, how did you two meet?"

"Well, it's kind of a funny story, actually," said Captain Gregory, visibly relieved to talk about something else, anything else besides the accident. "We were at an amusement park in Veracruz. A shipmate and I were going down an old wooden slide on plastic runners. Then I saw her. She was this vision of loveliness standing at the bottom of the slide. I just had to get down there as soon as possible to meet her. Before I knew it, I took off down the slide without the runner. Well, needless to say, I got a pants-full of splinters. She was a nurse at the time and plucked all of the splinters out of my pants," said Captain Gregory, suddenly glassy-eyed, not knowing whether to laugh or cry.

Visibly moved, Dr. Royale shifted her weight and nearly tripped over the IV line. "You mean she plucked them from your buttocks?"

Captain Gregory smiled, amused by her clumsiness. "Yes," he said, wiping the moisture from his eyes. "In this case, you might say that love was a many-splintered thing."

Dr. Royale laughed until there were tears in her eyes, and Captain Gregory thought for a moment that he saw a kindred spirit somewhere in the depths of her royal blues, and then it vanished. Captain Gregory sighed. "What's the point of all of this, Dr. Royale? You can't bring her back."

Dr. Royale got up, backpedaling away from Captain Gregory's bed so that he wouldn't see the tears in her eyes, buying time to restrain the emotions that were so vividly on display. "Yes, that's true, but maybe I can help you learn to love again," she said, as her shoe got caught in the IV line. Panicked, she kicked up her heels to disentangle it, and suddenly, as if in a slow-motion ballet, she lost her balance. "Uh, ohh, ooohhhh!" she cried as she fell into the Demerol stand, knocking it over and nearly ripping the IV out of Captain Gregory's hand.

Once he saw that she was all right, Captain Gregory laughed so hard that he thought he'd burst his stitches. Dr. Royale laughed, too, and Captain Gregory found her laugh to be completely contagious. Everything seemed so much funnier when you weren't supposed to laugh. Captain Gregory hadn't laughed like that in a long time, and it was all due to this clumsy beauty sitting at his feet.

As the laughter subsided, he felt the stitches on the back of his head. "Youuch," he said, rubbing them. "Maybe you'd like to check the stitches on my head, too? Or better yet, the stitches on my backside," he added, surprised at the ease with which he was casting lines with the winsome doctor once again.

"You haven't been sliding down any slides lately, now have you?" said Dr. Royale as she slowly picked herself up. "No, that's okay, don't answer that question. I'm not here to assess your posterior, Captain Gregory. I'm here to assess your anterior."

"My what?" said Captain Gregory.

"Your anterior lobes. You know, your state of mind. How is it, really?"

Captain Gregory recovered quickly. "Well, it's much better thank you, since you walked in the room."

Dr. Royale nervously searched through her purse, found a cigarette, and lit it. She puffed on it, blowing a protective cloud of smoke in front of herself. Embarrassed by all the attention, yet seeming to love it at the same time, she said, "I'd love to flirt with you all day, Captain Gregory, but unfortunately, we need to keep this on a professional level."

Captain Gregory was amazed at how quickly she changed tactics, like a boat tacking in a fickle wind. It was as if she was two persons, alternating between doctor and damsel. Unlike Dr. Royale, he would not change course once it was set, if he could help it. "Oh, now that's a shame. Okay, what else do you want to know?" he said, trying to conceal the fact that he was studying the curvature of her figure as if following the fine lines of a nautical map.

"Stick to the subject please. Do you have any questions?"

"Yes. How in the world did I get here?"

"You were rescued and brought here."

"Ah, then it must have been my good man, Manuel. He was always loyal, to the end. Which is more than I can say about that good-for-nothing Cranston. When I get my hands on him, I'll wring his neck." Captain Gregory looked at the hospital gown he was wearing. "But first I have to go home and change out of these things."

"There now, Captain Gregory, please calm yourself. If you don't mind, I have to ask you a few questions for the record." Dr. Royale pulled out a clipboard and filled out a few items on a rather official-looking document. "Tell me now, do you know where your home is?"

"I live on my boat."

Dr. Royale appeared stunned by this revelation, as if water was the domain of only the fish, who lived below the surface. After thinking about it for a moment, she asked, "Why do you live there?"

"Well I'm not much of a land lubber."

"Land lubber?"

"Yes. What I mean is, I love the sea... Oh, you wouldn't understand. Look, I'm a fisherman by trade, and all my life I've been looking for the perfect catch," he said, gazing at her as if she were some precious pearl being gently bathed by the sea itself.

"Oh, I see." Dr. Royale looked at Captain Gregory with a glint of unprofessional mischief in her eyes, crossed her legs, and said, "Well, when you find her, you let me know."

"That I will, missy," said Captain Gregory, smiling.

Although she had invited the attention, Dr. Royale seemed embarrassed by it, as if she was struggling with her own feelings. In a moment she was composed again, ignoring the captain's advances. Captain Gregory could tell that their romantic interlude was over, and he wondered if the Doctor had won out over the damsel for good. "Just one more question," said Dr. Royale. "Do you remember where you kept your boat?"

"Sure its, its...why no, now that you mention it. I have no idea. In fact, I can't even remember in what state it's docked." Captain Gregory scratched his head, amazed that he was revealing so much to this alluring newcomer.

"I see. But you remember names and faces."

"That's right."

Dr. Royale shook her pen, coaxing the ink. "But apparently not places. For instance, where do you get your fishing supplies, tackle, nets, and whatever else it is you fishermen use to do your kind of work?"

"I can't remember."

"I see. That's really all I need for now." Dr. Royale quickly wrote on the form and then made an entry in her notebook: "Systematic amnesia. Site complex."

As he glanced at the clipboard, Captain Gregory could not make head or tail out of the notes. He shrugged, realizing that doctors had a language all of their own. That didn't explain everything, though. His curiosity was almost as strong as the itch in the wound at the back of his head. Captain Gregory scratched it and asked, "How did you know that I am a fisherman?"

Dr. Royale smiled. "Simple. You were talking out loud in your dreams."

"Oh. What else did I say?" asked Captain Gregory, uncomfortable in the knowledge that he had shared his innermost thoughts and dreams with a complete stranger, a completely beautiful stranger.

"Not much, for the most part you were unconscious."

Captain Gregory stared at her. He could read a face as well as he could read a map, and there was something that the good doctor wasn't telling him. "Dr. Royale, do you know the nature and extent of my injuries?"

Dr. Royale gently shook her finger, all the while staring at it as if she had never seen one before. "I said I'll ask the questions, thank you, remember?" Then she looked at Captain Gregory and her demeanor changed from admonishment to pity. "No, from a purely physiological standpoint, I don't.

That's for you and your doctors to resolve. Their job is to repair your brain. My job is to understand your mind."

"Well then, you'll have to do it quickly because I'm getting out of here. Now where are my clothes?"

Dr. Royale shook her head. "Captain Gregory, I regret to inform you that you are not going anywhere."

"Like hell, I'm not," said Captain Gregory. He raised himself in bed, reached over his bedside for his shoes and started to put them on, forgetting to change out of his hospital gown.

"You don't understand," said Dr. Royale. "You are going to be here for a while. You are suffering from an unusual form of amnesia." She puffed on her cigarette, blowing another luxurious cloud of smoke in front of herself.

Captain Gregory stopped for a moment. "What kind is that?"

"Systematic. You remember names and faces, but none of the places associated with them. If you were to leave now, where would you go?"

Wearing bandages wrapped around his head and a hospital gown complemented by his dock shoes, Captain Gregory started up from the bed. "Lady, all you have to do is point me in the direction of the sea, and I'll find my way."

"You are forcing me to do this," said Dr. Royale. She grabbed the remote attached to the hospital bed but dropped it along with her clipboard and folders. Both she and Captain Gregory crouched at the same time to pick them up. He handed her the remote, not knowing what to do with it.

"Thank you... Now hold it right there, or I'll push the button." Dr. Royale was breathing heavily, excited by the challenge of her newest patient.

"You wouldn't," said Captain Gregory, annoyed that he had trusted her. Even so, he couldn't help but notice her bosom swell and the gentle undulations of her skin.

"Oh, wouldn't I?" She placed her finger on the button and accidentally pressed it.

Almost instantaneously, two orderlies entered the room, each dressed in blue-green uniforms with their names embroidered on them. The first spoke. "Are you ready to transport the patient?"

Dr. Royale shook her head. "No, I am not. You were told not to come in here until I was through talking to the patient."

"But you pressed the button," said the orderly.

"What do you mean, talk to the patient? About what?" said Captain Gregory, angry about the secret being kept from him.

"Please hold on a second, Captain. I promise I will explain." She turned to the orderlies. "I must have accidentally pressed the button. I'm sorry. Now please wait outside." With rather perplexed looks on their faces, the two orderlies filed out of the room without a word.

"Am I being kept here against my will?" asked Captain Gregory.

Dr. Royale puffed on her cigarette, and by the time the smoke cleared, she was standing in another corner of the room. "That all depends on your definition and your view of reality. If you're talking about when you first came here, I would say that you didn't have much say in the matter, and if you had, you would have been glad to be here."

Captain Gregory grabbed her by the arm. "You know what I mean, I'm talking about now," he said with fire in his eyes. He was red hot with anger, yet fully in control, the result of years of military training.

Dr. Royale tried to peel his fingers away, but his grip was too strong. "I'm afraid the answer is yes. You must stay here in your present condition. Now please let go of my arm."

His amorous feelings replaced by suspicion and anger, Captain Gregory let go with a huff and walked out the door. After a few steps, he was met by the two orderlies, who grabbed his arms. He struggled for a minute but was quickly fatigued by the whole ordeal and was gently escorted back to bed. Tired, but not broken, he asked, "Why are you doing this?"

With all of the human compassion that she could muster, Dr. Royale said, "You are suffering from amnesia. You would be lost, wandering the streets. We can't let you go in your present condition."

Captain Gregory pounded his fist on the night stand. "You have no right!"

"I'm sorry, Captain Gregory, but I do." Dr. Royale took out a pen, and with a grand sweep, signed the form on her clipboard. "These commitment papers give me the legal right to care for you."

Captain Gregory scowled. "For how long? A day, a year, forever?"

Dr. Royale paused as if she didn't know the answer. "Until you are better."

Captain Gregory knew that she didn't have the guts to tell him the truth, whatever that was. "You know, when we first met. I thought you might be different," he said turning away. "But now I can see that you're nothing but a lousy, two-bit shrink."

Dr. Royale tried to place her hand on his head, but he wouldn't let her. She looked down at him with gentle eyes. "Captain Gregory, I *am* different. And I do care. In time you will see that. I am sorry about this. I really am. But now it's time to go." She motioned to the two orderlies, one of whom left the room and came back momentarily with a wheelchair.

"You're not putting me in that." Captain Gregory folded his arms defiantly.

Dr. Royale sighed. "Captain Gregory, you're making this most difficult." She summoned a nurse, who came into the room with a syringe in hand. The two orderlies held Captain

Gregory down in his bed while the nurse injected him with a sedative.

"This will calm you down," said Dr. Royale, while the two orderlies began to strap Captain Gregory to the bed. Dr. Royale held up her hand to stop them. "I don't think that the straps will be necessary as long as you two accompany us." She turned to Captain Gregory. "Am I right?"

Captain Gregory nodded. Then the bed rails went up, the brakes were released and, before he knew it, he was rolling slowly down the hallway. As they turned the corner from his room, he asked, "Where are you taking me?"

"To a different part of the hospital."

"I *know* that. What part of the hospital?"

"For people who are recovering from head injuries and other maladies."

Captain Gregory's eyes narrowed. "Don't give me that double-talk, doctor. You mean the psychiatric ward, don't you?"

"Yes, if you wish to call it that. We call it the Neurology and Neurosis Wing."

Captain Gregory imagined long white corridors, nurses in white uniforms, and antiseptic music in the air. He also expected to hear the stereotypical screams from behind closed doors and see sedated inmates wandering the halls. Keeping his ears pricked for any signs of the crazies, he turned to Dr. Royale. "How long?"

"I'm sorry, Captain Gregory, but I don't know the answer to that question."

"I should have known," said Captain Gregory, feeling a bit more relaxed now. The drugs were beginning to take effect. "Well, I just know that I am going to hate my room and everything about this place."

Dr. Royale's face brightened as if she had hit upon a wonderful idea. "If you want your room changed, I have the power to change it to your liking."

"I don't suppose you could make it like a Captain's Quarters?" Even in his altered state, Captain Gregory knew it was a ludicrous request, so it came as no surprise that Dr. Royale didn't answer.

The orderlies put a card through a reader, and the doors to the Neurology and Neurosis Wing swung open automatically. Captain Gregory felt a bit woozy now, and he imagined himself drinking a whiskey on the rocks on his boat in the Atlantic, though he was well aware that the current journey would leave him land-locked. He made believe anyway, saying to anyone who would listen, "Look sharp mates, you're pitching low to starboard; trim your sails."

Dr. Royale and the orderlies looked at each other and nodded. As they rounded the corner on the way to his room, Captain Gregory noticed the nurses in white uniforms, the white walls, and the soft music playing in the background. "Ah yes, the sea sirens are at it again. It must be near time to retire to my quarters. See you in the morning, bright and early."

Dr. Royale smiled at Captain Gregory, tucked in his covers, then gently held his hand as he struggled to stay awake. His mind clouded, he looked at her with weary eyes. "Who are you? Doctor or damsel? You know, we don't allow any damsels on board, not even in distress. Or that dress either." He laughed a full-bellied laugh and held onto her hand a little tighter. The corridor lights seemed to be getting brighter and brighter, and they were beginning to bother his eyes, which were getting heavier and heavier.

When they got to his room, Captain Gregory was almost asleep, his eyes slit like a baby's just before a nap. Suddenly, his eyes opened wide, and he looked around. There was a table for laying out maps, a sextant, shelves filled with nautical books, a bunk with a fresh-water basin beside it, and a porthole for looking out on the seascape. "This room. It's perfect." He looked at Dr. Royale sleepily. "How did you know?"

Dr. Royale smiled a most alluring smile. "I do my best to anticipate the needs of my patients. So if you need anything, anything at all, just drop me a line...only make sure there's no hook on the end of it."

Captain Gregory smiled and rubbed his eyes. Everything seemed so bright. Dr. Royale motioned for the orderlies to lower the lights in the room. The bright light faded into darkness, and finally, Captain Gregory was asleep.

Six

Cranston took the egg out of the jar and held it up to the light, curious if there was anything inside, half-expecting to see a gold sovereign embossed on the outside. After all, this egg was his ticket to fame and fortune, his dream and destiny. First he would sell the egg to the Boston Biological Research Institute; interest was so great, they'd be willing to pay fifty thousand for it. Then he would go after the mother, a designation that seemed inadequate for a 100-foot plus leviathan. She was more than just your run-of-the-mill mother. She was the mother of all mothers, a Queen, a "big red" Queen whose market price could be counted more easily in gold coins. He had some connections, who had some connections, who might pay dearly for such a catch.

Certain that this was his lucky day, and growing impatient waiting for the buyer to show up at the appointed time, Cranston impulsively threw the egg up in the air. In what seemed like an eternity, the egg spun around its short axis, slowing on the way up, pausing at the top, and speeding on the way down before landing in Cranston's outstretched hand unscathed.

His change of fortune was almost too good to be true. With the captain gone, he had moved into the Sea Horse and found it much to his liking. As he sat on the bunk in the Captain's Quarters, he held the egg between his thumb and index finger and brought it up to his nose, as if he were a man of culture and refinement about to sniff the bouquet of a fine "big red" wine. Unexpectedly, the wind slammed the door shut, startling him. The egg squirted loose from his finger tips, and he watched in horror as it fell onto the bed and slowly began to roll. As it fell off the side of the bed, Cranston dove onto the floor with hands outstretched and caught it just before it landed.

He cradled the egg in his hands, held it up to his cheek, and breathed a sigh of relief. That was a close call. Perspiring heavily, he returned the egg to the jar and went outside for some fresh air. It was dark and in the corner of his eye, Cranston thought he saw someone lurking behind the nets and trolling equipment. He looked at the nets and scratched his chin, hoping to find someone there to throw overboard. That would calm his nerves. Seeing no one, he turned away, disappointed, and headed back into the Captain's Quarters.

He grabbed Captain Gregory's pipe from its stand, lit it, and took a few puffs. After relaxing for a few moments, he took the egg from the jar once more, held it up to the light, and said, "You and I are going to do great things together." He turned the egg over and over and reviewed his plan of attack...

First he would kill the giant beast and sell the parts for a king's ransom. Next, he would go after the great whales, some of which he knew commanded phenomenal prices in the Japanese black market. Then, like any good businessman, he would diversify into racketeering, "persuading" the business owners along the wharf to donate a percentage to his favorite charity. If they refused, he knew of several surgical methods that could be used to persuade them, all of which involved knives. Racketeering, of course, was an important part of the grand plan. But the part that really excited him, the part that fueled his imagination, was the thought of killing rare and endangered species. The thrill of the kill. The power to extinguish an entire species. That was ultimate power, the kind of power that even fame and fortune could not buy.

With ultimate power would come ultimate wealth. He pictured himself running his empire from the deck of a fancy yacht — not just any yacht, his yacht. There would be beautiful women everywhere, and they would adore Neil Cranston, "the eel". Yes, the eel. Let them say it behind his back. It suited him just fine. The name would be a compliment to the green suit he would be wearing, his favorite color. Not a wrinkle would show on the green linen pant legs, cream-colored silk shirt, and green linen suit coat that would lightly drape his rather thin, serpentine body; and the diamond-studded French cuffs would sparkle in the light when he took off his green leather gloves, the same gloves he would use in "surgery" to stab his victims between the eyes, as he had done many times with octopuses. This would be his trademark, a sign to anyone who knew him that he was a man of business and not to be trifled with.

The clock on the wall chimed and snapped Cranston out of his daydream. It was 9:15. His buyer, a college professor, was more than a full hour late. Perhaps this wasn't his lucky day after all. Maybe the lousy professor was going to welch on the deal. In fact, he was sure of it. Frustrated, Cranston took the egg out of the jar again and contemplated smashing it when, suddenly, the wind slammed the door and then opened it again. Annoyed, Cranston wheeled around to shut the door and was startled by the sight of another man.

In that instant, he dropped the egg. They both watched in horror as it landed on Cranston's foot and made the sound, the sound that neither wanted to hear, the sound of an egg cracking. To Cranston that sound might as well have been the sound of his own head cracking. The egg rolled off the end of his shoe and landed on the floor and, because the boat was listing slightly to the left, it rolled underneath the bed. Cranston stood there and just stared at the bed.

"Oh no. You've broken it! You've broken the egg!"

Cranston tried to appear calm, even though he dreaded looking under the bed. "Just take it easy, Professor. It is Professor Holloway, isn't it?"

Clearly agitated, Professor Holloway said, "Yes it is. But I don't see how you can be so nonchalant about it."

Cranston didn't quite understand Professor Holloway, but he got the gist of it. "Don't worry, Professor, we'll fix it, good as new," he said as he looked under the bed.

Professor Holloway shook his head. He hated dealing with idiot fishermen. "Well, you can't just 'fix' a rare egg. It's either in one piece or it isn't."

As he carefully took hold of it, Cranston breathed a sigh of relief to discover that the egg was still intact. He brought it out from under the bed. "I'll put it under the light. Let's see if it's broke."

"Broken," said Professor Holloway.

Cranston shook his head and waved his hands in exasperation. "Whatever you say, Professor." He placed the egg under the floor lamp, and they both bent over to look at it, their heads bumping slightly.

Professor Holloway backed away, exasperated. "May I, please," he said as Cranston handed him the egg.

Professor Holloway examined the egg with a magnifying glass, finding only a hairline fracture of the transparent, paper-thin shell, which was really a hardened membrane. He followed each and every line in the hairline crack as if it were a road to a destination, a destination of fame and fortune resulting from discovering a rare species. "Fascinating. This is, without a doubt, Octopus Giganticus."

"Speak in plain English, would you Professor," Cranston demanded, not liking the secretive language that college professors used.

"I believe that this is a female specimen of the giant octopus!" Professor Holloway tried to contain his excitement.

"Well, I could have told you that," said Cranston.

BENEATH FIFTY POUNDS OF SHRIMP NETS wrapped around his body like some sort of naturalist garb, crouched Claude Fountainbleu, a Frenchman and a card-carrying member of the Save the Ocean Society (SOS), a former weapons specialist in the French Navy, who was on special assignment to investigate the Sea Horse for suspected violations of the Endangered Species Act. A rather tall, wiry, birdlike sort of man with long hair and horn-rimmed glasses, Claude had sat patiently there for hours.

Earlier, when Cranston had grown suspicious, Claude had closed his eyes and curled in his toes to avoid betraying his position. With the gentle rocking of the boat acting on him like a smooth narcoleptic tonic, he had fallen asleep, something he was prone to doing on boats unless he kept himself busy. It was some time later-he didn't know when-that he was awakened by loud voices coming from the Captain's Quarters. Slowly, he emerged from the nets and moved to the porthole to listen.

"What do you mean you can't pay full price, Holloway?"

"Well, Mr. Cranston, the specimen has obviously been fractured. It's not as valuable to me in its current condition."

Claude slowly inched up to the porthole, wishing that his hair wasn't so bushy and long, making it easier to be detected. The two parties, however, were intent on the egg and nothing else, and so his presence went undetected.

With a night vision camera, he took a couple of snapshots of Cranston and Professor Holloway and several closeups of the egg. The professor was a short, stumpy man wearing a wrinkled business suit that looked like he had slept in it. There was several days of stubble on his chin, and his hair was slicked down and slightly askew.

Cranston grabbed the egg and held it at arms length away from Professor Holloway, giving Claude another perfect opportunity to take a few quick snapshots. "Okay fine, if it's not worth anything, I'll just smash it to smithereens." He placed it on the floor and raised his shoe just above it.

Professor Holloway held up his hands. "Wait. Don't do that. I didn't say I wouldn't pay."

"How much?" Cranston lowered his shoe until it just touched the top of the egg.

"$25,000."

Cranston's eyes narrowed. "We agreed to $50,000 beforehand. If you've got that much maybe I'll just take it."

Professor Holloway fidgeted, smiling nervously. "Ah, my friend, you do not know much about the art of commerce. The first rule is never to steal from your customers. It's bad for business, and you turn customers into enemies."

"Is that a threat?"

Professor Holloway waved his hands, dismissing the question. "Who me, threaten you? Now why would I bite the hand feeding me with rare and endangered species? Does that make any sense? No, Mr. Cranston, since Captain Gregory appears to be out of the picture, you and I are in this for the long haul, so we better make the most of it."

Cranston hesitated, and it was obvious to Claude that the money was much less than he had hoped. "I'll take it."

Professor Holloway paid him the money and then held the egg up to the light once more and examined the three white rings encompassing the long axis of the egg. "At last, a specimen of Octopus Giganticus." He placed the egg in a jar, put it in a small black bag, and said "Come home to daddy."

Claude was sickened by the transaction, but he was not there to intervene. He was there to establish the evidence. He had done so, and it was time to leave. He edged away from the porthole and then quickly hoisted himself over the side of the boat and into the cold, dark night water just as Professor Holloway came out of the Captain's Quarters. Within moments he had swam behind another vessel and was safely out of sight.

AS HE WALKED ALONG THE DOCK TOWARD HIS car, Professor Holloway thought with satisfaction at how he had saved the institute $25,000. The small fracture in the exterior of the egg would not in any way deter the research he would do on the occupant. The outside wasn't important; it was what was inside. The simpleton sailor had fallen for his bluff, and Professor Holloway reveled in his fine piece of trickery.

CRANSTON NEEDED FRESH AIR THAT NIGHT after the exhilaration and disappointment of his first sale, so he brought the money outside to count it again and to look into the depths of the sea where his next prize, the Queen, was undoubtedly lurking. With the dock lamps lighting the water, he almost expected to see the monster rise from the depths but instead saw only his own reflection.

SEVEN

Claude Fountainbleu swallowed hard as he walked up the ramp leading to the grand entrance of Manchester General, a huge hospital with 1500 beds. Man was so concerned with saving himself. Saving other species, however, was a different matter. As a Frenchman in a foreign land, Claude had little hope of convincing Dr. Bellwether to help him, but he had to try. There was another species, besides man, that needed protection, that deserved protection. Given his background, Dr. Bellwether would certainly be able to identify the egg, and that was a start.

At the end of the ramp, Claude was surprised as the doors opened sideways, beckoning him into the old building. He walked in slowly, looking at the wonderful carvings in the ceiling and marveling at the impressionist artwork on the walls. An adjacent hallway had portraits of benefactors, board members, and the heads of the various disciplines. He looked at each one, finally finding the portrait of Dr. Niles Bellwether, head of Neurosurgery. He was a light-complexioned, serious-looking man with deep, penetrating, dark blue eyes, and a cap of sandy blonde hair in full recession. He looked too young to be the head of any department. Claude decided it must have been an earlier portrait and returned to the main hallway.

Approaching a woman at the information desk, he wiped the sweat from his brow and tried to look calm. "Could you tell me which floor is for Neurosurgery?"

"Fifth. Access is restricted to family members only." The woman barely looked up.

"Oh, that's not a problem," said Claude, determined to find Dr. Bellwether. He quickly merged with a stream of people headed for the elevator deck and squeezed into an elevator with an assortment of residents and nurses. A man at the controls held the "Hold" button until a patient in a wheelchair had been wheeled in backwards, and then proceeded to punch buttons as people called out "Two, please...Eight...Maternity." No one called out Neurosurgery, so Claude said quietly, "Fifth, if you please."

When he got out of the elevator, he followed the arrows to neurosurgery until double doors secured by a card reader blocked his entry. He ducked into a utility closet and came out with a face mask and gown on. He then waited and pulled out a pad of paper as if he were writing out case histories. Soon an orderly wheeling an empty bed ran his card through the reader and walked through the doors. As if he belonged there, Claude followed quietly behind and then paused to write more notes.

Two interns passed him in the hallway, and he followed them through several hallways. They turned the corner ahead of him, and Claude could hear a creaky door opening and closing. When he got there, the door was closed and the interns were gone. He slowly opened the door and entered a large, square observation deck above an operating room. A gallery of interns were watching three doctors, an anesthesiologist, and a team of nurses below.

He had the right place, and Claude was confident that the surgeon with the intense eyes leading the operation in the room below was his man. Dr. Bellwether was a very difficult man to contact. Claude had left several unanswered messages on his answering machine and had even staked out his house for several days, all to no avail. He concluded that Dr. Bellwether virtually lived at the hospital. It seemed odd, too, that a man who had been renowned in the field of cephalopod research many years ago was now a neurosurgeon. Perhaps he had turned to medicine after his theories were ridiculed, and he had lost his teaching position at Boston College. Claude had read about that.

"We will now excise the damaged ganglia of the cerebellum opposite the frontal occipital lobes," said Dr. Bellwether over the conference speakers. "The remaining tissue will then be rejoined by my colleagues."

Claude didn't understand a word but that didn't matter. He couldn't stand to watch another minute, so he turned away, doodling on his notepad the logo of his family's shrimp business in France, a business he hated with a passion. He continued to draw and soon lost track of the time. After a while, he realized that Dr. Bellwether was no longer speaking, and the interns in the gallery were beginning to disperse. Worse yet, Dr. Bellwether had left!

Claude hurriedly exited the room and looked in the hallway but could not find him. So he followed the arrows on the wall to Neurosurgery. He went straight to the patient ward and approached a woman at the Nurses Station. "Can you tell me where I might find Dr. Bellwether?"

"He is just finishing surgery."

"May I see him?"

"May I inquire as to why you wish to see him?"

"No, I am sorry Madame, I am not at liberty to discuss the case." Claude felt bad about deceiving the nurse, but this was for a good cause. If he was to carry out his mission, he would have to do whatever was necessary.

She looked at him with suspicion. "Well, I'm sorry, but unless you can tell me...say where is your badge? I thought you were a doctor or something."

He fiddled around in his pockets buying time. "I know that I put it here somewhere."

"In fact, I don't recognize you at all." The nurse's eyes narrowed. "Do you know that this ward is restricted?"

"Yes, I do. Did you know that I am Dr. Bellwether's new associate?"

The nurse did a double take, the etched lines on her forehead sketching a singular frown. "He doesn't have any partners. I'm sorry, if you can't show me some ID now, I'm going to have to call security."

At that moment, Dr. Bellwether went by the Nurses Station on his way to the elevators after a grueling day of surgery. About fiftyish, he was a tall, lanky man with a rather large forehead that angled outward to a huge cranial capacity, every inch of which was no doubt used. His hair formed a neat hedge that went around his head from ear to ear. The back of his head was adorned with a large bald spot, which glistened in the fluorescent light. The dark blue eyes were large and penetrating and seemed almost sad. Dr. Bellwether appeared to be the man Claude was looking for, except in one respect: he looked too young. Perhaps he just looked much younger than his years; Claude had once met a 101-year-old man who looked like he was in his seventies. After that experience, he had learned that just about anything was possible.

The nurse motioned to him. "Dr. Bellwether, I'm sorry to bother you, but this man claims he's some sort of associate of yours."

Dr. Bellwether glanced at Claude and shook his head. "I've never seen this man before in my life."

"Oh, I'm so sorry to have bothered you," said the nurse.

Claude knew that he had to act quickly, so he got up his nerve just as the doctor was turning away from him. "Dr. Bellwether, I'm told that you might be able to help me identify the egg in this picture." Claude shoved the photo in front of him, but Dr. Bellwether turned his head, refusing to look at it.

Dr. Bellwether turned to Claude, chastising him. "I am not a chicken farmer, son. I am a neurosurgeon. You obviously have the wrong man. Now if you'll excuse me." He waved his arm in front of him, pushing Claude's outstretched hand away.

"No, but wait. This is a rare octopus egg." Claude stepped in front of him, and Dr. Bellwether tried to walk around him as he headed to the elevators.

"Young man, do you have any idea what I've been through the last fifteen hours? Lateral incisions of the frontal lobe. And microsurgery of the ganglia. Now, please don't bother me, I'm not interested."

The nurse picked up the phone and asked, "Doctor, shall I call security?"

Dr. Bellwether held up his hand to signal for her to wait. "Just a second." He put his hands on his side, and turned to Claude. "Now look—"

"But I was told that you know something about cephalopods. You are supposed to be an expert in the field."

"That was my father. Why don't you call Dr. Holloway at Boston Bio or his partner, Richard Pearlman? They're renowned in the field of cephalopod research. Now please go, or I'll have the nurse call security," he said, brushing him aside, continuing toward the elevator.

"You don't understand. Dr. Holloway is the man I saw purchasing this egg."

"Perfectly understandable. That's his field. Now please, I'm a busy man." Dr. Bellwether reached for the elevator button.

"But he paid $25,000 for it."

Dr. Bellwether paused for a moment. He looked at Claude incredulously. "For an octopus egg?"

"Yes. A very large octopus egg that is obviously an endangered species that has been poached from its environment."

"I met Richard Pearlman at a cocktail party once, and he hardly seems the type to be mixed up in that kind of business."

"I don't know if he is or not. All I know is that Dr. Holloway was there and I saw him pay the money with my own eyes."

Dr. Bellwether relaxed a bit and pressed the elevator button. He turned back to the nurse. "I can handle this, Doris. Thank you."

The nurse looked at Claude suspiciously. "Are you sure, Dr. Bellwether?"

"Quite."

The elevator door opened, and the two got in. After the doors closed, Claude continued, "They said the name but it wasn't clear. If I heard it again I would know it."

"Let's go to my office." Dr. Bellwether's tone and attitude had completely changed by the time the elevator doors opened. He quickly led Claude into his office and closed the door as if he was about to be briefed on something top secret. He turned on the overhead light and then went straight to his desk and turned on the desk lamp. "Now let's take a look at what you've got."

He looked at the photos closely and became very excited. "I can hardly believe it. These photos are real?"

"Yes. What kind of octopus is it?"

"This is the egg of an Octopus Giganticus, a species believed to have died off twenty years ago. Do you know where they found it?"

"He mentioned something about No Man's Land."

"I'll take the day off tomorrow. Can you take me there?"

"Sure. Meet me at the harbor at 8:00 a.m."

They shook hands and Claude left. As he was winding through the hallways between him and the grand entrance, he planned the next part of his mission. First his boat, the Sea Kelp, would have to be thoroughly scrubbed. It wasn't every day that a renowned neurosurgeon set foot on his humble schooner. Next, he would check that all of the gear was in working order. Then he would make sure that he knew the exact longitude and latitude of No Man's Land. Rather than waiting to tail Cranston's boat, it would be better to establish a position right away. Armed with cameras, they would gather evidence against anyone trying to exploit this magnificent creature.

Claude also had another ace up his sleeve: Dr. Bellwether. He had read the infamous article in the January, 1962 edition of Science and Nature magazine and was intrigued by the elder Dr. Bellwether's hypotheses about the incredible intelligence of the creature. He also knew by Dr. Bellwether's reaction to the photos that he was well acquainted with his father's work. It would be a real advantage having Dr. Bellwether assist him in finding and identifying the creature. Once that was done, Phase 1 would be over.

The plan for Phase 2 was plain and simple: destruction of the enemy target. Back at the harbor, he would attach a suitable device to the hull of Cranston's boat, and when no one was around, set it off. Then Phase 3 would be launched. A rotating eight-hour patrol of SOS boats would be established to protect the creature while the evidence of the violations would be presented in court.

DR. BELLWETHER SPENT THE EARLY HOURS OF the morning searching for his old scuba gear. After looking through cupboards, rummaging in old desk drawers, and rifling through inventory lists of personal property, he was about to give up. Then it came to him; he snapped his fingers and ran up to the third floor attic.

He went directly to an old trunk, grabbed the keys from a hook on the wall, and attempted to unlock it. At first the lock wouldn't budge, so he turned with both hands with all of his might until it relented. With great anticipation, he opened the lid, took out the top drawer, and after sifting through some musty clothes, pulled out an old wetsuit.

The heat was stifling, so he stripped to his shorts. Then he put the wetsuit on and sat there wiping the perspiration from his brow, and the naiveté from his mind. What a fool he had been. What if Claude were some kind of lunatic who was out to discredit him, ridicule him, and force him to resign the way they had forced his father to resign? His intellectual curiosity had gotten the best of him the night before. It was all a joke and he wouldn't go. He wasn't being paranoid, never, just prudent—that's all. On the other hand, this could be the only opportunity he would ever get to vindicate his father. He sat there for a while, thought about his father, and realized that he had to take the chance.

His mind made up, he quickly put the clothes away and rushed to the garage with wetsuit on and face mask and flippers in hand. He started the car and hurriedly left the house, fearing that he might be late for his appointment, something he would have never tolerated from his students.

He sped all the way to Boston Harbor and went straight to the boat, boarding it at precisely 8:00 a.m., wearing the old wetsuit that had not been worn for years. That didn't matter. He was ready to go scuba diving.

Claude looked at the wetsuit and smiled broadly. "Good morning, Dr. Bellwether. Are you ready to go?"

"As ready as I'll ever be," said Dr. Bellwether, trying on his face mask, adjusting the straps, and then taking it off with a snap. He wished the emotional string inside of him was nearly so elastic for he was being pulled in opposite directions by his curiosity and better judgment. This better be good kid.

They were soon under way and, when they got out into the mild swells of the open sea, the first thing that Dr. Bellwether noticed was that he had lost his sea legs. He was feeling a bit queasy, a feeling he had never been afflicted with as a youth. On top of that, there appeared to be storm clouds gathering on the horizon.

"Can I get you anything? Some Dramamine perhaps?" asked Claude.

"No, I'll be all right." Dr. Bellwether wasn't going to take any chances taking pills from somebody he didn't know very well. Claude didn't appear to be a lunatic, but you could never tell. Besides, it wasn't his stomach that Dr. Bellwether was worried about: it was his diving capability. As a youth, he had been scuba diving often with his father, but that was many years ago. He had assumed that it was like riding a bike: you never forget. With his stomach acting up now, he was beginning to wonder what would be next. Maybe these were psychosomatic symptoms, reflections of nagging doubts he had about going on the expedition. "You know for a few moments after I got home last night, I nearly convinced myself not to go."

"What made you change your mind, Dr. Bellwether?"

"No, please, call me Niles." He inspected the underwater camera, pointed it toward the sea, and looked through the lens. "I found my father's papers and read them all. And I realized that he was a dreamer, whose wildest dream came true: the discovery of a truly amazing creature whose abilities in some ways are much greater than our own."

"Yes, I read his hypotheses in Science and Nature magazine."

"He had many more writings on the subject. The first one was viewed with great skepticism by the scientific community.

He could never get another one published and, as a result, he lost his teaching post at Boston College."

"That's too bad."

"He had a dream but nobody believed it. Well, I decided that I'd make believers out of them all. But first, I guess I had to believe."

"And do you?"

"That's why I'm here." Dr. Bellwether gazed at the point of land in the distance, while reviewing his father's theories concerning the creature. All of the evidence his father had accumulated, including the specimen itself, had been completely destroyed in a fire. His father had somehow reconstructed all of the evidence and theories without the proof in the infamous Science and Nature article that was his greatest triumph and his greatest defeat. The theory that had piqued Dr. Bellwether's interest the most dealt with the creature's abilities. He played that over and over in his mind:

"The octopus has a wide array of abilities. It can replicate color better than any camouflage artist on land or sea. On the top layer of skin are specialized cells called chromatophores which open and close to produce virtually any color in any pattern, blending in precisely with its environment. It can secrete inks of different colors to ward off attackers. It can emit chemicals to mimic the chemicals emitted by other sea creatures or to neutralize its own smell and confuse its enemies. In fact, there seems to be no shortage of functions that the octopus can duplicate at will, either to defend itself against its enemies or to communicate with its prey.

"Hints about its communication abilities are the most intriguing; for instance, we witnessed hundreds of crabs routinely gather at the entrance of the cave where the great octopus would gather them in. If no mating sounds or chemical markers are used to attract the crabs, how does she do it? There were no ready clues until that fateful day when a specimen washed ashore. Upon examination, we found that a small decentralized portion of the cephalopod's brain, a part that is attached by thin bands to the main brain mass, is virtually identical to the nerve tissue in it's favorite prey, the crab. Perhaps these ganglia masses located at the base of the brain are used to communicate somehow with its prey or to trick it into thinking that the octopus is another crab—albeit a very large one. If this hypothesis is correct, then Octopus Giganticus is the only octopus known to develop sub-brains used for communication with other species. The rest of the female's brain is far more complex and diverse, making her a remarkable animal with extremely complex brain structures, three hemispheres, and a size that is several magnitudes larger than our own.

"The male, on the other hand, at two-feet wide is quite small and unremarkable. Given the sheer magnitude of the females, it is conceivable that the males might actually be organized around a single female, a queen, if you will, who is the dominant individual in each society, if in fact a societal structure exists. This, of course, is just a hypothesis and has yet to be proved..."

"There it is," said Claude. Dr. Bellwether's thoughts were interrupted as Claude pointed to the jut of land known as No Man's Land. They would be there soon, and so Claude locked the steering wheel and went below to get the scuba gear. Momentarily he came up with two tanks and a wetsuit.

While helping Claude with the tanks, Dr. Bellwether asked, "Why are *you* doing this?"

"Well, Dr. Bellwether, my father was a fisherman, and my grandfather was a fisherman, and I used to be a fisherman too."

"What happened?"

"The commercial vessels began to use drift nets, you know, the kind that catches everything, including the fish you don't want and can't sell. They drove the price lower and lower. Pretty soon everyone was doing it, including me. We were catching shrimp and everything else—grouper, porpoise, Mahi Mahi. Then one day I caught a leatherneck turtle, you know, the big one that is very rare, only it didn't survive the net. It had bit a hole in the net but could only get its head through. Its neck was broken, lacerated, nearly cut clean off. That's when I quit."

"To preserve what's left?"

"No, to conserve what's left. I'm not a fanatic. We have to eat, too, and though I've become a vegetarian, I try not to be preachy about it. But I can't see wasting these resources. There has to be forces that counter those who would exploit everything."

"I see."

As they neared the point of land rising from the sea, they came upon Captain Gregory's old boat but saw no one aboard. Claude was visibly concerned as he lowered anchor about 50 yards away from the other boat.

"What's wrong?" asked Dr. Bellwether.

"You see that boat over there?" said Claude. "The transaction took place on that boat when it was in the marina. You can stay onboard and wait for me if you want. I'd understand."

Dr. Bellwether hesitated, not knowing what to do or say. His first impulse was to head back to shore and let the authorities handle the situation. Then he remembered how his father had been ridiculed by the scientific community and ostracized for his views. After his grant money had dried up and he had lost his teaching post, he ended up selling used cars to help make ends meet and to help put his son through medical school. The treatment his father had received from his peers had always stuck in Dr. Bellwether's craw. Now was his chance to vindicate his father.

Dr. Bellwether held up a hand. "No, that's okay. I want to do this... I need to do this. Look, I *have* to do this. So, let's go take some pictures of her." He snapped a mini-light attachment to his camera and tied the camera strap around his wrist. Taking pictures wasn't the only reason he was going. He was beginning to admire Claude and wanted to help. He tightened his face mask, his straps, and his tanks. He knew every strap and adjustment and was pleased that Claude had taken note of it. There would be no tutorials needed.

Dr. Bellwether motioned for Claude to check his tanks. He adjusted the control valves and mixture and then sat backward on the ledge. "Let's go," he said. He then placed the mouthpiece into his mouth and dove backward into the sparkling blue water, and Dr. Bellwether quickly followed.

They descended until they reached the ocean floor, about 75 feet below. The vegetation was lush, and there were many nooks and crannies that were undoubtedly the splendid homes of many a mollusk. Dr. Bellwether noted that it was a perfect feeding ground for fish and crabs and, of course, their predator, the shy but highly resourceful octopus. Dr. Bellwether knew that these were the homes of smaller cephalopods, but not the immense creature described by his father in his journals. She would have a much larger home, a home large enough to house a creature that was 100 feet long, weighing in the neighborhood of 1500 pounds. The home of such a creature could only be a cave, and so Dr. Bellwether motioned to Claude to head for the sea cliffs.

As they got closer, Dr. Bellwether was stunned at the variegated beauty of the cliffs with its patchwork of purple and red sea urchins clinging to its surface. He paused to examine the clinging vines at cliff side and was startled as two manta rays nearly tickled his feet as they nonchalantly swam below him. After Dr. Bellwether had regained his composure, Claude motioned to him to move on to the other side.

They had just started for the other side of the island when, suddenly, they heard an explosion from around the bend about a quarter mile ahead. They swam quickly toward it, though it seemed to take forever to negotiate the distance. As they turned the corner, the cliff side gave way to an area with a great deal of small rocks, sand, and silt in the water. The explosion had raised so much silt that at first Claude and Dr. Bellwether held hands so as not to lose each other in the turgid water. When the sand and silt began to settle, they let go and Dr. Bellwether swam the remaining 15 yards or so along the cliffs to the opening of a cave to investigate. He stopped at the mouth of the cave when he sensed that Claude was no longer following him.

He looked back and saw Claude motionless by the cliffs, as if suspended by some fisherman's line. He moved away from the mouth and looked over at Claude again, seeing nothing but the great expanse of sea cliffs before them. He motioned to Claude to follow him to the cave, but curiously, he did not. Then he understood why.

He felt a presence, the same presence that had no doubt stopped Claude in his wake. The cliffs were not the only thing behind Claude. It was her, a majestic mountain of a mollusk with a head larger than any he had ever seen—on anything! Dr. Bellwether didn't know whether to laugh or cry. He didn't know what to do. If he moved to help, maybe she would think he was trying to attack; after all he was only fifty feet away, an arm's length from her awesome, massive head.

She was clinging to the side of the cliff with arms spread to their fullest, flattened out so as not to protrude too far from the rock, but to blend perfectly with it. Dr. Bellwether reasoned that she had ventured from her cave after the explosion. But why? Perhaps falling rocks had frightened her out into the open or, more likely, the silt had forced her to find clear water for air. But why didn't she just swim away? She was a much faster swimmer than they. Hoping for an answer, he turned to Claude, who slowly pointed to a rock not far away.

A man emerged from behind the rock, aiming a spear gun directly at the cephalopod. To protect her, Claude swam without hesitation in front of her. The man waved his hand furiously at the Frenchman to move away, but he would not move. Only the sound of the ever-increasing stream of bubbles from

Claude's mouth broke the silence that ensued. The man moved a little to the left, then the right, trying to get a clean shot between her eyes but he could not. He tried swimming a little closer so as to intimidate Claude, but Claude did not give an inch... Dr. Bellwether was amazed at the Frenchman's courage.

He snapped several pictures of the confrontation, and in response, the man pointed the spear gun at Dr. Bellwether, prompting him to drop the camera. As he did, the wrist band snapped, and the camera fell to the ocean floor. Dr. Bellwether froze, and the spear gun slowly turned back on its original target. After a seemingly endless stretch in which the three stared at each other, the man apparently decided not to kill Claude or the cephalopod—for some unknown reason. Instead, he turned around and quickly swam away, fading into the ever-darkening waters as Claude and Dr. Bellwether breathed a sigh of relief.

Claude slowly inched away from the giant cephalopod and swam over to Dr. Bellwether. They both backed away from the cliffs, hoping that she would go back into the cave. Dr. Bellwether thought about taking a picture, but he decided against it. The magnificent creature was undoubtedly traumatized enough, and he did not want to startle her.

After a few moments, she did move...only toward them, as if to get a better look. She looked at them both for a moment, turning her head slightly while maintaining the horizontal position of her eyes so as to keep her gaze upon them. She then pointed her head and with a tremendous burst of speed, jettisoned to the entrance of her home. While amazed at her power and grace, Dr. Bellwether was stunned by the feeling that the swim-by was a thank you of sorts. In that moment, he decided that whether or not he got a picture of this magnificent creature, just knowing that she existed and that they, or at least Claude, had done something to save her was all that mattered. His father had been right: she was a magnificent creature who deserved to live in her habitat without interference, and he decided that he would do everything in his power to see that she did.

After she had made it into her cave safely, Dr. Bellwether picked up the camera he had dropped, and the two began their swim back to the boat. They heard another boat take off at high speed, and Dr. Bellwether thought that this was rather odd. After all, the man with the spear gun had nothing to fear from them. They were unarmed. Yet he sped away as if he were in a hurry.

Then suddenly, as they rounded the bend, there was a tremendous explosion ahead of them. It was their boat! Judging by the bits and pieces of motor windings, frame, propeller, cabinet doors, and other odds and ends, the engine compartment had been blown apart. After the debris settled, they swam toward the boat, only to find that it was sinking. Dr. Bellwether and Claude looked at each other, both realizing that the man had had one more explosive device in his arsenal.

The first feeling that Dr. Bellwether had was one of sheer panic. He and Claude swam to the surface and pulled off their masks. It was raining, and the skies were getting quite dark. The swells were starting to pick up, and they realized that they had to do something soon to save themselves.

"What are we going to do?" asked Dr. Bellwether, trying to think of something, anything. He stared at Claude, who said nothing as he watched the boat sink into the ocean. "Do you have a battery operated radio?"

Claude motioned as if he had already thought of that. "No. The radio was powered from the juice on the boat."

"What about the oxygen?"

Claude quickly confirmed that they were nearly out, leaving them no opportunity to ride out the storm under water. "Perhaps we can find a spot on No Man's Land," he said. The seas were getting rough, so they swam under water toward the point, but soon, Dr. Bellwether was out of oxygen. He borrowed from Claude until his supply was exhausted, and then they rose to the surface.

Dr. Bellwether was gasping for air. "I can't keep my head above water for much longer."

"We've got to cut loose the gear."

"We can't just dump the oxygen," said Dr. Bellwether, knowing that the tanks were empty. That wasn't the point. The tanks were like a security blanket, and he was reluctant to let them go.

"What difference does it make? There is none left," said Claude. After some convincing, Dr. Bellwether finally agreed. With some regret, they unfastened each other's scuba gear and let it sink to the bottom of the ocean.

The thunder resounded in the distance like a mighty giant clearing his throat. It began to rain much harder, and the sea was heaving heavily with swells rising ten to fifteen feet. All of a sudden, the rain came down in torrents and it became difficult to see where they were going. As each swell would come and go, it seemed as if they were getting nowhere.

"Claude, where are you?" shouted Dr. Bellwether. Claude grabbed his hand and said, "Here, hold on so we don't lose each other." Dr. Bellwether was only too happy to oblige as they struggled to stay together and find the point of land that could not be far.

On the next swell, they were battered against a rock extending from the point, and they lost contact. Another wave came crashing in on top of the previous, battering Dr. Bellwether against the rock, knocking him unconscious. Like a large clump of seaweed, he slowly began to sink...

DAZED AND CONFUSED, CLAUDE SHOOK HIS head a couple of times, got his bearings, and then realized that Dr. Bellwether was no longer holding his hand. In a panic, he shouted, "Dr. Bellwether, Dr. Bellwether. Where are you? Please answer!" He dove in the water and looked around but could only see a few feet in front of his face. He tried again and did not find him. Then suddenly he felt something brush against his back. Turning around, he saw Dr. Bellwether face down in the water. Faster than the whippets on a cuttlefish, Claude put his arm around Dr. Bellwether's chest and swam away from the steep rocks.

The rain had begun to let up, and he looked for a more suitable spot to seek refuge, but there were none. He looked again and saw a small ledge extending from the cliffs not far away. That would have to do. He swam over with Dr. Bellwether in tow and made several attempts at getting him onto the ledge. He tried lifting one leg onto the ledge and then rolling the rest of him onto it but was unable. He was beginning to weaken. Things were looking pretty bleak, but he thought he would give it one last try. With all of his strength, he pushed Dr. Bellwether up. This time, Dr. Bellwether flipped up onto the ledge, as if he had been thrown! Claude could hardly believe how much lighter Dr. Bellwether felt that time.

He struggled to pull himself up onto the ledge. Once there, he placed two hands on Dr. Bellwether's stomach and pushed down to evacuate the water from his lungs. It came gushing out in torrents. Putting his lips to Dr. Bellwether's, he then administered mouth-to-mouth resuscitation. With a couple of coughs and a gasp for air, Dr. Bellwether was breathing again but unconscious. Claude held onto him with one hand and onto a rock with the other, trying to stay balanced on the narrow ledge.

As he clung to the cliffside, he looked at the sea, and for a moment, he thought that he saw her hovering in the blindness below. It had to be a hallucination. He looked again and saw nothing but the sea rising and falling like an upset stomach. The lull in the rainfall was replaced by a tremendous display of lightning and renewed sheets of rain. The swells picked up, the waves battered the ledge, and the wind howled.

Wave after wave came crashing in upon them. Claude lost his grip momentarily, and they almost fell into the sea. As if encouraged by the near fall, the waves came in with ever greater vengeance, pummeling them time and time again. As the sea closed in on them, Claude did not know how long he could hold onto the slippery ledge, but he knew that he must hold on to save their lives.

Eight

Captain Gregory woke up that morning, stretched, and went to the porthole to look out. There was no salt water or smell of the sea, no gulls, no musty wood planks creaking and whispering nautical tales, and no wind blowing through his gray hair. In fact there was nothing to greet him, except walls and flowers in the garden outside his room. It was enough to make him sick. He longed for the sea, where the only flowers were the occasional jellyfish rising to the surface and the only walls were man's own limitations. He longed for his boat at anchor, moving from side to side, rocking him gently to sleep at night. Everything about the sea suggested movement, and this movement was his lifeblood. The stationary floor at the hospital made him dizzy, even nauseous.

Even more than his boat or the sea, he longed for a chance to be with Dr. Royale—not as doctor and patient, but as soggy, old, salt-of-the-earth sea captain and dazzling young damsel. Perhaps that was why he had turned down her repeated requests for a session, either alone or with Jane, whom he had not yet met. He was just kidding himself though; she would never see him as anything *but* a patient. He thought about leaving, but he just couldn't do it. Maybe they would stop him if he tried. Or maybe, he would stop himself so that he could be with Dr. Royale a while longer. It was not because he needed help—he didn't. It was because he had caught a live one, and he wasn't going to let go until he found out what he had.

Someone knocked on the door, and Captain Gregory opened it. He knew that it would be her, and he knew that opening the door would be like opening Pandora's box. He shouldn't, but he just had to see what was inside. Dr. Royale was dressed that morning, not in a prudish full-length dress, but in a double-breasted, dark pink business suit with white pin-stripes. The hem line of her skirt was tastefully above the knees, at high tide, exposing her lovely sand-white skin through sheer stockings. Her beautiful auburn hair cascaded down like twin waterfalls along a V-neck blouse that exposed the twin inner slopes of her bosom, which was gently heaving. Standing there in her high heels, Dr. Royale was a dazzling sight to behold—and to be held—as far as Captain Gregory was concerned. He was completely stunned by her beauty. It was as if he had discovered treasure buried at the bottom of the sea, and she was standing before him.

"May I come in, Captain Gregory?"

"Oh, yes, I'm sorry." He stood there, hypnotized by her charms.

She checked the silver buttons on her suit. "You're staring at me. Is there anything wrong?"

The room seemed lighter; there was music in the air, and the feint hint of perfume. Captain Gregory was nearly drunk on its sweet smell. "No, nothing's wrong."

"There is something wrong," said Dr. Royale, slowly circling him in a symphony of celestial motion.

"No, everything is right. Just perfect. It's just that every time I see you, well it's kind of hard to explain." Captain

Gregory was almost dizzy as he watched her. "It's as if my world revolves around you."

"If that's true, would you do anything I ask?"

"Right now, I think I'd do anything you would ask."

"Anything?" asked Dr. Royale, her lips slightly pursed in a smile. "Well, that's quite a compliment coming from you Captain Gregory. I think that being the shy, retiring type, I'm going to have to take advantage of that. Would you, for instance, sail the seven seas for me?"

"That's easy, I'd be honored to my lady."

"Would you walk the plank for me?"

Captain Gregory laughed, wondering what she would ask next. "That depends. Are the waters shark-infested?"

She nodded.

"Maybe I'd take the chance."

Dr. Royale rubbed her hands together as if she was about to hit the jackpot. "Well, if you would do all of those things, I have one more request. Would you meet me for an appointment?"

The lines on Captain Gregory's face twisted into knots. "You mean a shrink session? Now that's one drill you won't get me to do."

Dr. Royale stomped her foot lightly. "Please?"

"No," said Captain Gregory, waving his finger.

"Why not?"

"Simple. There's nothing wrong with me," he said, looking up at the ceiling.

"How about a group session? You know, I have two new patients who will be joining the group soon."

"No, I'm not interested in group therapy either." Then suddenly his face brightened. "But I wouldn't mind taking you for a spin on my boat."

Dr. Royale smiled and ran her fingers through her hair. "Why, Captain Gregory, are you asking me out on a date? You know I can't do that; it wouldn't be ethical. But perhaps we could make believe. You can call it a date. I will call it a session."

"Well, I don't know."

"Oh come on, Captain," said Dr. Royale, beckoning with a half-bent index finger. "You won't feel a thing."

"They probably said that to the first dental patient, too, just before the drilling began."

"No drills, I promise."

"Okay, where do we go?"

"First, I have to hypnotize you."

"You've already done that," said Captain Gregory, his eyes sparkling.

"Not just your libido," said Dr. Royale, smiling. "Now take my hand."

Captain Gregory was completely surprised by the request, but he extended his hand anyway until their hands met, palm-to-palm, forming a tight seal. Her hand was soft and supple, and she gently drew him in, closer and closer, until they touched, and Captain Gregory let himself be swept away in the moment. For the first time, she was looking at him as a man who had distinguished himself in military service to his country, not as an amnesia patient who couldn't find his boat in a bathtub.

"Now look at me," she said.

He turned away for a moment, wondering whether she was wooing him, and if so, what would come next. He looked at her sleek, slender, sensuous figure. There were gentle curves everywhere, the kind that suggest movement, a movement accentuated by her gentle swaying from side to side that made Captain Gregory feel as if he had never left the sea. "I'm looking. I'm looking."

"No, look into my eyes, and dream about being back on your boat. Look deeper, deeper," she gently encouraged. He gazed into her eyes. Behind those stylish half-glasses—the ones Captain Gregory longed to take off—were royal blue eyes many fathoms deep protecting an entire sea-world of secrets. He was entering her hypnotic world now, on the open seas. Closing his eyes, he wished he were back on his boat.

THE MUSIC HAD STOPPED, AND SO CAPTAIN Gregory opened his eyes. Dr. Royale's eyes were open, and she had a smile on her face. He moved in closer to kiss her, but with seeming reluctance, she slowly backed away. Then he realized that things were going too fast. Or maybe they weren't "going" at all. Maybe she had used her feminine wiles to do her dirty work, to trick him into therapy. With disgust, Captain Gregory went over to the porthole and looked out. He was greeted by a splash of salt water, and that beautiful smell that he knew so well, the smell of the sea, filled the air. He breathed in deeply, while the wind blew through his gray hair. A dirty old gull seemed to call out his name, and the musty wood planks beneath his feet were creaking and whispering nautical tales. He knew that he was home once again. "I can't believe it," he said, pinching himself. "We're back on my boat. How did you do that?"

"You did it actually. You're imagining that we are somewhere else."

Captain Gregory looked at her skeptically. He never did believe in that hocus-pocus, but on the other hand, he couldn't explain how they had dropped anchor several miles offshore. "If this is my imagination, maybe you could explain to me why you're here."

"Because I am a part of what you are imagining. Let's begin the session, shall we?"

Captain Gregory frowned. Although he didn't believe that it was just his imagination, he decided not to fight with Dr. Royale about whether this was a date or a session or whether or not it was his imagination or not. No, he would turn this thing into his advantage, not because he wanted to dominate her, but because he wanted to change the nature of their relationship. Of course, there was one nagging question that had to be answered. If she didn't like water, there could be no relationship between them. "Okay, Dr. Royale, we can play that game. But let me ask the questions this time. Tell me, how do you feel about the sea?"

"I love it; it's like home to me." She lit a cigarette and took a few puffs, averting his eyes. The smoke hovered like an ink cloud above her head.

"Really." Captain Gregory was positively captivated by her response and pleasantly surprised that she was letting him ask the questions. There weren't very many women who were fond of the sea, though he knew there had to be a few of them out there. "Why do you love it?" he asked.

"It's like the air that I breathe. I love it and all the creatures in it."

He could tell that she was telling the truth, and her answers were stirring up a whirlpool of feelings inside. Only once had Captain Gregory ever fallen in love with a woman before, and only once had he ever been remotely interested in spending the rest of his life with one. It wasn't that he didn't like women. He did. It's just that so few were his type, yet this time he was sure he had found one. Although he was not the impulsive sort, he was feeling very impulsive, and he took her hand and very slowly drew her in, saying, "I love it too. Dr. Royale, if I may say so, women like you are a rare and endangered species."

With a wary look, she took a puff and blew another cloud of smoke in his direction. "You know, I've encountered a few fishermen in my life, and you guys are all alike. You feed us a line and expect us to fall for it hook, line, and sinker. I was hooked once by your sort, but I got away, and I vowed that I would never let it happen again." She took another puff from the cigarette, and resisted, only this time Captain Gregory could tell that she was having trouble.

He drew her in more slowly so as not to alarm her, like a winch pulling up a treasure chest from the bottom of the sea, and just as that treasure was about to make it to the surface so that Captain Gregory could see what was in it, it fell. But it was not the draw that did it. It was her high heel, and it had punched through a knothole, causing her to momentarily lose her balance and fling her cigarette out of the porthole nearby. She took her hand slowly out of his, shook her leg, and dislodged the heel. She backed away and reached into her purse for another cigarette.

In a single motion, Captain Gregory lit his lighter and with cupped hands, brought it up to the new cigarette dangling from her trembling lips. He sought to reassure her. "You needn't be alarmed. I may be an old salt, but I am a gentleman."

"I'm sorry, Captain Gregory. It's just that a woman can never be too sure. I've always been afraid of the so-called gentle man."

"I understand. Would you like a tour of the boat?" he asked, hoping to switch the subject. The first rule of love and war was never to telegraph your moves. Since she knew what was on his mind, the element of surprise was gone. It would be better to bid a hasty retreat and wait for another opportunity.

"I would like that very much."

He led her outside and extended his hand to help her up the stairs, which had no railing. They went around the exterior of the Captain's Quarters to the galley lined with storage cabinets made of beautiful old mahogany with brass rims and porcelain knobs. He wasn't quite sure what was inside and it disturbed him that he could not remember. The cabinets had to be used for something quite large, like the spare sails perhaps. He screwed up his courage and opened the cupboards, smiling with satisfaction at the sight of the sailing gear. There was nothing wrong with his memory, and he was going to prove it to her. "Here are the spare ropes for the sails, an extra main sail and jib in case one of them tears."

"I see, but I thought this boat had a motor."

"Yes it does, and that's what we use to get around. But this boat is a sail boat that has been retrofitted for fishing. If the motor breaks down, it's pretty handy to sail to port."

"Are most of the fishing boats larger or smaller than this one?"

"The commercial boats down the coast are a good deal larger."

"How large are the nets that you use?"

"Well I was just about to show you the nets. But if I tell you all my secrets, you have to promise not to go into business for yourself."

Dr. Royale shifted her weight several times. Wide-eyed and flushed, she said, "Captain Gregory, I wouldn't dream of it. I'm just curious about you and your work, from a professional standpoint, of course."

Captain Gregory led her along the starboard side. "This is a V-board centerline sloop, about 55 feet in length." He looked proudly over the length and breadth of the boat and ran his hand along the beautiful wooden hand rail along the side. They went a few feet further and then they stopped at an oyster dredge. "Here's an old dredge net. We don't use this contraption much anymore."

"A dredge net?"

Captain Gregory noted that Dr. Royale seemed a bit uneasy and wondered whether the tour of the boat was such a good idea after all. "Yes, my father and I used to fish oysters." He hoped that she didn't turn out to be one of those crazy environmentalists. You never knew who might be one. They came from all walks of life, and he detested them. Several had even jumped into his nets once and nearly drowned, forcing him to cut his nets to save them.

"How does it work?"

"Well this iron frame has a chain net at the bottom and twine at the top. The whole thing is connected to a powered winch, which hauls the net over the bottom of the sea."

Dr. Royale studied it closely but kept her distance, as if she were afraid that the large steel frame was a pair of jaws that might snatch her up at any moment. Captain Gregory gently led her away from there. He headed toward the stern, nearly tripping over a collection of lobster pots. "Here are the pots we use to catch lobsters."

She picked up a pot and studied it. "You catch lobsters, too?"

"Yes. Over the past fifty years, this boat has been retrofitted many times. At one point or another we've caught just about everything."

"I see."

He led her around to the stern, to the starboard quarter, and then to the nets. "And here are the nets we used when we converted her over to a shrimper."

Glistening in the sunset were the nets, designed to catch anything and everything, even small droplets, which cascaded along the fine thread. A long time ago, Captain Gregory and his father had used them often. Now they were there for show more than anything else. He was proud of those nets and it brought back fond memories of childhood. Even now, they came in handy when he would use them to catch squid or other fish. Often, though, he left the nets, the pots, and the jars behind and went diving—his first love—to catch his prey. This seemed to him to be the most honorable way to catch a rare prize.

Captain Gregory turned away from the nets and looked at Dr. Royale, who seemed quite agitated. She sighed, flicked her cigarette into the sea, and stared at the net. Captain Gregory put his arm around her. "You look a bit frightened by this."

"Yes, I am."

"I don't have to show you this or any of the tackle for that matter, if it's going to upset you."

"I'm sorry, it's just that these nets make me shudder when I think of what it would be like to be trapped in them."

Captain Gregory did not understand. After all, that was the point of using a net. "But why should it? It's just a net to catch fish. It's not like we're killing humpback whales or anything."

"Yes, but surely other creatures are trapped in it that you didn't intend to catch. What do you do with those?"

"We always throw them back," he said, puzzled.

Dr. Royale frowned. "Yes, but how many of them are alive? I eat seafood, too, but I don't believe in wasting it."

Captain Gregory did not answer her for fear that he would say something that he might regret. Despite their differences— or maybe because of them—Captain Gregory wanted very much to establish a relationship with her no matter where it might lead. She was the perfect woman: she loved the sea and she hated fishermen. That only meant that she had good judgment.

"Speaking of seafood, let's talk about dinner." Captain Gregory led her away from the nets to the bow of the boat.

Dr. Royale smiled. "Not this time, thank you, but maybe next time. Right now I have a few more questions to ask you."

"Okay," he said, his voice lowering with disappointment. Asking her out was not going to be as easy as he had hoped. He had never backed down from a challenge, though, and he was not about to now.

"Well, Captain Gregory, you've shown me the ropes, the gear, and the tackle. Are you sure that you've shown me everything?"

"I've shown you most everything that I could remember about this boat."

"Think hard. Is everything in its place? Is anything missing?"

"Well, there is the egg," he said, staring into the water.

"The what?" she said, her mouth wide open with surprise.

Captain Gregory looked up at her. "The octopus egg, and a rare one, I'm sure. I lost it."

Dr. Royale was incredulous. "You lost it? How? Did you take it?"

"No. Well, at first I did."

Dr. Royale glared at him. "You did? How could you do that? How could you take the egg of a rare and endangered species?" she said, her voice raising. As it did, it seemed to resonate in his head.

"Don't get upset. Say, how do you know about this?"

"I know the whole story," she said, regaining her composure.

"You mean you read minds?" he asked, half hoping that she would say yes so as to explain why she was always a step ahead of him.

"When you were delirious, you told me the whole story from your hospital bed. You were like an open book."

"You know about the octopus and the egg?"

"I know the whole story," she said softly. "All except the egg. I didn't realize that you had taken it."

Captain Gregory was astonished. "Why should you care?"

"Captain Gregory, I care about the world we live in. You wouldn't know this, but I happen to be an environmentalist and a supporter of SOS. You took an egg from a rare and endangered species. Now, suppose you tell me where it is, so that we might put it back where it belongs."

Captain Gregory sighed. His worst fears had been realized. She was one of them! A liberal environmentalist, and a supporter of the Save the Ocean Society. "I don't know where it is right now."

"But you just said that you took it."

"But then I lost it. The mother came after me and shook me like a salt shaker. The egg dropped out of my pouch and in the commotion my good-for-nothing shiphand, Cranston, took it."

"Do you know where we can find him?" she said hopefully.

"No. Anyway, it would do you no good. He's undoubtedly preserved the egg in formaldehyde."

"Oh, I see," she said, crestfallen.

Captain Gregory put his hand on hers. "There now, I only took one. There were two others I gave back. Funny thing is, I would have given them all back. When she had me in her arms, she could have killed me right away, but she didn't. She had this very sad look in her eyes, as if she were in pain. At that moment, I had a change of heart, not because I feared for my safety, but because I realized that what I had done was wrong."

"It was wrong," she said, withdrawing her hand.

"I know, but I would have given it back, really I would have, and I think that she knew that I would too. That's why she let me go."

Dr. Royale looked away. "Well, I was hoping that we could work together, but I'm not sure that I could ever work with you, knowing this."

Captain Gregory scowled. "Come on, you eat seafood, you said so yourself," he said, hoping with one simple rebuttal to reveal the hypocrisy of the entire environmental movement.

"You and I are worlds apart in our thinking," said Dr. Royale, shaking her head. "While you would kill the young of rare and endangered species, I have worked all of my life to support their cause."

"Since when did this start?"

Flushed with anger, Dr. Royale pointed her finger at him. "Captain Gregory, I'm beginning to lose my patience with you.

Surely you must realize that I do have a life outside of my practice."

"Okay, okay, I see. But you've got me all wrong. I really do love the sea and all of the creatures in it."

"You couldn't prove it by me. You may think that I am going overboard with this Captain Gregory, and if you do, then you don't know me very well. The sea is very important to me, and all creatures great and small. You see, I am an animal lover."

"In that case, I am sorry," said Captain Gregory, hoping to change the subject but not the lady. Though he hated her viewpoint, he admired her conviction. In a strange way, Dr. Royale's nurturing instincts, her love for all of God's creatures, and her passion struck a nerve. He began to pull up anchor, turning the crank slowly and trying to figure out how in the world he could get her to go to dinner with him.

"So am I. Captain Gregory, you might as well leave the anchor right where it is. It is impossible for you and I to go on together this way."

"But how will we get back to shore?"

With an undercurrent of anger, she said, "That, my dear captain, is your problem. I am releasing you from my care. I thought that perhaps we could work together. But once again, you've proven that there's ample reason why fishermen can't be trusted. Now, if you will excuse me, I have many things to tend to."

Captain Gregory looked dumbfounded as she went down the stairs into the Captain's Quarters and closed the door behind her. She had caught him completely off-balance. That was rare, because he was almost always on an even keel. He went over their conversation several times in his head and came to the conclusion that Dr. Royale had very deep feelings. No doubt that was why she was a psychiatrist: She really could feel the pain of others, and maybe even read minds, a thought that made him very uncomfortable at the same time that it intrigued him.

Undaunted, he walked slowly to the Captain's Quarters. He stood there and, after several moments, knocked on the door. There was no answer. He knocked again and then again, but there was no answer. He called her name. Again no answer. He knelt down, turned his head, and looked through the keyhole, hoping to see her, to peer into her heart, mind, and soul. Maybe she really wasn't angry with him. Maybe it was all a joke. If that was so, perhaps she wanted him to come in. His imagination went wild as he envisioned her waiting on the bed. With a good deal of anticipation and trepidation, he slowly opened the door and looked around the room... She was gone!

He knew that that was impossible, but nonetheless he was impressed. What tricks this woman could play! If she was playing at all. He looked under the bed, in the bathroom, in the closet, everywhere, but she had vanished. He looked across the room and smiled as he saw that the porthole was open. He measured the opening: 15 inches wide. His smile quickly turned into a frown. Dr. Royale had an hourglass figure, but that opening seemed too small for even her to have gotten out. But there were no trap doors, no other means of escape, nowhere to go. Captain Gregory concluded that she must have wiggled her way out, and was below deck, perhaps in the engine room.

He went down into the engine room and turned on the lights. She was nowhere in sight. He looked behind the giant encasement of gears and pistons but found no sign of her there either. He scratched his head and went back on deck. He searched the deck, the cupboards, and in every nook and cranny but she was nowhere to be found. He called out her name, at first a bit cautiously and then with the full force of a Navy sea captain. Finally he looked overboard, half-expecting to see her hanging onto the side of the boat—or floating beside it.

Slowly but surely panic welled up deep within. He dove into the water and swam around the boat looking for her, checking to see if she was underneath. It all seemed so futile. He climbed back into the boat and leaned up against the mast.

Dr. Royale was gone, vanished into thin air, or maybe drowned. Captain Gregory tried not to think about it. It was getting late, and it was time to get back to shore. He looked around but nothing seemed familiar. He felt disoriented. It was most peculiar. For the first time that he could recall, he couldn't tell which way was the shore. Worse yet, it was quite cloudy, and so he couldn't tell which way was the sunset. He knew that he had to be off the Atlantic coast; after all, that was where his boat had been docked, although he could not recall at which marina. He pulled out his binoculars and adjusted them for the furthest distance and slowly scanned the horizon, but there was no sign of the coast, only water as far as the eye could see. So he went to the brass-tipped wheel at the stern of the boat and pulled out the sextant, only to find the index arm broken and the horizon mirror cracked. That was the last straw; he would stay put for the night and wait for the clouds to clear, and the sunrise to show him the way out of there.

Captain Gregory walked over to the wheel and spun it. He had to admit it. He had lost his sense of direction, his inner compass, his built-in sextant. In fact, he had not only lost his inner compass, but he couldn't even remember where he had left it. Dr. Royale had been right all along. He could remember a name, and even a face, but he could no longer remember a place. All he knew was that he was out in the middle of the ocean, and he would not be making it back to shore for dinner.

He was hungry, so he put out a few fishing lines and sat and waited and thought about his predicament. If only he hadn't told her about the egg! That was a big mistake. If she had gotten that upset over one little egg, it would have been an even bigger mistake if he had shown her his chain of octopus teeth, or his "baby teeth" as Cranston used to say. He looked around to make sure that she wasn't watching and then reached into his shirt and pulled it from his neck to look at it. It was rather barbaric; he didn't know what he had seen in it, and he certainly had no use for it anymore. So he flung it into the sea...and watched as it sank slowly.

The wind let up and the sea was flat, like a mirror. All of a sudden, in the water below, he thought he saw Dr. Royale's face, and the necklace settle around her neck. She smiled and then slowly faded away, taking the necklace with her. Captain Gregory rubbed his eyes and thought *this can't be happening. I must be going crazy.*

"OKAY. YOU WIN. I give up. I admit it, I need help. Please help me. I think I'm losing my mind. Bring me into the group. I promise, I will help you do your work. Please..."

But there was no answer. He looked again, and this time he nearly jumped out of his boots as he saw the giant octopus hovering in the dark waters below. He could hardly believe his eyes. So *she* had taken Dr. Royale! It was as if he had brought the sunken treasure up from the bottom of the sea, and just when he was about to open it, *she* had taken it from him forever. *She* was probably waiting there, plotting her next move, or maybe *she* was waiting for him to come into the water and have it out one more time. *She* knew how to lure him in too. Dr. Royale was the first woman in a long time that he had cared about, and that devilfish had probably snatched her from the porthole, to exact revenge for what he had done. He had to do something, so he quickly grabbed a spear gun and dove into the water to get her back and to settle the matter with that devilfish once and for all...

A shiver went up his spine moments after his splash-landing. He turned on his flashlight in the darkened waters. He thought he heard something. He turned around quickly. Just a bird grabbing a scrap from the deck rail. He looked around for a few more minutes. Still nothing, but so still that there had to be something lurking about. The sea was still, the wind was still, and the conditions were perfect for lurking. After a few more minutes, though, Captain Gregory began to realize that the only thing lurking about was him, and he was getting cold. They were gone, and there was nothing he could do about it. Breathing heavily, he climbed back onto the deck.

He sat down in his chair at the helm and spun the wheel with his foot. He ran through the various scenarios, trying to make sense of what was happening to him. Maybe he had imagined he had seen them in the water. Maybe, just maybe he was imagining the whole thing. Or perhaps she was some sort of magician, some grand illusionist, who had somehow managed to bring them into an altered state of mind. All psychiatrists were illusionists in some way or another, at least those who practiced hypnosis. She could probably see him, hear him, bring him out of it if she wanted. She was probably right in the room with him right now, only he didn't know it. That's what was going on! He was being hypnotized... But if he was being hypnotized, how come Dr. Royale had been there on the boat with him. No, it had to be a dream—a bad dream—that was testing his mettle. Well, he wouldn't crack under the pressure. As a Navy captain, he had been in tight spots before. This one was different, though, because the battleground had shifted from the high seas to a much more delicate location, his mind. It was a battle all right. A battle for his sanity, and he would need help.

If it was all a bad dream, then he knew of only one way to end it—to get some sleep. He went into the Captain's Quarters and headed straight for the liquor cabinet, but it was locked. Now where were those keys, those lousy keys?! He wanted a drink to calm his nerves; no, he *needed* a drink to calm his nerves and regain his composure. He went over to his night stand and opened a small chest and rummaged through the many personal items inside. He smiled when he found his compass, and quickly put it in his pocket for safekeeping. Now for those keys. Where were they? At last he found them amongst some old Spanish doubloons. He opened the cabinet and poured a glass of cognac. It had been some day. Instead of enjoying a nice moonlit dinner on the marina with Dr. Royale, she had left him stranded in a bad dream, one he was eager to get over. With a heavy sigh, he took a few sips and then laid down and fell fast asleep.

NINE

Claude awoke, rubbed his eyes, and saw a beautiful but strange woman holding his hand. He thought for a moment that he had died and gone to heaven and that a beautiful angel was holding his hand, about to lead him through the pearly gates. But there were no pearly gates in this place, just a white door in a room with sterile white walls, and a white curtain separating him from the patient in the next bed.

Claude lifted his head off his pillow. "Where am I?"

"You are in the hospital," said Dr. Royale.

"How did I get here?" he said, looking a bit bewildered.

"You were picked up by a seagoing vessel off No Man's Land, about 50 miles from the coast of Maine."

"I see. How do you know this?"

"I am in contact with your rescuer."

"My rescuer?!" said Claude, as the cobwebs cleared from his mind. "May I speak with him?"

"No, she wishes to remain anonymous."

"She?! Who is she? And why does she wish to remain anonymous?"

"I am sorry," said Dr. Royale, "but I am not at liberty to say right now."

Claude motioned for a glass of water, and she poured him a glass from the pitcher on the night stand beside his bed. He extended his left hand and then withdrew it after noticing the IV attached to his arm was being stretched. As she gave him the glass, he noticed her auburn red hair. Like most redheads, her skin was a beautiful sandy-white, almost translucent, and the hint of capillaries pulsing near the surface gave it a feint mottled appearance. She was dressed in a conservative, white double-breasted, full-length business suit, and burgundy shoes. Her burgundy blouse was buttoned all the way to the neck, and she wore no jewelry.

"Are you some sort of concierge or something?" he asked, sipping on the water.

"I am one of your doctors."

"Was I injured?" he asked, half-knowing the answer to the question.

"You were. You suffered a head trauma from which you are now recovering," she said looking at him as a mother would her child.

It was odd, even strange, but somehow comforting. Claude winced and then felt the bandages that encompassed his head. "Will I make a full recovery?"

"That depends on your definition of full recovery. But I would say yes."

A nurse came in and looked surprised that Claude had awakened. "When did this happen?" she asked.

"Just now. I had alerted all personnel. If you had been plugged into the cellcom, you would know," said Dr. Royale.

The nurse made a note in her chart and then took his temperature, listened to his chest, and took his blood pressure.

After she left the room, Claude turned to the woman in the white suit. "Did you perform the surgery?"

"I was present during the operation."

"Then you are my doctor."

"No, I am your psychiatrist, Dr. Royale."

"My psychiatrist?!" said Claude, nearly spilling his water. "Mon ami, you are mistaken. I do not need one of those."

"You suffered quite a blow to the head. Trust me dear. It will take time to recover from such a trauma."

"Oh, I see," said Claude, as the extent of his injuries began to register.

"For instance, there may be things that you have difficulty remembering."

Claude wanted to shake his head but was afraid that something might shake loose. "I don't think so. I am a French citizen living in the U.S., where I have found a new home as a member of the SOS society. My family owns a fishing business in the south of France. There were three brothers, and I am the youngest, and as it turns out, the most adventurous, I guess. So you see, I remember everything."

"Do you know your name?"

Claude belly laughed. "My name?!...Why of course I know my name. My name is...Hmm. Now that you mention it, no."

"Well, I am sure that you will before long, but these things take time. I would like to schedule an appointment with you for tomorrow, when you feel better."

"I guess I have nowhere to go, Doctor."

Dr. Royale smiled. "You get some rest now, my child." She gently brushed the palm of her hand along his cheek as a mother would to her own son. Claude thought that this was very strange, but all the same he didn't mind her motherly touch. It was comforting, even reassuring, and reminded him of his childhood, when his mother tucked him in bed at night.

Dr. Royale turned off the light and began to pull the curtain around his hospital bed.

"Dr. Royale, do you know if they picked up my companion?"

"Yes," said Dr. Royale, touching his hand to reassure him. "You needn't worry about that. He is in the bed next to yours."

"What is his condition?"

"He is in a coma."

"Oh, I am sorry."

"But he is expected to recover. Now get some sleep please. The other doctors and nurses will be in shortly to check on you both. And I will see you tomorrow. Good night."

Dr. Royale shut the door to their room. Claude raised his head and looked over in the direction of the other bed obscured by the curtain. Forgetting about the IV, he thought momentarily about getting up to see Dr. Bellwether. He tried raising his head from the pillow again but this time the effort tired him out; so he closed his eyes and went back to sleep.

THAT NIGHT, DR. BELLWETHER OPENED HIS EYES for the first time since the accident. He wasn't the least bit groggy or disoriented. He was magnificently lucid, the same as always. It was as if a light bulb had been switched on, and the massive, gray filament inside his head was burning brightly indeed. His head felt fine, and the only thing that hurt was his ear, which was also plugged. So, he turned to his other side and saw a woman sitting there, calmly, patiently, anticipating his awakening. He noted that she was a lovely woman, but he had always been married to his work and was in any event more titillated by all things cerebral. So her overwhelming beauty did not overpower him. "Where am I?" he asked, working the controls to raise the top half of the bed.

"You're in a hospital," said Dr. Royale.

"I know *that* young lady. After all, I am a doctor. I mean *what* hospital?" He was a bit exasperated, but the woman seemed to take it all in stride.

"You're in NML General."

"Oh, Newport Medical Laboratory and General Hospital? Must be in the new wing. What in the world am I doing here?"

"You were rescued at sea and brought here. You had suffered a head trauma and had to be saved. Several procedures were performed, including reconstructive surgery using a regenerative process—"

"Wait a second," said Dr. Bellwether, his face narrowing considerably. "Are we talking about neurosurgery here? Because if we are, you should know that you can perform reconstructive surgery on bones and certain types of tissues but certainly not on the brain, unless you're cloning brains with stem cells on a molecular scaffolding, in which case I would surmise that you would be dead by the time they were done because man won't be able to accomplish that feat for another couple of hundred years."

"I thought that I was using a fitting terminology."

"You're obviously not a doctor. Now I don't mean to be rude but where is *my* team of doctors?"

"I am a part of that team. I am Dr. Royale, your psychiatrist."

Dr. Bellwether could feel his blood pressure rising as he began to raise his voice. "I do not need a psychiatrist. I am well aware of post-operative stress and traumatic syndromes. I need to know whether they operated on the cerebrum, cerebellum, or the brain stem. If it was the cerebrum, then was it the frontal lobe—"

"Or the occipital lobe?" said Dr. Royale, smiling.

"Yes, or the parietal—"

"Or maybe the temporal lobe?"

Dr. Bellwether smiled. He was never one to turn down mental games, particularly when they were on his playing field. "And if it was the cerebellum, what parts would I be interested in?"

"The vermis or one of the hemispheres."

"Okay. And what about the stem?"

"Do you mean the medulla oblongata, the midbrain, or the pons?"

Dr. Bellwether studied her carefully. "Yes, exactly. So you know a little about neurology. Very good, someone in your field should. But I need to know whether tissue was excised, pressure was relieved, and where. In short, I need my doctors, the surgeon who performed the surgery, someone who can speak my language so that I might learn the nature and extent of my injuries," he said, waving his arms for emphasis, causing the IV to tangle around the bedrails.

Dr. Royale put her index finger to her lips, gently shushing him. "It is the middle of the night, and we don't want to wake the other patients."

Dr. Bellwether relaxed and quietly disentangled the IV, punching the pain button on the IV pump to dispense increased quantities of Demerol. "Well that's a first," he said, laughing. "I've never been shushed by anyone smoking an imaginary cigarette."

"You know what I mean, Dr. Bellwether."

"Normally," he said, ignoring her, "I would feel compelled to launch into a diatribe to convince you to quit smoking, but smoking air is all right. It's the perfect cigarette if you think about it. I'm not sure what to make of it, but it is interesting." He looked at her as if he were examining her and then abruptly turned his attention to another subject. "You mentioned other patients. Could you please tell me what happened to my companion?"

"Do you know his name?"

"Of course I do." He looked at her with disdain, wrinkling his forehead. "If this is a test, I can tell you this: My memory is fully intact. I am Dr. Niles Bellwether, Dean Emeritus of the School of Medicine at Manchester University. I also have my own practice in Neurosurgery and am affiliated with the teaching hospital at the university. My father was a renowned researcher at Boston College, and then finally, at this very same institution. He built the home at 1503 Cherrywood Drive, in Manchester, where I live. Do you need any more proof?"

Dr. Royale stared at him. "Very impressive. It appears that you have no amnesia at all, even though everyone else who has had the same procedure has had some loss of memory. But you show no signs of memory loss."

"No, I have always had a photographic memory, and thank goodness, that seems to be intact. So you see, it is not necessary for me to see a psychiatrist."

"Trust me, Dr. Bellwether, maybe not today, but someday soon you will see the need. I will be in to see you alone the rest of this week, but I would like you to join a group session that I am putting together next week, if you feel up to it. Can I count on you?"

Dr. Bellwether flicked his fingers, waving her off. "I can't really say right now. But you haven't answered my question. How is Claude?"

"Oh, he will be fine. He is sleeping in the bed next to you. You two can talk in the morning."

"Well, that's a relief," said Dr. Bellwether, shaking his head. He felt his ear again, recalling the pain it had given him whenever he went scuba diving as a child. He punched the pain button again, only this time no more Demerol was dispensed. He had reached his limit.

Dr. Royale headed for the door, gliding across the room with great momentum. Her mental alacrity, her presence, and her mannerisms intrigued Dr. Bellwether. For that reason, he decided to join the group. He had been to many psychiatrists in his lifetime, and she was not like the others. In fact, he was not sure whether she was really a psychiatrist at all, though she obviously was a woman of many talents.

As she closed the door Dr. Royale said, "Good night, Dr. Bellwether. It is gratifying to have someone as knowledgeable as you in my little group."

Dr. Bellwether reacted with surprise. He got the eerie feeling that Dr. Royale *knew* that he would join the group. Or did she? Perhaps she was just an overconfident young lady. Perhaps she could read minds. Dr. Bellwether didn't really know, but he thought that something strange was going on at the hospital. Perhaps Claude wasn't even in the next bed. He calculated the distance from his bed to the next, and the length of IV line available; there was probably enough for him to peak through the curtain. He tried raising his head from the pillow but the effort tired him out. Instead, he stared at the ceiling, contemplating how this mysterious young woman had entered his life.

Ten

When Captain Gregory woke up, he found himself back in his hospital room. He looked around and realized that he was just a patient again, and worse yet, Dr. Royale was gone. He rushed to the door and looked out but found no one in the hallway either. He ran his hand through his hair as if running a fine-tooth comb through his mind to look for answers. But he only found questions. How did they go from his hospital room, to his boat, and back again? And how did she disappear so quickly? Was he dreaming? If so, the dream was vivid. He remembered everything about it, and this upset him greatly.

He had finally found the woman of his dreams, only to discover that she was some kind of spineless, invertebrate lover. She had convictions, though, as strong as his own, and he admired that. Besides, he didn't want some patsy, some disagreeable woman who agreed with him all the time; he wanted someone who would challenge him. She did, so much so that he forgot about his original quarry. He really didn't care about the egg anymore; in fact, he regretted taking it in the first place. He only cared about her, and he was determined not to lose her.

He got up from bed and looked at the clock—nearly 10:00 a.m., time for the group session. As he moved from the bed, he felt something bulging in his pocket. He reached inside and pulled out the compass! So, it wasn't a dream after all. It had to have been hypnosis, then, or some other sleight of hand. It really didn't matter anymore how she did it. The only thing that Captain Gregory knew was that he had to find her and start all over again. He headed for the hospital room door, glancing at his compass. The needle was moving steadily as if the true north position was moving. He stood still at the door to see if the needle would settle down, but it didn't. It kept on moving. For some reason, a marvelous notion popped into his head: Perhaps the needle was pointing to her! Perhaps she was his shining star, his true north, and his inner compass. The more he thought about it, the more he knew it was true, a sailor's intuition. There was only one thing to do. Follow the compass and see if it was true that all paths led to Dr. Royale's office door.

DR. ROYALE OPENED THE DOOR TO HER OFFICE and smiled gamely, as she struggled to keep a large carrying case, brief case, and purse under wing. Her patients were seated around a large oval table, Jane reading a book in a comfortable-looking couch-chair, and Dr. Bellwether and Claude in not-so-comfortable-looking wheelchairs with IVs attached. The men had husky attendants who rushed to help Dr. Royale unload her gear on the table. She thanked the attendants for their help and then excused them, indicating that she would ring them with the office call button if needed. As she went to her desk to rummage through some notes, her patients quieted to near-whispers, waiting for her to start the session.

She looked at her watch. A few minutes early. Puffing on her ever-present cigarette, Dr. Royale thought about how she wanted to handle the group session. She was a bit nervous since this would be her first. The private sessions with her patients had gone well, but she didn't know what to expect from a group session. She was particularly concerned about not making any mistakes, and under no circumstances revealing her little secret, a secret that would no doubt shock them in their fragile state of mind. No, she would have to wait to tell them, if indeed she would ever tell them at all. If she told them the truth, would they think of her as their enemy? Would they hate her for shattering their hopes for an early release? She dare not think of it at all, in case any of them could read her mind. After all, she could read theirs.

"Good morning," said Dr. Royale, her voice overpowering the other voices in the room.

"What's so good about it," said Dr. Bellwether. "I am a world-renowned neurosurgeon and am well-versed in the maladies of the mind. There is nothing wrong with me, and I do not belong here."

"It is not so bad, mon ami, the sun is shining outside and there is a beautiful woman here to help us. It could be worse."

"You are too kind, Claude," said Dr. Royale, smiling. She turned to Dr. Bellwether. "I'm glad to see you could make it, Dr. Bellwether."

"Make it? It looked to me as if I had no choice. Did you see that orderly? He had to have been over 300 pounds. Hospital food must be pretty good here."

Dr. Royale got up from her desk and took her place at the head of the oval table. "I assume that you've introduced yourselves, yes?" They nodded. "Good, now that we all know each other, let's get started, shall we?" She began to unzip the case and then hesitated when she saw the look of confusion on Jane's face.

"Didn't you tell me that there would be another?" asked Jane.

"Oh yes, there was, but I released him. But I suspect that we will be seeing Captain Gregory again soon." Moments later, they heard a knock and the door opened. Captain Gregory stood in the doorway, looking up from the compass in his outstretched hand. "May I come in?"

"What are you doing here?" asked Dr. Royale, blowing a puff of smoke toward the door, as if to prevent entry.

"Well, young lady, it's like this. My ship has gone off course. I was looking for the North star to bring me back, and low and behold, it turns out to be you," said Captain Gregory with a wry smile on his face. "The reason I've come here is to admit that I have a problem, and I would like to join the group."

"You have a problem? What is your problem?" asked Dr. Royale.

"I can't stop thinking about her."

"You mean Jane?"

Deep lines and pock marks formed on Captain Gregory's face, like notes composing a measure of frustration. "No, of course not," he said. "I've never even met Jane. I'm *talking about the octopus*."

"The octopus!" she said as she rifled through her purse for a pack of cigarettes.

"Yes, you see Dr. Royale, I'm a fisherman and have been all my life; we catch fish and we eat them too. But instead of wanting to catch her, I want to protect her. Now, considering that I am a fisherman, wouldn't you say that I've got a problem?"

"No, I would say that you are evolving," said Dr. Royale, the corners of her lips curling into a barely perceptible smile. "Now I've already released you Captain Gregory; you are free to go, and I have a lot of work to do here."

Captain Gregory shook his head. "I don't believe it. You brought me back here, or I'd still be back on the boat. You brought me back from hypnosis to make me a part of the group. We're in this together, Dr. Royale, and we have an obligation to each other. I don't want to leave; I want to be with you; and I need you to help me get well. Now what do you say? Can I rejoin the group?"

Dr. Royale gazed into Captain Gregory's eyes, trying to fathom his intent. After a few moments, she said, "Well...okay. You are sure you want to help the group?"

"I'm sure."

Dr. Royale turned to the other patients. "I would like to present to the group Captain Montague S. Gregory, former Captain of the Seahawk Navy vessel stationed off of San Diego Harbor in California. He received several medals of honor in the military. After a long and illustrious career, he continued a small fishing operation that his father had begun. His extensive knowledge of the sea and great leadership capabilities will no doubt be a great asset to us."

Captain Gregory smiled and shook his head in amazement. "You know more about me than I do," he said laughing.

Dr. Royale turned bright red with embarrassment. Captain Gregory had never told her about his naval career before. He may have laughed off her display of telepathy for her benefit, but how would he really react? Would he think that she had spied on him, had read his personal diary, or had requisitioned his personnel file from the Navy? More importantly, had anyone else noticed the slip? Dr. Royale quickly glanced at Dr. Bellwether, who was staring intently at the two of them. He had noted Captain Gregory's reaction and her subsequent embarrassment. Claude, on the other hand, was too busy getting acquainted with Jane to have noticed anything. It was Dr. Bellwether, though, that she was particularly worried about; nothing ever got by him. She had made her first mistake and they were barely into the first group session. She would have to get a grip on herself. Regaining her composure, she lit a cigarette and nonchalantly blew smoke rings above the group, as if nothing had happened. It was a small mistake, nothing really. They would never know if she could keep from blushing and showing the true color of her emotions.

"Okay, so we've done the introductions. Very nice, but can we just get on with it please?" asked Dr. Bellwether. "This meeting makes no sense to me whatsoever. Why do we need to be here at all?"

"Give the lady a chance," said Captain Gregory, glaring at Dr. Bellwether in a way that showed that he meant business. Dr. Bellwether shrank in his chair sullenly.

Dr. Royale nodded her head, thanking Captain Gregory for his intercession. "Perhaps I can best answer that by asking each of you what you hope to achieve here."

"I want to regain my memory so that I can find my lover and resume our field studies," said Jane.

"I want to find the perfect catch," said Captain Gregory, winking at Dr. Royale.

"I want to protect rare and endangered species," said Claude.

"And I want to get out of here," said Dr. Bellwether, "so that I can resume my father's work."

"Very good. In order to do most of these things, we must all regain our memories. Each of you is suffering from some form of amnesia, either total, partial, or systematic. Jane here is suffering from total amnesia, and the rest of you are suffering from systematic or partial amnesia which manifests itself in many ways. Captain Gregory has systematic amnesia with a site complex; he can't remember locations. Claude also has systematic amnesia with a nomenclature complex; he can't remember names. Dr. Bellwether has partial—"

"That's ridiculous," said Dr. Bellwether. "I've been to plenty of psychiatrists in my day, and I've never heard of site or nomenclature complexes. I don't think you know what you're talking about."

"Please bear with me, Dr. Bellwether. I think that with today's exercise, you will begin to understand." Dr. Royale unsnapped the carrying case and opened it. Claude stood up, IVs and all, to help her place a large wooden board onto the table and dump thousands of jigsaw puzzle pieces onto it.

"A puzzle? We're here to do a lousy puzzle?" asked Dr. Bellwether.

"Haven't you ever done one before, as a child perhaps?" Dr. Royale asked with a knowing look.

Dr. Bellwether put his fingers on his chin and stewed. "As a child...of course I must have. Come to think of it, I can't remember ever doing a puzzle as a child. In fact, I can't...I can't remember a single event of my childhood. My childhood is gone! You knew! But how did you know?!"

Dr. Royale turned bright red with embarrassment once more. She had made yet another mistake. How could she explain to him that she knew that he had lost his childhood? It would be impossible. In her panic, she lit another cigarette and began to puff in earnest, blowing smoke rings above the table, until the rings banded together into a large cloud above the table. Momentarily, she regained her composure and looked around the table to see if anyone had noticed that she was flustered. Good. It appeared as if no one noticed, except Dr. Bellwether and the others didn't trust his judgment yet.

She turned to Dr. Bellwether. "Don't most children do puzzles?" But he wouldn't answer. She went to his side and put her hand on his shoulder. "Don't worry, Dr. Bellwether, we will help you restore your childhood, but you must trust me." From his reaction, Dr. Royale could tell that she had caught Dr. Bellwether off guard. He looked at her with curiosity and said nothing, his resistance weakening temporarily.

Returning to the head of the table, she held up a puzzle piece. "Now, if we may proceed. I want you to think about a puzzle. It is filled with thousands, perhaps millions, of pieces and they all have to be put together to make any sense. That's just one puzzle. Think if you had millions of puzzles to put together, and the pieces were three-dimensional, some unique and some shared with many other puzzles. Each of your memories is like a puzzle, and all of your memories are interwoven together into a rich tapestry that is your mind. That, my dear patients, is the problem and the solution. Each of you has lost a part of your memory, but do not despair. In most cases, we have all the pieces. We just have to put the puzzle together to make sense of it. In order for me to help you, I need each and everyone of you to help me piece together these puzzles. I thought that we could start by putting together an actual puzzle for practice. By seeing the interrelationship of space, shape, and color it may give us some insights into our own memories."

"You really think that putting together this puzzle will bring back our memories?" asked Jane.

"No," said Dr. Royale, "but I think that it will give you the skills you need to piece together your memories. And you might learn something about yourselves and your situation in the process. Now let's begin, shall we?"

With a good deal of interest, the group picked up the pieces and looked for matches, but they found none at first. "Well, if we're going to do this thing, we ought to do it right," said Dr. Bellwether. "Gather the border pieces; gather the pieces with the same color, lines, or shape; and gather the concave and convex pieces."

Claude frowned. "What do you mean, concave and convex?"

"You know," said Dr. Bellwether, "the innies and the outies. Every puzzle has loads of them."

"For someone who can't recall ever doing a puzzle, you sure seem to know a lot about them," grumbled Captain Gregory.

"You should listen to my friend, monsieur Captain, he is a very smart man."

"I'm sure he is, but—"

"All right you guys, knock it off," said Jane, looking exasperated. "Putting together a puzzle of this magnitude is going to take cooperation. Since you were a leader in the Navy, Captain Gregory, why don't you take command of the operation; since you are a great neurosurgeon, Dr. Bellwether, why don't you suggest the best way to execute; and since you are always looking out for others, Claude, even with your IVs attached, why don't you assist?"

"With pleasure," said Claude, always the gentleman, "but where do we start?"

With pipe in hand, Captain Gregory took command of the operation, surveying the office like a Navy captain in search of a periscope. He turned to Dr. Royale. "Are you going to help us?"

"No, thank you Captain, I'll just watch."

"Okay then," said Captain Gregory nodding, "some of us here are not too mobile yet, but with four of us we can each take a side. Each of you is responsible for your own border, and each is responsible for the image area directly in front of you. That means we'll need plenty of coordination. When you identify an image or color that stands out, speak up so the others can send the pieces to you. We must keep the supply routes flowing and the communications open."

Dr. Royale pulled out a notebook and began to take notes. She was particularly impressed with Captain Gregory's take-charge attitude. She was glad that she had brought him back into the fold, but she was worried about whether she could separate her personal feelings from her professional duties. She couldn't help herself. She loved Captain Gregory, and she hated him. She was attracted to him and repelled by him, like the sea to the coastline, and the harder she pulled away the more intense the counterwave of desire. Perhaps it was because he was like the father she never had, a concept that intrigued her at the same time that it frightened her.

She turned her attention to the puzzle again and noted that the group had begun to piece together the border pieces. All of a sudden, Dr. Bellwether looked as if he had discovered the new world, or perhaps an old world. Claude also noticed. "Why do you look that way? What is it?"

"I can't take credit for the suggestions I made. It was my father who taught me how to put together puzzles. I have just recalled a small piece of my childhood."

Dr. Royale scribbled in her notebook furiously. "That's excellent, Dr. Bellwether."

"Perhaps doing a puzzle isn't such a bad idea after all," he replied.

Captain Gregory patted Dr. Bellwether on the back. "That's the spirit, Bellwether. Now, what do you need to get going?"

Dr. Bellwether began to pick up a few pieces. "I've got a few orange pieces here, looks like the sun."

In his best Navy voice, Captain Gregory ordered, "Okay, send your orange pieces to Bellwether. How about the rest of you? Does anyone see any images yet?"

"Oh, this is interesting. I see lots of brown pieces with bits of pink in them. The brown is obviously sea grass, but I don't know what the pink is," said Jane.

"Okay, send all of those to Jane."

"There are too many of them," objected Claude.

Captain Gregory smiled and took a puff from his pipe. "Then you can help her, my friend."

Jane had two pieces put together as Claude began to help. Soon there were four pieces and they speculated as to what it might be, but neither knew. Dr. Royale wrote some notes in her notebook and smiled occasionally, obviously pleased with the level of cooperation between the troops. After acclimating them to their new environment, she would work with them to restore their memories to a reasonable facsimile of what they were before. Then and only then would they be ready for the simulations, which would be designed to give her the information she needed to keep everyone's hopes and dreams afloat. Dr. Royale looked down at the puzzle to check on the group's progress. She was sure that they would identify the central character, and the other characters in the puzzle soon. All were busy at work, except Jane who was staring at her. "What's wrong, Jane?"

"Well, I think this whole thing is a bit unfair. After all, we've told you about our hopes and dreams, but you haven't told us what you hope to accomplish."

"All right," said Dr. Royale taking a deep breath. "I will tell you. This puzzle is designed to help you learn to work together in your new environment."

Several previously unseen wrinkle lines registered on Jane's forehead as she tilted her head quizzically. "New environment? You mean the hospital?"

The entire group paused for a moment, waiting for Dr. Royale's response. "Yes, but it's more than that. You see, you all have something in common. You all suffered a head trauma that caused a permanent change in your condition. Even after you recover, nothing will be the same. You will view the world through a different lens."

"Well, you're right about that," said Jane. "Nothing seems the same to me."

Captain Gregory nodded in agreement. "That's the same for all of us no doubt, and we could talk about that all day. But why not treat us separately and send us on our way? Why do we need to work together?"

"To survive," said Dr. Royale.

"What do you mean by that?" asked Dr. Bellwether.

"That's simple. I mean that I need you to help me help you."

The group looked at each other, not knowing what to make of her comments. Captain Gregory studied her carefully and said, "I don't know what you're talking about Dr. Royale, and right now if you'll pardon the expression, I don't care. We can only solve one puzzle at a time."

Dr. Royale nodded and looked at the puzzle. It was about one-quarter complete, and the group was passing pieces back and forth quite quickly now. Dr. Royale was amazed at the cooperation between group members, most of whom had only just met. She was also pleased that Captain Gregory had changed strategy on the fly. They were no longer working on the area in front of them, but instead, were piecing together the parts of the puzzle which would later be fitted into the overall framework. In her studies of nature she had seen many animals show problem-solving capabilities, but she always marveled at how human beings solved problems. They were unlike any other animals in nature. They were creative, resourceful, flexible, analytical, and always cunning.

She could tell that Captain Gregory was delighted to be at the helm again, even if they would never leave shore during this training exercise. He winked at Dr. Royale, nodded at Claude, and then frowned at Dr. Bellwether and growled, "Bellwether, get rid of those brown and pink pieces and send them to Claude." Dr. Bellwether began to object, but Captain Gregory cut him off. "Anybody got people pieces? Send them to Bellwether; he's working on some old guy right now." Dr. Bellwether's look of anger turned quickly into a smile once Captain Gregory showed his support. Captain Gregory was like that; he could turn on a dime, backhanding a sailor one minute and helping him back on his feet the next. It was apparent that Captain Gregory was a tough taskmaster, but he was fair.

Dr. Bellwether looked at the brown and pink object that Jane and Claude were putting together. "Someone should step back from the table every so often to see where these images fit within the border and to see if there are any images that we are missing," he said, looking for Captain Gregory. He turned around and saw that Captain Gregory had already stepped back from the table.

"Good idea, Bellwether," Captain Gregory said.

Jane and Claude continued working on the sea grass, trying to figure out what was obscured. All of a sudden, Jane jumped. "I know what's hiding behind the sea grass...it's a giant cephalopod!!" She placed the giant cephalopod in the center of the frame.

"My God, she's right," said Claude. "What kind of cephalopod is it?"

"I believe it is the giant octopus," said Jane.

"I don't understand," said Dr. Bellwether. "Is this some kind of Rorschach test or something to see how we will react?"

"In a way, yes. I would be interested in discussing your reactions when you are finished," said Dr. Royale.

"Well then," said Captain Gregory, "let's finish it."

As they made progress, the group became more animated, and they all began to speak at once. "Hey, there's somebody else in this puzzle," said Jane. "I've got a woman's hand, and here's a pipe," said Claude. "Let me see that," said Dr. Bellwether, "I think that fits in with mine." He laughed uproariously and turned to Captain Gregory. "That old man you were talking about is YOU!"

"ME?!" Captain Gregory stared at the puzzle. "What am I doing in the puzzle?"

"There's at least three people in this puzzle, isn't there?" asked Jane without looking up.

"Four," said Captain Gregory, "there's an SOS badge over here."

"My goodness, that's me. This is about us, isn't it?" asked Claude, looking up at Dr. Royale.

"Yes."

"Why?"

She held up her finger. "For now, I want you to develop your impressions of the piece. Then we'll discuss it."

"I knew it was about us all along," said Dr. Bellwether.

"Then why didn't you say so?" asked Claude, his lips turned up in a wry smile of disbelief.

"I didn't want to spoil it for everyone else."

"Mais bien sur," said Claude sarcastically.

"All right," said Captain Gregory, "let's finish the puzzle."

Jane was working on her golden-haired counterpart in the puzzle, but could not find the piece for the midsection. She held a pink piece up to the light and looked at it closely. "Oh, my God, I know where this one goes." She fitted the piece into the midsection, revealing that the giant octopus was holding her in the puzzle.

"She's holding me too," said Claude. The group got quiet as they realized that the giant octopus was actually holding each one of them in her arms.

Captain Gregory stood back and stared at the puzzle. Dr. Bellwether indicated that he too wished to be wheeled away from the table so that he could have a better perspective. Jane pulled his wheelchair back and then Claude's, and all of them stared at the puzzle.

It was a beautiful puzzle with hundreds of pieces. At the center was the giant octopus in pink with white pinstripes, partially obscured by tall sea grass. She was looking up at the surface of the water, above which she was holding each in the group. On the horizon, behind them was a bright orange sun with a single piece missing.

Dr. Bellwether held the last piece of the puzzle in his hand. Before putting the piece in the puzzle, he looked at Dr. Royale. "I want to know whether this is the sunrise or the sunset?"

Dr. Royale diverted her eyes from him. "That would depend on your perspective."

"And why is the octopus holding us above water?" asked Dr. Bellwether.

Dr. Royale smiled as she stood by the table and looked at the puzzle. She was amazed at the remarkable speed with which they had put together the puzzle. "I would like to get your observations on that before I reveal mine. But first you have to put in the last piece," she said, wanting more time to collect her thoughts.

Dr. Bellwether indicated that he wished to be pushed into the table again. As Dr. Royale wheeled him back to the table, he dropped the puzzle piece on the floor. They both bent over to look under the table at the same time. After a few moments, she picked up the piece and turned toward him. "I found it."

As Dr. Bellwether turned toward her, his mouth dropped open. "Oh my God! What's wrong with your eyes?"

Dr. Royale quickly righted herself, barely able to keep her balance as a wave of panic swept through her. "Oh, I suffer from Duane's disease."

"That's not Duane's disease."

"Well then, I suppose I should have it checked," she said, hoping to diffuse his curiosity. By the way he looked at her, though, she knew that she had made a big mistake, her third. She would have to leave now before he cornered her and demanded the whole truth. No one else had noticed, and perhaps later on Dr. Bellwether could be persuaded that he had just been imagining things. Dr. Royale placed the last piece in the puzzle and looked at her watch. "I have urgent business to attend to," she said, heading toward the door.

"Wait," said Jane. "We're supposed to discuss the puzzle."

As she closed the door, Dr. Royale said, "You can stay and discuss the puzzle amongst yourselves, and then we can talk about it in our next session."

"But you can't just leave," said Dr. Bellwether, but he was too late. The door slammed shut, and the group just sat there not saying a word, dumbfounded by the abrupt exit. All of the men instinctively looked to Jane for an answer. She raised her eyebrows as if to say, "Just because I'm a woman, don't ask me why she left." She then buried her nose in the ever-present book in her hands, a book she had open half of the time, looking up occasionally to add something to the conversation before retreating back into its papyrine pages.

Captain Gregory turned to Dr. Bellwether. "What did you do to her?" he demanded.

Dr. Bellwether looked innocent. "Me? I didn't do anything. I merely asked her what's wrong with her eyes."

Captain Gregory looked at him sternly. "There's nothing wrong with her eyes; they're beautiful. Why would you say such a thing?"

Dr. Bellwether bristled. "Oh yes, there was too something wrong with her eyes. Even though she was bent sideways, her eyes were horizontal." The group looked at Dr. Bellwether as if he was crazy.

"Don't you get what I'm saying? THEY WERE ROTATED IN HER SOCKETS!"

Captain Gregory frowned. "Oh, hogwash, Bellwether. You just imagined it. We've all been imagining things. Now give it a rest, would you?"

Jane looked up from her book and stared at Dr. Bellwether with wide eyes. "There is only one species that I know of that can rotate its eyes like that and it isn't man." Dr. Bellwether and Claude waited for her to say something more, but she didn't.

"What species is that?" asked Claude.

"The octopus," said Jane. "Maybe she's some sort of circus freak or something. I knew something was different about her."

Captain Gregory laughed. "Oh come on. If she's an octopus, then I've been looking in all the wrong places for the perfect catch. Now let's forget about this nonsense and figure out what this puzzle is all about."

The group just stared at Captain Gregory. He had been put in charge through their acquiescence, and now no one was willing to question his authority or his position as de facto leader of the group. So they all turned their attention to the puzzle and stared at it. After a while, Jane said, "I think she's trying to tell us something."

"It seems odd, though, that we are the only ones in the picture," said Dr. Bellwether.

"I don't think so; after all, we're the only ones with head injuries. Nobody else was even near the accident," said Jane, who then resumed reading.

Dr. Bellwether's eyes lit up. "You're not getting the point. I mean *where* are our rescuers?"

Captain Gregory smiled, as the long arm of truth lifted him from an ocean of ignorance. "At first I thought that I was rescued by Manuel, but I don't believe that I was rescued by *anyone*. She's trying to tell us that we were saved by the giant octopus."

"The octopus!" they all said at once.

"Yes, the octopus," Captain Gregory said. "Dr. Royale doesn't want to shock us. It's her way of telling us and letting us come to grips with it."

Dr. Bellwether shook his head. "It doesn't mean that at all. I think she's trying to tell us that we're trapped here and there's no way out. What do you think, Jane?"

"Oh, I agree with Captain Gregory. I think that the octopus saved my life. It would explain a lot of things."

"And I thought that I saw her in the waters just before I was knocked out. Maybe she rescued us too," said Claude.

"Well I don't buy that at all," said Dr. Bellwether, looking around the room to see who, if anyone, was in agreement. Much to his dismay, Jane was reading her book again. "Would you please put that book down, Jane? We're trying to get to the bottom of this." As Jane put the book down, Dr. Bellwether looked at her quizzically, his nose crinkling and forehead furrowing.

"What's wrong now?" asked Jane. "It's a Tale of Two Cities. Don't you like Dickens?"

"It's not that. Don't you notice anything peculiar about this book?" asked Dr. Bellwether.

"No."

"The title is misspelled. The word 'Tale' is supposed to be T-a-l-e, not T-a-i-l."

"That's curious," said Jane. "I hadn't noticed."

"May I," said Dr. Bellwether as he reached out his hand. Jane handed him the book, and Dr. Bellwether opened it to the first page.

Captain Gregory shook his head at Dr. Bellwether. "I'm beginning to feel like I'm the captain of a floating asylum. I mean, what does this have to do with the price of tea in China?"

Dr. Bellwether ignored Captain Gregory. He was too engrossed in the first page. "Look at this. It's got misspellings all over the first page." He motioned for Jane to hand him another book from the shelves.

"Which one?"

"Any of them. Bring a few," said Dr. Bellwether. She handed him the books and he quickly scanned the first page. He did this with several books, stacking one on top of the other.

"So," said Captain Gregory, "it just means that maybe the book is worth a lot. But I don't see what—"

"No, I don't think so. Look at this book. And this one. And this one," he said pointing to each. "They are all misspelled."

"What does that mean, mon ami?" asked Claude.

"I don't know, but there's something fishy going on around here. I think we should leave this place, at once. Who's with me?"

Nobody answered and it was so quiet you could hear a water bubble pop. "Now let's not panic," said Captain Gregory.

Dr. Bellwether shook his head. "Are you nuts, Captain Gregory? We've got to get out of here. Come on, now, who's with me?" he said in tones that resonated throughout the room. "I believe this place is an insane asylum and we are trapped here."

"Yes. I've gotten that feeling before. Perhaps we should leave. I want to go see Richard...Richard? Yes, Richard, that's his name!" said Jane jumping for joy. A smile as wide as the continental divide parted her lips. "I remember. I remember my lover's name!"

"Well then," said Dr. Bellwether, "let's go see Richard. Let's go see Dr. Holloway. Let's go anywhere, but let's get out of here! Now, what do you say. Are you with me?"

"I'm with you, mon ami," said Claude. "If you could just unhook our IVs." Dr. Bellwether unhooked the IV line from the needle on Claude's arm. He then quickly took out the needle, and applied pressure with a handkerchief. "Here, hold this there for a minute," he ordered Claude as he took out his own IV.

Captain Gregory took a few puffs from his pipe. "Well, you can go if you want to, but I don't think you will get very far. Besides, I think we owe it to Dr. Royale to stick it out with her."

Jane quickly wheeled Claude out into the hallway and then came back for Dr. Bellwether. As she wheeled Dr. Bellwether to the door, she turned to Captain Gregory. "Are you sure you want to stay?"

"I'm sure," said Captain Gregory.

At the doorway, Dr. Bellwether looked back at Captain Gregory. "You can go down with the ship if you want to, but I say we abandon, now!" With that, he closed the door, leaving Captain Gregory behind.

In the hallway, Jane oriented the wheelchairs back-to-back and then slid between them, butting the handles together so that she could wheel both men at once with Dr. Bellwether facing forward. They went down the hallway past gurneys and rolling utility carts toward the EXIT sign. As they approached the door, Jane parked the wheelchairs. She then tried opening the doors, but they were locked!

"They are locked from the inside?" asked Claude.

"No, I don't think they are locked, only stuck," she replied.

"I knew it," said Dr. Bellwether. "It is an insane asylum and we are trapped here. Try again. We've got to get out of here."

Jane tried again and managed to open the doors just enough to trigger an alarm. Moments later, three rather large attendants opened the door to the hallway. Two went over to the patients and the other quickly turned off the alarm.

"I am sorry," said one of the attendants, but you are not allowed to leave the premises without permission from Dr. Royale.

"I want to see Dr. Royale right now. No, I demand to see Dr. Royale right now," said Dr. Bellwether.

"You may see her tomorrow during your regularly scheduled session. You can take it up with her then. My orders are to escort all of you back to your rooms." He motioned to one of the other attendants. "Buzz up for a nurse. We'll need their IVs hooked up again, too."

Dr. Bellwether looked at the others in silent disbelief as the mutual realization hit home that they were not patients, but *prisoners*, of Dr. Royale.

AT DR. ROYALE'S OFFICE, CAPTAIN GREGORY pulled out his compass, hoping to use it to find her. He looked at the hand and headed toward the door to the hallway, but when he got there, the hand shifted and pointed back toward the room. Captain Gregory paused at the doorway and scratched his chin. He went back to the oval table. No one was there, yet the compass pointed toward it. He circled the table, and to his astonishment, the needle made a complete circle. In a moment of inspiration and befuddlement, he realized that the needle was no longer pointing to Dr. Royale, but to the giant cephalopod in the puzzle...

Eleven

Standing at the bow of Captain Gregory's ship, which was now his, Neil the eel Cranston looked at the tiny jut of land in the distance, No Man's Land, and thought of the crown jewel that lay in a cave beneath it. He was happy to be at sea once more, tired of dealing with Professor Holloway and the condescending professors at Boston Biological. They always acted as if he were working for them, as if he were their lackey. But now that he was back on his boat, he was in charge, and he had several sailors to boss around to smooth his ruffled scales.

As the wind blew in his face, Cranston carefully thought through the details of his plan. The trick was to kill the "big red" without damaging the carcass. The head would be sold to the research institute, and the arms would be sold through the black market in Tokyo.

The boat veered off-course and did not correct. Cranston looked back at the helm and yelled, "Watch your bearing, Manuel."

"Yes, boss," said Manuel as he swung the wheel to bring the ship back on-course toward No Man's Land.

"All right now. Hold her steady," said Cranston.

As Manuel sat down at the helm, his knee nudged the wheel, and they were off-course again.

"I said hold her steady, you stupid Mexican jumping bean," said Cranston, his eyes shooting poison darts at the helm.

Manuel quickly turned the wheel again and muttered a few words to himself, none of which Cranston could make out, except "gringo" which was sprinkled throughout like hot peppers on a tortilla. He had a good mind to toss the ingrate overboard, except right now he had more important things to do.

Instead, Cranston went to the nets near the bow and ran his fingers along them, testing the size of the holes to see if he could fit his fist through it. He could, but just barely, and he estimated that they were not large enough for the octopus's head to squeeze through, but just large enough to entangle her arms. Soon they would sweep the area with the net and see what turned up.

FROM BEHIND HER DESK, DR. ROYALE LOOKED apprehensively at her patients and their attendants, whom she had summoned to her office in the middle of the night, causing a good deal of grumbling amongst them.

"What's the big idea," demanded Dr. Bellwether, scratching his head.

"I was right in the middle of a beautiful dream, mademoiselle," objected Claude.

Captain Gregory smelled the air, not for salt spray, musty oak planks, or rotting seaweed, but for trouble. "Something's bothering you, isn't it?"

"Yes. There is something I need to tell you." With a wave of her hand, she dismissed the attendants and got up to close the door behind them, perspiring profusely, and dragging her feet in a kind of walking crawl. She then headed for a sink in the corner of the room, presumably to grab a glass of water. Before she could make it, though, she collapsed on the floor, laying there unconscious, pale as a ghost, nearly sheet-white, as if she were fading out. Captain Gregory and the others leapt up to assist her.

"What in the world is happening?" asked Jane.

"I don't know," said Captain Gregory, "but something is seriously wrong. Somebody hand me a glass of water—now." Jane handed him a glass and he splashed some onto Dr. Royale's face. No response. "See if she has some perfume in her purse," he ordered.

"Why?" asked Jane.

"Just do it," said Captain Gregory gruffly. Jane rummaged through Dr. Royale's purse, found a small bottle, and handed it to him. He dabbed some on a handkerchief and held it under her nose. That didn't help either.

Dr. Bellwether handed a blanket to Captain Gregory, who covered Dr. Royale with it. Suddenly, as quickly as the sun drops into the ocean at sunset, she turned whitish-blue and appeared to be fading fast.

"Oh my God, do something," said Jane.

"Call a doctor," said Claude.

"I am a doctor," said Dr. Bellwether.

"No, I meant a doctor from this hospital."

"For crying out loud, just do something," ordered Captain Gregory.

Dr. Bellwether knelt over Dr. Royale and began to check her vital signs. After checking and rechecking, he became very alarmed. "There isn't time for that," he said as he knelt over her and began to administer CPR, alternately breathing into her mouth and then pushing on her chest with the heel of his hand.

"Somebody count, for God's sake. And call the nurses station and tell them to get over here NOW!!"

Jane immediately jumped up to call for help. "Hello, hello, is anyone there," she said, tapping on the phone. "We have a medical emergency here." She then pressed the red emergency button repeatedly but no one answered. As Captain Gregory counted, Dr. Bellwether continued to push, but Dr. Royale did not respond. After a few more minutes, Dr. Bellwether felt her wrist but could not find a pulse. He resumed and this time began to push harder and harder on her chest.

"Where is everybody? Did you call the nurse's station, Jane?" asked Dr. Bellwether, continuing to push on her chest.

"Yes. It's almost spooky. It's as if the staff are here, but nobody is listening."

"Well, call again."

"I did, they're all gone."

After a few more minutes, Dr. Bellwether checked Dr. Royale again and shook his head dejectedly. The entire group was in shock. Captain Gregory gently rubbed Dr. Royale's hand as if by doing so she would be revived, like a Genie from a long lost bottle. "I can't believe this. Isn't there anything we can do?"

Claude pulled the blanket up over Dr. Royale's head. "What did you do that for?" asked Captain Gregory, pulling the blanket back down. He turned to Dr. Bellwether. "There's some hope left, isn't there, Doctor?"

Dr. Bellwether ignored the question and raised his voice. "Where are they? They should have been here by now. She needs a shot of Epinephrine injected, now. Are you sure you called them, Jane? Call them again. No, on second thought, someone get a gurney. I'll wheel her down to ER myself."

All of a sudden, Dr. Royale sat up. "That won't be necessary." With those words, she turned pink again, only a bright-reddish pink, and got up to her feet so quickly that they were all taken aback.

"What in the world?" said Dr. Bellwether.

"Are you all right?" asked Jane.

"It's a miracle," said Claude, clapping his hands.

"What happened?" said Captain Gregory. "You had me worried sick."

Dr. Bellwether looked at Dr. Royale suspiciously. "I hope this wasn't some sort of joke. That had to be the weirdest feinting spell I've ever seen, if that's what it was. You should have seen the colors you were turning."

Dr. Royale checked the color of her skin. "Oh that. I'm sorry about that. I never intended to show you my true colors," she said lighting a cigarette. "You see, I am in crisis. I really did feint, and I'm afraid I'll need your help, or I will feint again, and the next feinting spell may be permanent."

"Permanent! What are you talking about? What's wrong?" asked Captain Gregory.

Dr. Royale took a deep breath and stared at the group. "Well, I never meant to share this with you, but I have no choice. It's a secret I've been keeping from you, one that will undoubtedly shock you even more than the shock you just had."

"I doubt that," said Captain Gregory. "Please share it with us. If it's some sort of problem perhaps the group can help you with it. You've helped us with ours."

"Well, here goes. You see, we are all one...I am a part of you, and you are a part of me, and we are all part of each other," said Dr. Royale.

"What do you mean by that?" asked Dr. Bellwether.

"Yes, tell us in plain English," said Captain Gregory. "WHAT IS IT? WHAT'S THE BIG SECRET?"

She turned to them. "That *is* the big secret: You are *all living in me*. You are living in an illusionary world, a living dream-state, and you occupy a corner of my brain known as the sub-neurals, which are ordinarily used in communicating with males, sending messages, and reading minds. I am an ambassador to you and have come in your image to learn from you and to teach you."

Too intimidated to look Dr. Royale in the eyes, Jane stared down at her book, "A Tail of Two Cities". Dr. Royale's assertion would certainly explain the misspellings and the fact that the library only had titles that were familiar to her. But even so, it was hard to believe. In fact, too hard. "You've got to be joking," she said.

Claude was too confused to know what to think. He did note, though, that there were many fanciful women in France and that with Dr. Royale's romantic notions of the sea, she would fit right in on the French Riviera. "She's fantasizing, or perhaps, hallucinating," he said.

Dr. Bellwether knew exactly what to think. He didn't buy it at all. There was no proof. It was more likely that this was all a bad dream. Some bad whiskey. Or both. He had never trusted Dr. Royale. He knew something was fishy about her from the start and was not about to give in without a shred of evidence to support her claim. "I told you," he said. "She's not hallucinating; we are. She's been drugging our coffee and now she's going to have us do her bidding."

The only one who believed Dr. Royale was Captain Gregory. He knew that she was telling the truth. That was why his compass always pointed to her—she *was* True North. That was why they were able to go back to his boat from his hospital room. And that was why he no longer had a desire to catch octopi. He had caught the perfect catch—or she had caught him. Captain Gregory concluded that it all depended on your viewpoint. "What species?" asked Captain Gregory.

"Now everyone please calm down. I assure you. I mean you no harm." She took another puff from her cigarette and took a deep breath. "Now, in answer to your question, Captain

Gregory... I am a mollusk, order of cephalopods, sub-order of octopods, species Octopus Giganticus, to use your own terminology."

Captain Gregory looked at Dr. Royale and then Jane and put his arm around her. It was amazing. All of the pieces of the puzzle finally fit together. "Then you must be Jane Seabury, the woman missing at sea off No Man's Land."

"Why yes," said Jane. "That's true."

Using his arm like a fishing pole, Captain Gregory cast in the direction of Dr. Royale. "Then we are not your patients...We were your catch of the day!" Captain Gregory laughed deliriously.

"Well, that's not exactly true, but I haven't got time to explain."

"She hasn't got time to explain." Captain Gregory looked at the other patients. "Well, Dr. Royale, in light of the circumstances, I think you *owe* us an explanation."

"I don't think any of us can fathom what you are talking about," said Dr. Bellwether.

"Don't you get it, Bellwether?" said Captain Gregory. "She didn't save us; she ate us for dinner! What a grand joke! You are what you eat!!"

Dr. Bellwether circled his index finger around his ear. "You're crazy, Gregory. I don't believe a word you're saying. You don't just reconstruct a magnificent mind like mine by popping it into your mouth like an hors d'oeuvre. It's physically impossible."

"Then how do you explain that I am now a squid lover, or that we were all rescued at sea, or nobody has come to visit us in the hospital, except Dr. Royale and her flunky doctors and nurses?"

Dr. Royale turned red with anxiety. "Listen, all of you! *I need your help*!! Don't you see how I look? First I was white and now I am red. This is my second alarm state. You don't understand the predicament I am in. That we all are in. I am caught in a fisherman's net and am being dragged to the surface at this very minute."

"So, if that's true, and I'm not saying it is, what do you want us to do about it?" asked Jane.

"Does anyone have any suggestions on how to get out?" asked Dr. Royale.

Dr. Bellwether shook his head angrily. "This is utter nonsense. If you're some sort of ambassador from some giant invertebrate biosphere in which we're all reluctant guests, how come *you're* not in a state of panic? After all, you're being dragged to the surface, right?"

"Dr. Bellwether, *I am in a panic*. You've seen my colors. I'm telling you the truth. I'm pleading with you. *Don't you see, I need help*," said Dr. Royale as the blush in her cheeks increased dramatically.

"Okay, so you can turn red in the face. Why should we help you?" asked Dr. Bellwether.

"Because if you don't, you will be killed too."

Dr. Bellwether shrugged. "What difference does it make? If what you say is true, we're already dead. Why shouldn't you join us?"

"That's not really true. You can live a normal existence here if you want." She turned to Captain Gregory to appeal to him. It seemed odd to her that her sworn enemy was now her only hope, her last hope. "Captain Gregory, surely you don't want to go down with the ship, do you?"

"Don't listen to her, she's some sort of devilfish," pleaded Jane.

Like a main mast on a steady ship, Captain Gregory stood there, unwavering, unmoved, and unaffected. "To be precise, she is the first known female specimen of the Northern Atlantic species of Octopus Giganticus, known in the folklore as the red giant."

"The what?" asked Claude.

"The red giant... octopus," replied Captain Gregory matter-of-factly. But he offered no answers to her dilemma.

Dr. Royale turned away. She felt that if she could not win the battle within herself, there was simply no hope that she could overcome the spider's web that entangled her outside of her cave. It didn't really matter now if they saw her true colors or not, so she turned bright crimson red with white pinstripes from head to toe. She turned to Captain Gregory to appeal to him one more time. "Captain Gregory, will you help me or not? I am drowning. I am telling you that I can barely catch my breath in this net and they will have me at the surface in a matter of minutes. Now, for the last time, will you help me?"

Captain Gregory lit his pipe and took a long puff, keeping Dr. Royale waiting. Everyone in the group waited to hear what their leader had to say. The longer he made them wait, the more certain they were that he would come to his senses and tell Dr. Royale to leave them alone. To go take a hike. To quit playing with their emotions, and telling them these preposterous tales. At last, Captain Gregory turned to her. "Yes, I have never turned down a lady in distress, and I am not about to start."

"Are you nuts, Gregory?" exclaimed Dr. Bellwether.

"Shut up, Bellwether," said Captain Gregory. He turned his attention to Dr. Royale. "Now, can you disentangle yourself?"

"No, it is hopeless."

"Can you attach to any rocks?"

"I'm clear of the rocks."

"Look above you, is there anything you can entangle the net on?"

"No, please help me, they've almost got me to the surface."

"Well, I'm trying. You mustn't let them get you to the surface in that net. He'll harpoon you or shoot you right between the eyes for sure, and that will be the end of it."

"I can see them. *Oh, help me!*"

"If only I could see what's going on."

"That's it! I should have thought of that before," said Dr. Royale.

All of a sudden, the lights went out in the room, and they saw nothing but water and bubbles, as if the sea were churning. In the confusion there were many voices, adding to a crescendo of cries for help. "Hey what's going on, turn on the lights, we're under water, get us back to the office, okay we surrender, just tell us what you want from us. This isn't funny. Everyone calm down. What's going on here. Tell us what's going on. Please."

Outside, her massive arms were struggling to get free of the net. Inside, her guests, to their amazement, could see what was happening as if they were in a giant Sensurround theater. Two of her arms were hopelessly entangled in the net but she had managed to free the others.

Captain Gregory was in awe at the sight of her; the others were in varying states of shock. Her arms were crimson red and tentacles were massive. She was writhing and twisting, trying mightily to get away, but to no avail.

"Can you spray?" he asked.

"Yes."

"Fire when I give the command, and then jettison in the opposite direction."

She was nearly at the surface now and could see the boat. A shiphand was dutifully cranking the winch, whose motor had apparently failed. Captain Gregory's mouth fell wide open as Cranston and Manuel also came into view. Seeing Manuel brought about all sorts of feelings—elation, sorrow, anger, and betrayal. It was as if they had staged a mutiny and made him walk the plank; and now he was coming back as an octopus, which they were hellbent to catch. It was too unreal, being trapped in a fisherman's net looking up at them, and the unreality of it made him feel as if he were in a trance.

Cranston checked the firing mechanism on the spear gun, and slowly raised it. As the spear gun reached position, Captain Gregory realized that he wasn't just shooting at *her*, he was shooting at *him*...and *them*, and that was enough to snap him out of it. Cranston slowly put his finger in place and was about to pull the trigger...

"DO IT NOW," shouted Captain Gregory. At that moment, she sprayed gallons of black ink onto the boat, covering Cranston, Manuel, and the other shiphand from head to foot. From their watery view below, they could see that in the confusion, Cranston slipped, tottered backward, and fired the spear gun...It was a direct hit, piercing the man at the winch, who staggered backward and then fell.

Seeing her opportunity, the giant octopus pointed her head away and jettisoned from the boat with such force that the net came unfurled, and she landed, net and all, a good 100 yards away, out of range of the spear gun.

"Quickly now," said Captain Gregory. "Work on one arm at a time." They watched as she struggled and struggled but was unable to break free.

"What about biting the net?" he said. She tried but the material was too strong, appearing to be made of some sort of new high-tech composite fiber.

"Maneuver around so that I can see how your arms are tangled," Captain Gregory ordered. One of the arms appeared to be looped through the net; the other was hopelessly tangled.

Captain Gregory examined the arms closely. "It looks as if your one arm is looped in a simple sailor's hitch. Pull it back, that's it. Now over. Now under. And back again." As her arm was freed, the rest of the group came alive and cheered.

But Dr. Royale was not celebrating. "They're hauling us in again. What should I do about my other arm?"

"I don't know how to put this delicately, but it's already mangled. You should sever it."

"What?"

"Pardon me, Mon Captain, you can't ask her to do that," objected Claude.

"Don't you get it," shouted Captain Gregory. "We have no choice. If she doesn't swim away, neither do we. It's sink or swim. We've got to get out of here, now!"

"What about the bleeding?" asked Dr. Royale.

"I think that it will stop and you'll be all right," said Dr. Bellwether. "Do you have the ability to regenerate? Some cephalopods do you know."

"I can't speak for Dr. Royale," said Jane, "but virtually every species of octopus can."

"I wouldn't know, over the past few hundred years, I haven't had to bite off an arm that often," said Dr. Royale sarcastically.

"Just do it," commanded Captain Gregory. "They haven't left to care for their wounded, and unless I miss my guess, they will not."

She moved her mantle toward her arm and opened her large mouth underneath, hesitating only for a moment, and then bit down hard. A cloud of red filled the water, only this time it was not ink, but the true color of anguish.

Dr. Royale let out a terrible scream and fell to the floor. Captain Gregory knelt down and reached out instinctively to put an arm around her, to comfort and protect her. Not a word was spoken. They all knew now that what was happening to her was also happening to them. Mesmerized, they all watched as the giant octopus pointed her head toward the cliffs, and jettisoned toward her den.

❖ ❖ ❖

IN THE BOAT ABOVE, MANUEL WAS KNEELING beside the fallen shiphand, wrapping his wound to stanch the bleeding. Intent on his catch, Cranston reeled in the net containing a single arm. As he hauled in the partially ripped net, his eyes grew wider. He took out a tape and measured the arm. "Fifty feet! What a monster!" He dragged it on deck and handed it to Manuel. "Here put this on ice."

Manuel took the arm. "Okay, but then we head home, right boss?"

"No, we've got to go after her."

"What about Jack?"

"What about him?"

"You shot him."

"So what? It's not my fault he stepped in front of the spear gun. Jack wasn't too nimble, and Jack wasn't too quick."

"This is no joke, amigo. We've got to get him to a doctor."

"He's a goner, Manuel, leave him be. We've got bigger fish to fry. Now I want that big red and I want it now."

"No, we've got to leave now." Manuel started to pull up anchor.

Cranston grew rabid. "Now you listen to me, if you don't do as I say, I'm going to report you to the INS faster than you can say wetback. You get the picture?"

Manuel thought about it and shrugged. "Okay, boss, whatever you say. But we got no net, and she won't be coming up for *air* any time soon, so how do you think we're going to catch her?"

"We're going to reset the spare nets," snarled Cranston.

At that moment, Jack regained consciousness and groaned. Manuel pointed to him. "You tell him that we're not going back." Seeing that Jack wasn't a goner yet, Cranston grimaced and spat in disgust. "Oh, all right, let's take him in."

❖ ❖ ❖

BACK IN HER OFFICE, DR. ROYALE ADDRESSED the group again. "This has been a long and difficult day for all of us. I am going to be recuperating, so I will blink out so to speak and you will find yourselves back in bed. We will meet again in a few days, at which time, after we have all calmed down, I will be happy to answer your questions and make you feel as comfortable as possible. Oh, and one other thing. Thank you for helping me. Your kindness will not be forgotten."

In an instant, Dr. Royale blinked out. Her guests found themselves in their beds, left to contemplate their ambassador to the new world, a "red giant" planet upon which they alone were the inhabitants. The lights were turned off and all but Captain Gregory were soon asleep, a state that they would stay in for the next few days while the queen of the cephalopods recuperated.

Captain Gregory sat up in his bed and lit his pipe, reflecting on the events of the last few days and making a mental note of each of the things that he had learned. It seemed hard to believe but it was true that—

- His new home was in the corner of the magnificent mind of a full-fledged giant cephalopod,
- He and Dr. Royale had been on a date on board a mirror image of his boat,
- His new enemy, Cranston, had been his enemy all along.

Saving this magnificent creature was the least that he could do. After all, she had saved Jane, and Dr. Bellwether and Claude from drowning. That's what she had been saying all along in the puzzle. She made that claim about him too, but he remembered the sharp pain in the back of his neck. He had not drowned; she had *incorporated* him, or so it seemed. It was not her fault, though; she was just protecting her offspring, as any other mother would do. Captain Gregory puffed on his pipe and said, as if Dr. Royale were right there in the room with him, "You may have saved the others, but you killed me, didn't you?"

"No, you were chosen," came a whisper in his ear.

Captain Gregory turned but no one was there. "Chosen for what?"

"To lead my troops against the enemy."

"Who might that be?"

"The fishermen, of course."

"But why me?"

"Who would know the moves of the enemy better than the enemy himself?"

"Yes, but how do you know I won't betray you?"

"Simple. Self-preservation. You are now the enemy of the fishermen too. And the enemy of my enemy, my dear Captain, is my friend. Now please, get some sleep. Sweet dreams..."

Twelve

The Queen had been home now for several days and was busy making preparations for the hatchlings, who were due any time now. Her arm had quit bleeding shortly after she severed it, and the pain had largely subsided. Much to her delight, she had found out that Jane had been right; she did have the ability to grow it back. The wound had healed and new skin had formed around a nub that was growing longer by the day.

Her guests were tucked safely in bed, and she was enjoying their dreams. Dr. Bellwether was dreaming about the Dance of the Sugar Plum Fairies, who were tiptoeing like ballerinas from flower to flower, opening one after another, as each note in the Nutcracker Suite was faithfully reproduced in his mind.

The Queen imagined that she too was tiptoeing as she crept along the ocean floor, moving from one point to the next, in step with the melody that resonated in Dr. Bellwether's mind; and each time the bell rung to resolve a chord progression, she would pirouette, and then move on, until finally she arrived at the rock behind her table. She gently moved it away and looked at the two large eggs, wishing that they would open like the petals on a flower so that she might see her children for the first time. She gently touched the eggs, watched intently for any movement and aerated them. She then went into the long tunnel at the back of the cave and "tiptoed" amongst the millions of eggs that she had laid, wishing that they too would blossom like flowers in a vast hydroponic garden. It would be soon, but not soon enough as far as she was concerned. She was eager to begin their training.

There were other dreams going on at the same time too, each of which she found rather amusing. Claude was dreaming about setting up a flotilla blockade to prevent Japanese fishermen from slaughtering the great whales. Jane was dreaming about marrying Richard, taking him into her arms, and gently kissing him at the altar, while church bells played beautiful music. But it was Captain Gregory's dream that interested her the most, so much so that she turned blush red as he dreamt of Dr. Royale with the passion of a man who had been at sea for a long, long time.

As she contemplated the unspoken love that was developing between Dr. Royale and the captain, an unspoken love that called to them in their sleep, another unspoken love called to her, and it resonated through her entire being. It was the feint sound of an egg cracking, a sound that she hadn't heard in fifty years, a sound that made all of the church bells in Jane's dream toll to announce the birth of an infant, a queen, who was just now extending a small armtip probe from the small opening she had chiseled in the top of her egg, the first royal to lay claim to a new world.

The Queen's eyes grew wide, her pupils like dense celestial objects pulling in the light before them, so that none of the vision that she had longed to see would go unseen. She touched the probe, and it did not retreat, but instinctively attached to her arm before going back to work on the exterior of the egg. Another arm came a moment later, followed by another, and another, and soon the inhabitant popped out of her egg. The small, five-inch hatchling turned and gazed at her mother for the first time, blinked several times, and began to crawl toward her. The Queen gathered her in her arms and held her to her head, and for the first time in a long time, she was at peace with herself and the world. For the moment, she was no longer aware of her guest's dreams; the only dream that she was aware of was the little dream that she cradled in her arms, her little bundle of pink with white pinstripes, her little dream come true...

She fed the infant and after it was satisfied, it closed its eyes and fell asleep in its mother's arms. Instinctively its small delicate arms adhered to its mother, and she was moved to weep the silent tears of happiness that only a mother can weep. Soon she fell fast asleep, too, but not before naming her first born with a name her guests could understand and appreciate, Elizabeth.

Some time later, in the midst of a dream about her daughter, she felt her move and tap one arm, then the opposite arm, and then both at once. Groggy and confused, she stirred a bit, wondering how Elizabeth had managed such a trick. A moment later, she felt suckers attaching to both arms, and she awoke with a start. Elizabeth was attached to one arm, and her sister was attached to the opposite arm! Another child was born!!

The two baby queens crawled up their mother's arms and met on her mantle, tentatively touching their arms and staring at each other. The Queen was overcome with emotion as she gently cradled the two in her arms and began to feed them with some morsels left over from dinner. She looked over at the rock that used to shelter the two and, sure enough, there were now two sets of broken eggs, the last remnants of an intimate, secure world.

The Queen touched her daughters, fed them, and tucked the little sleepyheads in the small holes she had prepared in the wall of the cave. She then rubbed up against a rock and settled down in the corner near her daughters and went back to sleep.

She began to dream again, only this time it wasn't about her children. It was about Captain Gregory. They were back on a boat together, only it wasn't a boat, at least she didn't think it was. She wasn't sure. She had never seen one like it. It was a boat that was sailing underwater. The Queen thought that the dream was a strange one. Whoever heard of a boat that sailed underwater? As the thought crossed her mind, she became aware of Captain Gregory's dream again, which had picked up more or less in the same place as hers. In fact, her dream was interacting with his dream, and certain elements were being transported back and forth between them. It was strange that she was aware of this in her subconscious, but nonetheless she was aware of it. She was also aware that his dream was far more suggestive than hers, far more interesting, and so she boarded the boat in his dream, a willing participant...

It is wartime, and Dr. Royale and Captain Gregory are on a submarine, not a nuclear submarine, but a biological submarine that is their only hope for survival. She is in her quarters, undressing, when suddenly she realizes that he is watching her through a special periscope that sees inside the submarine. She turns away but continues undressing, until she is standing naked with her back to him. Moments later, the hatch door to her quarters slowly opens, and he is standing there. She is just about to turn around when suddenly an alert is broadcast throughout the submarine that the enemy has launched a torpedo. Captain Gregory leaves immediately to go on deck, but there is no one there. He orders the boat to dive anyway and it obeys, almost magically, settling on the bottom of the ocean floor. The torpedo barely misses them, and the submarine takes refuge in a long underwater cave. Fully clothed again, she joins him on deck. Not a word is spoken between them. It's as if they know what each is thinking, and it sends tremors up and down her sleek, nubile body. They move slowly toward each other, hesitate, and then embrace, his arms slowly encircling her with a surprisingly strong grip considering the lack of tentacles. He looks into her eyes, drinking in the royal blue color that is many fathoms deep. He moves toward her slowly, and her lips are quivering like a schoolgirl about to have her first kiss.

As their lips come together in a dizzying rush, Dr. Royale is taken aback by the powerful feelings sweeping through her body like a Tsunami wave. Her first kiss seems to last forever, and yet, as Captain Gregory's lips part from hers, it does not seem long enough. But at least she knows now, for certain, how he feels about her, and it makes her ecstatic, confused, and fearful at the same time, a Molotov cocktail of emotions that are completely different from any she has ever experienced before.

Before Captain Gregory can kiss her again, they become aware of an enemy battleship on radar above them. Captain Gregory calls the men to their battle stations, but not a single man is on board. He asks her where all the men are, and she replies that none of them have "hatched" yet. But they have to have troops or they cannot defend themselves. "Where are my troops?" he asks again. As he does, there is a crackling noise that fills the air around them...

The crackling noise was so loud that it filled the water around her, too, and the Queen awoke to see no less than eight small males escaping from their eggs. Then eighty. Then eight hundred—a whole regiment. Her eyes grew wide as the eight hundred became eight thousand. Eight thousand warriors in their traditional pink and white pinstriped uniforms! This was the proudest day in a mother's life. She turned bright yellow to attract her warrior sons, who soon linked arms and formed a circle around their queen mother, slowly swimming around her in an instinctive ritual, like a vast array of celestial bodies orbiting the sun at the center of their universe. The popping sound continued and soon, the eight thousand warriors became eight hundred thousand strong. The birth of a nation of cephalopods whose world revolved around the Queen and her daughters. As the males filed past her out the entrance of the cave in search of food, she sighed. Soon they would return, and they would begin their training. Her fifth and final hatching was complete... It was an event that she had waited for these past fifty years and she was rejoicing in it, ringing bells in her mind and implanting messages of love and peace in her guest's minds. With the birth of a nation, the birth of an eight-armed Navy designed to keep the peace, she and her guests were no longer alone in the world.

Thirteen

---✦---

They were in Dr. Royale's office again, tired from the emotionally-wrenching experience of finding out that they were living a kind of double-existence, one of half-human and half-octopus. Though tired, almost all of them felt at ease from the ebbing and flowing of soothing messages and images that they had received while asleep, like a gentle brook lapping at the interwoven roots at the shore of their collective mind. All except Dr. Bellwether, who knew that there could not be another species as intelligent as man, and no other intellect superior to his own. He knew the kind of tricks a mind could play, and he felt certain that this was a hallucination of immense proportion, so large that it occupied all of their minds.

They had all been having dreams that were interwoven with messages of love and understanding and images of children, broadcast through the Queen's mind. With each of the Queen's hatchlings, she had sent out more and more images of babies, and more babies, until there were babies everywhere, and that was all that they had been able to dream about.

"I had the strangest dream last night," said Dr. Bellwether. "I was in a garden and before I knew it, there were babies blossoming from flowers everywhere. They were all crying, as if they did not belong in the flowers, and the flowers did not belong in the garden, and the garden did not belong in the dream."

"My dream had babies in it, too," said Captain Gregory. "It was crazy. I was calling my men to their battle stations, but no one was there. All I could hear were the sounds of a whole regiment hatching from their eggs and singing a recruit song."

"How strange," said Jane. "I dreamed that I got married to Richard, and when we got home from the church, our house was full of babies, and they were all laughing."

"You, too?" said Claude. "In my dream, we set up a blockade to spare the whale calves from the fishermen. But we didn't need to. Their boats were full of sleeping babies to remind them to spare the young."

"Who would have thought we would all dream about babies?" said Jane.

"I don't know. All I know is that the crying was awful," said Dr. Bellwether.

"The singing was beautiful," said Captain Gregory.

"The laughing was wonderful," said Jane.

"The quiet was deafening," said Claude.

They wondered aloud what it all meant. The door opened and Dr. Royale walked in wearing a burgundy silk blouse that looked stunning against her royal blue eyes. "I'll tell you what it all means. Last night the Queen gave birth to 800,000 infant soldiers who will defend you against the enemies of the realm."

"Oh, sure, and last night I performed brain surgery on an amoebae," said Dr. Bellwether.

"You may not believe it, but I did," said Dr. Royale, flushed with pride.

"*You* did?!" said Dr. Bellwether, clicking the roof of his mouth in disbelief.

Jane looked reproachfully at Dr. Bellwether. "You know and I know, Dr. Bellwether, that many octopus species are capable of that."

Dr. Bellwether knew that the notion was ludicrous. It was time to draw a line in the sand. "Ah, but octopus is the operative word here now, isn't it? I mean, are you all blind? Can't you see that Dr. Royale is a beautiful flesh-and-blood woman and not some eight-armed bulbous-headed beast?"

Captain Gregory glared at Dr. Bellwether. "Look, Bellwether, you don't have to be here."

"He can stay," said Dr. Royale. "Because I know that for Dr. Bellwether, understanding is believing. So I will show you things, so that you will come to understand this place."

"Good," said Dr. Bellwether, "because I want some answers."

"Then let's begin, shall we." She headed for the wall without slowing down, so that the others thought for sure that she would run right into it. At the last moment, the cherry wood wall parted, revealing a seamlessly integrated sliding door to a secret elevator. She walked through the opening and beckoned the others to join her, and they did so hesitantly. Once everyone was in, the door closed automatically. There were three buttons on the wall—Tour, Simulator, and CC. Dr. Royale pressed Tour and the elevator began to drop.

"Where are you taking us?" asked Dr. Bellwether.

Dr. Royale smiled. "On a journey." The doors opened and they were at an old-fashioned train station. Moments later, a train of open, ultra-modern magnetic levitation rail cars appeared out of nowhere. It was so quiet that it had taken all of them by surprise.

"Looks more like an amusement park ride," said Dr. Bellwether.

"Give the lady a chance," said Captain Gregory.

"Yes," echoed the others, as Dr. Bellwether made a face at them. That gesture struck him as peculiar, because he hadn't resorted to making faces since he was a child. For some reason, though, he seemed to have lost control of his emotions, as if he were going through a second childhood. There was nothing wrong with his faculties, however. In fact, the filament inside the giant bulb in his head was burning more brightly and more energetically then ever.

Captain Gregory helped Jane into the first car, which had only one seat, and Dr. Bellwether and Claude got into the second. "Keep an eye on him," said Captain Gregory to Claude. "He's acting very strange." There was only one car left, and so he and Dr. Royale climbed into the car and sat down, his broad shoulders barely touching hers. In the back of his mind, he wondered if she had planned it that way.

"This morning will be your indoctrination into your new world. First, you will learn the ABCs of this world in the Holodome. It is based on the collective knowledge and experiences that you yourselves have already had, but this experience, I can assure you will be quite different. Tomorrow we will go to the Training Simulator, and after that Command and Control..."

"Excuse me, Dr. Royale, but what do you mean by the ABCs?"

"Well, I don't mean ABCs in the conventional sense. It's an acronym for Answers to Biological Conundrums."

"What?" the group said in unison.

"You will see," said Dr. Royale as the first car took an abrupt turn. In succession, the other cars took a sharp curve to the left and then they went through a long tunnel. At the end of the tunnel, they entered a large geodesic dome. The cars moved quickly inside, and as they whizzed by, Captain Gregory and the others could just barely make out the small slender objects in the walls—books, the collected titles of all that they had ever read.

"We are now in the Holodome, which is an advanced virtual library run by a computer of sorts. Ask the computer any question in any field and it will provide the answer in a three-dimensional virtual world," said Dr. Royale.

The cars slowed down considerably so that they could make out row after row of books mounted in shelves that appeared to be built into a cone-shaped mountainside inside the dome. Gradually, the cars followed a slow upward spiral as if they were climbing the mountain of books, one shelf at a time. "Looks more like a dusty old library in a dusty old mine shaft," said Dr. Bellwether.

"Unless I miss my guess," said Captain Gregory, "there's more to it than meets the eye."

"I suppose there's only one way to find out for sure," said Dr. Bellwether. "Okay computer, where are we?"

"You are in the Holodome," a very pleasant-sounding voice responded. Dr. Bellwether could not tell whether the voice was male or female, nor could the others. He had a hunch it was female, though he couldn't quite put his finger on the reason.

"I know that," Dr. Bellwether snapped. "But Dr. Royale claims that we are also inside her head. Is this true?"

"Yes. We are inside her head."

"How can that be?!"

"It's sort of like being in a mini-submarine."

Dr. Bellwether looked skeptical. "I don't see a mini-sub in here. There's no entry hatch, no portholes; no pump, no engine, or jet tubes. I don't see a radio antenna or a telescopic projector. And there's no pincer arms or control levers."

"You will find none of those gadgets here," said the voice. "This submarine is far more advanced, since it is biological in origin."

"A biosub! Who would have guessed?!" said Captain Gregory. "Can't say I've ever been on one of those!"

"Would you let me do the talking?" demanded Dr. Bellwether.

"Go ahead, be my guest," said Captain Gregory, waving his hand as if it were a magic wand conveying some authority to Dr. Bellwether.

"All right, supposing that what you say is true, then tell us what *is* inside her head."

"Let's take a look, shall we?" the voice said. The cars veered suddenly to the right and the scene around them changed instantaneously. At once they were inside a long dark tube, barely illuminated.

"Where are we?" asked Dr. Bellwether.

"This is the funnel. It is used to blow water at great velocity and to eject ink, among other things."

They were forcefully expelled from the funnel into a large cavity. In the distance was a large object that resembled a giant pink caterpillar.

"You are now in the muscular septum of the ventral mantle cavity."

"It looks like a cave," said Claude, recalling the many fine adventures he had had spelunking the underwater caves off the Mediterranean coast.

"Above you is the ink sac. The ink is used to conceal the direction of travel, when evading predators."

"What colors do you have?" asked Captain Gregory.

"What colors would you like?"

Captain Gregory raised his eyebrow, obviously impressed. "Really, you can do any color?" he said, scratching his chin, thinking about the battlefield potential of such a weapon.

"Yes, but black or red are the colors most often used."

The cars slowly climbed the giant pink caterpillar, up one side and down the other, as if they were on some giant pink roller coaster. As it traversed from one segment to the next, the voice said, "You are now traveling along the gills."

"Amazing," said Jane.

"Fantastic," said Claude.

As the cars finished traveling the gills, automatic seat belts and overhead restraints secured the occupants. The first car left the last segment of the gills, and Jane screamed as it fell onto a rounded platform below amidst the thunderous sound of muscles expanding and contracting in a constant, rhythmic beat, which was most reassuring to Captain Gregory, who had undergone heart surgery in the Navy. Suddenly the platform rose at great velocity, and the car was launched forward onto another organ. Each of the cars in succession were launched, and each car came to a rest next to each other. An access door on the bottom of the cars opened to reveal a glass bottom, and they all watched in awe at the great river of fluids running below them.

"No doubt you know that we just saw the heart up close, and that we are now looking through the kidneys. Next, we will tour the digestive tract. You will see in order, the stomach, pancreas, and caecum, and the opening to the intestine."

The cars began to move again, and they quickly went along the digestive tract organs until they were riding along a narrow bridge, high above a large brown organ below.

"I don't believe I will be having a taste for sausage for a while," said Claude.

"You are now traversing the crop, and that large organ below is the liver."

"Or liver and onions," laughed Captain Gregory.

The cars began to slow down again until they were moving at a crawl as if there was some giant traffic jam at the end of the narrow bridge, and perhaps, some toll to pay. Dr. Bellwether was growing impatient. He knew all about the anatomy of the octopus; he had read all of his father's books. It was all a sham, an elaborate trick, and it was time to call Dr.

Royale's bluff, or the computer's, or whoever the illusionist was behind this elaborate scheme to keep them from returning to their homes, their careers, their lives, and to everything familiar.

Apparently the others were wondering, too, whether the tour would be just another interesting amusement park ride. "Ask her how she does it," said Claude.

"I'm getting to that. Now please let me ask the questions," said Dr. Bellwether, who turned around to Captain Gregory for reinforcement. Captain Gregory was silent as was Dr. Royale, who had barely uttered a word throughout the tour. Annoyed, Dr. Bellwether turned ahead once more. "If we're inside her head, how does she do it?"

There was no answer at first. The cars moved forward slowly, and after traveling a few feet, a large bony structure appeared before them. "You are now occupying four of the eight sub-neural ganglia masses at the base of the octopod-equivalent of the cerebellum. These axions are biologically wired to billions of bioprocessors in the base cerebellum of the brain," said the voice.

A small opening in the bony structure allowed the cars to go through. They then veered to the left, nearly throwing the passengers. As they recovered, the scene around them changed instantaneously, and they were surrounded by pink tissue, following the neural networks inside the brain of the octopus. "Where are we?" exclaimed Captain Gregory. "It's beautiful," said Jane. "It's like cotton candy," said Claude. "Its putrid," said Dr. Bellwether.

They began to slowly move up a steep mountain of neural tissue, some of which was pinker than others, attracting greater blood flow in the capillaries embedded within. "We are traveling up the vertical lobe. Directly below is the posterior basal lobe, and the posterior chromatophore lobe or skin color processing center." The cars arrived at the top of the mountain of neural tissue and began to move down the back side of the brain. "We will now be traveling through the superior, inferior, and buccal lobes."

"If you've seen one lobe, you've seen them all," said Captain Gregory. "Let's see something else."

"Be patient," said Dr. Royale.

"I am your patient, remember?" said Captain Gregory, his eyes glinting. Dr. Royale lit a cigarette and took a puff, blowing a smoke ring around Captain Gregory's head. She smiled and then suddenly their car vanished.

MOMENTS LATER, THEIR CAR REMATERIALIZED in another strange place, or perhaps their car did not vanish at all but the scene around them had changed. The rail car doors closed and sealed shut, and they slowly floated along on green, swampy water. For the first time in a long time, Captain Gregory was alone with Dr. Royale.

"What is this place?" he asked.

"Why don't you ask the computer?"

"Because I'm not too fond of computers, especially make-believe ones. I'm asking you, what is this place?"

"This would be the poison gland."

"The poison gland?!!"

"You *said* you wanted to see something else."

"Well, if that doesn't beat the rats out of the bilge. Biological weapons! You're a woman of many hidden talents, Dr. Royale," he said, noticing that her dress had moved up from her calves to just slightly above her knees. She had beautiful legs, the kind of legs that could only result from evolution having worked out the finer details over a very long time—perhaps a millennia or so.

"Please, call me Isabelle," she said laughing.

Captain Gregory looked up. "Now we're getting somewhere. That other stuff was beginning to bore me. The problem with Dr. Bellwether is that he'd like to prove you're wrong, but he knows that you're right. He just can't accept it. On the other hand, I know what happened to me, and I accept it. Sometimes you do battle and you lose. And it's only afterward that you find out who the real enemy was."

"Your shipmate?"

"Exactly. I wouldn't mind giving him a shot of your poison rum, here. How does it work?"

Dr. Royale extended her long, sinewy arm, pointed an index finger, and slowly tapped her thumb on it.

Captain Gregory smiled. "Oh, I see. Like a gun."

"Yes, it can be shot from the funnel."

"Range?" he asked, as he looked at the green swamp below the amphibious car.

"Just a few feet."

Dr. Royale felt a strange feeling as she looked into Captain Gregory's eyes, the same feeling she had when listening in on his dreams, and when she was on his boat. It was as if what they were talking about was only secondary to the nonverbal communication between them. She was picking up on his compliments, the ease with which he had come to terms with his new existence, and his smoldering attraction to her. Human communication was altogether different from invertebrate communication, and she particularly enjoyed the subtext. Yes, there was something about this one-man one-woman thing that was oddly attractive to her, and she decided that she would like to try it, even if it was against her better judgment. The feelings were too strong, and they had stayed that way for a long time, so there was no avoiding it anymore. But why didn't he make a move? Perhaps she should give him a sign that it was okay. That she wanted him to kiss her. She slowly pointed her finger at him again and lowered her thumb trigger and held it steady.

"What are you shooting now?"

"Arrows."

Captain Gregory smiled, and the muscles flexed in his legs and arms, as if they were clearing the cobwebs off the memories of what it was like to be intertwined with a woman, a woman whose alter ego had eight arms it was true, but nonetheless a woman. And what a woman she was. Perhaps it was time to settle down, maybe even start a family with this beautiful woman, this beautiful woman of the sea. On the other hand, perhaps he could be court-martialed for such an obvious violation of Navy protocol. It was forbidden for him to have a relationship with a female officer on the same ship, especially if the officer was also his commander-in-chief. He could picture the court martial with the military judge handing down the sentence that he himself would be forced to sign with a quill dipped in the poison swamp. Then again, he was no longer in Uncle Sam's Navy; he was in the Queen's Navy and there was a new set of rules. Captain Gregory weighed the consequences of his actions against the strength of his desires that had been so strong for so long. There was no avoiding it anymore. "I don't see any cupids," he said.

"You never do."

He put his arm around her and was both excited and repelled by the notion of making love to this half-woman, half-cephalopod, this magical mistress of the deep, this woman of the sea. He looked into her eyes. "I don't know how I feel about kissing the woman who did me in."

"I did not," Dr. Royale protested.

"Oh come on, you had me for lunch, and you know it." His eyes narrowed as if aiming at a very difficult target: the truth.

"I did not have you for lunch. But I wouldn't mind having you for dessert," she said her lips pursing slightly.

Captain Gregory moved in closer and decided to take the plunge. "I don't know. If I make love to you, you aren't going to sprout eight legs in the middle of it, are you? Because if you do, that would be a real turn off. Especially if they've got those suction cups. Now if they're like Betty Grable's legs that could be interesting. But suction cups, that would definitely spoil the mood."

Dr. Royale hesitated for a moment, trying to decide if, as a woman, she should be offended by Captain Gregory's remarks, whether they deserved a rebuttal, or whether she should spar with him at all. She looked at him with deep pools of hurt in her eyes, as if she were greatly wounded. "Captain Gregory, I thought that you were a prince among men, but now I'm not so sure."

Realizing his mistake, Captain Gregory said a bit awkwardly, "Oh but I am. I am a prince among men."

"Well, that's a relief," said Dr. Royale wiping her brow dramatically, her eyes dancing with mischief. "Because I was afraid that if I kissed you, you might turn into a frog or something. And that, my dear captain, would definitely spoil the mood for me."

"Very funny."

"No offense, Captain, it's just that I have this thing about men who can't make up their minds. Amphibians are the worst, of course."

Captain Gregory smiled and decided that although a poison gland would not have made his top ten list of places to romance a lady, under the circumstances it would have to do. He moved in and firmly planted his tough, weather-beaten mouth on her quivering lips. He felt a sudden wave of desire engulf him, like a rising tide as he moved slowly along her sensuous ruby lips and glistening pearly whites, probing gently inside as if exploring the nooks and crannies of some new undersea cave. After several, long, luxuriant kisses, he opened his eyes. The green swamp had turned into a sparkling golden waterway. Captain Gregory dipped his finger in it, closed his eyes and tasted.

"It's very sweet," he said. "What's in this swamp anyway?"

"Poison for the enemy," said Dr. Royale as Captain Gregory's eyes grew very wide. "And honey for the prince."

Captain Gregory laughed nervously, realizing the awesome power of this deadly beauty. He put his arm around Dr. Royale and looked into her eyes. What a woman.

She crossed her legs and looked into his eyes. They were gentle, kind, strong. She lit a cigarette and settled back against his shoulder. What a man.

THE CARS PICKED UP SPEED ON THE BACK SIDE of the brain and were now moving with great speed. "We have just left the buccal lobe," said the voice. "Next are the anterior chromatophore lobe, the brachial lobe, and the pedal lobe." The cars whooshed through the undulating tissue, making a long curve to the left and then another long curve to the right as they moved from one lobe to the next. "And if you look just above to your left, you will see the olfactory, pedunculate, and optic nerves."

They all marveled at the large optic nerve which was like a giant pink-gray city suspended in the sky. "This is all fine and dandy," said Dr. Bellwether. "But can we get to the sub-neural ganglia masses at the base of the brain? That was the central focus of my father's research, and frankly, the only part I'm interested in."

"Please bear with me Dr. Bellwether, not everyone in the group has read your father's research," said the voice. The cars came to a stop at the first of eight smaller lobes. "You are now in the octopod-equivalent of the cerebellum, which is at the base of the brain. Soon you will be in the sub-neural lobes, which are a relatively recent evolutionary development. To understand this evolutionary path, one must know a little bit about the social structure of these invertebrates. Their society is made up of colonies of individuals, one female to a colony and several hundred thousand males. The female is the dominant individual in the society; the males gather food for the females and protect her at all costs. Three major developments have occurred in the history of the species. The first is the differentiation between males and females. Over the millennia, the female became larger and larger as did her brain. Eventually she became much more advanced intellectually than the male and lost the ability to communicate with him. The behavior of the males became instinctual; the behavior of the female became more and more logical."

"I don't believe it," said Dr. Bellwether. "No animal society is organized in this manner. You make it sound as if we are living in the midst of a bee colony." Dr. Bellwether shook his head. "And how could you possibly know these things. You haven't gone under the knife, you haven't dissected yourself, have you?"

"No, but your father has done so with one of my species."

"Yes, but how do *you*—whoever you are—know that this is how she works?"

"That's simple. I don't."

"What?"

"I know everything that your father learned from his research. Things that you once knew but have long since repressed; it's all there. I've also deduced a few things on my own based on his research and what I know. I'm just laying it out before you in a slightly more colorful way," the voice said as the sparks crackled all around them, not from brain activity around them but from the sudden entrance of Captain Gregory and Dr. Royale's car.

"I still don't believe it," said Dr. Bellwether.

"Yes, but I do," said Jane.

"You would believe anything to get back to Richard," said Dr. Bellwether. Jane slumped back in her chair and her eyes welled up with tears.

"What an awful thing to say. Take it back, my friend," said Claude.

"I don't mean to hurt anyone," said Dr. Bellwether. "It's just that it's true. Dr. Royale has somehow trapped us in this world, and it's a world run by women."

Jane sat up valiantly and wiped her tears away. "Let's just forget it. Can we get back to the tour? I want to know, what was the second development?"

"In a minute, Jane," said Captain Gregory. Everyone turned around and looked at the sudden reappearance of Captain Gregory and Dr. Royale. With his chest thrust forward like a big red robin, Captain Gregory shook his fist at Dr. Bellwether. "Now, you listen to me you little sea serpent with spectacles. I won't have you addressing the ladies in this way."

"Why not? Just who do you think you are?" said Dr. Bellwether. He stared at the red lipstick on Captain Gregory's cheek. "And where have *you* been?"

"We took a little detour to the poison gland."

"The poison gland! Looks more like you've been through the tunnel of love. What is that on your face?" asked Dr. Bellwether.

"Nothing," said Captain Gregory, who quickly wiped it off.

"It's lipstick isn't it? Isn't it?" said Dr. Bellwether excitedly. "Don't you get it Gregory? She's not kissing you, she's poisoning your mind. She's poisoning your mind against me, against all of us, so that you will do her bidding."

"Now that's enough, Bellwether."

"Isn't it ironic. You set out to catch a rare prize, and you get caught instead!!"

"SILENCE!" said the voice authoritatively. "You are here to learn, not quarrel." The group looked at each other, frightened, not knowing what the voice might do to them. A long pause occurred and then the voice said, "Now in answer to your question Jane, the second development was the maturation of small buds at the base of the cerebellum, the sub-neurals. Right now there are four mature sub-neurals, and you will note an immense amount of electrical activity around them."

The cars began to move again from one sub-neural lobe to the next. To the left and right were electrical "storms" of activity that reminded Captain Gregory of the great lightning displays at sea he had witnessed on so many occasions.

Dr. Bellwether was fascinated as they literally sailed into a fierce electrical storm brewing within the sub-neurals. "Why did these buds develop?" he asked.

"This happened in response to ever-greater competition over territory. As the species prospered, the search for suitable homes became more intense, and whole colonies went to war. Eventually, some females regained the ability to communicate with the males by spontaneously growing an inferior lobe at the base of the brain that was like those of the males. Those who could communicate with their male "armies" gained advantage. They could help them organize, coordinate their otherwise haphazard responses, and develop and convey sophisticated troop movements."

"Fascinating," said Captain Gregory. "Who would have thought that war would bring about such a change."

"War is the birthplace of change," said the voice.

"What was the third development?" asked Jane.

"After developing a replica of the male brain, the species developed the ability to replicate the faculties of other species."

"I find that far-fetched," said Dr. Bellwether.

"You've heard of Darwin haven't you, Dr. Bellwether," the voice said. "The female of this species can already replicate the mind of the male; it was only a matter of time before she could replicate the minds of her prey and predators, and with it, the knowledge of how they think, feel, and communicate. Those queens who lost whole armies in the wars had to learn to feed and protect themselves. By learning to mimic the female crab, she was able to lure herds of male crabs into her den for bulk feeding. By learning about her predators, she was able to learn how to better defend herself."

"You mean man?" asked Captain Gregory.

"Precisely. The only mechanism that was missing at first was the delivery system."

"Ah, I see. You mean the means of getting the DNA to replicate these buds." Dr. Bellwether thought about it for a moment and then smiled. "The bite on the back of the neck," he said triumphantly.

The rail cars exited the electrical storm and suddenly were inside a cylinder-shaped object. There were hairs everywhere, and a strange vast network of what appeared to be honeycombs. The rail cars entered the honeycombs following the hair through an endless maze of tunnels.

"That is correct," the voice said. "Your father did some research in this area; but he was only exploring hypotheses that he was unable to prove. I have deduced from his work that the gland we are now in is at the base of the mouth. You will note that the gland has two basic commodities: hair and honeycomb-shaped objects called neural coordinates located at the far end of the gland. The hair are actually flexible microscopic syringes and the honeycombs store donor neurodendrons and neuroaxons on a complex coordinate system. When fully developed, these honeycombs are a new bud that grows into the sub-neural ganglia mass at the base of the brain of the host."

"But what about the DNA?" asked Dr. Bellwether.

"After the bite is administered, the small hairs extend a great distance to the donor's cerebrum, and inject a fast replicating combination of cloning receptor agents and mapping agents. Like a virus, they invade the cell membrane of the donor and make copies, modified somewhat," said the voice. Suddenly, millions of agents were released from the ends of the hairs, filling the air everywhere around the cars, like the spawning of coral reefs in the ocean depths.

"These agents are a highly efficient means of extracting DNA from the donor and delivering snippets of DNA to the host," the voice continued. "The double helix from the donor DNA is decoupled and paired with a specialized version of the host DNA. After the pairing, the host DNA splits from the donor and remakes the second half of the double helix, building an exact replica using the host's biological material and cells. This DNA is then delivered to the host at the sub-neural bud forming in the honeycomb, which then grows into a mature lobe, and a biocopy of the host's brain. After the lobe has matured, billions of synapses are reconstructed in the host from a map derived from the complex coordinate mapping of the synapses in the donor. Eventually what emerges is an exact replica of the donor's cerebrum, who must then be assimilated as a guest into a new world."

The rail cars exited the tunnels and the group just looked at each other, speechless. After a while, Captain Gregory said, "Well, that's certainly a mouthful. That should be enough to even satisfy the likes of you, Bellwether."

"Hardly," Dr. Bellwether sneered. "If what you say is true, that we are nothing but sub-neural blobs at the base of some lonely outpost in your brain, then how can we see? We are not biologically wired to your optical nerves. We have no eyes, no ears, no mouth, nothing."

"That is correct," said the voice. "Remember that you exist in a conscious dream-state, a new world. In fact, after your accident, you were transformed into something like a blind, deaf, paraplegic, who can only see and hear in a different conscious state. You touch and feel the same as you would in a dream, though you are not dreaming; and mental images are sent to you instantaneously with physical properties on a minute physical scale."

"So we only see what you want us to see," said Dr. Bellwether.

"Yes, but you also see what *you* want to see, too."

"I don't see how there can be any law and order to such a universe."

"That's easy. You have a complete working knowledge of physics, chemistry, and biology, Dr. Bellwether. Every image is built on those principles."

"No wonder I keep dreaming that I'm teaching class," said Dr. Bellwether. "But I don't see how you could put all the pieces of our fragmented memories together. Prove it to me. Let me see the rest of the old world. Release me, release us all, from the hospital."

"I can't do that. Because of your amnesia, the old world is a mess. All of the names and places are scrambled. And not one of you was good at geography. So if you don't let me know where you are going, you could sail over the edge of reality and be swallowed into a sea of darkness."

"Then forget about the old world," said Captain Gregory. "Build us a new one."

"Yes, and give us our freedom," said Dr. Bellwether.

"That could be done, but even then, you would not be free to go," said the voice. "You see, you will all be needed for a mission that Dr. Royale will brief you on at command and control in a few days."

"You make this sound like some sort of military operation," said Dr. Bellwether, his head turning slightly to the left as if the truth were a prism, and if he looked at the right angle he would see the light.

"We are going to war Dr. Bellwether, and we all need to stick together," said the voice.

Dr. Bellwether looked frightened. He had never fought a war before, and he was not about to start. People lost arms and legs in war, and he had already lost those. The only thing he had left was his mind, his magnificent mind, and he was not about to sacrifice that. "Not me. You can fight your own wars, all of you. This is all just an elaborate ruse to keep us trapped in the hospital, and I don't believe a word of it," he said. He felt like jumping ship that instant, only he could not bare the thought of being swallowed by some giant bowel, and being slowly devoured by the microorganisms that resided there.

"Oh, I think you are already convinced about what happened," said Dr. Royale. "That's not the problem. The problem is that you can't accept it, so you're going to leave just when we need you most."

Dr. Bellwether threw his hands up in the air. "You know something, you're right. I can't. I can't accept the fact that I traded a world-class career for a lifelong cruise on a floating biosphere. It would have been better to let me drown. I have nothing to live for."

"You have everything to live for," said Captain Gregory, lighting his pipe.

"That's easy to say when you've got the hots for Dr. Royale," said Dr. Bellwether, pursing his lips to mock Captain Gregory.

Captain Gregory puffed his pipe, half hoping that the resultant rings might collar Dr. Bellwether. "I don't think that you should refer to our commander-in-chief that way," he said in a near-whisper, trying desperately to put out the fuse that would soon ignite the incendiary anger he had been famous for on occasion in the Navy.

"Oh, come on, I've seen the way you look at her, and I have to admit that I am a bit jealous. I think that the only reason it took you so long to steal a kiss from her is because you were afraid she might sprout eight legs on you, and you wouldn't have the testicular fortitude to deal with it!"

Captain Gregory puffed up his chest and stuck his jaw forward. "I'm more of a man than you'll ever be, you sniveling neuro nutcase!" he shouted.

"HA! That's just it. The joke's on you, Gregory, because we're not men at all. We're just a bunch of pink-gray blobs talking to each other. The whole world is an elaborate construction, a grand illusion."

"I believe that it is real."

"Even if we are real, and I'm not sure that we are, what we are seeing is definitely not."

"So what? Get used to it," said Captain Gregory. He turned to Dr. Royale. "Do we have to stay here and listen to this nut? I think we get the general idea of how this all happened. I don't know about the others, but I want to get back."

Dr. Bellwether held his hands out in front of him as if he would stiffarm anyone who got in his way. "Nothing doing. I'm not budging until I get to the bottom of this."

"I agree with Captain Gregory," said Jane. "Let's go."

"Me too," said Claude.

"Et tu, Brute," said Dr. Bellwether to Claude. The Frenchman said nothing, carefully avoiding Dr. Bellwether's scowl as he joined Jane. He felt bad about abandoning his friend but could no longer tolerate him at this moment.

"Perhaps Dr. Bellwether needs a moment alone to adjust to his new circumstances," said Dr. Royale. "The tour for today is over. Tomorrow, we will show you the Training Simulator." In an instant, there was a low rumbling sound, and the other cars zoomed out of sight down a series of synapses that were firing in succession.

After they left, Dr. Bellwether called to them. "Oh fine, go ahead and leave me. See what I care." He looked around at the giant lobes that surrounded him and felt a bit scared and all alone. Everything seemed quiet and the solitude was driving him crazy.

"Dr. Bellwether," said the voice, "you need to accept your new place in the new world."

Hearing a voice, even a disembodied one, was a great relief. "What's the use," said Dr. Bellwether, putting his hands on his face with great resignation.

"You have a great opportunity."

"What great opportunity?"

"A great opportunity to do research."

"I've done research before."

"Yes, but for the first time in history, you can do it from the inside. Think of the possibilities, Dr. Bellwether; you can vindicate your father. I've even set up a special lab just for you."

Dr. Bellwether looked up. "I don't understand. Why would you care?"

"Because you are a part of me now, and your research will help us defeat the enemy."

"Maybe there is no enemy. In fact, I don't even know if I'm real. Maybe this isn't really us at all. Maybe it's just the Queen's way of dealing with her own multiple personalities and these sub-brains she hatches every once in a while. She watches a few people, eats them and then makes believe that they are somehow reincarnated in her. Only it's not us at all. We're gone. It's only her and her wild imagination. The main brain getting acquainted with the sprouts." Dr. Bellwether smiled, knowing that the voice couldn't possibly top his argument. It was a battle of wits, a debate, and he was sure to win. Not because he believed what he was saying necessarily but because he wasn't going to let some cephalopod outwit him.

"Not even close," said the voice. "You'll have to do better than that."

"Okay, maybe we're just in the midst of a dream that she's having about herself, about a queen that eats her subjects and then becomes them."

"Maybe the Queen's not here either," said the voice. "Maybe she's in a dream that another queen is having about a queen who eats her subjects. Maybe we're the figment of the imagination of a succession of a hundred queens having dreams about a queen eating her subjects. And these dreams are not happening in a linear fashion, they are happening simultaneously in the mind of one queen whose mind is building and supporting 100 different worlds and millions of characters at one time for added stimulation and enjoyment. Maybe each of the queens is within the dream world of the queen who is dreaming her, all supported by the first in line, the only one who is actually real."

"An interesting scenario," said Dr. Bellwether, who, for the first time in a long time, could not think of a reply. "Are you quite through with this interesting exercise in the world of make-believe?"

"Oh, but there's more. Maybe none of us are real and the land and the sea and the earth are all created as sensory stimuli in the mind of the great Spirit I've been reading about in your minds. It only seems real to you and me because we are in it. Maybe the milky way is just a part of His great mind. Maybe matter only has physical properties that we attribute to it, but whose real nature is an entirely spiritual world. Then again, maybe we are all real. What do you think, Dr. Bellwether?"

"All right, Dr. Royale, I get your point."

"What?" said the voice.

Dr. Bellwether smiled. "Oh come on, I know its you, Dr. Royale. You win. Show me the lab."

"I thought you'd never ask."

Fourteen

Neil Cranston felt uncomfortable as he rode in the back seat of his old, weather-beaten shark-fin Cadillac. It was not the ride down to Boston that made him uncomfortable, and it was not the poor driving skills of Rhub, his ever-faithful gopher, though these were enough to make any sane man ill at ease. No, it was an appointment that evening with a certain Japanese "businessman" known only as Mr. Oh; and it was the smug attitude of the oriental secretary who called him back earlier in the day to inform him that Mr. Oh would be willing to hear his offer. Mr. Oh was a very important man she said. Mr. Oh would only give 15 minutes of his time. Mr. Oh did not usually do business with people he did not know. Mr. Oh was only willing to meet at his favorite restaurant at the appointed hour, and don't be late. A suit coat and tie was mandatory for a meeting with Mr. Oh; a full bow was not. And one more thing: Mr. Oh should never be called by his first name, only Mr. Oh. By the time he had listened to all the rules of the meeting, Cranston had had his fill of that so-and-so Oh, even though they had not yet met.

He nervously tugged at the lousy tie he was being forced to wear. As the car pulled up to Matsura's, a small Japanese restaurant tucked away in a dimly lit alley off of restaurant row, Cranston checked his watch. Five minutes early. He would wait in the car for a couple of minutes.

"You sure you took care of everything, Rhub? The snapshots, the sample, everything?"

"Don't worry boss, I took care of it."

"Just checking."

Rhub turned around. "Boss, would you like me to go in with you, you know, as back-up?"

Cranston raised an eyebrow. His shiphand was so dumb you could prick his head with a needle and watch it deflate. "Rhub, this is a business proposition, not a drug deal. You been watching too many movies."

"Just checking, boss."

Cranston looked at Rhub and shook his head. "You look like last week's catch, Rhub. You haven't shaved in a week, and your mustache looks like its growing out of your nose. Now why would I bring in a scum-sucking, bottom-dweller like yourself into a million dollar deal?"

Rhub just stared at his boss, obviously not caring about the insult, having developed a thick skin long ago. "Uh, that's a good point, boss. And uh, did you know that the bottom-dwellers are very important to the ecology of the ocean?" Cranston just stared at him in stony silence until finally Rhub added, "Do you want to know why?"

Cranston couldn't care less. His stomach was turning he was so hungry. Who ate dinner at eight-friggin' o'clock anyway? It was uncivilized. "No, I don't want to know why."

"Well, it's because they crap so much."

"I said I don't want to talk about this before dinner."

"Yea, they eat a bunch of fish eggs, swim around a little bit, and then pop one out every minute or so. Blanket the whole sea with them. Better than a crop duster. Bet you never knew that."

Cranston sighed. "No, Rhub, I never knew that."

"See, I knew deep down you wanted to know bein' as smart as you are and all."

Cranston shook his head. He had very little patience and tolerance for people, especially dunderheads. But Rhub was a useful reminder of his own superiority. Cranston looked at his watch again: 8:01. His blood began to boil. "Rhub, you fool. Now look what you've done, you've made me late." He quickly exited the car, putting his suit coat over his head in the drizzle, and ducked into Matsura's Restaurant.

Matsura's was fairly unusual, at least by American standards. Dimly lit, crowded, filled with so many waterfalls that Cranston half-expected Geisha mermaids to pop out at any moment. It was the meeting place for Japanese businessmen and their associates, some of whom were big in the Japanese underworld. It was also one of the few public places where the fine art of Japanese deal-making was done out in the open, if you could get in, and that was a big if. The waiting list was a year long, so effectively, the restaurant could pick and choose its guests, mostly Japanese, or their invited guests.

Cranston exchanged glances, but not coats, with the coat-check lady and then was quickly approached by a short, fat, bald oriental man in a tuxedo. "Good evening sir, ah, may I help you?"

"Yea. I'm here to see Mr. Oh."

"Ah, very good. He is waiting for you. Follow me." The man led him past dimly lit booths with lamps hanging from the ceiling, through a maze of rooms shielded by sliding walls, and to a fancy back room with a waterfall adorned with oriental artwork at the entrance. It was definitely not Cranston's type of restaurant. There was no piano, no topless women, no main bar. There were no mermaids either, only two very ugly bodyguards, probably ex-Sumo wrestlers, at the entrance.

The man in the tuxedo made the introductions, and the two bodyguards quickly frisked Cranston. "Hey take it easy," he said. "I'm not that kind of guy." Neither of the guards even cracked a smile. After a thorough search, they gestured to Cranston to enter.

Mr. Oh was sitting on a small pillow in front of a rectangular table that was only a few inches off the ground. He was a fat cat all right. He owned Matsura's along with hundreds of business establishments in Boston, San Francisco, and Tokyo, and he was chairman of their holding company, the Kashimoto Corporation. He was flanked by two underlings who were in the midst of bowing their heads to Mr. Oh when Cranston stood in the doorway.

Everyone was so low to the ground that Cranston did not know whether to walk or crawl into the room. He approached them slowly, smiling, head bowed, hiding his distrust of oriental men in general. The way they looked at you was like a pair of beady little eyes peering from half-closed window shades. It gave him the creeps. It seemed rather odd to Cranston, though, that he found the same look to be rather enticing from an oriental woman.

He stood in front of them, hoping that one of them would say something, anything. There were so many rules of protocol with these guys, that he wasn't sure how to proceed. As he waited, he was disgusted at the sight of three live lobsters, claws and tails pinned to the wooden plates, and tail shells split open down the middle. It wasn't that he was squeamish. Not in the least. It was just that he hated the Japanese custom of eating raw meat.

Mr. Oh noted the American's bowed head. "We have been expecting you, Mr. Cranston," he said, as if expecting Cranston to apologize for being late. He then lowered his chopsticks into his meal.

"Yea, I know." Cranston looked up at Mr. Oh and the ever-present subordinates trading glances, wondering whether it was an omission not to apologize. He didn't care. No matter how bad he wanted the deal, he would rather sabotage the meeting then bow to Mr. Oh and his yes men.

"Please sit down, and tell me what you wish to offer." Mr. Oh clapped his hands and two Geisha girls came in immediately with small decanters of sake and some Sushi.

As he sat down, Cranston shook his head no thank you to the Geishas and watched the subordinates carefully for their reaction. Rejecting an offer from a gracious host. Another transgression apparently. The subordinates traded glances again, as if expecting a signal for the two thugs at the door to throw the American out, but the signal never came. It was obvious to Cranston that he had something of interest to their master.

"Did you get the sample?"

"Ah, yes, our chef was most impressed by the picture. The board of directors found the octopus arm to be a bit too undressed for consumption, however."

Neil Cranston turned red with embarrassment. Rhub was supposed to drop off the picture to the secretary, and the sample to Matsura's, a restaurant famous for its sushi. Instead Rhub dropped off a piece of raw meat at the front desk of the Kashimoto Corporation. No rice, no proper cuts, not even a strand of seaweed wrapping. If Rhub screwed up this deal, he would kill him.

Mr. Oh could see Cranston's reaction, and as a gesture of good will he said, "Not to worry, Mr. Cranston. We sent for the chef, and he prepared the delicacy in the cafeteria."

"Good," said Cranston without acknowledging the gesture. This omission was not lost on his host, and Cranston could tell that Mr. Oh found Cranston's complete lack of etiquette rather amusing. Cranston swallowed hard and decided to get to the point. He had thought about it over and over again. A one-of-a-kind specimen of this size and distinction should be worth at least a hundred thousand dollars. He would offer it for a million dollars and bargain from there. "I don't want to take up your time, Mr. Oh. This is a one-of-a-kind catch, and I want a million dollars for it. Fifty thousand up front for my expenses," he said, expecting to be turned down.

Mr. Oh never batted an eye. "What expenses do you have?"

"I'll need a much bigger boat, some special gear for trapping, and a harpoon gun."

Mr. Oh waved his hands. "No harpoon. We do not want a massacre. We want the octopus fresh and intact."

"No harpoon?!! What am I supposed to catch it with, my bare hands?"

"Perhaps you could catch it with a net and put it in a holding tank."

"You mean keep it alive? Are you joking? That octopus is 100 feet long. How long do you think it would take for it to escape?"

"Ah, but you see, that is not my problem. You are asking for a lot of money."

"Okay, supposing I agree to your terms. How long do I have to keep it alive?"

"Until you get to shore. That way the delicacy will be fresh. That is very important to my client."

"Who is your client?"

"Ah, Mr. Cranston, that is privileged information that I am afraid I am not at liberty to discuss."

Cranston frowned. "Okay, maybe I don't want to know anyway."

"Then do we have a deal, Mr. Cranston?"

Cranston could hardly believe his ears. A million dollars, and they didn't even blink. Maybe he should have asked for more. Maybe they hadn't agreed to the million dollars. He had heard that to the Japanese, sometimes yes means no, and sometimes no means yes. He had better agree to the deal before they changed their minds.

"Yes," he said, extending his hand. "You can call me Neil." They shook hands and the subordinates grinned. Cranston didn't like doing business with the Japanese or with any guy who preferred to keep his first name secret, as if he were someone high and mighty. He had already closed the deal. Screw the secretary. He was going to ask. "And I didn't catch your name?"

"Mr. Oh."

"I know that. I mean your first name."

His question was met with stony silence. Mr. Oh dropped his hand, and the subordinates cowered. Mr. Oh smiled for the second time that evening, apparently amused by Cranston's utter ignorance and blatant disrespect for tradition, or at least his tradition. He pointed both of his cupped hands to his chest, "Mei."

Cranston sighed. "Yea, you, who else do you think?" The subordinates looked at the ground, as if expecting Mr. Oh to finally lose his patience. Instead, Mr. Oh suddenly burst into laughter. Taking their cue, the subordinates joined him. Cranston looked at them with bewilderment. He was not sure what was so funny, but he decided not to repeat the question at the risk of insulting his host.

"Please go now," said Mr. Oh. "You may pick up the check from my secretary in the morning. But I will expect an expense report. Remember, this is not your money until you fulfill your end of the bargain."

Cranston shook his head yes. He had no intention of filling out an expense report, but he was catching on very quickly to this yes-means-no, no-means-yes way of doing business. He quickly said his goodbyes and left the room, escorted by another huge bodyguard he hadn't seen before. These guys were coming out of the woodwork, like elephant seals on a beach. Cranston concluded this so-and-so Oh must be a big-time

Charlie after all. With fifty clams in his pocket, and a "big red" in the bag, he would soon be the talk of the town himself.

Fifteen

---✦---

After breakfast that morning, the guests gathered around Dr. Royale, eager to find out what they would be doing that day. She would not tell them, except to say that it was part of their training. Her evasiveness only added to their anticipation, and when she got up to leave the cafeteria, they quickly followed close behind. Single file, they walked past a nurse attending a patient in a wheelchair and dodged around hospital beds, cleaning carts, and gurneys abandoned in the hallway. People were wandering aimlessly about the hospital, one waiting for a child to recover from surgery, another waiting for a loved one to come out of a coma, and yet another, waiting for his wife to come out of an emergency c-section. They had learned the stories of many since they had entered the hospital, and there were new stories every day. Their new world was populated with people who were much like the people of the old world. Even the faces seemed oddly familiar.

Dr. Royale led them from the main hospital, along the hallways with color-coded arrows painted like fine lines etched on a printed circuit board, back to the psychiatric wing, and to her office. As they gathered there, the secret elevator revealed itself again and she went in, beckoning them to follow. Everyone went in, except Dr. Bellwether. "Not me," he said. "I already took that tour, and I don't care to get inside your head again. I'm not a shrink; I'm a surgeon."

"Dr. Bellwether, there are three floors below the hospital. You have only seen the first. Aren't you the least bit curious to find out about the others?" asked Dr. Royale.

Dr. Bellwether thought about it for a moment. "Yes, I suppose so," he said, slowly joining the group.

"Good, then let's begin shall we?" She pressed the Simulator button with conviction.

The door closed and the elevator began to drop. It seemed to Claude that it was taking too long to get to its destination, and he began to feel a bit apprehensive. Then again, he always felt that way when he was in an elevator. "I'm feeling a bit claustrophobic. Why isn't the door opening?"

Jane took his hand. "Don't worry, it'll only take a minute." Claude looked at her and smiled. Her feathery, honey-blonde hair flowed down to her broad, swimmer's shoulders that angled dramatically to a thin waistline and curvaceous hips, the kind that no doubt would be excellent for child-bearing. For the first time, he realized that he was smitten. He did not know exactly when he had become that way, or why, but maybe it was the knowledge that besides Dr. Royale, Jane was the only real woman on the planet. It didn't matter. She was madly in love with Richard, who was a very lucky man indeed. He knew that the hand-holding was just a kind gesture. He would have no chance, and he was resigned to that reality. Just spending time with her, as one gentleman to a lady, was enough. It would have to be enough.

"How soon will we be there?" he asked like a child who could not wait to disembark.

"We are already there. Open please," said Dr. Royale matter-of-factly.

The door opened, and they exited the elevator into a long hallway. As they went along, Jane noticed a bank of elevators marked "1" through "5". "What are these for?"

"These elevators go directly to your rooms," said Dr. Royale, continuing down the hallway. "But they will not be operational until you have toured all of the floors with me. Then you may come and go between floors as you please."

They stopped at a large set of double doors flanked by a security station. Dr. Royale sat at a chair and typed in a code on the touch screen. Moments later, it began to flash and a laser scanned her retina. Then the double doors opened, and Dr. Royale led them in. The room was immense. An acrylic floor dominated the center and consoles were at either end. As they stood at the perimeter, the floor in the center began to move, prompting exclamations of surprise. As it slowly receded, it revealed another acrylic floor below with holes spaced evenly apart.

"This is a giant aquarium," said Dr. Royale stepping out into the center of the room, the water gently lapping through the holes at her feet.

"Looks more like a giant fishbowl to me," said Dr. Bellwether.

"Oh, it's much more than that," said Dr. Royale. Seconds later, eight small octopuses slowly appeared near the surface of the water. One put its arm through one of the small holes, trying to touch Dr. Royale's foot. It put one arm after another through the hole, like an escape artist who had done it a hundred times before. Finally, it pulled its head into the hole, elongating considerably while going through and then returning to normal size. Though some of them had seen similar feats before, the guests just stood there in awe at the octopus's ability to negotiate small places.

Dr. Royale picked up the octopus and brought it over to the others. "I would like you to meet one of the children." Captain Gregory stared at it, sure that it was the ugliest child he had ever seen. The others didn't know what to say. At some level they knew the truth, but the shock of seeing Dr. Royale pick up the octopus as if it were one of her own took a few minutes for everyone to digest.

"Do we have to see them up close? Couldn't you just beam in the picture like you did before?" asked Dr. Bellwether, who had never particularly liked handling octopuses.

"I know how you feel, though I do not understand it," said Dr. Royale. "But I thought that it would be best if you got to know them personally. These from the tank are a bit larger than the rest; they are known as horn-rims, because of the black markings around their eyes."

Dr. Bellwether studied them closely. "But these aren't really her children. They are on the outside. So they are merely representations."

"Mental replicas to be exact. The Queen is looking at the horn-rims in her world, and projecting them exactly as they appear into your world," said Dr. Royale.

Even Captain Gregory, who had handled a few octopuses before, was initially repulsed by its sight. His initial repulsion turned to an odd attraction, though, as he reached for the horn-rim in Dr. Royale's arms. The horn-rim immediately grabbed his arm as if it were grabbing a log. Startled, Captain Gregory let go of the horn-rim, but its grip was so strong, it did not fall off his arm. Regaining his composure, he gently stroked the horn-rim's head. It winked at him, and he and the other guests laughed in amazement.

After the laughter subsided, his demeanor changed on a dime. Looking very serious and sounding very official, he said, "Okay, what can they do?"

"What do you mean?" asked Dr. Royale.

At that moment, Captain Gregory put on his military hat, figuratively, and turned on that part of his mind that was remarkably adept at recording fine detail, even minutiae. Like a bazooka loaded with questions instead of ammunition, he asked a series of questions in rapid fire. "Can they shoot ink?"

"Yes."

"What colors?"

"Black only."

"Range?"

"Ten to fifteen feet."

"Can they spit poison?"

"Yes, a paralyzing agent. Kills crabs. Don't know what effect it has on humans. Haven't tried it yet."

Captain Gregory was intrigued. "Range?"

"Close range. A foot or less. Usually administered with a bite. Unless the prey is behind a rock. In that case it is ejected into the water and breathed in through the gills by the victim."

"Any other weapons?"

Dr. Bellwether frowned. "Can we forget about the weapons roundup? That's not what is going to save us."

"Do you mind, Dr. Bellwether? I'm trying to get an inventory of the troop's weapons capabilities, something you know little about," said Captain Gregory.

Dr. Bellwether drummed his foot impatiently. "Oh, this is so typical. You military men are all alike. You always want more weapons. But what you *need* is a strategy."

"Strategy? Huh, I've studied war strategies most of my naval career. What could you possibly know about strategy that I don't already know?"

"Plenty," said Dr. Bellwether, smirking.

"Is that so? You think just because you're a regular Dr. Frankenstein that you're smarter than me?"

"No, I didn't say that, you did. I'm smarter because the synapses in my brain are much more dense."

Captain Gregory's eyes lit up. "You're more dense all right. I'll give you that."

"Very funny."

"Well, go ahead and tell me your strategy. I'm listening."

"Well, the way I see it, we're sitting ducks down here. We should not wait for things to happen to us. We should take the offensive. Send the pawns out early, you know, the foot-soldiers. Follow with the knights; that would be the horn-rims. Then the bishops in the flank, which would be the probes. Then when the enemy is subdued, have the Queen move in for the kill."

"What are you talking about?" asked Captain Gregory.

"What do you mean? I've won many a chess match with that very same strategy."

Captain Gregory looked at him as if he were off his rocker. "Chess? Chess!! Are you crazy? This is not a game of velvet gloves with polished brass pieces. This is war, Dr. Bellwether, and our Queen is in very real danger. We are all in danger if we don't begin preparations to defend ourselves."

"Dr. Bellwether's plan sounds pretty good," said Claude.

"Yes, they would never expect it," said Jane.

"That's why we should do it," said Dr. Bellwether.

"You guys don't get it, do you? We have 800,000 horn-rims to command—"

Dr. Bellwether held up his finger. "That would be eight horn-rims, 799,992 soldiers to be exact."

"Whatever. My point is we don't have 32 chess pieces. We have an entire army."

"Fine let's put them on offense, not defense."

Captain Gregory was incredulous. "That would be disastrous. We need to defend our position. Not leave ourselves vulnerable to attack. It won't work." He opened up a notebook and turned to the others. "Now let's begin the simulation, practice the maneuvers that I have already planned, and forget about this neurosurgeon's nonsense."

"Hey, just because you kissed the Queen doesn't make you the King," said Dr. Bellwether.

"Oh, is that what this is all about? You want to be leader of the group? Or is it that you're just plain jealous? You know, I ran into guys like you in the Navy. They couldn't understand why I dated girls in the Army. Well you never plan these things. They just happen."

"He sees so little, yet he knows so much," said Dr. Bellwether, cupping his hands over his eyes.

"Come on admit it. This is about Isabelle, isn't it?"

"Oh, *Isabelle* is it now? How familiar. Well, for your information, it's not about Dr. Royale. You can have your eight-legged woman."

"Eight arms, to be precise."

"Oh, excuse me. I forgot. You always did go for those *army* women!"

"Gentlemen, gentlemen. Have you forgotten, Mademoiselle Royale is in this room. It is not polite to say such things in her presence. Please apologize," said Claude.

"Oh all right, but he started it," said Dr. Bellwether.

"Typical male egos run amok. Must you two argue about everything?" asked Jane.

"YES!" answered Captain Gregory and Dr. Bellwether.

Dr. Royale stomped her foot on the acrylic floor. "All right, that's ENOUGH!!" No one said anything. Dr. Royale's voice was like a clarion call for sanity through the din of disharmony, argument, and bickering that echoed throughout the aquarium. It also scared the daylights out of her guests. Although she would never harm them, it was best not to let them know that. If they really knew how she felt about them, they might become unruly, difficult to control.

They were all afraid to say a word, especially Dr. Bellwether, who feared that he had gone too far and that she might sprout eight arms and wring their necks, funnel a shot of ink in their eyes, or worse yet, spit poison in their faces.

"Now we need to have some semblance of order and discipline around here, and I want the leader of the group to establish it," said Dr. Royale.

"Yes, but who is the leader? It would seem that we have two," said Jane.

Captain Gregory took a step forward. "There is only one choice. It's me."

Dr. Bellwether stepped in line with him. "It most certainly is not. It is me."

"So that's what this is all about, isn't it Bellwether? You think that you should be the captain of this ship. You think that just because you got some Ivy League education that you're smarter than me." Captain Gregory fixed his gaze on Dr. Bellwether, trying to unnerve him. "Well, I've got news for you, Professor Egghead. I've seen a lot of you guys come and go, and you eggheads all got one thing in common: you always crack under pressure, and then the yoke is on you. In fact it's all over you."

Captain Gregory's gaze had no effect on Dr. Bellwether, but his words made his blood boil. "All right that's it, I challenge you."

"What'll it be, Bellwether? Pistols at twenty paces, swords, or simple hand-to-hand combat?" said Captain Gregory, rubbing his hands together.

"Not guns, you Navy Neanderthal. A battle of wits. Winner take all. Whoever wins calls the shots."

"Would you guys quit fighting?" said Jane.

"If you're talking about chess, Bellwether, you can forget it. But I will agree to face you in a different battle of wits, the only one that counts, a war game." He lit his pipe and turned to Dr. Royale. "Can you set it up?"

Dr. Royale thought about it for a moment. She really wanted Captain Gregory to lead and the group to follow. But it was more important for them to believe that they lived in a democracy, even though it was more like a benevolent monarchy. "I can, but I'm not sure that I should. If I do, will you agree to quit fighting?"

Captain Gregory and Dr. Bellwether stole glances and then nodded reluctantly. After acknowledging their agreement, Dr. Royale asked Jane and Claude to take their seats in the gallery. She then pointed down at the aquarium. "The war game that you are about to play is unlike any you have ever seen. It does not use cards, it does not use chess pieces, and it does not use big burly men in helmets and uniforms. Instead, you will be commanding real horn-rims, shooting real biological weapons, and using real defense mechanisms to achieve your goal. This is a war game, gentlemen, designed to assess your ability to command an army. It will more closely resemble the actual wars between the colonies that pitted octopus against octopus, rather than man against octopus. Even so, it will have real-world application to the current danger we face. You will be using many of the same weapons, countermeasures, and strategies that you will use in actual combat situations. It is a winner-take-all proposition. There are no consolation prizes. The winner will be the undisputed leader of the group..."

As Dr. Royale spoke, Captain Gregory imagined what the war of the colonies must have been like in all its grandeur and horror. The camouflaged troops, the ambushes, and the entanglements of huge networks of soldiers holding tight to one another to form an impenetrable web around the Queen to protect her at all costs. The rounds of ink that were undoubtedly fired, clouds of color mixed with other clouds of color, in a mad ink-fog that defied the sense of direction. The legs torn off, bitten off, discarded. The untold suffering in terms of cephalopod losses. And the tragic waste of the war-torn valleys with their spoils squandered by the victors and quickly devoured by the fish, the sharks, and last but not least, the scavengers and the parasites. It was a grand vision. It was a tragic vision. It was what he had trained his whole life for, and now that he was on the eve of leading his troops into battle, his ability to lead was being challenged, before he had even had the chance to prove himself.

Dr. Bellwether was titillated by the thought of leading the troops to defend the realm. It was a new challenge, and a new beginning for him. His surgical career was over; there was no use in playing at it in the new world. It was time to take up a new vocation, and maybe, just maybe, playing a game of "chess" on this grand scale would be worthy of his strategic skill. After all, chess was war and this was the ultimate game of chess, where he was playing for his life, where winning was everything. If he should lose, then Captain Gregory would be in charge, and they would no doubt end up in some fisherman's net. If he should win, then he would lead surgical strikes against the enemy, and prove to his new friends that he alone was the grand master.

As she gently stroked the horn-rim, Dr. Royale said, "We need to establish a few ground rules. As part of the war game, you will each have a control console, which has buttons for all of the traditional arm-to-arm combat and special force maneuvers. You will also have configurable buttons which you may use to devise new movements. Each button triggers an infrasignal command to the horn-rims."

"What is the object of the game?" asked Dr. Bellwether.

"I was just getting to that," she said, placing the horn-rim onto the floor. "The object is to capture the queen."

"THE QUEEN!" they said.

"Yes, that is the object of our enemy, and so it is ours for this exercise."

"But where are the queens?" asked Captain Gregory.

With a slink, a slop, and a kerplop, two baby queens popped out of the holes in the floor at either side of Dr. Royale. She picked them up and held them to her face as a mother would to her own children. "May I introduce you to Elizabeth and Victoria, the baby queens." Dr. Royale beamed with pride. "Aren't they beautiful?"

They all hesitated for a moment. With their distinctive pink pinstripes, the babies were beautiful, for cephalopods. But it took a little time to get used to the idea of oohing and ahhing over bulbous-headed "babies" with eight arms and pink pinstripes running from tip to top. By the time Dr. Royale looked up to see why none of them had responded, they had all begun oohing and ahhing, carrying on as if the babies were their own.

Even Captain Gregory, who at another time had been averse to the ungamely features of the octopus, had to admit to himself, and to Dr. Royale, that they were rather cute. As the notion settled in his mind, one of them crawled up his leg and onto his chest and looked him in the eye, as if reading him like a book. It was Victoria. Captain Gregory made a face at her, and she batted her eyes at him. At that moment, a tidal wave of joy swept away his revulsion. He felt great joy in having the honor of holding such a rare creature, the hope, the dreams, and the destiny of an entire species, whose very survival was in his hands; and he felt great sorrow at having been instrumental in destroying her sister, and the colony that would have been. There was no time for sorrow now, though. He had a job to do. He had to prove his worthiness, and he was determined to do so.

"How exactly do we capture the queen?" asked Dr. Bellwether.

Dr. Royale took a deep breath and began to recite the features of the game. "You capture the queen by having one of your troops spray her with ink, though not in the eyes please. You may also spray your opponent's horn-rims, too, to immobilize them. But if you spray and miss, your horn-rim will be without ink for the remainder of the period, in a highly vulnerable position."

"Your control console will be used to convey orders to your troops. Each console will have default Control Buttons for troop movements and close-range firing and Custom Buttons that can be configured to suit your needs. Each of these buttons are pressed in conjunction with a player button in order to request a player to perform a function. In addition, players can be moved manually by moving their applicable icons on the touch-sensitive control screen before you. The control screen provides a 3-D map in miniature of the aquarium. By moving the icons on screen, players can establish positions that could not be achieved using the control buttons, which are limited to specific commands. You may try all of these control buttons before the game begins so as to determine their function and logic."

"There will be rounds of 15 minutes each, plus a warm-up minute at the beginning of the game to establish your positions in secret. The first to capture his opponent's queen, wins the game. Any questions, gentlemen?"

"Yes," said Dr. Bellwether. "How do you know that the reactions of these horn-rims would actually be the reactions in a combat situation?"

"Good question. The aquarium is the mirror image of the outside world in the immediate vicinity of the cave. Any commands you give will also be carried out by the horn-rims on the outside. When the game starts, their movements will be projected exactly by the horn-rims here in the aquarium; this will give the game an exactness that could not otherwise be duplicated.

"One more question. How do you see the movements of the troops well enough to establish their positions in the simulation?"

"Easy," said Dr. Royale. "I am currently attached to the cliffside at the perimeter of the playing field, approximately fifty feet above the sea floor." She looked at the horn-rim in a peculiar way, and he immediately escorted the baby queens into their holes and back into the aquarium.

By the way the horn-rims moved when she looked at them, Captain Gregory knew that she was communicating with them. As he stepped up to the control console, Captain Gregory saw four horn-rims swimming below the console, as if waiting for orders. Suddenly, they dove, and when they came up, they were in a fairly tight formation, linked arm-in-arm in a circle. In the center of the circle, their arms were interwoven, forming a hammock of sorts, on the center of which sat Victoria, who was already a good deal larger than any one of them. They were giving her a ride.

Captain Gregory smiled and saluted them. The gesture reminded him of his years in the military, his rise to the top of the officer corps, and his subsequent commission to captain a ship, only to have it taken away at the last minute. It was patently unfair then, and it was unfair now. Gambling his years of experience and training to a single game. Yet he had no choice. He had to play. To play against Dr. Bellwether was ridiculous; to lose to him was unthinkable. This was the first real challenge to his leadership of the group, a leadership he himself had declared. Now, just as he was about to assume command, he might lose it once more. Captain Gregory could not bear to think of it. There was only one thing to do: to get on with it. So, he looked at the console and contemplated his next move.

START	TUTORIAL	INTERCOM	ON-SCREEN	HELP
LOCATE	DISTANCE	ACQUIRE	FIRE	CAMOUFLAGE
Q	R1	R2	R3	R4
COVER	ADVANCE	HOLD	SLOW	GRAB
CONFIGURE	CONFIGURE	CONFIGURE	CONFIGURE	CONFIGURE

```
                    AQUARIUM MAP

              Enemy Positions
         (Unknown before Start of Game)


                      MIDWALL

         R1                        R4

                 Your Positions
         Q                         R3

                       R2
```

Captain Gregory pressed the START button, and a message appeared. *"Welcome Captain Montague S. Gregory. Please read the following rules, and press any button when you are ready."*

- Rule No. 1. A player is "hit" if a direct shot of sprayed ink touches any part of the body
- Rule No. 2. A player who is hit turns bright red, is identified with an "X", and is immobilized
- Rule No. 3. A player's ink is replenished with each shot that results in a hit. A player's ink is exhausted by a single miss

Captain Gregory pressed TUTORIAL, and a short tutorial of the buttons and other features were explained. Two were most interesting. INTERCOM would allow him to talk to his opponent. ON-SCREEN would allow him to see his opponent in the upper right-hand corner of the console screen. In most Naval battles, you never got to see your opponent; you only detected him. After the tutorial, another message appeared. *"Waiting for opponent to get ready. Any questions before we get started?"*

"Can any of the horn-rims shoot farther than any of the others?" asked Captain Gregory, hunting and pecking at the keys.

"Good question. It is possible to find out the answer without firing your weapons."

Captain Gregory thought about squirting water from straws, something he had done often as a kid. Usually the greatest distance could be achieved by using thinner straws, although there was a point at which a straw became too narrow. Two ink shots of equal force might not travel the same distance if the funnel size differed. "Who has the smallest funnel size?" he inquired.

"Congratulations. You have asked the right question. The size increases from Horn Rim No. 1, who has the smallest, to No. 4, who has the largest."

Dr. Bellwether read the rules and looked apprehensively across the room at Captain Gregory. He could see Captain Gregory's fingers busily tapping away at the keyboard and his eyes light up. He wondered what Captain Gregory had discovered. Dr. Bellwether typed in a few meaningless questions and got a few meaningless answers back. He had to win. Not to satisfy his ego; he knew he was the intellectual superior to the old sea barnacle. That wasn't it at all. He had to win because he had to have control of the ship. He had to be in control of everything in his life, and it had driven him to get his private pilot's license and various other licenses so that he would always be at the controls. Now that his survival was at stake, he couldn't leave it up to chance; he had to be in charge once more.

As Dr. Royale joined the others in the observation deck above the aquarium, the two signaled that they were ready.

Suddenly the control consoles, along with a calm Captain Gregory and a panicky Dr. Bellwether, lowered into waterproof tubes at opposite ends of the aquarium below. Within moments, the horn-rims and the baby queens surrounded the tubes, staring at their commanders with curiosity.

Captain Gregory was amused by the new twist that Dr. Royale threw into the game. He was used to the tight spaces, having spent so much time on subs, although he did feel a bit like a torpedo loaded in a tube. He looked across the aquarium at Dr. Bellwether who was not amused.

A message flashed across the screen. *"You will have one minute to establish your positions after which the game will begin."* A large midwall rose from the floor of the aquarium, sectioning the aquarium into two chambers, forcing the combatants to start on opposite sides of the aquarium.

Captain Gregory noted the landscape of the aquarium, with its sand on the bottom, coral reefs along both sides, sea brush everywhere, and a cliff on the right. He touched the "Q" icon for the queen and moved it with his finger to the end of the aquarium on-screen. When he looked up, Victoria was staring directly into his eyes. He smiled, and she blinked back at him. He looked at the screen again, and noticed that the other icons were identified as R1 through R4 on screen, corresponding to their control button counterparts on the console. He moved his long-range shooter R1 to Victoria's side, and R3 and R4 behind small coral reefs at the east and west sides of the aquarium, near the midwall. He sent R2 up to the ceiling of the aquarium to adhere to the top lid.

He pressed the COVER button and the player buttons simultaneously, and they all adjusted their positions to take cover, Victoria hiding behind the tube and R1 behind some brush nearby. He pressed CAMOUFLAGE, and they all turned the color of their surroundings immediately. He looked for other color buttons, but found none. So, he pressed a blank configuration button, which called up the prompt, *"Please*

Describe Configuration". Captain Gregory typed in "All Red". Another question came on screen, *"You Wish to Sacrifice one of your Men?"*. "No, Turn Red, but Continue Playing."

"Processing Request... Configuration Accepted. Defined Properties are Assigned to Button labeled 'RED'". Captain Gregory immediately pressed the R1 and RED buttons simultaneously and the R1 icon turned red on screen but no "X" was on it, the sign of an enemy hit. Captain Gregory looked into the aquarium and verified that R1 had turned bright red. He smiled and asked the console, "Can Victoria move to a location above the ceiling?"

The answer *"No"* appeared on screen just as the midwall lowered, becoming a midline, revealing a giant boulder on Dr. Bellwether's side of the aquarium. Captain Gregory quickly scanned his screen. No enemy Bellwether horn-rims had been sighted by his players. They were out there, but where? Captain Gregory looked far across the aquarium at Dr. Bellwether to pick up a hint, but Dr. Bellwether was intent on his screen. There was plenty of kelp and sea brush scattered throughout the aquarium, and lots of good places to hide along the floor.

Captain Gregory slowly advanced horn-rims R3 and R4. The control screen showed that they were slowly advancing, but they were disguised so well that he could no longer visually confirm their positions in the aquarium. Apparently the enemy could see their location because as soon as he looked at the screen again, the R4 icon turned red and a large X was placed on it. Captain Gregory breathed a heavy sigh and pounded his fist against the console. "That Worm!" he shouted. "He's drawn first blood!!" Captain Gregory stared at the console hoping that one of his other men might spot one of Dr. Bellwether's. No such luck. He made R3 "hold" position so as not to give away its location and contemplated his next move.

This was nothing like his training to command a submarine. None of the old strategies applied. He would have to think on his feet. He would have to quit worrying about the body count and concentrate on protecting Victoria while going on the attack. He quickly asked the console, "Can horn-rims leave the aquarium?" There was a long pause, and another message appeared, *"Processing Question, Please Stand By"*. Captain Gregory laughed as he read the message; as if he had anywhere else to go at that moment. Then the message that he had been waiting for appeared, *"Horn rims may leave the aquarium."*

Captain Gregory quickly pressed a second CONFIGURE button, and typed in, "Surveillance from ABOVE aquarium". *"Button is configured improperly. Queens are not allowed to leave the aquarium."* Captain Gregory clarified the request, "Surveillance of Elizabeth by transparent-colored Horn-Rims above the Aquarium."

"Processing Request... Configuration Accepted. Defined Properties are Assigned to Button labeled ABOVE." Captain Gregory immediately moved R2 above the aquarium; the icon for R2 turned transparent on screen with only an outline to define its shape. Without tilting his head, Captain Gregory looked up at the ceiling of the aquarium, trying to locate R2, but was unable. His troops were experts at camouflage and subtle movement.

He heard the sound of suction and looked up in time to glimpse a head popping through one of the holes in the middle of the ceiling. The message *"R2 is now located ABOVE aquarium"* was displayed. Moments later an icon identified as B1 appeared on screen. His troops had located one of Bellwether's horn-rims, at long last! Captain Gregory punched the ACQUIRE target button, and rested his index finger on the FIRE button. Two seconds later the button turned red and a message below read, *"Target Acquired by R2 "*. In a flurry of button punching, Captain Gregory went into action. R2 fired upon B1 as R2 and R3 quickly moved to new positions. Shoot and run, a strategy that Captain Gregory had used effectively many times.

A flash of red ink came from the ceiling, striking B1 as he was about to jettison away. As the B1 icon was Xed out on screen, Captain Gregory looked across at Dr. Bellwether and shouted, "Yes! Take that four eyes!!"

Before he could revel in the moment, B2 appeared on screen. Captain Gregory acquired the target, rested his index finger on the FIRE button, and waited. Two seconds later the button turned red with the message, *"Target Acquired by R3"*. Captain Gregory fired at the enemy and saw the flash of red shoot from behind a boulder deep in enemy territory, except he did not see the intended target. Puzzled, he looked for the X to show up on the console, but it did not. He quickly pressed the button again and the console responded, *"R3 is out of ammunition"*. His horn-rim had missed! Perhaps he had taken too long to press the FIRE button or the acquired target had moved at the last minute.

Captain Gregory could hear Dr. Bellwether's voice carrying through the water, "You missed, you old crustacean!"

Captain Gregory quickly configured another button as "Sand Grenade" and waited for acceptance.

"Processing Request... Configuration Accepted. Defined Properties are Assigned to Button labeled SAND." Captain Gregory configured a fourth button labeled UNDERCOVER to command a horn-rim to take cover in the sand. He then commanded R3 to throw sand grenades and go undercover.

When the sand had settled, Captain Gregory could not see R3, but he knew that he was buried in the sand by looking at the icon on screen, which had turned into two round eyes. Captain Gregory saw B2 move into the vicinity of the hole to investigate. He looked at B2's icon on the console and tried to acquire it...

"*Target is Located by R3 but Not Acquired. Out of Ammunition,*" read the message at the bottom of the screen. Captain Gregory checked the distance.

"*Target is approximately three feet away.*"

Without a moment to lose, he configured a PLUG button to command a horn-rim to stick an armtip in the opponent's funnel, making it impossible to fire a shot. After that, he asked for distance again.

"*Target is two feet away.*"

Captain Gregory advanced R2 above the aquarium to a position directly above the boulder. R2 was above the boulder, R3 was below, and B2 was right there. Captain Gregory tried to acquire B2 again but was unable to acquire. Apparently, the boulder was in the way. Captain Gregory could tell by the way they were moving that B2 was aware of R2 above; the two were jockeying for position to acquire and shoot. The messages "*Target Acquired by R2*" and "*Target Lost by R2*" were flashing at the bottom of the screen as B2 took refuge and refrained from shooting at the Swiss cheese ceiling above. Captain Gregory asked for distance again.

"*Target is within reach.*"

Captain Gregory leapt into action. He commanded R3 to grab and plug, R2 to acquire, and then rested his index finger on the FIRE button. He could see ahead that a titanic struggle was ensuing by the boulder; R3 had grabbed B2, who was struggling to break free while keeping an eye on the ceiling.

Seconds later, R2 acquired the target. Captain Gregory fired and saw a flash of red come from the ceiling, striking its intended target below. As B2 was Xed out on screen, Captain Gregory let out a loud whoop. Two down, three to go!

It was not time to celebrate, however. Moments later, another of Dr. Bellwether's horn-rims, B3, was located near some sea brush on Victoria's side. Captain Gregory commanded R2 to acquire, and waited to fire. Seconds later, the message read, *"Target Acquired by R2"*.

This was too easy! Captain Gregory became excited as he sensed that the tide was turning and victory would soon be his. He would take out B3 and then there would only be one more horn-rim to dispose of before capturing Elizabeth.

Captain Gregory pressed the FIRE button and saw a flash of red shoot from R2's location on the ceiling. At the last second, B3 jettisoned away from the curtain of ink, taking refuge in the coral reefs. He must have been hit, Captain Gregory reasoned, and the console would confirm it momentarily. He waited for the confirmation, but none came. Captain Gregory quickly fired again, but nothing happened, no flash, no ink, no nothing. The console informed him, *"R2 is out of ammunition."*

"No!" shouted Captain Gregory. "That can't be. He couldn't have gotten away. That's not fair. I've lost one soldier and two are out of ammunition now. Just take the one, but don't leave the other two defenseless." But there was no response. If only he hadn't fired. Perhaps he was too far away, giving the enemy ample time to dodge the ink torpedo. It was a stupid move, and he could not believe he had made it.

Captain Gregory quickly recalled R2 and R3 to Victoria's side. They were shooting blanks now, and their only use would be as army shields. He configured a SHIELD button to have them wrap themselves around the queen; then he commanded them to shield her. He posted the red R1, whose funnel was loaded, about 15 yards in front of Victoria's position, out in the open, as a decoy for R4, who was already hit.

At the console at the other end of the aquarium, Dr. Bellwether laughed. "You won't be captain for long, Ensign Gregory!" He reveled in the thought but then realized that first he would have to capture the Queen. There would be plenty of time for gloating later. Dr. Bellwether sent both B3 and B4 in pursuit. They moved in slowly, from opposite sides of the aquarium, like bishops in a chess match, Bishop B5 to Queen G8, checkmate. He kept looking on the console for the location of R1, but the horn-rim had not been sighted by his men. Victoria, on the other hand, was hiding behind some sea brush. It would only be a few seconds before his troops would be in shooting range...

Captain Gregory located B3 and B4 on his console. He could see them slowly moving in toward the queen from his vantage point in the tube. They were barely 15 feet away from R1, who was motionless. He commanded R1 to acquire, and the console posted the message, *"Targets B3 and B4 are Acquired by R1."* But Captain Gregory did not fire, and the console repeated the message, adding *"Do you wish to fire?"* Again, Captain Gregory held his fire, waiting until he was certain he would not miss.

B3 and B4 looked at R1 but did not fire, apparently thinking that the red decoy had already been hit. They went over to investigate and were right in front of R1. A perfect setup. Captain Gregory was breathing so hard that he wondered if the enemy would notice. Then he pressed the FIRE button twice and R1 let out two tremendous blasts of ink from short-range, hitting both B3 and B4. "Yes!!" said Captain Gregory, and he immediately looked over at Dr. Bellwether, who put a loaded finger to his head.

At his console, Dr. Bellwether was in a panic. R1 was advancing along with Victoria toward Elizabeth, who would be no match against the two of them. Dr. Bellwether requested to configure a button to allow Elizabeth to crawl into the tube with him, where she would be safe. A tie would be a victory of sorts. After all, if Captain Gregory could not win the match, he could not be declared the captain. He waited for the response to his request. A question appeared on screen, *"You Wish to Protect the Queen, yourself?"*

"Yes," Dr. Bellwether responded.

"*Processing Request... Configuration Accepted. Defined Properties are Assigned to Button labeled "TUBE"*. Dr. Bellwether commanded Elizabeth to climb into the tube. He came face to face with her as she climbed onto the console. A clammy row of suckers encircled him, followed by another and another. He shuddered. She was scared. "Hey cut that out. Keep your slimy arms to yourself," he said, but she kept her grip on him. Within moments, she was on his chest with her arms around him. She was hugging him. "Come on, now, that's no fair," said Dr. Bellwether his revulsion weakening. She was kind of cute in an ugly sort of way.

All of a sudden, Captain Gregory's face popped up on screen. "I see you've found a friend. May I congratulate you both on a good match."

"The bet is not quite over yet," said Dr. Bellwether, checking the clock, which flashed a two-minute warning. If only he could engage Captain Gregory in conversation for two more minutes, the period would be over, and he could regain his men.

"Oh, but it is," said Captain Gregory. "It's checkmate. And I would respectfully request that you surrender, or I will be forced to shoot the queen."

"Never," said Dr. Bellwether. "Not while my queen is safe with me." He smiled, noting that the console showed less than two minutes left in the period.

"Don't make this so hard on yourself," said Captain Gregory. "Now, this is your last chance. Do you surrender?"

Dr. Bellwether checked the console again. One minute to go. He could see something moving above them, so he would have to do something quick. A disturbance maybe. "No! Not to the likes of you. You're just a big blowhole. Nothing to say, but plenty of air coming out."

"Why you spineless little—"

"I've got news for you, we're all spineless here."

"Well, I know *that*. I was talking about your lack of honor. You can't admit when you're beaten."

Just thirty seconds to go, and they would have to go to Round 2. Dr. Bellwether fidgeted. "Okay, you've got me. If I give up, will you share command?"

"Times up, Dr. Bellwether. You just violated the first rule of the sea. Never negotiate with the enemy. Close your eyes."

Dr. Bellwether looked up and saw a horn-rim with its funnel pointed directly at them. He closed his eyes and a split-instant later was splattered with a heavy shot of ink. When he opened his eyes everything was red, including Elizabeth. He had lost, and worse, he had gotten red ink in his eyes. He began to wipe furiously with his handkerchief. "You got ink in my eyes!"

"I'm sorry. I told you to close your eyes. Use a little spit," suggested Captain Gregory.

Dr. Bellwether spit on his handkerchief and rubbed furiously until he found relief. "That helps, a little. Thank you."

"Your welcome. Before we go up, I want to settle this."

"It's already settled. You won, Gregory."

"That's not what I mean. I want you to let me lead this ship without interference, and I will not interfere with your work in the laboratory. That's really where you belong. You've had your glory. You're a famous neurosurgeon."

Scowling, Dr. Bellwether stuck his index finger in the air and rotated it. "Big deal. I never really wanted to be a neurosurgeon. I only did it to wreak revenge on my father's detractors. That's how I got used to being in control. It's not that I want to lead the ship, it's just that I have to be in control. It's nothing personal. I've never really known what I want to do, but I've always been accomplished."

"That's funny. I've always known what I wanted to do, but never been accomplished."

"Then why should I trust you?"

"You have to trust me. It's not about intelligence, Bellwether. If it was, this game would have been over long ago. It's about seeing the playing field, knowing the enemy's strengths and weaknesses, and capitalizing on opportunities. That's one thing I can do better than you, and you've got to let me do it. Now, what do you say, are you on board or not?"

"Okay, Captain Gregory, just ask Dr. Royale to take this slimy sack of eight-string potatoes off my back."

Immediately the tubes rose, the doors opened, and the two combatants emerged. Captain Gregory felt elated. With Elizabeth clinging to him, Dr. Bellwether had felt like some sort of octopus sushi dipped in red sauce. The defeat was bad enough, but being splattered with red ink was humiliating. It would take weeks to get those spots out. Dr. Bellwether wondered whether there were any dry cleaners in the new world.

Dr. Royale gently took Elizabeth from Dr. Bellwether. She unlocked a hatch door to the aquarium, gave her a kiss, and then gently lowered her into the water. She turned to Captain Gregory and Dr. Bellwether. "Gentlemen, may I congratulate you on a most interesting match. Both Jane and Claude thought that you would win, Dr. Bellwether, which is indeed high praise. And I must say that I was most impressed with the ingenuity you displayed in configuring your buttons, Captain Gregory."

Dr. Bellwether wiped the ink from his face with a red handkerchief. Captain Gregory acknowledged Dr. Royale with a salute.

"Now Captain Gregory, I would like to officially declare you the captain of this ship."

"Yes sir," said Captain Gregory, saluting. He paused for a moment, looking at her quizzically. "Or should I call you ma'am?"

"Or your highness?" said Claude.

"Or your majesty?" said Jane.

"Yes," said Dr. Bellwether. "We haven't talked about protocol. What should we call you? Should we bow, should we salute, or should we play military music when you come in the room? And if so, what is your favorite song?"

"Oh, I think 'God Save the Queen' has a nice ring to it, don't you?" said Dr. Royale, smiling the smile befitting of a woman who was at last sure of herself, and in charge. They all laughed, even Dr. Bellwether, who managed a respectable "ho-hum". When the group had quieted, she added, "In answer to your question, Dr. Bellwether, you may call me *Isabelle*, but you should think of me not only as the lady ambassador to your world, but as the *Queen*—your Queen—because that is also who I am. Now Captain Gregory, if you would, please give the other officers of this vessel their assignments."

"With pleasure, my lady," said Captain Gregory. He turned to Dr. Bellwether. "Dr. Bellwether it is my great privilege to offer you a commission as Chief Science Officer in our great Navy. Do you accept?"

"I do," said Dr. Bellwether, looking rather subdued.

Captain Gregory smiled and turned to Jane. "Dr. Jane Seabury, Professor Emeritus at Boston Biological Research Institute, it is my great privilege to offer you a commission as Communications Officer in our great Navy. Do you accept?"

"I do, Captain Gregory."

Captain Gregory turned and placed his hand on Claude's shoulder as if he were his own son. "Monsieur Claude Fountainbleu, it is my great privilege to offer you a commission as Chief Weapons Officer in our great Navy. Do you accept?"

Captain Gregory was about to wind up and give the great speech that he had prepared for all of his life when he noticed that Isabelle seemed preoccupied. "Is there anything wrong, Isabelle?"

"I hate to bother you about this during the ceremony, but I'm afraid something has come up."

"What?" asked Captain Gregory.

"A boat, about fifty yards east, but I don't think that it is the same boat that was here before," said Isabelle.

"Order your troops to surround you and return to stations immediately. We can't take any chances."

"Yes Captain, I will see to it that your orders are carried out."

Sixteen

Toward the end of his class that morning, Richard Pearlman looked out upon the sea of faces, hoping that something, someone, might cheer him up. It was no use. It was as if he were looking through dark-colored glasses, though he wore none. Everything and everyone was drab. Nothing and no one could cheer him up, not even his best student, the lovely Nancy Boudreaux, a twenty-two year old ROTC student from the Coast Guard whom he looked upon as his own daughter, though he had none. She and the other students made life bearable, but for life to be worth living, it had to be more than bearable. It had to have a purpose. That morning, a year to the day since his fiancee, Jane Seabury, was found drowned 50 miles off the coast, he realized that he had none. And there was only one thing to do about it.

Without the great flourishes of the arms to which his biology students had become so accustomed, he slowly wrote out the word "Cephalopod" on the chalkboard and then painstakingly wrote out the mollusk class structure. "Our next topic, ladies and gentlemen, will be cephalopods. These creatures are invertebrates and are among the most mysterious animals in the sea. When nature made these creatures, it was as if she left out a backbone by accident, a most marvelous accident that gave these creatures an array of unique capabilities, not the least of which is the ability to negotiate very small spaces. While the rest of the world is trying to get out of a tight squeeze, they are trying to get into it, so to speak," he said without smiling.

Richard Pearlman knew that this was the part of biology class that Nancy had been waiting for with great expectation. Her look of disappointment belied the fact that she, more so than the other students, picked up on his gloomy mood, non-characteristic monotones, and utter detachment from the topic.

She raised her hand but didn't wait to be called upon. "Excuse me, Professor Pearlman, but will we be studying octopods or decapods?"

"Both. Actually the number of arms vary greatly among cephalopods, but the aforementioned will be the main classes that you will be studying," he said, the sparkle gone from his eyes. He held up a book. "I would like you to skim through this book that I wrote. Read any part you would like, any part that wets your appetite to learn more about these creatures."

"Will there be a quiz?" asked one of the students.

"No, no quiz, no regurgitation of facts, just learning about an extraordinary class of animals. As you read through the book, consider it my gift to you, sort of like a long letter written to each of you personally," he said. Class was nearly over, and although no one there realized it at the time, Richard Pearlman planned on this being his last class. With great sadness and resignation, he looked at his class, wished them well, and dismissed them and himself.

He waited and waited until everyone had left but Nancy, the one student that he had hoped he wouldn't have to face. Kind and caring, she was the wonderful daughter he had never had, and he didn't want to lie to her. Besides, this was a private matter and he didn't wish to burden her with it.

She approached him slowly, studying his face intently, as if she were counting the circles around his eyes. "Professor Pearlman, is anything wrong?"

"Oh nothing, Nancy. Really, I'm all right."

She looked at him skeptically. "Come on now, Professor Pearlman, I had you in Biology 101, 201, 301, and now 401. You can't stand there and tell me nothing is wrong. I know better."

Richard Pearlman managed a feint smile. He never was any good at fooling Nancy; she could always see right through him. "Please, after all these years, I think you should call me Richard. In fact, I don't know why I never suggested it before. It seems that there is no need now for formalities. I might as well tell you; you would find out soon enough anyway. I miss Jane. Everywhere I go, I think of her. Everything I do, I think of her. Everybody we used to know, reminds me of her. So you see there is no reason to go on."

Nancy took a deep breath as if she, too, shared his burden. "Oh, Professor Pearlman, I mean, Richard. I am so sorry. I had no idea that you were still tormented by her loss. You know how I felt about her," she said, moving close to put her arm around him.

"Yes I do, and it gives me some comfort to know that you miss her too. But nothing fills the void. I suppose if I had a gun, I would blow my brains out," he said, wiping an overly moist eye.

Nancy stopped in her tracks, shocked by the revelation. "Please, Richard, that kind of talk scares me. Is there anything I can do? Perhaps you could come to my Aunt's house for dinner this week."

"Oh, that's kind of you to offer. But you needn't worry. I don't own a gun."

"Please don't talk that way. You've got to pull yourself together. You know, there is a reason for you to go on: your work."

"My work serves no purpose anymore," he said, heading toward the door.

"You said that you and Jane were on the brink of a great discovery. Don't you think that she would want you to carry on that work? Perhaps I could help you."

Richard Pearlman paused at the open door. "No, Nancy, but I appreciate your concern, I really do."

"But you need the company. Look, Richard, you've been like a father to me these past four years; it's the least I can do."

He put his hands on hers and managed a feint smile. "You were always my favorite student, Nancy, but I am afraid my dear that this is something I need to work out on my own. So, if you'll excuse me, I need to go to my office."

Richard Pearlman headed straight down the hallway to his office and closed the door behind him. Alone at last, he retreated into his own little sanctuary where he could contemplate his fragmented hopes, his broken dreams, his shattered life. He felt like an empty vessel, the spirit having gone a year ago, along with his hopes, his dreams, and his life. Even the ghosts had abandoned the vessel and now it pitched to and fro, like a boat scuttled on the rocks, rudderless, and about to take on water from the tide pools swirling around it.

Water was all he saw, water was all he could hear, and water was all he could feel as he took out the newspaper clippings from a folder, laid them on the desk and the floor, and pinned them to the tackboard. They were all about his fiancee, Jane Seabury, who had been scuba diving near No Man's Land, had turned up missing, and who was subsequently found drowned. He had identified the body. She had two wounds, one on her forehead from a rock and the other a mysterious wound on the back of her neck from an octopus bite. It was all too strange. There were no signs of struggle. There were no lacerations or deep suction wounds. It was almost as if the octopus had only gently touched her before administering the bite, like a nurse administering a shot to a patient. Even more startling was the bite itself. It came from a very large specimen with not one but *two* large teeth spaced several inches apart.

Richard Pearlman scratched his head. There was not a single recorded incident of an octopus attacking a human unless provoked. In fact, man had given the creature every reason to hate him, and yet, the octopus had remained a curious friend. If it had attacked her, why hadn't the octopus devoured her after the bite? Why had it bitten her at all, unless she had tried to handle it? Judging by the beak size, though, this was unlikely. He had asked himself these questions hundreds of times since the accident. Once again, he came to the conclusion he had always come to: there was no reason.

When Jane had gone diving that day she had taken his spirit, and now, there was no reason to go on, and there was no reason to stay. There was only a reason to leave, the hope that by taking his own life he could once again join her. It made sense to him. Perhaps others would not understand, but that didn't matter. If he killed himself, he could reclaim the restless spirit prowling the sunken wreckage of Jane's boat and begin his search for Jane.

Before he could begin his new life, he would need to end the old one. That was the problem, and the opportunity. He could use poison, but convulsions did not appeal to him. Nor did jumping off a bridge. Strangely enough, the one method that did appeal to him was to shoot himself, but he didn't have a gun. He determined that he would remedy that soon enough. It was all settled then, a gun would be the modus operandi. First though, he would have to say good-bye, but not to friends, families, or relatives. They would try to talk him out of it, and he had made up his mind. No, he would say good-bye only to the laboratory animals whom he had cared for, who would not understand, and who could not talk.

Richard Pearlman pulled a bottle of Cognac from the bottom drawer of his desk and drank a toast to his decision. He took a few sips, and then a few more, and thought about Jane. He was actually enjoying himself for a change, and he was in no hurry anyway, so he indulged himself even more and settled back in his chair, his spirits lifting with every sip. Soon he would be reunited with Jane, and that was the only thing that had given him a moment of peace in the last year.

RICHARD PEARLMAN AWOKE WITH A JERK FROM another of his endless bad dreams and looked at the clock. 10:30 a.m. He had been napping for almost an hour. He went down the hallway to the bathroom and splashed water on his face. Looking in the mirror, he pondered his next move. It was time to say goodbye to the animals and get on with it. He headed down the hallway to the laboratory in the basement of the Marine Sciences building at the Boston Biological Research Institute. Just as he was about to put the key in the door, he heard someone inside, which was strange, since no one else had access besides Professor Holloway, who had the day off. Putting on his "spy hat" for a moment, he slipped into the laboratory through the utility room, and peered in from behind a row of file cabinets. To his great surprise, it was Professor Holloway. Richard Pearlman's first impulse was to make his presence known, but he hesitated. His partner had been acting very suspiciously, and he rarely came in on his day off.

Professor Holloway carefully removed an egg from a jar of formaldehyde and examined it, looking amazed that he was in possession of such a rare treasure. He examined the markings on the egg but seemed dissatisfied. He placed the egg into a compact magnetic resonance imaging machine, positioned the subject, placed a new tape cartridge in the drive of the computer, and turned on the machine. Moments later, he removed the subject from the machine and examined the image on the monitor.

Richard Pearlman had seen enough. As if from nowhere, he walked up behind Professor Holloway while he was examining the image. "What do you have there?" Startled, his portly partner popped up and tapped his head on the overhead lamp. "Where did *you* come from? And why are you sneaking around?" he asked, turning off the monitor, visibly unhappy to see his colleague in the lab.

"Heard some noise, and thought you were a vandal. So, I came in through the utility closet. Now tell me, what do you have there?" said Richard Pearlman, craning his neck to get a better view of the egg.

"Oh nothing, just something a local fisherman gave me."

"Come on now, let's have a look at that egg," he said, looking at his colleague reproachfully.

Professor Holloway put the egg in his lab coat pocket and then reluctantly took it back out. "Oh, all right. You might as well know. You were bound to find out about it anyway." He handed him the egg and turned the monitor back on.

Richard Pearlman examined the egg and shook his head. "This is quite unusual. I don't believe I've ever seen anything like it. What is it?"

"What do you think?"

"I have no idea."

Professor Holloway pointed to the screen, beaming like a proud parent. Richard Pearlman's mouth dropped open as he looked at the image, immediately recognizing the inhabitant in the egg. "My God, it's a giant octopus, and it's a..." He examined the size closely. "Yes, it's a female. This is quite a discovery," he said as the excitement welled up within him. In fact, he became so excited that, for a moment, he completely forgot about his troubles and immersed himself in his other love, the pursuit of biological discovery. "Where did you get this?"

"Ah, ah, ah," said Professor Holloway, waving his finger. "I'm afraid I can't let you in on that."

"Yet you intended to keep the egg itself a secret from me?"

"I was going to let you in on it, eventually."

"I've never seen one like it. It must be rare."

"Extremely rare I should think."

Richard Pearlman frowned as he examined the egg once more. "My point exactly. This egg should never have been taken from its mother. You know it, and I know it."

Professor Holloway shifted from one foot to the other. "Well, I don't believe the fellow who found it knew what he had."

"That could be. But don't you realize what the discovery of this egg means?"

"Yes, it means that the first thing to do is to get a specimen."

Richard Pearlman shook his head. "No, no. The first thing to do is to study the mother in her habitat."

"Oh come on, Richard, you know that you can't really know about the biology of an animal without invasive research."

"Yes I know. But it's one thing if you're referring to amphibian research. There's millions of frogs out there. But it's quite another if you're talking about dissecting an undoubtedly rare species of octopus. It would be like killing a blue whale to do cerebral cortex research. It just isn't done."

"That's because we already have a cerebrum preserved. There's plenty of tissue to go around."

As he examined the lines in the egg, Richard Pearlman remembered the article about the once-abundant male octopus and the claim that the males were subordinate to a giant female, a queen of the species. "That's not the point. Do you remember that article about Octopus Giganticus? Before this, we didn't even have evidence of the existence of the female of the species. The one that laid this egg might be the *only one* for all we know. We can't destroy it, we must protect it."

"And if it is, so what? There are so few, it's doomed to inbreeding with its own progeny. The species will be genetically weakened and die a slow death."

Richard Pearlman slowly held the egg up to the light. "You don't know that. Perhaps the species has a mechanism for dealing with that. You can't just go around killing an entire species indiscriminately before you know what you have. We don't know their numbers, feeding habits, nesting traits, mating rituals, societal organization."

"All I know is that if there's only one, I want to be the one to dissect it, to make the discoveries, and to go down in history. If there's more out there, then I want to be the one to help the seafood conglomerates harvest them. Either way, I'm going to be famous. You know, it just came to me, if the males were once abundant, and the females were scarce, they must be like giant eight-legged hens laying millions of eggs. This could be worth a fortune."

Richard Pearlman bristled. "What has happened to you, Harry, don't you feel any responsibility, any stewardship toward the animals that you are studying?" He held a magnifying glass to the egg, carefully examining its transparent-thin membrane.

"Richard, the difference between you and me is that I only care about one species, man, and one subject, me. Every other species is here for one purpose, to be used in the manner that we see fit to benefit us. That's the natural order of things. We have won the evolutionary race and now we are reaping the rewards. And I intend to get mine. And if that means extinguishing a species, then let me be the one to do it, instead of some idiot fisherman, who will leave the carcass to rot. If we let that happen, then no one will benefit."

"Least of all, you."

Professor Holloway smiled. "That's the point isn't it?"

"No, the point is that we must protect this find because it is one-of-a-kind, like Jane," said Richard Pearlman, pointing to the egg. His face brightened a bit as he realized that at long last he had found a reason—a reason to fight, a reason to hope, and a reason to live. It was as if his hopes and dreams, which had long been submerged with Jane's drowning, were suddenly resurfaced by this new discovery, like an underwater lava flow creating a new island upon which life could be rebuilt. Now, he could abandon the cause he had taken up the last year, one of self-denial, pity, and despair. Instead, he would fight to help protect this new species, to learn about it, and to preserve its habitat. The only problem was that he and Holloway were drifting apart.

Professor Holloway shook his head. "Oh, I don't see it that way at all. Richard, you've gone soft. Ever since you lost her, you've been no use to me at all. You've lost your appetite for discovery."

Richard Pearlman's eyes narrowed and the corpuscles in his cheeks ignited. It had been a long time since he had felt this kind of red-hot anger, a long time since he had cared about anything in the land of the living. So, even as the anger welled up within him, he had the presence of mind to recognize that this was in fact a healthy thing. He had rejoined the human race and was reveling in it. He half-wondered if this passion for living would last, or whether it would be a fleeting respite from the overwhelming fog of despair that had immobilized him for the past year. He took the egg and held it close to his chest. "Now you listen to me, Holloway, you're forgetting that my name is on that grant too. I won't let you do this. I'll shut down the project."

"So what? I don't need your money or your self-righteous attitude anymore. You'll have to do better than that." Holloway laughed, half-taunting his reluctant colleague.

"You know a simple dissection isn't going to answer all of the questions about its behavior: it's eating habits; its mating habits; its predators if any; its social structure, communications, and habitat. But together our research could paint the entire picture. Perhaps we could win a Nobel prize for Biology. It's a pity you can't wait. If you don't want to share in the glory, though, that's fine with me."

Professor Holloway thought for a moment. "Do you really think we could win the Nobel? There's a sizable award that goes with that."

"Yes, I do. Now come on, Harry, this could be the discovery of the century. What do you think?" he said, handing the egg over to Professor Holloway.

Professor Holloway carefully rotated the oval egg in his hands. He stopped rotating the egg and smiled as if a wonderful idea had just hatched in his head. "All right, I'll tell you what. You can keep it alive in an aquarium for as long as you like. But you know and I know that's not going to be very long. The female of practically every species dies shortly after it lays its eggs. So you see, there's really nothing to argue about."

"Then it's settled, and I'll be joining you for the capture," said Richard Pearlman.

Professor Holloway looked at his watch and frowned. "I don't know. I'm supposed to be at the boat right now. You don't know the guy we're dealing with. Sort of a tough customer."

"We're paying him, right?" asked Richard Pearlman. He detected a slight nod from his partner and a sigh of resignation. "Well, then he has no choice."

NEIL CRANSTON PACED IMPATIENTLY ALONG the deck of the old whaling boat he had rented at the harbor, looking at his watch every few minutes. 10:00 a.m., Boston time. Holloway was already 15 minutes late, and the boat was being charged *by the hour*. What was keeping him? Never mind that it would be better to wait until the afternoon to catch their prize. It was the principle of the thing. He could only imagine what surprise the egghead professor had in store for him this time. Hang that bastard, Holloway, he was late again. If there was one thing he hated, it was waiting. No, it was eggheads. No, it was eggheads who made him wait.

While waiting for Holloway, he began to second-guess his decision about how to capture the overgrown beast. He had been wavering all week. He knew of several methods. There was the giant jar, intended to lure the octopus in as a potential new home; the piece of lead upon which many giant hooks and a giant lobster could be attached; the long bamboo pole with hooks and a red cloth at the end; the plain old-fashioned spear, or better yet, for the really big prey, a spear gun; and finally, there was the possibility of using a net baited with crab or lobsters. Cranston would have preferred to use the spear gun; it was the safest way to dispatch the creature, though a bit too clean for his tastes since there would be no struggle. He would have preferred to somehow tie the creature down and bite it between the eyes, as he had done many times before with its lesser cousins. But he was not that stupid.

This time he would have to forget about the thrill of the kill. In the end, Cranston decided that it would be best to use the net. Mr. Oh would want a picture of the beast to ensure that the catch was authentic, and he would want to know that the meat was kept fresh until they got to port. When they were ashore, he would merely drain the holding tank, the beast would suffocate, and that would be the end of it. He waited impatiently for Professor Holloway, who had insisted on going along to inspect the cargo and to ensure that the head was preserved properly. As if he didn't know how to put a pod on ice. He would be glad when this deal was over. Holloway and his kind had grown tiresome, and if it wasn't for the money, he would have nothing to do with them.

Cranston pulled out a large green tarp from a cupboard and then laid it out on the deck, glistening in the mid-day sun. After inspecting it, he looked to the marina one more time, and then gave Manuel the signal to shove off. Forget Holloway. Who needed him anyway.

WHEN HE AND HOLLOWAY ARRIVED AT THE harbor, Richard Pearlman had completely forgotten about Jane for the moment, having been so excited by the prospect of seeing a female specimen of Octopus Giganticus. They hurried along the wharf, almost running to the landing where the sign read "Boats for rent". Nearby was an empty slip, and they soon discovered that Cranston had already headed out to sea.

Professor Holloway was furious at his colleague for making them late for their rendezvous. They'd missed their opportunity, missed the "goose" that laid the golden egg. After arguing for a while, they decided to take Richard Pearlman's boat. After slipping the ropes from the mooring, he took the helm, and they headed out to sea.

There was something magical about the sea that lifted Richard Pearlman's spirits. It was hard to believe that two worlds so entirely different could be adjacent. Mother nature was as spectacularly varied as she was miraculous. The world above the surface was vast and barren while the world below the surface was a teaming metropolis going through its daily routine, mostly unaware of the world above.

The thought of studying a whole new species sent tingles down Richard Pearlman's spine at the same time that it sent chills back up, especially when he contemplated the size of Octopus Giganticus. It had to be immense, based on the fact that its egg was hundreds of times larger than even those of the giant Pacific octopus, octopus dofleini, native to Puget Sound.

It seemed to take forever but after a few hours in which very little was said between them, Richard Pearlman and Professor Holloway saw the little jut of land in the distance and a rather large boat anchored nearby.

As they got closer, they studied the old whaling boat with its multiple boom arms and winches. The seas were calm, so they pulled up near to it and dropped anchor. Then they dropped a small dinghy into the water and covered the remaining distance to the whaling boat, fastened the dinghy to it, and climbed the steel ladder to the main deck.

They approached Cranston, who had just finished attaching the ends of a heavy-duty cable to the eyering of a trunk and to a boom arm with a motorized winch. He placed a green tarpaulin, four cement blocks, and four bundles of cable in the trunk and then closed the lid. He looked up, obviously surprised to see Professor Holloway with a companion aboard the boat. "What's the big idea Holloway, you're late. You get lost on the way to the convention?"

"What convention?" asked Holloway a bit puzzled.

Cranston glared at him. "You know, the convention for eggheads and uninvited eggheads. What's the big idea bringing him along?"

"Oh, that one, I see," said Holloway, nervously itching his nose. "Thought you could use another hand, so I brought along my partner. Don't worry, he won't cause any trouble."

Cranston looked at him suspiciously. As he finished with the trap, he motioned for Manuel to bring the wetsuits.

Richard Pearlman wandered over to the makeshift holding tank. He measured its width and length. "This pool is twenty-five feet. Why so large?"

As he put on his green wetsuit, glimmering in the mid-day sun like an electrified eel, Cranston smiled. "You mean, why so small."

The comment made the hair on Richard Pearlman's back stand up. "Surely she can't be more than twenty-five, thirty feet across."

"Try fifty foot an arm."

"You're joking," said Richard Pearlman, but he could tell by the scowl on Cranston's face that he was quite serious. "Oh, I see, well then, when did you make contact?"

Cranston spit into the wind, having grown weary of the conversation. "You ask too many questions," he said, throwing a couple of wetsuits at him. Then the hint of a smile crossed his face. "Here, you and Holloway put these on and see for yourselves if you're so curious. The old devilfish could probably use a snack about this time of day."

Cranston mounted his spear gun and slowly climbed down the ladder into the water as Richard Pearlman and Professor Holloway put on their gear. When they were ready, Manuel handed them several cages with crabs and they climbed down the ladder. It had been almost a year since Richard Pearlman had gone on a dive, and for Professor Holloway, it had been even longer. It didn't take long, though, for them to reacclimate themselves to diving. Soon they had reached the ocean floor where Cranston was looking up, waiting impatiently for Manuel to swing the boom arm over the boat and lower the trunk into the water.

After the trunk thudded onto the bottom, Cranston quickly offloaded the bundles of cable, and Richard Pearlman and Professor Holloway helped him spread the tarpaulin trap out on the ocean floor. Richard Pearlman had never seen a trap like it before. He understood that the tarpaulin would make it virtually impossible for the octopus to climb out, but he hadn't yet figured out how it would work. They put cement blocks at the corners of the trap and then followed Cranston's lead as he covered the entire surface with a thin layer of sand. He took out one crab at a time from the cages and tied them to the button eyes in the tarp, using fish line. Next, he untangled the four cables and tied each to a corner of the trap. Each of these cables were then uncoiled, wrapped in kelp, brought vertically to the surface of the ocean, and looped around a single buoy, allowing for at least another 25 feet of slack. The slack ends were drawn to the center of the square formed by the buoys and hooked to a center ring, which was attached by a center cable to the main winch.

When they were finished, Richard Pearlman followed Cranston and Professor Holloway back into the boat and marveled at the ingenuity of the device.

From the boat, the cable apparatus and buoys looked like a large x in a square figure. That x marked the spot where directly below, Richard Pearlman and his rather reluctant companions would make history by capturing a beautiful new species to protect and preserve for generations to come. It was a new beginning for Richard Pearlman and a new reason to live.

Seventeen

---◆---

She was dressed that night in dazzling white adorned with a scintillating array of ruby sequins announcing her joyous mood. As she peaked tentatively around the corner of the entrance to her cave, she was surrounded by a regiment of her adoring children, who instinctively encircled her as though she were going out onto some battlefield where the flanks were to be carefully protected. Tonight, though, there would be no preparation for war, only preparation for a grand celebration, a tradition that had been handed down through many generations. It was a celebration of the birth of her hatchlings, a celebration of life, and a celebration to honor her children, the generation that would serve and protect the colony and do anything to ensure the survival of its queen. It was only fitting that for a celebration on this scale, there would be a feast, a feast fit for a mighty queen and her subjects. So tonight, and only tonight, as tradition dictated, the Queen would catch a sumptuous feast of lobster and crab and serve her children, indeed thank her children, before time and the elements and the war against the enemies of the colony would begin in defense of the realm. Yes tonight, the Queen felt like celebrating the birth of her children and the glimmer of hope that she and her children, and her children's children, might live in peace. This was her fervent hope, one that she would share with her children alone, while her guests were sleeping. They would be awake soon enough, and then the training for all of them, guests and children alike, would begin in earnest.

She moved slowly with her youthful escort encircling slightly above her so as to allow her sparkling colors to attract the crustacean delicacies crawling along the ocean floor. She crept along the floor with her mantle slightly higher than usual to accommodate the baby queens, who were along for the ride on their very first outing. Like her mother, and her mother before her, the Queen brought the baby queens along to see the celebration.

She could have called to the crabs, left chemical markers, and had them marching to the mouth of her cave. Tradition, though, called for her to catch the prey with her bare arms, and she was not about to turn her mantle on tradition. So she began a systematic search in all the places they liked to hide. Much to her surprise, she found a whole congregation of crabs not a few hundred yards away. She sensed that the crabs were in distress, and this made her suspicious. So she changed colors, dimmed the sequins, and crept slowly toward them. Sensing danger, her children closed ranks around her and attempted to escort her back home. The Queen, though, was in charge, and with an intricate series of infrasounds, she let it be known that there was going to be a feast. Her children were just following their instincts, the little darlings. Surely their senses were not as keenly developed as her own.

Everything appeared normal, except that four new strands of kelp had taken root nearby. That was nothing to be concerned about. New plants were always taking root in the floor of the ocean. The crabs were on a wide open stretch of sand with no one in sight, nothing so unusual about that either. Yet, for some reason, the crabs seemed to be struggling to get away but were unable. She surreptitiously approached the crabs and grabbed three or four at once, only to find that they were somehow attached to the floor! She thought about Dr. Royale's tour on the boat with Captain Gregory and she turned pale white. Immediately she turned her head and was about to funnel away at full stream, when the strands of kelp were pulled up taught, and the floor moved up from the ocean and collapsed around her! It was a trap. Another trap!! And she had fallen for it!!! She struggled mightily to climb up, but she was caught in a slippery noose in which she thrashed back and forth.

Her regiment was caught too, though most had been washed out as the water was squeezed out of the trap and the lines were drawn taught. The Queen quickly checked under her mantle. Her babies were safe under her mantle, thank goodness. Then she realized, NO! They were not safe. They were all being drawn up to the surface!

The Queen looked at the top of the noose; there was a small opening, but maybe she could get them through. With great panic, she lofted them up toward the opening, only to have them slide back down and scurry underneath her mantle. They signaled distress as she pried them away once more and lofted them through the noose, just before the top was drawn tight. Yes, they had gotten away! She breathed a sigh of relief. At least her babies had made it. That was what mattered most. Through the trap, the Queen ordered her troops to take the baby queens back to their home and leave her to do battle with the enemy. Before she had uttered an infrasound, though, her troops had already found the baby queens and were escorting them back.

"I SAID BRING IT UP SLOWLY, RHUB," CRANSTON shouted to his shiphand. "Get up there and give him a hand, Manuel, before he drops it on top of us." Manuel quickly headed to the top deck to give Rhub a hand with the boom arm and winch. The octopus was thrashing violently, writhing and twisting in a vane effort to break free of the giant trap. The boom arm was by now swinging wildly and the apparatus and trap had swung directly above Richard Pearlman's boat.

"No, no, watch out for Senõr's boat," yelled Manuel as he climbed the stairs.

"And keep her steady, before she gets hurt," said Richard Pearlman, who was even more concerned for the specimen.

"Bring it over to the tank, you idiot," barked Cranston. "No, not there, I SAID THE TANK!"

"He said, the tank, can't you hear?" repeated Holloway.

In the confusion caused by so many people giving orders at one time, Rhub panicked. He lunged for the controls, hitting the wrong button just as Manuel reached him. The cable was suddenly released and the octopus, tarp and all, fell about 15 feet onto Richard Pearlman's boat, smashing it to bits.

"Forget about the boat," said Richard Pearlman. "Bring up the cable or she'll get tangled and drown." Manuel grabbed hold of the controls and brought the cable up slowly, lifting the limp mass into the air. She was not moving at all, exhausted from the fight, or knocked out, Richard Pearlman reasoned. Manuel carefully lowered the trap into the tank. Climbing the ladders to the top of the holding tank, the men carefully looked inside at the creature.

"She's unbelievable," said Holloway, his eyes blinking like dollar signs on a slot machine.

"I hope she's all right," said Pearlman.

"She's mine," said Cranston.

Once the octopus was buoyed by the water, the men quickly unhooked the cables from one side of the trap. Cranston then signaled to Manuel to raise the other side of the trap. The octopus slid off, and began to shake off the effects of the fall.

"Close the lid," screamed Cranston. The octopus stared at them and turned bright red. They shut the huge, Plexiglas lid on top of the tank and quickly put the pins in the latches to secure it.

"We've gotcha, you monster," yelled Cranston, pounding on the side of the tank triumphantly.

"She's not a monster, she's beautiful!" said Richard Pearlman.

"You've got to be joking," said Cranston. "She's as ugly as they come."

They sat on deck for a while, staring at the sad-looking creature in the tank. Richard Pearlman couldn't help but feel sorry for her, being torn away from the familiarity of the sea, and being forced to live in a fishbowl.

Holloway was beaming as he looked into the tank. "There's my ticket to fame," he said.

"My ticket to fortune," added Cranston.

"My ticket to the future," said Richard Pearlman, noting to himself that only that morning he had had nothing to live for, and now he had everything to live for. What a difference a day makes. He stood and watched in awe, in wonder, in ecstasy.

Some time later, Manuel poked his head from the bridge below. "Dinner is ready, Senõr." Never one to miss a free meal, Holloway headed downstairs followed by Cranston. As he left, Cranston said, "Why don't you keep an eye on the monster, Manuel, while we eat."

Manuel backed up, staring at the floor. "Sorry, Senõr, but that thing gives me the creeps."

Cranston glared at Manuel. He was just about to say something when Richard Pearlman intervened. "You go back downstairs with them, Manuel. I'll watch her for you. I'm not hungry, anyway. Too excited."

Cranston pulled a gun from his jacket. "I assume you know how to use this. If she makes a move, blast her to kingdom come."

Richard Pearlman nodded, though he didn't know the first thing about a gun. The thought that he would harm such a beautiful creature was repulsive to him, but he took the gun anyway, not wanting to upset his reluctant host.

A moment later, he was all alone with this beautiful, fearsome creature that was staring at him with such intensity, as if she were studying him, and not the other way around. Slowly, she turned away from him and looked at the lid on top of the tank. She pushed at it first with one arm, and then another until four were pushing on the lid and the others were being used for leverage at the bottom of the tank. Richard Pearlman felt sorry for her, feeling that captivity was a great injustice, a great price to pay for the advancement of science, though a necessary one. He even went so far as to empathize with his captives, envisioning himself in a tank or in a water world. This gave him great insight into their plight and a means to devise methods to make them more comfortable.

The lid was beginning to rattle a bit as she made several Herculean attempts to pry it open. Richard Pearlman went around to each of the latches, checking the clevis pins. Everything was secure, so far. Pausing in her attempts to escape, she looked at him closely and pointed to the lid. Richard Pearlman was stunned. He put the gun in his belt and quickly jotted a few notes on a notepad.

Amazingly, she seemed to have already figured out that the lid had three latches. To prove it, she pointed at all three of the latches and looked at him. Surprised, Richard Pearlman shook his head. "I'm sorry, I can't."

She abruptly turned on him and adhered to the side of the tank, exposing the underside of her mantle. Richard Pearlman looked closely at her beak. She had not one, but two! A double toothed beak! At once he realized the truth. This creature, this horrible creature, had killed his fiancee! He stepped back, his mouth dropped open and, turning away, he muttered, "A double beak! It can't be true." He looked again. It was there. It did not...it had not...it would not go away, as much as he wished it so. "But it *is* a double beak. You are the one...the one who killed Jane, you, you treacherous beast!" In a fit of rage, he pulled the gun out and pointed it at the tank. She abruptly turned and stared at him with those large, eerie yellow eyes.

"Why, why did you kill her? It wasn't for the food, because you left her alone. I know that. So tell me why, why did you take her away from me, WHY??"

The brief calm that had descended on him had now turned back into a swirling whirlpool of anguish in his mind. It had been a false calm, the kind found in the bottom of a whirlpool, and the bottom now revealed its occupant for the first time. It was her all along. She was the source of the torment that wrapped around his soul like some evil centrifugal force. There was only one thing to do, and he spent the next few moments contemplating it.

AT NOON, NANCY CALLED HER AUNT AND arranged to have a dinner set up for Professor Pearlman that Friday. This was just the thing he needed: a night out; new people to meet; a different setting; and above all, no waterfront beach house. Anything to take his mind off of the water and Jane.

After making plans, she hurriedly went to his office to invite him, but when she got there, the door was closed. As she knocked, a student passing by informed her that Professor Pearlman had canceled his afternoon classes. That was very strange indeed, because Professor Pearlman had not missed a class in 15 years. Something was wrong. She stood by the door for a moment, trying to decide what to do. Finding it unlocked, she went in to use the phone. After dialing a few numbers, she abruptly put the phone on the receiver when she noticed the newspaper clippings on the desk...on the floor...and on the tackboard. They were all about Jane's drowning at sea. He had never come to terms with her loss, and it was evident that he had been hiding his feelings all along. But why would he all of a sudden bring out all of these clippings and put them on display in his office?

She read the headlines: "Boston Research Institute Biologist Lost at Sea", "Drowning Victim Found Near No Man's Land", "Biology Team Loses Key Member", among others. One of the clips read: "Jane Seabury, a member of the noted biology team that discovered a new species of mollusk in the Nautilus family, was found near the point of land known as No Man's Land, 50 miles off the coast of Maine."

After reading the article, she realized that this was the one-year anniversary of the accident, and suddenly, she got a very bad feeling. She quickly tried calling Richard Pearlman's home, but he wasn't there. She called his favorite coffee shop, where he often wrote his articles, but he wasn't there either. Then something told her to go to the harbor. She checked to make sure that she had the keys to the Coast Guard boat and left immediately.

At the harbor, she ran straight to his slip and found that the boat was gone, just as she had expected. She hesitated once more to consider if perhaps she should not interfere. The hesitation only lasted for a moment before she decided that she had to help. She rushed over to the Coast Guard boat secured to a mooring that was 15 slips away. There was no time to ask for permission, so she quickly untied it, and headed for No Man's Land.

CAPTAIN GREGORY AND THE OTHERS WERE standing in their night clothes in Isabelle's office once again. It seemed all too familiar to them. A call in the middle of the night, summoning them to meet in her office.

"All right," said Captain Gregory, wiping the sand from his eyes, "what is it this time?"

"Yea, every time you give us a wake up call in the middle of the night, we're about to be chopped up into little bits of sushi," said Dr. Bellwether, looking bleary-eyed.

"This is no laughing matter," said Isabelle. "I'm afraid we're all in danger."

"Perhaps you could give a little advance warning before it becomes a catastrophe," said Captain Gregory.

"Let her speak," said Jane. "What is it you're trying to tell us?"

"Yes, please tell us," said Claude. "We're here to help."

"Well I don't know how it happened, it happened so quickly. But he netted me again."

"He what?! Who netted you?" asked Captain Gregory.

"What does that matter, anyway? If they've netted us, we won't get away. We're goners," said Dr. Bellwether dejectedly.

"*Who* netted you?" repeated Captain Gregory.

"The one you call Cranston and another man who looks vaguely familiar," Isabelle said.

"With your permission, I'm taking control of this rescue mission." She nodded her approval. "In that case, bring it up on scope," Captain Gregory ordered.

Immediately a screen dropped down from the ceiling, and they were shocked at what they saw, once the outside world came into focus. Through a fishbowl lens, they were staring at Richard Pearlman, who was waving a gun wildly, talking to himself.

Then it hit Captain Gregory like a wave on a sea wall. "We're not in a net! We're in a *tank*!!" he exclaimed.

"First they netted me, then they dumped me in a tank—"

"Never mind," barked Captain Gregory, whose eyes grew wide. "Whoa, look out, he's got a gun."

"He's going to blow *our* brains out!" said Dr. Bellwether.

"Oh my God, it can't be. It is. It's Richard," said Jane.

"I don't care if it's the King of England, he's got a gun pointed right at our head!" said Dr. Bellwether.

"No, he's not. He's turning it on himself," cried Jane. "We can't let him do that."

"Do you think we can take that chance?" shouted Captain Gregory. "We got to open the lid of this tank and take him out now."

"Tried that before," said Isabelle.

"Then squirt the tank with ink and lay low, flat to the tank."

"Then we can't engage him," said Jane.

"Are you crazy? We need to *disengage,* immediately. Who's in command here? Now, squirt the blinkin' tank, your highness, this instant!!"

The Queen turned on a dime, and all of a sudden, everyone in the room was disoriented, as if *they* had turned sideways. A moment later, there was complete darkness in the water.

"What's going on? I'm seeing spots," said Claude.

"That's because she squirted the ink," said Dr. Bellwether.

"Oh, I see. I'm seeing ink spots."

"No you aren't, now just be quiet," said Captain Gregory.

"Richard can't hear us," protested Dr. Bellwether.

"No, but I'm trying to figure a way out of this mess, and I can't with you two babbling about ink spots."

"Now you listen to me—"

"That's it!" said Jane. "That's the answer. He can't *hear* us, but maybe we can communicate with him. Isabelle are you still with us?"

"Yes dear."

"Can you think of a way to communicate with him?"

"I don't see how."

"Use your colors," said Captain Gregory.

"My ink?"

"He means your chromatophores," said Dr. Bellwether.

"The colors on your skin," said Jane.

"Oh. What do you want me to do with them?"

"Jane, you think of something that only you and Richard would know about," said Captain Gregory. "Perhaps you can draw a picture."

Jane slapped her thigh. "I've got it. On our first date, we saw the New York Philharmonic Orchestra performing Beethoven's Fifth."

"I know every note to that symphony," said Dr. Bellwether.

"Then think of the first measure," said Jane.

"Okay, I'm thinking of it."

"Do you *see* what he's thinking, Isabelle?" asked Captain Gregory.

"Why yes, I do."

Just then the ink began to settle and they could see Richard Pearlman standing by the tank and talking to himself. "What's he saying?" asked Jane. "Can you hear him?" asked Claude. "Let us hear him too," said Dr. Bellwether. "Yes, give us your eyes *and* your ears," said Captain Gregory.

Richard Pearlman looked very despondent as he slowly raised the gun and pointed it not toward the tank, but toward his head. "I can't bring myself to kill you, but I can do something better," he said aloud.

"Quickly," said Jane. "Draw the picture."

"What?" asked Isabelle.

"Project the notes to the symphony on your skin," said Captain Gregory.

Isabelle began to repeat the famous notes to the first measure of the symphony, but Richard Pearlman did not look at the tank. Instead he closed his eyes and pulled the trigger...but nothing happened. He looked at the gun, checked the barrel and spun it until a loaded chamber was in place. He then redirected the gun to his head. "Tap on the tank, Isabelle, now!!" shouted Captain Gregory.

Just as Richard Pearlman was about to pull the trigger, they saw him, half-dazed, turn and look at her tapping on the side of the tank.

"Now that you've got his attention, are you projecting the notes?" asked Captain Gregory.

"Yes, but he doesn't seem to be responding. I'm projecting them over and over, and in different colors."

They looked intently at the scene playing out before their eyes. All of a sudden, Richard Pearlman slowly lowered the gun and pressed his face against the tank, looking directly at her mantle. The group breathed a collective sigh of relief.

"Now what do we do?" asked Claude. "We can't just keep playing music. He'll get tired of the notes."

"That's it," said Jane. "That's how we'll communicate with him. We'll write him a note."

"Of course," said Captain Gregory, "it's the perfect solution. But can you write, Isabelle?"

"If you can write, I can write. Say the words out loud, Jane, and I'll project them to him."

"Then you take it from here, Jane," said Captain Gregory.

For the first time, the group was quiet, wondering whether Richard Pearlman would respond, and if he did, whether he would believe Jane. Jane spoke slowly, collecting her thoughts. "Richard, it's me."

Richard Pearlman dropped the gun on the deck. He lowered his head slightly and tilted it, and his mouth opened in utter disbelief. "What are those words on your mantle? It can't be," he said, shaking his head.

"But it is. You must help me. I'm trapped inside the Queen."

"What? What Queen?"

"The one you see before you is a queen. If you trap her, you're trapping me."

"I don't believe, you, you treacherous creature. You don't have Jane inside."

"Test me darling. Ask me anything. Ask me something that only I would know."

He looked at her skeptically. "Okay, I guess I can play along with your game. Tell me the nickname you used to call me."

"The Pearl..."

Richard Pearlman said nothing, staring at the tank. Then he rubbed his eye as a single teardrop descended his right cheek.

"Excuse me for interrupting, Jane, but do you think that if I projected your image, that he would respond favorably?" asked Isabelle.

"Yes, but wait," she said.

Richard Pearlman wiped the tear from his cheek and looked at the tank again. "But how?"

"Please don't ask me that. It's a long story. You have to believe me."

"But I've got to know."

"The two bites on the back of my neck. They served a purpose, to gather a minute sample of my DNA. My DNA was reconstructed inside the Queen."

"That's impossible."

"I know. But how else would I know what I know? There's a whole world inside here, Richard."

"Well, then tell me this. I've got to know—are you a woman or an octopus inside there?"

"Both. I am a woman inside an octopus. But I look like myself. Let me show you, and then you can see me saying these words to you."

⊕ ⊕ ⊕

RICHARD PEARLMAN'S EYES GREW VERY WIDE, and he placed both hands on the tank as Jane's image became visible on the Queen's mantle. She moved in closer to him and the surface of her skin raised off her mantle, and "Jane" was actually touching the side of the tank, with only the glass separating "her" hands and his.

Richard Pearlman was both attracted and repulsed, excited and depressed, and encouraged and afraid at the same time, but mostly he was encouraged. "Well, that's a relief, I think," he said. "It looks as if you were faithfully reproduced."

"*Yes, Richard, DNA can work miracles. It can turn something into something else. And someone into someone else. Now, my darling, I want you to do something for me.*"

"What is it?" he said, watching intently as the words appeared on the Queen's mantle.

"*I want you to set us free.*"

"I can't set you free. But I promise you. You will be treated well. I will see to it."

"*But you've got to.*"

"You don't understand. I can't, Jane. I know this sounds strange—at least it sounds strange to me—but I don't want to lose you again."

"*But it's not just about you and me. She has a family to raise down there. The survival of the species is at stake.*"

"And so is mine," said Richard Pearlman, as he thought about the consequences of keeping Jane, the Queen, or whoever it was, or letting them go. The consequences were both personal and professional. If he kept them, he could at least talk to Jane, or at least the memory of Jane, if that's what it was; and he could learn about a unique and wondrous species. If he let them go, he would lose all that; but he might save a species from extinction. He decided that keeping them for the sole purpose of bolstering his career was not important. It all boiled down to whether he could bear to lose Jane again. He started to unclasp one of the hinges, and the Queen quickly moved the tip of her arm to the lid to be ready for the opportunity. Richard Pearlman hesitated, and then pulled his hand away from the clasp, realizing that he could not bear to lose Jane. The Queen would take Jane away from him again and he couldn't let her do that.

Richard Pearlman turned away from the tank, not wanting to look her in the eye. Suddenly, there was a commotion in the galley, and he overheard Cranston and Professor Holloway arguing down below...

"No, now you listen to me, Professor Egghead, the deal was to keep it alive until we got to shore and no longer."

"But I told my partner that he could study the octopus for a while before we killed it."

"You're not the only one who wants a piece of the "pi" you know. My buyer has a truck on standby, and they're waiting for my call."

"We'll double the price," said Holloway.

Cranston laughed. "You're only footing 10% of the bill right now. That will raise your stake to 20%."

"We can't go any higher than that."

"Then it's all settled. The prize goes to the highest bidder, and that's the Japs. They're not going to want to wait for their sushi."

"You'd better go up and tell your friend."

"I can't."

"Well, if you can't then I will."

"How will you kill her?"

"When we get to shore, we'll drain the water from the bottom of the tank. I figure, it shouldn't take more than 20 minutes after that."

Richard Pearlman had heard enough. He regretted doing what he was about to do, but he had to do it. Though the Queen was the only link that he had to Jane, he would not let them butcher her. He looked at the image of Jane and asked, "If I release you, will she kill me?"

"*No*," said Jane, her words painted on the Queen's mantle.

Richard Pearlman quickly unclasped the three latches and threw open the lid. The Queen moved slowly out of the tank and with her long arms grabbed hold of the side of the ship, slipping over the rail just as Cranston came up with Holloway.

"What are you doing!" Cranston screamed.

"Are you crazy!" shouted Professor Holloway.

"She escaped," replied Richard Pearlman calmly.

"Don't give me that. You let her out, you idiot," Cranston said, as he grabbed the gun off the floor and began to fire wildly into the water. Richard Pearlman lunged for the gun and grabbed Cranston's hand, fighting for possession. Their outstretched arms caused the gun to raise into the air, then lower, then point directly at Professor Holloway, who let out a shriek as he dove under a bolted-down bench. The gun raised again and fired into the air. As Richard Pearlman gained control of the gun, Cranston knocked it loose from his hand, causing it to fire once more as it fell into the ocean and sank quickly out of sight.

All of a sudden, the water turned bright red.

"I think you got her," he said, laughing wickedly.

"I did not get her," protested Richard Pearlman, looking over the side of the boat.

Cranston edged closer to Richard Pearlman and, with one quick motion pushed him overboard. On the way down, Richard Pearlman hit a glancing blow against the ship before landing in the water. "You got her and now you're going to go down with her," Cranston called down to him.

Richard Pearlman shook his head, a bit dazed. Momentarily, he regained his bearings and looked up at Professor Holloway, who was shaking his head. Pounding the boat, he said, "Are you going to go along with this?"

"Look Richard, I said I'd try to buy you more time, but I never, ever, not even once said to let it go free. This is your mess, not mine. If you can find her, I'm sure he'll let you back on the boat," said Holloway smiling, as he left to go back down into the galley.

Cranston gave the sign to Rhub, who was at the helm, to get started. Manuel went up to the helm and took the wheel from Rhub, stopping the boat.

"Let's get under way," yelled Cranston.

"We can't just leave him behind boss," said Manuel.

Cranston shook his fist angrily. "I *said*, let's go." Manuel shook his head. Cranston opened a cupboard and pulled out the spear gun. Slowly raising the tip, he aimed it at Manuel. "You come down here—now." In defiance, Manuel came down from the helm to the main deck at a snail's pace. As his shiphand stood before him, Cranston pointed to the water. "Next time you try that, you'll end up with him, you mutinous Mexican jumping bean." Manuel said nothing, but his eyes belied a simmering hatred for his boss.

As Rhub restarted the engine, Cranston looked down on Richard Pearlman. "There were enough pieces of the "pi" for everyone. But you had to screw it up."

"You're not just going to leave me here?" asked Richard Pearlman, knowing the answer.

Cranston untied the dinghy and pushed it toward him, smiling. "No, of course not," he said as he slowly raised his spear gun, took aim, and shot a hole in it. "You can have the dinghy."

Richard Pearlman cringed. "What about the octopus?"

"What about it?"

"I'm the bait, aren't I?"

Cranston had grown tired of Richard Pearlman's insulting questions. "You know and I know that she's long gone. That wasn't blood. It was ink. But I suspect you already knew that," he said, raising his voice as the boat throttled forward and crept up to speed.

JANE WAS VERY UPSET AS SHE ADDRESSED THE group in Isabelle's office. "There's no telling what they'll do with Richard." The tears began to stream down her face, but there were no other outward signs of crying. She had always cried in this way, a small leak in a dam of suffering that poured directly from her soul.

Though she had not given any indication, Isabelle knew exactly what they had done with him. She had detected the splash as she was heading toward home. In a moment of weakness, or compassion, or both, she said, "I'm sorry to be the one to tell you this, dear, but I think they threw him overboard."

"And you didn't tell me? Why didn't you tell me?"

"I didn't think there was anything we could do about it. One of them was shooting at us, you know."

"But we've got to try to save him. You've got to go back," said Jane, glassy-eyed.

"I'm sorry Jane. That's out of the question," said Captain Gregory. "Too dangerous. We're completely unprotected out here, and the last time she did that, well, you can see that it got us all into trouble."

"Please," said Jane pleading with her anguished eyes, pursed lips, and outstretched arms.

Isabelle listened to their arguments and pleas and then decided to do what any other independent-minded woman would do—she made up her own mind. "Well, all right," she said.

"You can't be serious," said Captain Gregory.

"It appears that Isabelle is a hopeless romantic," said Claude.

"No, just a good friend," said Jane.

"Oh this should be interesting," said Dr. Bellwether. "We haven't even gone through training yet and already we have a mutiny. Some Captain you're turning out to be, Gregory. Every decision you make is being overturned by a woman."

"Well, let me tell you something my scrawny little friend. That woman you speak of is our commander in chief. And if she tells me to charge up the hill with my soldiers, I will say 'Yes ma'am, and in what direction.'"

Dr. Bellwether scoffed. "Oh come off it, Captain. Don't you get it? This is a woman's world and we are being marginalized. Her Royal Highness here is in charge, and you're not. You can't even keep your own officers in line."

"Gentlemen, gentlemen, we must show the utmost decorum in front of the ladies," said Claude, but the two ignored his pleas.

"I can prove it to you," said Captain Gregory, "but it's against my nature to hit a spineless wonder like yourself."

"Go ahead and try it." Dr. Bellwether smiled, relishing the challenge. His first fight. On an intellectual level, the notion of pugilism at this stage in his existence excited him. On a visceral level, he had become attuned to his animal instincts and found them overpowering. The beauty of it was, no matter how badly he was beaten, in the back of his mind he knew it was all mind play in an illusory world.

"Please stop this now," said Jane. "We have more important things to do right now, and you might become a distraction to the Queen."

Captain Gregory ignored Jane. He had more important matters of male honor and pride to consider. Under normal circumstances he wouldn't have stooped, but Dr. Bellwether had gotten under his skin. The little self-centered-surgeon-turned-cephalopod was safe though; he couldn't really hurt him. The laws of physics might apply in this world, but there were no serious outcomes. Those could only come from the outside.

"Let's talk about rules," said Dr. Bellwether.

"Okay," said Captain Gregory. "The first rule is..." His arm snapped forward as if it were shot from a cannon, and his wide fist landed squarely on the bridge of Dr. Bellwether's nose, knocking him flat on his back. "There are no rules."

"Hey, that's not fair! What did you do that for?" said Dr. Bellwether, spitting blood. Isabelle and Jane rushed to Dr. Bellwether, whose lip and nose were bleeding. "Are you all right?" they asked. Isabelle gently wiped the blood from his lip and nose, and then cradled him in her arms. For a moment, Captain Gregory felt regret and wished he could trade places with Dr. Bellwether, not because he felt any pity for his Science Officer, but because he was quite jealous of the way that Isabelle was cradling him in her arms. Claude handed her a sponge to wipe away the blood that was pouring from his nose.

Dr. Bellwether shook his head a few times, tasting the blood trickling down onto his lip. He smiled. "Never felt better in my life."

He rubbed the wound and it felt a bit tender. Reconsidering, he said, "How long will it take to heal? Better yet, can you make it go away?"

"It'll take about as long as it normally would," said Isabelle, "and no I won't."

Dr. Bellwether frowned. He had never been punched in the nose, so he looked to Captain Gregory for some help.

"About three weeks," said Captain Gregory smiling. "You'll be as good as new, my friend, provided of course that nothing is broken."

"That's easy for you to say," said Dr. Bellwether, who had never been squeamish about other people's blood. He had an entirely different reaction, though, upon seeing his own. As

Isabelle wrung the sponge out into a basin, he felt a bit woozy and passed out.

SOME TIME LATER THEY WERE SEATED IN Isabelle's office, staring at the drop-down screen again. Captain Gregory was sitting in front of the "scope"—as he liked to call it—flanked on the left and right by the others. Dr. Bellwether was there too, looking very uncomfortable, his nose heavily bandaged with gauze. On screen, there were bubbles everywhere and then suddenly a pair of legs dangling close by.

"I've located him," said Isabelle. "Now what do you want me to do?"

"Take it up slowly," said Captain Gregory. "Close to 50 feet. Then surface for a moment and let him know you are there."

On screen, they could see that the seas were quite rough. Shivering, Richard Pearlman was fighting valiantly to stay above water, but he was losing the battle. He was staring right at them, looking petrified at the sight of her out of the tank, in the largest tank of all, her ocean home.

"I think he's frightened," Isabelle said.

"Let him know that you are not going to hurt him," said Jane.

"How?" asked Isabelle. "The seas are too rough to do what we did before."

"We could use sign language," said Claude.

"Give him the international sign of peace," said Jane holding up two fingers.

"What do you think, Captain?" asked Isabelle. Captain Gregory nodded his agreement.

Suddenly they saw the tips of five arms rise out of the water and gather together like the fingers on a hand. The fourth and fifth tips bent and were held in place by the first, while the second and third tips shot into the air, illuminating red.

Richard Pearlman looked a bit perplexed at first but then relieved as he flashed the peace sign back to her. He reached for one of her arms, but a giant wave swept him under before he could grasp it. He got back to the surface once more to gasp for air, but another wave crashed in on him and he began to sink.

"He's drowning," cried Jane.

"Well, don't just *float* there, grab him," said Dr. Bellwether.

"Yes, we must save him," said Captain Gregory, nodding in agreement.

The Queen quickly grabbed him, and with her tremendous strength, lifted him with one arm well above the waves, while she remained below looking up at Richard Pearlman through a fishbowl lens.

"What do we do now?" asked Claude, marveling at her strength.

"Do you detect any other boats in the area?" asked Captain Gregory.

"No," said Isabelle.

They all sat there for a while, saying nothing. Finally Dr. Bellwether said, "Why don't you just bite him in the neck and get it over with?"

"Dr. Bellwether! How can you suggest such a thing?" said Captain Gregory.

"Oh come off it, Gregory, everybody here has thought about it. One bite and she could bring him into our little holographic world. It's the perfect solution."

"But this man is not a drowning victim."

"Not yet."

"Just the same, we can't bring him here just for Jane's benefit."

Jane threw up her hands in exasperation. "Wait a second, you two. Don't you think you should ask *me* how I feel about this before making a decision? After all, he is my fiancee."

"Was," said Dr. Bellwether.

The others in the group groaned. "Now that was uncalled for," said Claude. "My friend, you must apologize to the lady."

"Oh, all right, I apologize," said Dr. Bellwether. "But there's no use candy-coating the situation."

"Okay," said Jane, "just forget about it." She turned to Isabelle. "I think we should ask Richard what he wants to do, don't you?"

Isabelle thought for a moment. "It would be better if we were to keep his head *above* water. I'm sorry my dear, but we need an ally on land."

"I'm afraid I agree with Isabelle," said Captain Gregory.

Jane put her hands on her hips. "I don't understand. Are you going to swim all the way to shore with him?"

"I don't have to," said Isabelle. "A rescue ship has just entered the vicinity."

"How do you know this?" asked Captain Gregory.

"I can sense the vibrations of the motor."

"Bring it up on scope. It could be a trap."

"She can't do that, we're below the surface, remember," said Dr. Bellwether.

"Actually, I can, with the fore-eyes on my arm tips," said Isabelle. They all looked at each other as the screen changed, showing a Coast Guard vessel getting closer.

"And I don't think it's a trap," she added. "There's a woman there who is waving to Jane's friend."

"Then release our friend to the Coast Guard vessel," said Captain Gregory.

"Is it okay?" Isabelle asked Jane.

"It's okay. It's Nancy. She's come to rescue Richard," said Jane, half-smiling, half-crying but completely relieved that he would be saved. She wasn't quite sure whether to be disappointed or happy that Richard did not join them. She made up her mind, though, that somehow they would get together again, whether on land or on sea or in a place somewhere in-between, a place where if not their bodies at least their spirits could reunite to sing the praises of their love.

Eighteen

The doors to the elevator opened and the crew followed their commander-in-chief into a large room with several huge displays on the walls. The front display showed the view outside. The sea was full of Isabelle's troops, some gathering food, some patrolling the ground outside the entrance to the cave, and others tending to the baby queens, who were trying to lose their escorts and making a game of it. The left-hand display showed an overhead map of the area with all of the main topological and strategic points, and an accurate display of troop movements and concentrations. The right-hand display showed a detailed layout of the cave. Two large consoles with numerous touch-sensitive membrane controls and built-in active-matrix screens were housed in a series of continuous work surfaces that curved around the back of the room. Another console occupied the center of the room.

"Welcome to command and control," said Isabelle. "I will be spending the next few hours briefing you on the 'war room' facilities. So sit back, relax, and listen, please." They all listened attentively as she described the intricacies of their new command and control center. The war room, the simulator, and the holodome were all part of a huge complex that included the hospital and the psychiatric ward. It was a military base, a strategic outpost at the edge of consciousness, and a think tank. It was also a sanctuary located on a small island off the coast of a great continent. And it was the place where all wars were started and ended, and won and lost.

Like any military base, this one had rules. They would need to be there the better part of each day to learn the capabilities of the troops and to help train them to perfect their maneuvers. New maneuvers would be added, and old maneuvers would be critiqued and modified as needed. At night, they would leave the command and control center on auto pilot, which would place the horn-rims in the highest state of alertness. The support staff that Captain Gregory referred to as "figments" would monitor their stations and notify them in case of an emergency.

Captain Gregory added a few rules of his own. Isabelle would have to inform command and control of her every movement. There would be very limited and heavily guarded excursions outside the cave. Last but not least, the captain would request a national security briefing from her each night. Captain Gregory knew that this last rule would seem self-serving to the others and they would be right, but he didn't care. The others knew about his relationship with her, and they would just have to get used to it. He envisioned their first "briefing" in a restaurant fashioned after an old ship where he could view the royal blue ocean lapping at the rocks below. Afterward, they would retire to his quarters, sit by a warm fire, sip cognac, and talk in passionate tones about the defense of the realm and the honor of a very great lady.

These thoughts were soon cast adrift as Claude looked up at the front display and said, "Captain Gregory, why are the troops moving around so quickly?" Captain Gregory looked up and noted that the troops were concentrating at the mouth of the cave, almost completely sealing it off.

"I don't know. Do you know anything about this, Isabelle?"

"One of the horn-rims saw something that was very large but could not identify it."

Captain Gregory looked very surprised. "It didn't show up on any of the displays, and it is not showing on the map."

"It came through the area so quickly that it only registered as a momentary blip on the display. That was all the information the horn-rim could give me. They are so young, you know."

"Perhaps it was a submarine," said Claude.

"Or a boat," said Jane.

"No," said Isabelle. "It was a life form."

WEARING CAPTAIN GREGORY'S OLD NAVY uniform that he had stolen from the captain's boat, Cranston walked into Mr. Oh's eighteenth floor office, half-hoping that he would finance a second expedition to capture the Big Red, but half-expecting to have his legs broken and his boat seized as payment for the money he owed for the first expedition.

The secretary in the outer office announced his arrival to Mr. Oh, but apparently the big man was in no hurry to meet with him. Cranston had to be there on time, but the same rules did not apply to the big man, who was fully prepared to make him wait and sweat. The secretary would not look him in the eye, nor return his smile. The Japs were definitely an oddball breed, but the one thing that he had learned about business was that you couldn't choose your customers. They chose you.

After what seemed to be hours, the secretary told Cranston that Mr. Oh was ready to see him. Cranston sauntered in as if he didn't have a care in the world. His eyes grew wide as he viewed the oriental tapestries, the intricately interwoven handloom rug, ivory and jade statues, and a music box with inlayed gold and mahogany. Behind the imposing desk of Mr. Oh were ceiling-to-floor windows.

"Good afternoon, Mr. Oh," said Cranston.

Mr. Oh held up his hands to cut him off. "My sources tell me that you failed to capture the giant octopus. This makes me very sad."

"Yes but you see—"

"And my investment is lost at sea. Is that not correct?"

"Yes, but—"

"There is no time for *buts*. You are a fool, Mr. Cranston, and we intend to get our money back."

"You don't understand, I don't have the money. I used it to rent the boat."

"To borrow a phrase, Mr. Cranston, a fool and his ship are soon parted." He made a few, short grunt-like Japanese commands over the intercom, and the two thugs from the restaurant were suddenly at the door.

"Now wait just a minute, Mr. Oh, look at this," said Cranston, pulling the photograph from his pocket.

Mr. Oh studied the photograph and his slant eyes became as round as saucers. "You know where to find this one?"

"Yes, now if you'll just give me another advance—"

Mr. Oh thought about it for a moment. "You shall have your money, and a new crew too." He looked at the two thugs and grunted some more commands in Japanese. The two bowed and looked over at Cranston.

"Oh no, not them. I don't need more men, I just need more money," said Cranston, not wanting to beg for more money from the research institute and that egghead, Professor Holloway.

"You don't understand, Mr. Cranston. I am sending my three finest sushi chefs. They will protect my investment at all costs. That is the deal, Mr. Cranston, take it or leave it."

RICHARD PEARLMAN WAS STANDING IN FRONT of his class relating his encounter with the Octopus Giganticus. He left out several parts, most notably his conversation with "Jane" and his subsequent rescue at sea. He had sworn Nancy to secrecy about that. No one would believe him anyway, so he ruminated aloud about the grand nature of the rare beast instead. Better to enlist the aid of his students purely on romantic grounds, not the least of which was the preservation of an entire species.

For the first time in a long time, Richard Pearlman was fully animated in the classroom. His eyes were dancing and his arms were waving with gusto. "She is a master of color manipulation. Her colors are spectacular and ever-changing, as if her skin were the canvas of some great impressionist painter. But she is more than just some piece of art. She is nature's masterpiece. She is poetry in motion, the ebb and flow of the sea. A gentle giant. An altruistic ally. An intelligent species. And maybe the only one of her kind left."

Nancy Boudreaux and the rest of the students sat there, mesmerized. Finally one of them raised his hand. "You say she, but how do you know that it was a she?"

"It was a female, all right. She had none of the enlarged sucker disks that are typical of male octopuses," said Richard Pearlman.

"Then you got a close look, is that right?"

"Yes, when she was in the tank."

Another student, Nathan Thornwell, leaned forward in his chair and raised his hand as if he couldn't wait to jump in to challenge his teacher. "On what basis do you say that she is intelligent or even altruistic? Surely you didn't have time to perform field studies or tests of any sort. How can you make such a claim?"

Before thinking, Richard Pearlman blurted out, "Because she was attempting to communicate with me."

Nathan dug his heels in deeper. "In what way was she trying to communicate?"

"When I was on the boat, she pointed to the clasps on the lid, in effect asking me to open it."

Nathan looked skeptically at Richard Pearlman; he stole a glance at the other students, and noting their incredulity, he grew bolder. "But don't you think, Professor, that you're reading too much into that? Couldn't it have been pure coincidence?" The other students nodded their agreement.

Richard Pearlman could tell that he was losing them. They didn't believe him, and why should they? He had not offered one shred of evidence as proof. He turned to Nancy Boudreaux. "What do you think, Nancy, should I tell them?"

From every corner of the room, his students cried out in unison, "Tell us *what!*" When Richard Pearlman did not respond, the room grew quiet, and the students leaned forward in anticipation.

Nancy reflected for a moment. "I don't see why not. It's the truth."

Richard Pearlman paused. If he told them the truth, no one would believe him. But if he didn't tell them the truth, they would think that he didn't trust them. It was a no-win situation. "If I tell you, you must believe that it is the truth. Do you agree?"

The students nodded their agreement. Richard Pearlman cleared his throat. "Okay there's more. The reason I know that she is trying to communicate with me is because... she rescued me."

His explanation was greeted with silence and then the sound of muffled laughter. There was a palpable undercurrent of skepticism in the room mixed in with concern. It was obvious from the looks on their faces that they believed they were witnessing the emotional breakdown of a once-great professor. "It doesn't make any sense," said Nathan. "You say that this giant octopus somehow rescued you? But I thought you said earlier that Nancy rescued you."

Richard Pearlman looked at Nancy. "That's true, but that's only half of the story. The giant octopus saved me from drowning and held me above water in rough seas for a while before she came."

The room became so quiet that Richard Pearlman imagined that it sounded like the inside of a conch shell. Finally, a student in the back of the room said, "Oh sure, I believe that she rescued you. And I'll bet she was looking for a date with you, too, Professor Pearlman."

The silence of the conch shell was soon filled with laughter that seemed like cruel waves crashing in on Richard Pearlman. He didn't know whether to be angry at them or not, but he could feel the tears well up as he thought about Jane. They hadn't believed him, and there was no way to make them believe.

Nancy Boudreaux read his thoughts and rallied to his defense. "Shut up, all of you! This was a very traumatic experience for Professor Pearlman. I was there, and what he is telling you is the truth."

Richard Pearlman fought back the tears in his eyes; the water crested and the dike held. His face brightened as he realized that there was a way to make them believe after all. He smiled as he slowly took off his shirt, revealing a very hairy chest. There were hoots and hollers, and the class looked at him as if he was crazy. Seemingly oblivious, supremely confident, he turned around and, for the third time that day, the class grew silent. In neat, double diagonal rows across his shoulder and back were huge, perfectly round, red welts, the size and shape of which could have only come from the arms of a very large octopus.

Several of the students appeared to be near tears as they gazed at the spectacle. "What can we do to help?" asked one. Her offer was soon followed by a trickle and then a chorus of offers.

Richard Pearlman smiled again, realizing that he had won them over. They were in the palm of his hand now, and he was going to take advantage of it. "As we speak, there are fishing vessels off of No Man's Land whose sole purpose is to kill this beautiful creature. I suggest that we observe the area near No Man's Land 24 hours a day, and that we get a court order under the Endangered Species Act to stop all fishing in the vicinity. These fishermen are a tricky bunch. If we merely watch them and wait for their next move, they'll sneak out of the harbor in another boat without our knowing. That's why we've got to be there ahead of them. Perhaps Nancy can persuade her superiors at the Department of Marine and Fisheries to declare the area a marine sanctuary. In the meantime, we must establish a presence and we must protect this individual. She is a beautiful cephalopod, and her existence is clearly the most important biological find of this century. Are you with me?"

The room thundered with pledges of assistance, and they set up a schedule at once. Riding a tidal wave of sympathy, adulation, and support from his students, Richard Pearlman began to feel that maybe, just maybe, there might be a way to save the Queen, to contact Jane again, and to rejuvenate the love they had together. In doing so, he would save his own life and ensure the survival of a rare and beautiful species.

Nineteen

---✧---

It had been several days since the Queen had ventured from her home, and she had a very bad case of cave fever. She had refrained from venturing out after her near-miss with the sushi knife at the hands of the fiendish one, Cranston. With each hour, however, she became more emboldened and more determined to overcome her fear. It was unnatural to stay holed up in a cave, even one so delightfully comfortable as this one. Today she would venture out to say hello to the world and to crawl amongst her children. It would remind them for whom they were fighting, their Queen mother. It would remind them of the cause. And it would remind them that they were, in fact, a colony, a colony whose survival depended on a system perfected over the millennia, handed down from generation to generation, and encoded in their chromosomes. These were important reminders because the troops were no longer just her children. Now they were soldiers. They were all part of a great undersea army, working in unison to support and defend the realm.

All that is except two, two baby queens that were equally curious about the world outside their home, who were privy to a great undersea conspiracy, working in unison to test, undermine, and upend the realm, as toddlers often do. The Queen did her best to entertain them, blowing herself up in the shape of a huge bell, rising slowly from the sea floor and then twirling her arms and untwirling them, like a beautiful dress on a belle at a ball. And they were having a ball, only the Queen did not know how long she could keep her mischievous babies entertained.

CAPTAIN GREGORY AND HIS CREW WERE IN THE war room putting the troops through routine maneuvers, special tactical unit training, and various attack strategies. In an ink attack, a horn-rim and his regiment would surround the target and spray ink and then retreat in all directions. In a poison attack, a squad would cover the target with bites from head to toe. In a creep attack, two regiments would approach the enemy by stealth from opposite directions and attack with ink, poison, bites, and any other weapon at their disposal. Then there was the battering ram, the arm-to-arm sling shot, and the noose. The noose was accomplished by linking arms and then twirling around the gills of the intended victim. These were effective weapons, but nature dictated that they would only be used in self-defense, no matter who commanded their use, the Queen herself or a lowly horn-rim.

The officers in command and control were as busy as the troops on the ground. Captain Gregory was firing commands almost as quickly as the troops were firing ink into the water; Jane was pinpointing troop locations and perfecting communications; Claude was studying the formations on the display and the weapons panel; and Dr. Bellwether was jotting down a few notes on troop behaviors. They had set up a virtual pentagon—no, octagon—by the time Isabelle had entered the room.

"I've come to inform you that I will be going out soon to visit my troops."

Captain Gregory could hardly believe his ears. Hadn't Isabelle learned anything from her ill-fated excursion with them? He crossed his arms and ground his teeth so that his jawbone oscillated in his cheek. "You shouldn't go out at all anymore after what happened the other day. The troops here are raw. They will need much more practice before they are combat ready."

"I'm sorry, Captain Gregory, but I need to get out."

"Why? You have enough food, don't you?"

"Yes."

"Then there is no need to go out."

Isabelle felt as if she would burst. "You don't understand. If I don't get out soon, I'm going to go crazy."

Captain Gregory looked at the troop configurations on the display. According to the map, the troops were in the appropriate defensive posture. "Why don't you confirm with the horn-rims that there are no boats in the vicinity before going out. I don't want to take any more chances."

"All right."

"And when you go out put your view up on the wall display."

Isabelle stood there impatiently like a school girl waiting to be released from class. "Can I go now?"

"Just stay out of trouble. But keep me posted please. I don't want to be talking to the walls in case there's trouble."

"All right, I'll be back in a minute," said Isabelle, smiling as she left the war room.

The view on the display changed from a dimly lit cave with small shadows moving back and forth to the wonderful world of the ocean blue. Once outside the cave, they could see the Queen's enormous arms project ahead of her as she slowly moved along the ocean floor. Everywhere she went she was greeted by her troops, who came up to her and touched her, cleared brush out of her way, and treated her like the great queen mother that she was.

She stopped by the cliffs, admiring the sea flowers gently moving in the current. She studied the colors, and then, like some beautiful watercolor painting, she matched their colors, blending in with the sea cliffs in an instantaneous blaze of glory. Her troops followed suit and they looked like a giant moving bed of flowers. After a while, she moved away from the cliffs. As she moved away, a horn rim picked one of the flowers from the cliff and brought it to her. She gently stroked his head and tucked it under her mantle as she crawled onward.

"The colors are beautiful," said Jane.

"Tres magnifique," said Claude.

"A masterpiece," said Dr. Bellwether.

Soon she caught sight of a hermit crab and gave a lazy chase around several rocks until she had him cornered in a hole. For a while, she poked in and out of the hole at the large hermit crab but then gave up. She had had plenty to eat.

"This is his lucky day," said Captain Gregory, lighting his pipe and putting his feet up on the console. He watched, enjoying the "ride" and the view of the seascape. At that moment, he even thought that perhaps he was being too restrictive about the Queen's comings and goings.

The next moment, though, his feelings were decidedly different as he noticed the front display momentarily go dim and then bright again. "What was that?"

"What was what?" asked Dr. Bellwether.

"Didn't you see it? The display flickered," said Captain Gregory.

"So, perhaps we're having transmission problems," said Dr. Bellwether, looking worried and not believing his own words.

"What did you see, Captain?" asked Jane.

"I think it was a shadow."

"A shadow? Oh, you're just paranoid," said Dr. Bellwether looking intently at the display.

"Perhaps a glass of wine to calm the nerves," offered Claude.

"Never drink on duty. Look, I hate to be the one to crash the party. But I'm telling you that something's out there," said Captain Gregory.

"I don't believe it," said Dr. Bellwether.

They watched as an eerie silence fell upon the room, like a brief lull before the storm. Suddenly, the scene on the display became chaotic as a large arm went around the Queen's head and pulled her violently backward. She was surprised, shocked, stunned, unable to move for a moment. Then she struggled valiantly as the view rotated back and forth amidst many bubbles and roiling water.

"What's going on?" asked Captain Gregory, raising his voice.

"Isn't it painfully clear to you, we're being attacked!" cried Dr. Bellwether, terrified.

"I *know* that. But what is it?" he asked. The pipe fell out of Captain Gregory's mouth and nearly burned his hand as he began barking orders. "Jane, acquire the target. Claude, arm the ink torpedoes and the poison cartridges."

"Yes sir!" they answered.

"What can I do?" asked Dr. Bellwether. "I'm not just going to sit here and go down with the ship. Come on, give me something to do. Anything!"

"You watch the display and try to figure out what we're dealing with!" barked Captain Gregory.

On the display, the Queen turned pink as two more gargantuan arms encompassed her. In response, she sent two arms around the rather large body that was wrapped around her, and the two were locked together.

Jane pushed a few buttons. "Target acquired, Captain."

"Fire fifty ink torpedoes," shouted Captain Gregory.

Claude punched in the number on the console and pressed the red FIRE button, but nothing happened. He pressed the button repeatedly but no torpedoes were launched by the horn-rims or the troops.

"Poison attack," shouted Captain Gregory. Claude pressed more buttons. They watched on the display, but nothing happened. "Why aren't they firing? I ordered a full-scale attack," said Captain Gregory.

"I don't know," said Claude. "I punched all the buttons."

"Try again," said Captain Gregory.

Claude tried again, but nothing happened. Dr. Bellwether looked puzzled. "It appears as if the troops are just watching."

Captain Gregory puffed harder and harder as if by doing so he might unleash the barrage of torpedoes that were inexplicably jammed in the troops' funnels. "I knew this was a bad idea. Next time she goes out, I'm putting my foot down."

"If there is a next time," said Dr. Bellwether.

The view changed to show the eye of the intruder as the two struggled. It was a huge, blue saucer that was glowing with fury.

"For the love of mike, look at that," said Captain Gregory, as shivers went up and down his spine. "Isabelle, where are you!!"

They heard running down the hallway, and the door to the war room burst open. "I'm here, I'm here, what's all the commotion?" asked Isabelle, hands at her hips.

"What's all the commotion?" said Captain Gregory, perplexed. "We're under attack, and the troops won't counterattack."

"Of course not," said Isabelle.

"WHAT??" they all asked at once.

"That's Archie. He's an old friend."

"An old friend!!" exclaimed Captain Gregory. "If your friends look like that, I'd hate to see what your enemies look like."

"They look like you, Captain Gregory," said Isabelle, eyes gently teasing, yet admonishing at the same time.

"Oh yes, of course, I almost forgot," said Captain Gregory, embarrassed that he had forgotten the new world order.

"What kind of a freakazoid is that?" asked Dr. Bellwether, scratching his chin.

"That 'freakazoid' is in fact a squid, Dr. Bellwether. You should know that," said Isabelle matter-of-factly.

"Wouldn't want to meet him in a dark alley," said Captain Gregory. "Where did he come from?"

"Off the coast of the land you call New Zealand."

"Why didn't you tell us about him," asked Captain Gregory.

"Yes, why didn't you," the others chimed in and nodded their agreement.

"Because I thought he was dead. But as you can see on the display, I'm happy to report he is alive and well. Archie and I go back a long way. We're sucker buddies, so to speak. He has saved me and my children on more than one occasion."

"Oh, that's preposterous. Who ever heard of an octopus and a squid being friends?" asked Dr. Bellwether.

"Oh sure, that makes a whole lot of sense coming from a world-famous neurosurgeon who was lost at sea and incorporated by a giant octopus. You find the friends that *she* makes preposterous? That's a laugh," said Captain Gregory.

"I can hardly believe my eyes," said Jane, writing notes on a pad. "You realize what he is, don't you Dr. Bellwether?"

"No, should I?"

"It's Architeuthis, and we are the first to observe him in his natural habitat."

"Well, bully for us," said Dr. Bellwether.

"Architeuthis?" said Claude.

"The giant squid," said Captain Gregory matter-of-factly.

"He looks like a big, giant head," said Claude.

"A big, giant swimming head," said Dr. Bellwether.

"A big, giant, swimming warhead," said Captain Gregory. "This is great. Now we've got some real firepower on our side."

As they marveled at the sight they were witnessing on the display, Archie turned bright cochineal, then turquoise, then aqua, and then alternated between black and white. He then turned multiple colors and continued to change colors in geometric patterns, like a kaleidoscope.

"Fascinating," said Dr. Bellwether. "What is he doing?"

"He's putting on one heckuva' light show," said Captain Gregory.

"He is communicating," said Isabelle.

"What is he saying?" asked Dr. Bellwether.

"He wants to know if I've incorporated anyone lately."

"He knows about that?" asked Captain Gregory incredulously.

"Of course, we have no secrets. I've told him everything about you. I hope you don't mind." They all looked at each other, but none could think of any reason why she would need to keep their new world a secret.

Captain Gregory figured that they must be chatting up a storm because more kaleidoscopic lights went on and off on the giant squid. At the end of the light pattern, Archie turned pink and began to blink.

"What's he doing?" asked Captain Gregory.

Isabelle smiled. "He's laughing. He says, 'If you don't watch it, you'll be sprouting extra heads before long. But then again five heads are better than one'. He is an old cut-up."

"Oh, great, a giant squid with a sense of humor. That's all we need," said Dr. Bellwether.

"Can we talk to him, if you translate?" asked Jane.

"Yes, it is possible. He'll have to be given a voice of course, but it can be done. Any time you're ready, Jane, go ahead."

"Hello," said Jane. "We understand that Isabelle has told you a little about us. We would like to get to know you, too, if that would be okay."

"What do you want to know?" said Archie over the com while turning bright orange on the display. Isabelle turned to her guests explaining, "He always turns orange when he's curious."

"What do you eat?"

"What's that you say?"

"What do you eat?"

"What do I eat?"

"What is he, hard-of-herring? asked Dr. Bellwether, laughing along with Claude.

Jane put her index finger to her lips. "Please, be quiet Dr. Bellwether. Give him a chance."

"Oh, he can't hear me," protested Dr. Bellwether.

Captain Gregory's chest puffed up, his chin jutted forward, and his eyes glared. "Yes, but we can. So shut up!"

"Did he get the question, Isabelle?" asked Jane.

"Yes, he did. I think he's thinking about it."

Archie twirled his arms around and then untwirled them. Then he looked directly at them, his eyes gleaming. "Oh, just about anything," he said.

"What, for instance?" There was no answer, so Jane continued. "That's okay, you're among friends here. You can tell us."

"No, I am not. The Queen tells me that there is a fisherman amongst you, and they are my enemy."

"Oh, I am so sorry. He cannot harm you. Besides he's on your side now."

"I eat small squid...and I eat fishermen, on occasion."

"You eat fishermen?!" they all exclaimed.

"One or two, here or there make a fine fisherman feast. But only the ones with the harpoons and the nets. I don't go looking for fishermen. But if I come across one with a spear gun or a net, well, my motto is, dine or be dinner."

Dr. Bellwether looked at the others. "Eating people, how barbaric. He should seek help."

Jane laughed. "My friend, Dr. Bellwether, says you should refrain from eating fishermen and try to seek help."

"I tried *sea kelp*. Trust me, it doesn't taste very good."

Jane laughed and said to Isabelle, "Your gentleman friend is pretty funny."

Isabelle looked up at the display with real affection. "I know. He's sensitive, kind, and gentle too. If he had had two less arms, I might have considered him for a mate."

"That's a good question to ask him," said Jane. "Do you have a mate?"

The giant squid turned blue. "She was killed in a fisherman's net. She is gone but I believe that her inner light lives on. I have been searching for that light for years and have seen it in the twilight waters on two occasions."

"I'm sorry to hear about your mate. That must have been horrible," said Jane.

"Yes it was."

"That's nonsense," said Dr. Bellwether.

"Dr. Bellwether! Have a little consideration for Archie," Jane responded.

Isabelle cleared her throat. "Let me explain something to all of you. All giant squids have an inner light that they only show to their mates or their loved ones. I believe that all animals have it. I believe that man does too, only you cannot see it. Archie and I have had many arguments about this."

"Archie says that all octopuses are really squids, only they are missing two appendages. He says that the jellyfish stole them and learned to walk on land and became a jelly fisherman. But that's all he got; he didn't get the light. We've got that. But he says, one day all of the creatures of the earth and the sea will be reunited. Then man will be reunited with his inner light and the octopus will get back her missing appendages. He's expecting me to grow back two any day now."

"What a bunch of nonsense. And just what does he mean by inner light?" said Dr. Bellwether.

"It means that the giant squid is a biolume. Fascinating," said Claude.

"A biolume. What's that?" said Captain Gregory.

"Most squid species have the ability to generate light from within," said Jane.

"Kind of the squid pro quo," said Dr. Bellwether.

"Very funny, Bellwether," said Captain Gregory.

"Better say something to him, Jane. It looks like he's getting impatient," said Isabelle.

"I know what it is like to be separated from a loved one. Mine is named Richard, and he and I were to be married. So you see, we do have something in common."

Archie turned a warm yellow that got brighter and brighter and then faded like a sunset being swallowed by the sea. Jane turned to Isabelle. "What does that mean?"

Isabelle's mouth opened up slightly with surprise. "Well, I would never have guessed that he would reveal this to anyone else. He's showing you his inner light."

"It's beautiful," said Jane.

"Like a sunrise in the Mediterranean," said Claude.

"Yea, very nice," said Captain Gregory, pondering what other hidden talents Archie possessed. "Ask him what kinds of weapons he has. Is it standard issue to have teeth on his suckers? Does he have ink too?"

"We shouldn't ask him that," said Jane.

"Why not?" protested Captain Gregory.

"Because you just met him."

Isabelle nodded. "I agree with Jane. Besides, I can fill you in on that."

"Well, then, fill me in."

Isabelle turned to Captain Gregory and in a near-whisper, she said, "He has teeth on his suckers. Teeth on his tongue, for ripping his prey apart of course. Perfect camouflage. Ink. Elastic arms. Fast swimmer. And he's a biolume. But he says he won't need any of that for long because soon there will be great land earthquakes, and the earth and the sea will be reunited and the jelly fishermen will be returned to the sea."

"Where does he get such utter nonsense?" asked Dr. Bellwether. "Just another biolume and gloom, I guess," he added, laughing.

Archie changed position and his eye loomed very large on the display. "Oh, I almost forgot, he also has very keen eyesight," said Isabelle, ignoring Dr. Bellwether.

"What do you mean, keen eyesight?" asked Dr. Bellwether.

"He can see through things. In fact, he's looking into my mind at you right now," said Isabelle.

"That's really creepy," said Dr. Bellwether.

"No it's not," said Jane. "He's looking with kind eyes." Jane addressed Archie. "It was an honor to meet a good friend of Isabelle's."

Archie turned yellow and pink at the same time, as if he was laughing. "The Queen was right. You are not like the others. I have looked, and I have seen. You have an inner light. Even the captain, too. So I guess that's one more thing we have in common. Until next time, my friends. Stay out of trouble. And remember, there's a suckerfish born every day." Archie turned away momentarily, looking for something. Then he found what he was looking for, the baby queens. Before leaving, he scooped them up.

"Just look at him," said Dr. Bellwether. "Aren't you afraid that 'Headfirst Harry' here might pop them into his mouth like a couple of hors' d'oeuvres?"

"No, of course not, I trust him completely. We're old friends," said Isabelle.

"Just the same, I'd feel better if he'd just look at them."

"Why Dr. Bellwether, I didn't know you cared."

Dr. Bellwether wasn't quite sure why it had happened or even when it had happened. But it had most assuredly happened. Perhaps he had become attached to the baby queens during his match with Captain Gregory. Since then he had felt as if he were their protector or perhaps their guardian. He sighed. "You become attached to the squirts; or they become attached to you. Sometimes I'm not sure which it is."

"Don't look now but he's bringing them up to his mouth," said Captain Gregory.

"Oh, I can't bear to watch," said Dr. Bellwether. "It's hideous. Somebody do something."

Archie gently wrapped a single tentacle around each baby queen, and brought them in slowly toward his immense head, nearer and nearer, until they were no more than a tongue's length from his gaping mouth.

"Look out," cried Dr. Bellwether.

A moment later Archie brought the baby queens up to his enormous aquamarine eyes, eyes with pupils like black holes that sucked in all of the available light and distributed it in a blaze of glory throughout his body. The baby queens were squirming with giddiness, delighting in the light show, not sensing any danger at all. He and they sized each other up and then began to nuzzle like an uncle with his baby nieces.

"See, Dr. Bellwether. I told you. There is no reason to worry about Archie. He is our friend, not our enemy," said Isabelle.

"I'm not so sure. Today's friend may be tomorrow's enemy."

"A friend is not a friend, unless he is a friend forever," said Isabelle.

ARCHIE LITERALLY GLOWED AS HE CHANGED the mosaic pattern on his moveable palette, and then swam slowly away, mesmerizing the soldiers and the Queen. The baby queens were perhaps the most mesmerized of all for they followed him out, obscured by his tentacles, which were like a tangled forest of sea kelp.

They did not get very far. A horn-rim spotted them and summoned a sea of octopuses to retrieve the mischievous baby queens and bring them back to a very grateful Queen.

TWENTY

Richard Pearlman waited with Nancy as the last of his students got into the Coast Guard boat. It was not official Coast Guard business; no one had given them orders to go out in the name of the government and stop the fishing boat from catching the great octopus. But Nancy had convinced the captain of the Coast Guard that if she could deter the fishermen and get a few pictures of the creature, they could get a court order to stop fishing in the area under the Endangered Species Act.

When all of the students had arrived, Richard Pearlman said, "I am gratified that your courage and conviction brought you here to save a species from extinction. I believe that we will make history this week. A history that we must all pledge to keep secret for a while. But there is something all of you should know. These fishermen are a rough lot, and they will stop at nothing to get what they are after. You may be in some danger if you go with me. Therefore, if any of you would like to leave right now, I will understand. Once we head out to sea there will be no turning back, except to shuttle people back and forth for different shifts."

He looked around to see if anyone wished to leave, but the students shouted their support for him and his cause. Their voices made Richard Pearlman's soul rejoice, and he began preparations to go out to sea.

WHEN THEY ARRIVED AT NO MAN'S LAND, THE coast was clear, the ocean was flat as far as the eye could see, and the wind had stopped blowing, save an occasional huff. As soon as their boat was anchored, thousands of small octopi came to the surface to inspect the boat and surround it. The students picked up a few and studied them. Richard Pearlman examined one and made the positive identification. "These are in fact the males of the species Octopus Giganticus."

His students were excited and took notes furiously about the native pink coloration of the animals, their strange, coordinated movements that resembled a kind of water ballet, and their inquisitive nature. Within minutes after they had arrived, though, the small octopi left abruptly, and the sea turned from pink to green once more, like a lily pad unable to make up its mind. They all wondered how soon it would turn pink again.

"They didn't look so big for a species with such a big name," said Nathan, skeptical about the professor's claims. "If the males are this small, the female can't possibly be as large as you say."

Richard Pearlman smiled. "That has always been the joke about this species. Big name, small octopus. But you must understand, there is precedence for this. For instance, in some species of the Argonaut, a close cousin of the octopus, the female is up to fifty times larger than the male."

"I don't believe it," said Nathan.

"Then why did you come here?" asked Nancy.

"To see for myself whether Professor Pearlman really saw something or whether he's just seeing things. After all, the notion that the female is fifty times larger than the males is hard to believe, don't you think?"

As if on command, two huge arms jutted out of the sea, then three more, and they twisted and turned until they made the sign of peace, just behind where Nathan was standing. The other students let out a collective gasp.

Richard Pearlman pointed. "Do you believe it now?"

Nathan turned around and stumbled backwards, he was so startled. "My God, what is it?"

The Queen slowly surfaced and Richard Pearlman literally beamed. "I would like to introduce you all to the Queen of this colony, the only one of its kind in existence, as far as we know."

The students moved away, afraid that she might swallow them all in one gulp. Richard Pearlman went over to the other side of the boat and touched a tentacle on the Queen's arm. "It is all right. She is not only harmless, she actually likes people, and she can communicate."

A few of the students ventured forward and began to gently touch the Queen's arms. "You're joking, right?" asked another of the students.

"I am quite serious. When she rescued me, I found out a lot of things about her. She has a multi-faceted personality, but that's really all I want to say about it at this time. Perhaps she will communicate with us, if she trusts us." He motioned for more of them to move up slowly to the side of the boat.

A couple came, and a few more, and then the rest of the students gathered up the courage to approach the Queen. Some touched her gently; some watched intently; and some took notes quietly. One remarked that she was beautiful; another said she was repulsive; and another thought that she was fascinating. "Stand back," said Richard Pearlman. "I want to show you something."

After the students had moved away, he turned to the Queen. "Your majesty, how are you today?"

The Queen tilted ever-so-slightly, flattened her head a little, and began to send notes on her mantle. "I am fine... You came back."

Amazed, the students recorded her words on anything that was handy—notebooks, handkerchiefs, and even a few sweaty palms. There were many questions to ask, but they would have to wait.

"Yes, we're here to help," said Richard Pearlman.

"I am most pleased."

"How is everyone?"

"They are fine. One in particular says that she misses you."

"And I miss her. When this is all over, we will talk."

"That would be nice."

"How may we help?"

There was no answer. The Queen held onto the boat and her eyes closed for a moment as if she were listening to the voices inside. "Perhaps you could signal us when there is danger."

"Excellent," said Richard Pearlman. "We will shine a red light in the water when the fishermen come."

"A sentry will be posted to monitor your boat to watch for the light, and, wait a second..." The Queen hesitated, as if awaiting instructions. Richard Pearlman waited patiently while the students looked at each other, not understanding the various personalities expressing themselves in the conversation. "Perhaps you could use a flashing red to indicate the presence of scuba divers," she added.

"Very good," said Richard Pearlman. We will also place a flashing yellow light in the water to indicate the presence of one of our own divers. You can identify them by the yellow stripe on their wetsuits."

"I will inform my men," said the Queen, her large yellow eyes blazing. She blinked once. "Then perhaps there is something I might do for you?"

Richard Pearlman looked around. They had just eaten, the boat was in good shape, and there was no sign of Cranston and crew. "I can't think of anything that you could do right now. Tell my friend that I will talk to her in private."

"That's not what I mean. I mean that surely you must be hungry. I will have my men send up crab for you."

Richard Pearlman laughed, several of the students cheered, and the rest sat there in awe. It would not be polite to turn down her generous offer. "That would be most kind, thank you."

BY NOW A WHOLE NEW WORLD HAD BEEN BUILT for her guests inside the Queen's mind. The hospital had been turned into a Naval base and like most, it was a world unto itself with a full complement of food, services, and support facilities.

Captain Gregory sat in the crow's nest overlooking the midship, the galley, and the Captain's Quarters below at the crowded naval Officer's Club, the last great bastion of civilization in this extraordinary, floating naval base that he and his shipmates now called home. He looked out the giant porthole of the elegant restaurant to the royal blue ocean lapping gently at the rocks below; he looked around at the series of interconnected rooms; and then he looked at his watch, oblivious to the low din being made by the clean-cut military officers and their dates and the man at the baby grand in the corner crooning old standards. Isabelle was late, fifteen minutes late to be exact.

Perhaps she wasn't coming at all, or maybe she was making him wait, just to tease him.

As he waited, he wondered if they would ever get together, and if they did, whether she was really a woman, a half-woman half-octopus, or an octopus masquerading as a woman or visa versa. This mystery was so unsettling and so thrilling, that he could hardly stay seated he was so full of anticipation.

She did not disappoint. Wearing a dramatic V-cut emerald sequin dress, Isabelle walked slowly toward his table, her auburn hair gently caressing the mother-of-pearl necklace, the last few pearls of which got lost in her cleavage. She was acutely aware that she was late, and she feared that Captain Gregory may have grown impatient waiting. After all, he was a military man who was used to punctuality. Getting dressed was a snap; it was figuring out what to wear that was the problem. If only she had talked to Jane before choosing a dress for the occasion.

As she walked across the room, she tried to pick up on Captain Gregory's thoughts but was unable. At least he was smiling, but she could not interpret its meaning. This made her feel most uncomfortable; and for once, she felt that she was at a decided disadvantage. But there was no turning back now. She continued to walk slowly, dragging her high heels ever so slightly in a seductive half-glide, half-crawl toward the table. People were staring—her own figments, hand-picked for the base—and it was making her acutely self-conscious.

As she went by the piano, the music stopped momentarily as if the syncopation had gotten stuck in mid-measure, and the crowd stopped talking for a moment to gaze. What were they staring at? Was it her dress? Was it her walk? Or was it her physical appearance? She had read Captain Gregory's dreams over and over and she thought that she had projected the woman of his dreams. Perhaps she had left something out. Perhaps not. The possibility was too upsetting, and she could not bare to think about it.

As she approached the table, Captain Gregory smiled but said nothing, which made her all the more nervous, so nervous that she dropped her purse. She quickly crouched down to pick it up, showing the dramatic bare back to her emerald sequin dress.

Captain Gregory leapt from his chair to help but hesitated as he caught sight of her exquisite frame. As she gathered up her lipstick and nervously placed it back in her purse, Captain Gregory once again noticed the beautiful milky-white skin, the slight curvature of her back, and the delicate undulations along the center that could only mean one thing: she had a backbone. Captain Gregory took a deep breath, as if drinking in her beauty, and said, "You look absolutely beautiful tonight."

Isabelle smiled as she got up, grabbing a cigarette from her purse. "Oh this old thing," she said with a sigh, "is hardly worth mentioning I should think."

Captain Gregory offered her a light. "If it is hardly worth mentioning your beauty, then all of the words of love spoken through the ages were hardly worth saying."

Clearly dazzled, Isabelle smiled and sat down next to Captain Gregory. She looked out at the ocean, and blushed. "Why you old silver-tongued sea devil, tell me more."

Before he could say another word, the waiter came to the table, introduced himself, and described the various entrees. "Tonight our specialty is roast octopus on an oak mesquite grill. These are in short supply, so if you are interested I would need to place the order now. Would either of you care to order this rare delicacy tonight?"

Isabelle was stunned. It was like a nightmare, yet they were both awake, and that is what puzzled her. In her conscious state, she would not have allowed such an entree to be placed on the menu; it must have bubbled up from Captain Gregory's subconscious. Regardless of its origin both she and Captain Gregory knew the answer to the question. They looked at each other in disgust and shouted, "No!"

❖ ❖ ❖

SOME TIME LATER, THEY WERE SERVED THE main course for dinner, New England dungeoness crab. The waiter apologized profusely for the shortage of shell-crackers but explained that there was nothing he could do about it. They were all being used, and until one turned up they would have to fend for themselves.

Captain Gregory decided that, in this case, the best course of action was none at all. As he waited for a set of shell-crackers to turn up, he thought about how wonderful it was to be at dinner with Isabelle and how sad it was that Jane could never enjoy this simple pleasure again with Richard Pearlman. As his mind wandered, it eventually made its way back to Isabelle, and how foolish he had been to be thinking about anyone else but this gorgeous lady in front of him.

While Captain Gregory's mind was wandering, Isabelle had been waiting patiently, and politely, for him to begin eating. Soon, however, her appetite overcame her decorum, and Isabelle attacked her crab with such ferocity that Captain Gregory thought that she might crack the plate instead of the crab. He was wrong. With a single well-placed bite, she cracked the upper shell of the crab.

Captain Gregory stared in amazement, noting that he was clearly out of his league. He didn't mind that she was so adept, but he didn't want to appear to be helpless. It was too unmanly. So, he drew the battle lines on his plate and waged war with the enemy crustacean. It was a grand and noble struggle. Captain Gregory fought gallantly, thrusting his fork into the foe like a sword between plates of armor, but it was a losing battle, and he knew it. Even so, he continued the struggle because the captain always went down with the ship.

Isabelle had thought about helping Captain Gregory but didn't want to embarrass him. Somewhere along the line, she had learned that men, in particular, did not like having their weaknesses exposed, especially by women. Finally, though, she could not bare to watch such an amateur in action. It was pitiful, and he needed help. Isabelle lunged across the table, pounced on his crab, and shattered the shell with one swift bite while deftly ripping the legs from the body one by one. As a reflex, Captain Gregory backed away from the table with his hand cupped between his legs for fear that one of his appendages might be ripped away by mistake.

Depositing the crab legs on his plate, Isabelle saw the funny look on Captain Gregory's face, but she was unable to understand it. "Why Captain Gregory," she said, handing him his plate, "you look as if you've seen a ghost."

Captain Gregory gulped. "Oh, I'm fine."

"Are you sure?"

"I'm sure."

"It's funny. I can read what the others are thinking most of the time, even when they are awake. But I can't seem to crack your shell."

"I'm surprised," he said recovering. "You look pretty good at it."

As she sucked a tender morsel from a crab leg, she said, "Well, it's true I've cracked a lot of shells in my day, but I must say yours is the hardest. Please tell me, what is on your mind?"

"Well, I don't know if I should mention it, but I was just thinking that maybe we should bring him aboard."

"Who?"

Captain Gregory was surprised. She really couldn't read his mind, at least not tonight, and that made him feel much more at ease. "Richard Pearlman, of course. He loves Jane, and she feels the same toward him. When two people love each other, they shouldn't be kept apart, don't you think?"

"Yes, but we can't do that. I only bring aboard those who are drowning."

"Or fisherman who make you very, very angry."

"Okay, I admit it. I was in a rage. But it was in self-defense."

"Are you still angry with me?"

"No, not really. I realized that you did not know what you were doing. It took me a while but I was able to forgive you. And now, I've even grown rather fond of you. I've discovered that it's a short crawl from anger to passion."

"I'm glad to hear that. But you haven't really answered my question. Why can't we bring Richard Pearlman aboard?"

Isabelle wiggled in her chair, feeling uncomfortable. "It's not right for us to change a life form, except to save its existence."

"We could get his consent, I'll bet."

"There is not enough room—all right?" said Isabelle, slightly annoyed at Captain Gregory's persistence.

"Ah, so the real reason comes out. There's not enough room...or maybe you don't want to *make* room. I suspect you could bring him aboard if you really wanted to," said Captain Gregory.

"I don't want to talk about it," said Isabelle, waving a crab leg at Captain Gregory.

"Well, that's a shame. Jane is such a nice lady. But what a fool I am for talking about another woman when I have the most stunning woman on the planet at my table."

That's all it took. Just the right words at the right time by the right man. With all of her warm feelings toward him returning instantly, Isabelle smiled. "Why Captain Gregory, flattery will get you everywhere."

Captain Gregory didn't know if it was the champagne talking or the simple fact that he had always been a real suckerfish for a redhead, but he had talked more that night than he had talked in a long time. Except for Maria, he had rarely been able to maintain a relationship with a woman, because another woman just as alluring had always beckoned him to her great adventure on the high seas. Now he had finally met the perfect woman from the sea, of the sea, and like the sea, a great lady with royal blue eyes, who glided across the floor effortlessly, and whose voice was a calm tonic in a world of noise—and he would not let her go. He took the bottle of champagne from the ice bucket stand and filled both of their glasses. Lifting his glass, he said, "I would like to propose a toast."

"What shall we drink to Captain Gregory?"

"Please call me Monty."

"Okay, Monty."

"All my life I have been searching the high seas for the perfect catch...and now I have found her." They raised their glasses and drank, and Isabelle felt a wave of warmth go through her body that caused her to simultaneously blush until she was literally glowing.

"I don't know what to say."

"Don't say anything. Just tell me what I can do to make you happy. What is it that you want out of life, Isabelle?"

Isabelle took a deep breath. "I want to survive. I want peace for my children and my children's children."

"Is that all?"

Isabelle thought for a moment before answering. She didn't know whether it would be too unladylike to say what was really on her mind, but she decided that she could trust Captain Gregory. "No, I left one thing out. I want you, Captain Gregory."

All of the lines on Captain Gregory's face connected into a giant nautical map with all points leading to a smile. Grabbing hold of her hands, he said, "Would it be too presumptuous of me to ask you back to my room for a night cap?"

"Why Captain Gregory, I thought that you would never ask."

Captain Gregory leaned forward to kiss her, and she leaned forward to meet him halfway until Captain Gregory finally saw the pearl at the bottom of the necklace nested in her cleavage. They kissed and both felt dizzy, as if they were at sea, going from one swell to the next. For someone who had only been kissed once before, Isabelle kissed amazingly well.

Isabelle felt a tingly sensation from her head to her toes; she was amazed that such a ridiculous-looking ritual could be so pleasurable. Captain Gregory gently ran his tongue along her teeth, and she responded by moving her tongue slowly along the contours of his mouth, making his blood move like a strong current through his veins. At the same time, he was quite relieved to find that her tongue was quite normal—no teeth, unlike so many of her species—and quite pleasantly surprised to find out that she was a wonderful French kisser, so wonderful that Captain Gregory wondered if her lineage was French Mediterranean. The kiss got stronger and stronger until finally neither of them could bare it any longer, and their lips parted. Isabelle fell softly into her chair, her breasts heaving. Captain Gregory just stood up smiling at her, his legs spread as if he were attempting to maintain balance on a boat that was heaving to and fro. He looked across the room, motioned to the waiter, and said, "Check please."

WEARING A SMOKING ROBE, CAPTAIN GREGORY waited impatiently for Isabelle to slip into something more "comfortable". Whether on land or in sea, women were the same all over, and it would take some time to get used to waiting for a woman again. The lights dimmed and the door opened, and Isabelle walked out slowly wearing a see-through negligee cut low at the bosom, which was lightly covered in beautiful flowing, auburn hair. It was worth the wait; Captain Gregory could hardly believe the stirring inside that she caused, like an old volcano, which had just become active after decades of quiet. As she gently laid down beside him, he pulled her hair away from her bosom and looked down, only to find that the negligee was cut just above his expectations. The secrets of the sea were not given up that easily. Ah, but she was a sight for an old sailor's eyes. He moved in slowly, caressing her back gently with his experienced hands, and they kissed amidst the sound of the sea that surrounded and echoed in their mind.

After they kissed, Isabelle said, "That's odd. I thought I would be nervous, but I'm not."

Captain Gregory was a bit offended. "You mean, I am not the first."

"No, you are the only. There will never be another."

Visibly relieved, Captain Gregory smiled and said, "You weren't the least bit nervous about me?"

"Well, yes, but from that moment we kissed in the holodome for the first time, I knew that you were a gentleman. But I must admit that I am a bit nervous about what the others will think," said Isabelle.

"Who cares what they think? Show a little backbone!"

She looked perplexed. "But I don't have..." Her eyes lit up. "Oh! One of those!" she said, slowly turning to show a beautiful curved back framed by the oval cut in her negligee.

His eyes glinting, Captain Gregory moved in from behind to kiss her again. He slowly moved his hand to the front of her negligee and caressed her breasts lightly. He tugged playfully at her negligee and peered inside as he kissed her neck. "You do have them," he said with relief.

"What did you expect?" asked Isabelle, smiling.

"I thought maybe you might have suckers."

"Oh, but they are suckers."

Captain Gregory swelled with desire. "Is that an invitation?"

"Why Captain Gregory, you *are* a gentleman. But you needn't ask when you already have permission."

One thing was certain about Captain Gregory. He rarely had to be told once, never twice. He had talked enough, it was time now to make a woman out of this seductive sea creature once and for all.

One thing was certain about Isabelle. When she wanted something, she rarely asked more than once, never twice. And because this was her first time, she was filled with anticipation and fear. If Captain Gregory didn't accept her invitation, she would not ask again. But if he did, she would make a man out of the jelly fisherman once and for all.

Captain Gregory kissed her lips and then slowly kissed her neck and moved toward her heaving breasts. With tremendous skill and precision that could only be born of experience, he deftly slipped her strap over one of her shoulders. He hesitated for a moment and looked into her eyes, just to let her know that he would be gentle and careful with her. Then he lowered his head...only to have it shoved unceremoniously away.

"Hey what's the big idea," he said, looking very surprised.

All of a sudden, Isabelle looked troubled. "I can't right now, Captain Gregory."

"Please, there's nothing to be afraid of," he reassured her.

Her face flushed with fear, she said, "It's not that. Something has happened—on the outside. My babies...they're gone!!" she said, quickly pulling the strap over her shoulder and hopping out of bed. She ran into the bathroom and a moment later, she came out fully dressed.

Even though Captain Gregory was very concerned about the baby queens, he couldn't help but notice that she had gotten dressed much more quickly that time. In that regard, Isabelle was no different than any other woman he had known.

The speed with which they got dressed was always related to the importance of the task at hand.

In a flash, Captain Gregory quickly buttoned his shirt, got out of bed, and headed for the door. "I'll send a special unit to go out and find them."

Twenty-One

Captain Gregory was alone in the war room while the others were taking an afternoon nap. They had been up late the night before, waiting for word about the mischievous baby queens who had run away from home. Captain Gregory had been up later than all of them, but he would not rest until the baby queens were found—if they were found. After all, he felt a little responsible; they had slipped away on his watch the night before, right in front of his troops, who had been trained to keep a watchful eye on the youngsters. While he was a bit upset about it, Isabelle was positively distraught. He had had several arguments with her earlier in the day, mostly about whether she would go out to look for the them herself or wait for the troops to locate them.

He lit his pipe and began to puff slowly, as if the pipe were the smokestack on some great steam locomotive beginning a long climb up a mountain. As he contemplated the whereabouts of the baby queens, the door suddenly flung open and

Dr. Bellwether and Claude stepped in, wearing only their night wear.

"We couldn't sleep knowing the little ones were in danger. Any news?" asked Claude.

"None."

"Where's Isabelle?" asked Dr. Bellwether.

"Isabelle is upset about the baby queens being gone. I should have never invited her back to my cabin. That's when they got loose."

Claude raised his eyebrows and glanced at Dr. Bellwether. "You didn't tell us that before."

"Yes, well, I left out that part of the story," said Captain Gregory.

"You slept with her?" asked Dr. Bellwether incredulously.

As soon as Dr. Bellwether asked the question, Captain Gregory knew that it was a mistake to have told them about his rendezvous with Isabelle. "Just because I invited a woman back to my cabin doesn't mean that I slept with her."

"You did sleep with her! How disgusting...was she any good?"

"Dr. Bellwether!" protested Claude.

"Hey, it's not every day that a man gets to sleep with a 100-foot-long octopussy."

"I told you I wouldn't know," insisted Captain Gregory.

"Oh, so she knocked you out."

"No, she didn't."

"Bit you with some venom? Maybe sprayed ink in your eyes? Then moved in for the kill." Dr. Bellwether smiled. He had caught Captain Gregory admitting to engaging in an action that was unthinkable. Well, maybe not unthinkable, but certainly inappropriate, outrageous, and disgusting.

Captain Gregory slowly, deliberately, clenched his fist. "No, let me explain as clearly as possible... It's none of your business!"

"Good for you, Mon Captain."

"Who's side are you on, Claude?" protested Dr. Bellwether.

"I am on the side of chivalry, my friend. And chivalry never plays kiss and tell."

Captain Gregory looked up at the display and pointed. "Uh-oh. We've got trouble."

Claude and Dr. Bellwether looked up. "What is it?" they asked.

"A red light over the port bow of Richard Pearlman's boat. The enemy has arrived. Claude, get on the cellcom and call Isabelle and Jane to the war room immediately."

Claude's voice reverberated throughout the complex. Moments later, Jane walked into the war room. "What's going on?" she asked, looking rather bleary eyed.

"The enemy is here," said Captain Gregory.

"What do we do?"

"First, we must find Isabelle. She must not leave the safety of the cave. Then we do nothing, for now."

The door opened and Isabelle entered quickly, looking very impatient. It had been too long, and she would not wait any longer. "I am going out to find my babies," she announced.

"It's too dangerous," said Captain Gregory. "Give the troops a chance to find them first."

"If it's too dangerous, it may be too late," said Isabelle. "We cannot afford to wait any longer."

"You are jeopardizing the entire colony if you leave the cave," said Captain Gregory.

"You don't understand, Captain Gregory. Without the baby queens, there is no colony."

"You can't leave now. You know it, and I know it. The enemy is here."

"Yes I know, and that is why I must find them before they do. I have made up my mind. Alert the troops, I am going out...now."

"I refuse."

"You are refusing an order from your commander-in-chief?"

"No, I am saying that if you crawl out of that entrance, I will resign. Because we are all as good as gone, anyway."

"For once, I have to agree with Captain Gregory," said Dr. Bellwether.

"Me too," said Claude.

"You too, Jane?"

She nodded her head slowly. "I know this must be unbearable for you, but it is for the best." She walked over to comfort Isabelle, who moved away.

Isabelle stomped her foot, startling Jane, who backed away. "That's not fair. I can't believe that you would abandon me at a time like this."

"You don't understand. We are not abandoning you, Isabelle," said Captain Gregory. "We are protecting you."

Isabelle looked at him with hysterical eyes, turned bright red, and stormed out of the war room, slamming the door behind her. Captain Gregory and his crew were speechless. It was the first time they had ever seen Isabelle lose control of her temper. Captain Gregory didn't know what to make of it, but he knew one thing for certain. The troops had better find the baby queens— and quick—before there were three queens on the loose.

THROUGH BINOCULARS, CRANSTON LOOKED over at the Coast Guard boat, hoping to divine the crew's intentions. He was angered by their presence, especially Richard Pearlman's, but he hadn't yet decided what to do about them.

There was too much to do right now, so he returned his attention to catching the big red. He would deal with them later.

Cranston looked down at the water, hoping to divine something more important—the location of the beast. The entire boat was a flurry of activity. Manuel was checking the water level in the tanks. The three sushi chefs that Mr. Oh had sent were readying the ice in the built-in freezers. Professor Holloway was busy putting on his wetsuit. Rhub was standing at the winch, awaiting Cranston's orders. And Cranston, who already had his wetsuit on, checked the gages on the oxygen tanks. Everything appeared to be in order.

"Lower the trap, Rhub," said Cranston. "And be careful. This time, no mistakes." Cranston nervously tapped his fingers on the side of the boat, anxious about their next attempt at killing the sea monster. It wasn't that he had suddenly felt pity for the beast. Quite the contrary. Nothing would have given him greater satisfaction then to tie the ugly beast down and bite it between the eyes, the way he had killed so many octopi as a teenager. It was the way she had looked at him before, as if she knew him, as if she were possessed by the ghost of Captain Gregory himself, who would no doubt try to thwart his efforts at capturing the beast. The conniving, old galley ghost; he would ruin everything. As he thought about the captain, the anger swept across his mind like a red tide, poisoning his attitude toward everyone and everything.

He slipped in his mouthpiece, mounted his spear gun to a shoulder harness, and slowly climbed down the ladder into the water, followed closely by Professor Holloway. They carefully guided the tarpaulin trap down toward the sea floor. When they got close, Professor Holloway pointed to the entrance to the cave in the distance. It was swarming with octopi. Cranston waved him off and pointed to the tarp. Better to set the trap and get out of there before they were inundated with the little eight-armed army.

Cranston quickly untied the bundle from the cable, and he and Holloway spread the tarpaulin trap out on the ocean floor. This time the crabs were already tied to the button eyes in the tarp, which made it much easier to set up the trap. They set it exactly as they had before, putting small blocks at the corners of the trap and then covering the entire surface with a thin layer of sand. One by one, they uncoiled the four cables attached to the corners of the trap. Each was brought vertically to the surface of the ocean and wrapped around a single buoy, allowing for at least another 25 feet of slack. The slack ends were drawn to the center of the square formed by the buoys and hooked to a center ring, which was attached by a central cable to the main winch.

As Cranston methodically set the trap, he thought about how he really didn't need Professor Holloway anymore. He had his money, and he could hardly stand his insufferable arrogance. He was expendable, really. His new client could pay a lot more for the prize, and they no doubt would be interested in the head too. In fact, he had heard Mr. Oh say as much. Perhaps he would tell Professor Holloway that he didn't want his money anymore, but then he would have to give back the down payment. Perhaps he would arrange for an accident. Or perhaps he would just welch on the deal. One thing was clear. The giant octopus would go to the highest bidder.

After the trap was set, Cranston pointed to go back to the boat and started to ascend. Professor Holloway indicated that he would explore around the island for the next 15 minutes. He swam away, going over to the cliffs to gather a few sea urchins in his net. As he did, he thought about what he would do if he were to come face to face with the giant. The best approach would be to simply observe her in her habitat. She didn't really pose any threat to him, unless he were to spontaneously grow eight arms and a hard shell. Then he'd be in plenty of trouble. He certainly didn't believe the poppycock Richard Pearlman had been spouting about her intelligence either. She was probably intelligent for an invertebrate, but that wasn't saying much. Professor Holloway chuckled as he swam further and further along the cliffs, away from the entrance of the cave and the boat.

He followed the cliffs, hoping to find another entrance to the cave where the giant octopus was no doubt hiding. Though she was not intelligent enough to match wits with man, she certainly wasn't dumb enough to be caught by the same trap twice. He was certain that if they were to catch their prize again, they would have to take her by stealth. If he could find a secret passage, perhaps they could send down a few of the deckhands with spear guns to dispatch her.

As he swam, he noticed that the sea floor was a beautiful mosaic of colorful sea flora, and it reminded him of a time when it was the pursuit of science, not money, that motivated him most. Something had changed along the way, though. It wasn't that the colors weren't as rich and vibrant as before—they were—and it wasn't that he didn't notice them anymore—he did. It was really more a matter of emphasis. The bright colors of the ocean just didn't hold his attention anymore. In fact, the only color that he was interested in was green, not forest green sea grass, nor lime green sea moss, not scintillating green fish, nor illuminated green eels, but plain green ink on paper denominations of presidents from bygone eras. Fame and fortune. That was what excited him the most.

He rounded the horn around the jut of land on one side of the island and looked at his watch. He would have to be turning back soon. There would be just enough time to see what was on the other side. He kept exploring every nook and cranny, but none were of any consequence. As he was about to turn around to go back to the boat, he noticed something in the distance moving and changing colors. He quickly swam over to the creature. As he got nearer, he realized that it was not one, but two octopuses crawling side by side along the ocean floor, two female specimens of the giant octopus! It was a stupendous find, if only he could catch them. After that, the crowning achievement would be the capture of the mother. That would make the discovery complete. Then he would have everything—the egg, the infants, and the head of the mother. With the infants in a tank of perfectly balanced, filtered water, and the head of the mother preserved safely in formaldehyde, he could dissect the mother and watch the infants develop in the lab at the same time.

At first, the octopuses did not appear to notice him as he swam up from behind. They were crawling along a stretch of wide open sand with few places to hide. Suddenly they paused, and he paused. Then they resumed swimming, and he resumed swimming. This happened several times, and each time they stopped, they turned various colors. The colors came in rapid fire, one in response to the other as if they were discussing what to do, like two females chattering away using light waves on some unknown invertebrate frequency. Holloway scoffed. Such a notion was impossible. They were only playing a game. One thing was certain, though; they had noted his presence and were keenly aware that his swimming pattern mirrored their own.

When they resumed swimming, he quietly pulled a nylon bag from his diving belt and opened it. He saw the trunk of a sea plant lying on the sea floor, scooped it up, and stuck it in the bag while keeping up the pace. He swam closer and closer, but they began to swim in opposite directions. He stopped swimming for a moment, hoping that the octopuses would do the same, but they were making a break for it swimming headfirst, full-throttle away from him. He would have to go after one and then the other.

He resumed swimming and quickly overtook the first octopus. Grabbing the stick from the bag, he stuck it out, touching her arms. She instinctively grabbed the object, and within moments he had thrown her into the bag and pulled it shut. Dark, heavy ink poured out of the bag, as Holloway quickly turned to catch the other octopus, who was leaving a telltale stretch of bubbles as she jettisoned through the water.

He quickly scooped up another stick, stuck it in his belt, and began to swim after her as fast as he could. It took a while to catch up to her, but finally she slowed down to a crawl. She stopped and turned toward him, bright red with anger. He approached slowly, extending the stick as if it were an olive branch. She slowly backed up to a rock and squeezed under it. He began to prod her arms with the stick, waiting for her to latch on. Come on, honey. I won't hurt you, he said to himself, looking her straight in the eye.

But she wasn't looking at him. She was looking past him, no doubt at the long shadow that was being caste by the clouds covering the sun above. Or was it the clouds? All of a sudden, Professor Holloway felt a presence behind him, and he realized that it wasn't the clouds that were casting the shadow from above. He turned around, and he nearly feinted when he saw it... He had never seen a real, live Architeuthis, but he knew from the size of the beast that indeed it was. He gulped hard, dropped the bag, and began to swim away.

In a whiplike motion, the giant squid extended its long arms and encircled Professor Holloway, and the teeth on the suckers ripped his wetsuit and sank into his flesh, taking hold. Professor Holloway tried to squeeze free, but it was useless. It was all a bad dream. If only he hadn't chased after those octopuses! Then he would have never met this terrible beast. A wave of panic swept over Professor Holloway like a Tsunami, and he scratched and kicked, all the while struggling to reach the knife in his diving belt. He was being shaken violently, and he could not get to it. Finally he succeeded and was about to stab the creature when another arm came by and batted the knife away. As the shaking subsided, Professor Holloway slowly watched the knife fall to the floor of the ocean along with his hopes of getting away. With his oxygen tanks hanging by a single strap, Professor Holloway's life dangled in the balance.

ARCHIE CLUTCHED HOLLOWAY WITH HIS RAZOR sharp arms and held him there for a moment, contemplating. Then he slowly brought him toward his gaping mouth, like a chocoholic bringing a chocolate candy to his mouth, fighting off the urge but losing. With all his might, he fought the temptation. He knew that he shouldn't eat this man, but not because he felt any pity. The man was a fisherman, and worse yet, he had caught him red-handed with the baby queens, about to destroy an entire colony. No, the real reason that he felt guilty was that he had been having far too many desserts as of late, and this one no doubt would make him feel bloated like all the others.

Soon temptation overcame Archie, and he slowly brought Professor Holloway into his gaping mouth, snapping the single strap holding the oxygen tanks and ripping his mouthpiece from his mouth.

Archie ate quietly, or at least as quietly as a giant squid can eat, all the while keeping an eye on the baby queen who was trying to open the bag to let out her sister.

CRANSTON LOOKED AT HIS WATCH AND SMILED. Professor Holloway's tanks were depleted by now and that could mean only one thing. There would be one less claim to the giant octopus. The loss of Professor Holloway had significantly simplified the transaction. There was now only one customer, a customer who had already invested a significant amount of money in the venture, and who was more or less at Cranston's mercy—not the other way around.

Cranston impatiently drummed his fingers on the race board of the hull, wondering why they had not gotten any bites. They had been there a full day now, and it would soon be nighttime. It was Rhub's turn to make the meal that night, so he would send Manuel down there, just to make sure that the trap was properly set.

He went forward to the bow where Manuel was checking the winching motor. "I want you to go down there and check the trap."

"Can't you send, Rhub, boss?"

"He's cooking tonight. You go."

"But boss, I can't."

"Why, you chicken or something?"

"No."

"Then go, and don't give me any more of your guff. And scout around a bit while you're down there. See if you can find another way into that cave."

"You think I'm crazy? I ain't goin' down there with no creepy, haunted devilfish," Manuel protested.

"Who says its haunted, anyway? Look, either you go down there, or I'm going to leave you behind. You got that straight?"

Manuel shook his head and mumbled a few words. He slowly put on a wetsuit, strapped on the tanks, inserted his orange mouthpiece, and checked his gages. He reluctantly climbed down the ladder attached to the hull of the boat and paused for a moment. Before plunging into the water, he blessed himself three times and looked up at the sky to say a quick prayer.

There was still enough sunlight to see everything, so he put his flashlight in his belt. After adjusting the spear gun strapped to his shoulder, he went down to check on the trap. He noticed a few small octopi swimming around him, watching his every move, and it gave him the creeps. Everything was in order. He thought about swimming back up to the boat, but he knew that there would be trouble if he came back that soon. So he swam away from the trap, which was attracting more and more attention from the octopuses in the area. He soon realized that he was the one who was attracting the attention, and so, he swam away as fast as he could, leaving the octopuses behind.

He swam around for a while, every once in a while doing a full circle to see if anyone—no, anything—was following him. Eventually he got more comfortable and adventurous, and he turned the corner around the cliffs. Taking a knife out of his pouch, he dug under some rocks for a while. He smiled when he found some abalone and stuffed his pouch full.

In search of more abalone, he swam around the small island but found no more. After a while, he checked his gages. Time to go back. Since he was at the end of the island, he would go back the other way just to see what was on the other side of the island.

As he rounded the bend, he nearly feinted when he saw a huge, monstrous beast about fifty yards away from the sea cliffs, trying to get at something hidden behind a rock. It hadn't seen him, and he quickly swam past it. As he swam away hurriedly, he ran into a rock jutting from the sea cliffs. Looking back to see if the beast was following, he nearly swallowed his Adam's apple as the beast began to whirl around. Manuel quickly ducked into a nearby cave. The beast began to swim toward the cave, and so Manuel went in deeper and deeper until the cave was so narrow he could barely pass through. He would be safe there, as long as his oxygen held out.

He turned on his flashlight and looked at his gages. He would have to leave the cave soon to get back to the boat, but to leave now would be disastrous. So, he turned on his flashlight and went deeper and deeper into the cave in hopes that it would lead to the other side of the island. As he pressed on, he was relieved to see the small, guppy-sized fish that greeted him. It was nice to be out of the land of the giants.

He followed one curve after another and made it through several rather tight squeezes, holding his breath to get by. Finally, he made it to a point where the cave split. He shined the flashlight in both directions, but neither tunnel would give up its secrets. One might lead to the open sea, the other to a cave of no return.

He had grown tired of squishing and squeezing through the narrow, winding tunnel so he chose the tunnel that appeared to have a widening in the distance twenty yards away. As he approached the opening to what appeared to be another much larger cave, he got a bad feeling about it and thought about turning around. He checked his gages again. Only ten minutes left. He would have to exit through the large cave ahead. His flashlight dimming, he tapped on it until the light brightened.

With his light showing the way, he swam into the cave and immediately froze—there at the other end was a large, ominous figure. His first instinct was to go back where he came from, but there was no time for that. She just sat there looking at him, studying him, deciding what to do next. Manuel knew how even the largest octopuses could slip and slide through the smallest of crevices. There would be no use in hiding. If she wanted to get to him, she could. He could shoot her with the spear gun, but if he didn't get her right between the eyes, she would surely kill him. She had not budged though, and it seemed to Manuel that as long as he did not move, she would not either. So he watched her, studied her, and tried to figure out his next move. As if by divine inspiration, an idea came to him, and he slowly blessed himself three times.

ISABELLE, CAPTAIN GREGORY, AND HIS CREW were riveted to the image of Manuel treading water at the other side of the cave, his flashlight flooding the water with light.

"Hold your fire," said Captain Gregory. "That's Manuel."

"I don't care if it's the Archbishop of Canterbury," said Dr. Bellwether. "You've got to get rid of him."

"I'm waiting for your decision, Captain Gregory," said Isabelle. "And I can't wait much longer. If he reaches for the spear gun, we will have no alternative but to rip him to shreds."

Captain Gregory was stunned by talk of disposing of his good friend. "You can't do that," he said, lightly pounding on the console. "Manuel is a good man."

"He may be a good man," said Dr. Bellwether. "But he is also a good fisherman, and they are a barbaric, spineless, ruthless bunch of squid eaters."

"That's enough, Dr. Bellwether," said Captain Gregory.

"Hitting a little too close to home?"

"No."

"Oh, I think so. Your problem is that you haven't decided whose side you are really on. Tell us, Captain Gregory, are you one of us, or are you one of them?"

Captain Gregory frowned. "What do you mean by that? I am a fisherman, of course."

"That's not what I am talking about. Come on, you have to choose. What are you, *fish* or *man*?"

Arms folded defiantly, yet clearly flustered, Captain Gregory said, "I was a fisherman, now I'm...I'm...All right already, I am a fish."

"Then you know what you have to do. Liquidate him," said Dr. Bellwether.

Claude was puzzled. "But how can we liquidate him if he's already in water?"

"That's *French* for kill him, you nincompoop," said Dr. Bellwether.

"There is no need for names," said Claude.

"Wait," said Jane. "He's getting something out of his pouch."

"It's a trick," said Dr. Bellwether. "Do something while you have the chance."

Isabelle looked at Captain Gregory, waiting for instructions. "Don't do anything," he said. "He's reaching for his abalone pouch. He's going to feed us, not kill us." They could see Manuel pulling a white substance from his pouch and putting it on the rock where the Queen had fed so many times before.

Dr. Bellwether threw his hands in the air. "Oh come on, this is not 'Guess Who's Coming to Dinner'. It's 'Guess Who's Going to be Dinner'! If we take the bait, he's going to kill us."

"Will you please shut up, Dr. Bellwether!" said Captain Gregory. He turned to Isabelle. "Now, project me onto your skin in neon lights with the words, 'Do not be afraid. It's me, Captain Gregory. I am alive in her. She will not hurt you.'"

"I am doing this right now," said Isabelle. Manuel dropped the abalone and stared at them. He blessed himself three more times.

"Now," said Captain Gregory, "slowly move away from the mouth of the cave, circle around the perimeter opposite Manuel, and head toward the abalone." As she did this, they could see Manuel slowly make his way opposite them to the front of the cave. In their field of view, they could see the Queen wave an arm. Just before he left the cave, Manuel waved back and then quickly swam out of the mouth of the cave.

"You did it," said Jane.

"Thank you," said Captain Gregory.

"Your welcome," said Isabelle.

"It was the right thing to do," said Claude. "I always say that one good turn deserves another."

"We shall see," said Dr. Bellwether. "We shall see."

Twenty-Two

---⊕---

Cranston waited impatiently on the side deck, nervously drumming his fingers on the gunwale, looking for bubbles to surface by the ladder on the port side of the boat. It was twilight now, and he was irritable, not having caught the mighty beast. Rhub had just finished getting dinner ready and had come up from the galley. The Japanese were playing cards on the foredeck. Holloway was gone. And now, where was Manuel? He would need a few deck hands to help him finish the job before double-crossing them all out of their money. Finally, a few bubbles came to the surface, followed by a few more, then many, and Manuel surfaced. As he climbed the ladder, his face was sheet-white, his hands shook, and he blessed himself three times.

"What's wrong with you? You look like you've seen a ghost," said Cranston, half wondering if Captain Gregory had come back as a blood-thirsty, bedeviled galley ghost out for revenge.

Manuel sat down and took off his goggles. "Nothing," he said, shuddering, holding his hands behind his back.

Cranston's eyes narrowed. Whenever he was lying, Manuel always held his hands behind his back, like a small child concealing pocket change. "Did you check on the trap?"

"Yes, it was fine."

"Did you see anything? Did you see the giant octopus?"

"No, just the little ones."

"And you didn't see the mother?"

"I just told you, I didn't see her."

"Listen here, you big smartass, just answer the questions."

"Did you find another door into the cave?"

"No."

Cranston knew Manuel was lying. When it came to lying, Cranston himself was an expert in the field. He had elevated the lie to magnificent heights, to unparalleled beauty, to an art form. He had gotten so that he could tell a lie exactly the same way that he told the truth, except that his lies sounded more like the truth than the truth itself. It was his greatest strength.

When it came to lying, Manuel was an amateur and like all amateurs, he was pretty transparent. It wasn't the lie that intrigued Cranston, though; it was the motivation behind it. Why had Manuel lied to him, other than the fact that he was a dirty, good-for-nothing wetback? Maybe the ghost of Captain Gregory had possessed his soul and conspired with him to sabotage the expedition. Maybe Manuel was planning on capturing the beast himself, now that he knew where to find her.

Whatever the reason, Cranston wasn't going to let him off the hook. "You're lying."

"No I am not, Senõr."

"Bull. You always hold your hands behind your back when you are lying, and I'm telling you, you're lying."

"I'm telling you the truth, Senõr. There is no secret passage into the cave. The only way to get to the octopus is to head in through the mouth."

The conversation caught Rhub's attention. "The mouth?" he asked. "Now why would a feller' want to stick his head in the mouth of an octopus?"

Cranston looked at his shiphand with contempt. "No, you idiot! The mouth of the cave!" he shouted. Red in the face, he turned to Manuel, puffed his chest out, and slammed his fist on the gunwale. "Now, I know you saw something, Manuel, so out with it."

"I did see something. But it was not another door. And it was not the giant octopus."

"Then what was it? We don't have all day," said Cranston. Manuel hesitated. "Out with it man. Or out with you," said Cranston, pointing his finger at him.

"It was a giant squid," said Manuel, putting his fingertips together in front of him as if he were about to pray.

"You're joking," said Rhub.

"No, it is the truth."

Cranston's eyes widened. He waited for Manuel's hands to slip behind his back, but they never did. He stared at Manuel squarely in the eyes. "Now we're getting somewhere. How big, and where did you see it?"

"About 100-feet long, on the other side of the island."

Cranston laughed. "A giant squid! Who would have guessed it. This is the best fishing hole in the world, and I'm the only one who knows it," he said, slapping the railing. "Disconnect the winch and head over to the other side of the island, Manuel."

"But, boss, what about the octopus?" asked Rhub.

"She's not going anywhere. We'll get back to her after I catch me a giant squid. Rhub, get the harpoon ready, and put together some bait."

"But what do giant squid eat?"

Cranston looked at his unwanted Japanese guests who were looking into the water, and, for a fleeting moment, the thought of using them as bait crossed his mind. "I don't know, tie a few crabs together and put a mirror on the bait bundle to catch his attention. We'll try to lure him to the surface."

Cranston cupped his hands. "You three," he shouted. The Japanese turned around. "Yea, you, No. 1, No. 2, and No. 3! Get the lights ready! Maybe the lights will attract it. Squid are attracted to lights." The Japanese bowed their heads and immediately went to get the lights.

"I hear tell a giant squid can swallow you up in one gulp," said Rhub.

"That's probably what happened to Professor Holloway," said Manuel, relieved that Cranston had turned his attention away from him.

"And of course you know that they glow in the dark," said Rhub. "Kind of creepy. In fact, super creepy."

Cranston sighed heavily with exasperation. He had no time for nonsense. "All right, that's enough."

"Super double-duper creepy!" said Rhub, determined to squeeze one more in before his boss blew a fuse.

"I said that's enough!" shouted Cranston. "Now you shut up, Rhub, and you put it in gear, Manuel, on the double." The anchor went up, and Manuel fired up the engines. The boat lurched forward and they slowly headed toward the end of the island.

BELOW DECK, RICHARD PEARLMAN, NANCY, and a few other students heard the whaling boat's giant engines turn over. This was followed by the sounds of shuffling feet as many students moved to the starboard side on deck, cheering, even taunting as the larger boat pulled closer.

Richard Pearlman, who knew Cranston's temper first-hand, rushed up the stairs with Nancy, waving his hands and shouting, "Be quiet!"

There was so much noise and confusion, though, that many of the students did not hear him. "Please, be quiet!!" he shouted again. "Do not provoke them. We have not won. They will not give up that easily. They will be back, I guarantee it." His second plea had a much greater impact, but by the time the students had quieted down, it was too late.

As he slowly went by, Cranston angrily shook his fist and yelled, "You ain't seen the last of me yet!! Gun the engines, Manuel." Manuel looked straight ahead, as if he hadn't heard the command. "I said, gun the engines," yelled Cranston at the top of his lungs, but there was no response again. Cranston quickly ran to the control console, pushed Manuel out of the way, and shoved the starboard and port engine throttles full forward. The front end of the whaler nearly lifted out of the water, and the Japanese fell out of their seats. The ocean churned white suds behind them as they sped by the Coast Guard boat. As he looked back, Cranston smiled with satisfaction as a series of large waves headed straight for them.

Richard Pearlman and his students braced themselves, holding onto the rub rail, sheer line, gunwale, cabin rail, and anything else they could get there hands on. As the waves hit, the boat rocked violently, and they all held on for dear life. Though the coast guard vessel did not capsize, several of the students fell over the starboard side, and were thrashing in the water. Several others cut themselves crashing into various objects onboard.

As the boat began to settle in the water, there were many calls for help. Richard Pearlman threw several life preservers into the water, and the victims latched on very quickly. With some help, he reeled them in, pulling them up and over the side of the boat and onto the deck, like waterlogged slugs, while Nancy attended the students who had cuts. After everyone had been helped and all were accounted for, the noise, confusion, and hysteria was transformed into a low din, and finally into an uneasy quiet.

Richard Pearlman breathed a heavy sigh of relief as he looked at his students reproachfully. "Let that be a lesson to all of us. This fisherman is crazy, and you must always treat a crazy fisherman with the utmost respect. Apparently he would think nothing of capsizing our boat and leaving us here to perish."

AS HE APPROACHED THE CAVE, ARCHIE KNEW from the white, frothy water at the surface that a boat had recently left the vicinity. He wasn't particularly interested in it, and he was only mildly interested in the small vessel anchored about fifty yards from the mouth of the cave. It had no fishing nets out, and so, he decided he would leave the boat alone. Besides, he had more important things to do, like return the mischievous baby queens who had eluded their mother and an entire army for a day.

Archie couldn't understand how the two had slipped out from under the watchful eyes of their mother. Then again, there were many things that Archie couldn't understand about the female of the species—any species. One thing was for sure. He would not tell her that her babies had nearly ended up in a net. They were safe now, and there was no reason to worry her. There was also no reason to upset her about the lovely little snack he had made of the fisherman. Admissions like that always seemed to upset her greatly. Females were funny that way.

As he approached the cave, a sea of small octopuses parted to either side, hovering and drifting together like a massive web of cephalopod flesh. He entered the cave and looked at the Queen who had been watching him intently. He turned a warm yellow that got brighter and brighter and then faded like a great sunset being swallowed by the sea. Slowly he unfurled two tentacles, revealing two squirming baby queens, and brought them to their mother.

In response, the Queen slowly turned a warm yellow that got brighter and brighter, as if Archie's inner light had penetrated her soul and she was reflecting it back on him, on her baby queens, on her troops, and on the entire sea world to see. She took the baby queens from Archie, gently winding her arms around them, bringing them up to her adoring eyes, and then hiding them under her mantle for protection. She was so happy that they were safe. There would be plenty of time to scold later.

The yellow glow faded, and she returned to her normal pink. One of her many huge arms encircled Archie while another scratched in his favorite location. A third arm began to tickle him gently. That was the great advantage of having so many arms. You could hug, hold, scratch, and tickle all at the same time. It was the least she could do for having her precious children returned. The two rolled around in a slow-motion loving sea ballet that lasted for a long while.

"THANK GOODNESS, THEY'RE HOME," SAID A much-relieved Captain Gregory, looking up at the display in the war room. Moments later his confidence, which had been severely shaken, returned, and he turned to Isabelle. "I knew there was nothing to worry about. Just the same, I'm glad it's over." It was over, both the search for the missing children and the protracted battle over what to do about it. They embraced, and he all but resisted the strong urge to kiss her at that moment, save to give her a gentle peck on the cheek. If there was one thing he had learned about women, it was that they were unable to switch gears as quickly as men. They both felt joy and ecstasy after the return of the children, but he alone felt that irresistible urge returning now that the danger was over.

She literally glowed, warming his soul and attracting him as surely as the sun warms the planets and pulls them into her orbit.

She shared her innermost thoughts with him, quietly whispering in his ear, though no one else was there, until he was quite intoxicated with her voice. There she was standing there, a lovely, sensuous sea siren, and he a salty seaman listening to that lovely voice, each word a song of herself. It was only propriety that held him back now, like a caged animal trying to break loose. Propriety be hanged, he was going to give her a kiss that she would not soon forget, not this century or the next. He moved in to give her a real kiss this time...

Suddenly, the door flung open again, and he reluctantly backed away. It was the others, in their night wear. "We couldn't sleep," said Jane. She looked up at the display and saw the baby queens playing under their mother's close supervision. "They're home!" she cried.

Archie was there too, ever-present, hovering nearby and watching the youngsters like a proud uncle. "Well, I'll be," said Dr. Bellwether. "Look at what the Giant Squid dragged in!"

"You can all go back to bed now," said Captain Gregory. "I'm happy to report that the baby queens have been rescued."

"Well, that's a relief they were found," said Dr. Bellwether.

"I am so glad," said Claude.

They were all busy celebrating, except Jane who was looking at the display, admiring Archie's lights blinking on and off in amazing kaleidoscopic patterns. "What is he saying?" she asked.

"He says that he found my children on the other side of the island. He also said that he saw a small boat nearby but left it alone," said Isabelle.

Jane seemed a bit disturbed by the news. She got up from her chair and began to pace slowly about the war room.

"He won't harm them," said Isabelle. "You needn't worry about that. I promise you."

Jane shook her head. "Oh, I'm not worried about Richard. He can take care of himself. It's your friend that I am concerned about. I think you should tell him to leave at once. He is in grave danger if he stays here. The fisherman's boat may be back any time now."

"You're right. But if I tell him this, he will be sure to stay," said Isabelle.

"No, you must not tell him about the boat at all," said Jane. "You must simply tell him that you want to be alone with your children."

The smile that had been plastered on Isabelle's face since the return of her children crumbled away. This advise seemed to greatly upset her. "I can't lie to him; he's my friend," she protested.

"Then just ask him to leave," said Jane. She went over to Isabelle and placed a hand on her shoulder. "Look, I know that it is hard to turn him away, especially at a time like this. It was hard for me to turn Richard away, but you must."

Captain Gregory waved his hands. "No, no, no. That is precisely why we should tell him about the boat, so that he can help protect Isabelle."

Isabelle thought for a moment. "This is not a military decision; this is a personal decision. So, I alone must make it."

"This *is* a military decision. He would make a great ally. I think it would be a great mistake not to tell him," Captain Gregory said.

Isabelle took Captain Gregory by the hand. "You are always looking out for my best interests, and I am deeply grateful. But I cannot jeopardize my friend's life to save my own. I don't know how I will ask him to leave but I must." She gave Captain Gregory a kiss on the cheek and left the room.

⊕ ⊕ ⊕

THEY HAD BEEN TRADING LIGHTS IN A glorious display, laughing and enjoying each other's company, the way they always did. All of a sudden, the Queen's demeanor changed. She did not flash-respond; she did not tear off into wild mosaic patterns; and she did not reflect color sequences. She merely turned yellow, the universal color of love, and asked him to leave without an explanation. Archie's kaleidoscopic color changes slowed and then turned into a pattern of triangles, the squid equivalent of befuddlement and misunderstanding. He turned to the Queen and looked at her, his bright inquisitive eyes attempting to divine the reason for the abrupt request to leave, but none was forthcoming.

Please do not ask me why, only know that you go with the love and affection of a Queen, her subjects, her children, and her colony, she communicated to him. Archie gently rubbed the baby queens and looked at his friend. Deeply offended, hurt and upset, he turned blue and headed toward the mouth of the cave. The Queen waved, but Archie did not look back. At that moment, if an octopus could have shed tears, she would have. Isabelle, though, had no trouble crying on the inside as she watched her dear friend leave the cave.

As he left the cave, Archie suddenly felt very depressed, and whenever he felt depressed, he could think of only one thing, food. So it was a welcome sight when he saw several crabs bunched together on the sea floor. He went over to investigate. Finding them to be of reasonable size, he quickly grabbed them with his sharp tentacles, but the crabs were somehow attached to the sea floor. Archie pulled the crabs and the tarpaulin up off the sea floor, but the crabs remained attached to the tarp. So he did the only thing he could do. He popped the crabs into his mouth and with one powerful bite, bit clean through the tarpaulin. One gulp later, he went on his way.

✦ ✦ ✦

LATER THAT NIGHT, AFTER RETURNING FROM their giant squid hunt, the entire crew had gone to bed, except Manuel. He walked about the boat, checking to see if everyone had fallen asleep during his watch. As he made his rounds, he was greeted by an odd symphony of the somnolent sounds of snoring. When he was sure that everyone had been rocked asleep, Manuel made his move. He quickly put on his wetsuit, saddled up a set of oxygen tanks, and lowered himself into the water. With his head above water, he slowly swam over to the Coast Guard boat.

As he climbed the ladder, he looked up and saw that a hand was extended. He grabbed hold of it and was pulled aboard. On deck were several students and Richard Pearlman, whom Manuel recognized immediately.

"Well, this is certainly a surprise," said Richard Pearlman. He gestured to one of the students, who handed Manuel a cup of hot cider.

"Gracias."

"Now suppose you tell us why you have come."

He took a sip and looked at Richard Pearlman. "I have come to help you. I do not want to kill the beast."

Richard Pearlman looked at Manuel suspiciously. "Tell me, what has made you change your mind?"

"It would be bad luck to kill the beast," said Manuel. The students were looking at him as if they did not believe a word he was saying, and a few of them said as much. "And the man I work for, he is a son-of-a-bitch," Manuel added, twirling his thumbs behind his back nervously.

Richard Pearlman glared at his students and then turned to Manuel. "There is no other reason?" he asked.

"Yes," said Manuel. "There is. Tell me, Professor, do you believe in ghosts?"

Richard Pearlman smiled knowingly. "That depends, Manuel, on what kind of ghosts you are talking about."

"I know this sounds crazy. But the octopus spoke to me. She told me that my old boss, Captain Gregory is living inside her. Crazy, no?"

Several students began to laugh at Manuel's suggestion, but Richard Pearlman was quick to raise his hands to hush them. "I believe that anything is possible, Manuel. So, if what you say is true, and if you are on our side, what can you do to help us?"

"I know a secret passage way to the cave."

Richard Pearlman leaned forward. "You mean, we can get to the cave another way?"

"Yes. It is on the other side of the island," said Manuel.

"That could come in handy. Could you draw us a map?"

"I can do better than that. I can show you."

Richard Pearlman looked over at the whaler, looming large in the night. "Yes, that would be good, but shouldn't you be getting back to your ship before the others find out you are gone?"

Manuel placed his hands together in supplication. "I do not want to go back. Do you have room for one more?"

Several of the students protested. "Are we going to let him aboard without even searching him?" one asked.

Manuel finished taking off his wetsuit and held up his hands. The student looked over at Richard Pearlman, who nodded his permission to search Manuel. The search turned up nothing special, except a few soggy rabbit's feet. "See," said Manuel. "No tricks. No trouble. I promise. You take me aboard, yes?"

"Why not? Welcome aboard, Manuel," said Richard Pearlman.

"Thank you, Senõr," said Manuel, and he blessed himself three times and smiled.

Twenty-Three

That morning, the second day since their arrival, Cranston looked out over the port bow at the small Coast Guard boat in the distance. Manuel was gone, completely disappeared. Cranston suspected that Manuel had gone over to the enemy, but he couldn't prove it. Even with binoculars, he had not been able to spot Manuel on deck.

That wasn't his only problem. Several of the cables attached to the trap had become entangled, so Cranston ordered Rhub to pull up the entire apparatus. To their surprise, not only was the bait gone, but the tarpaulin had been severely torn in what appeared to be a first-rate case of sabotage. "Those dirty rotten little octopussy lovers. I'll get them for this. We'll see how they like it when I sink their lousy boat," said Cranston as he began to turn the crank to pull up anchor.

He smiled at the thought of ramming and sinking the Coast Guard boat. He would head over slowly so as not to raise suspicions, and at the last moment, he would gun the old whaler's engines and slice the boat in two. The people inside the cabin wouldn't even know what hit them as they sank to the bottom of the sea, destined to be shark bait. Cranston laughed at the notion. It was, after all, vicious. Just the way he liked it.

Rhub approached him with the trap and spread it out on the floor. "Take a look at the hole in this tarp, boss."

Cranston stopped pulling up the anchor for a moment and looked. Along the edge of the toe were evenly spaced teeth marks, too big for an octopus. "What happened here, Rhub?"

"Got me boss."

Cranston wasn't sure either, but one thing was for sure. He was disappointed, even irritated that Rhub had shown him the evidence. It meant that those squid-loving land-lubbers hadn't destroyed the trap after all, and that meant there was no reason to ram their boat. But Cranston decided that he wouldn't let that stop him. Professor Pearlman had let the beast go free, and the students had been a nuisance ever since they had arrived. Then there was that double-crossing wetback, Manuel. Besides, the sheer thrill of the kill was reason enough to do away with the do-gooders. Nothing would start his day off better.

As he stepped up to the control console, Cranston stopped and looked through binoculars at the Coast Guard boat. No one was up yet, or so it seemed. It would be the perfect time to attack. Cranston started the engines, keeping his eye on the Coast Guard boat at all times. He figured that Manuel had gone over to the enemy, but he wanted the satisfaction of knowing for sure before sinking it. Just as he was about to put the old whaler in gear, he had his proof: Manuel's orange mouthpiece laying amongst some gear in the corner of the Coast Guard boat. Undoubtedly, he would tell Richard Pearlman everything he knew. That was some gratitude for you. If only he could find out what Manuel knew... Cranston let the engines idle for a while as he thought about his next move. Suddenly, he shut them off. He would let Manuel, the Professor, and his land-lubber friends go this time. They might lead him to the secret passageway to the big red.

Before that could happen, he had to take care of yet another problem that had just gotten worse. He was short-handed, and he would need to go ashore to round up more men. With more men, it wouldn't be necessary to set a trap, and it wouldn't be necessary for the beast to come to him. He would go to the beast.

CAPTAIN GREGORY PUFFED ON HIS PIPE AS HE looked up at the display and discussed strategy with Dr. Bellwether and Claude. That morning, Jane was helping Isabelle pick out accessories for her evening dresses, so that she could dress more appropriately. It seemed almost unimaginable that someone as talented in the fine art of camouflage, more talented then any chameleon could ever hope to be, could be so poor at color coordinating her outfits. Even Captain Gregory had noticed the odd assortment of colors that Isabelle was given to wearing, and he was certainly no fashion king himself.

Things were unusually quiet that morning, and that troubled Captain Gregory. The large, ominous whaling boat was still there, but there had been no sign of Cranston or his men, except when they came down to set the trap, a completely futile effort. Didn't Cranston realize that they were too smart for a fisherman's trap, especially one that had been used before?

These thoughts were soon interrupted by Dr. Bellwether. "I think we should enlist Archie to help us out," he said.

"No," said Captain Gregory. "Isabelle said she wanted to leave him out of it."

"But we can't just sit here and do nothing. We're sitting ducks. If we do nothing, sooner or later they will kill her. And where does that leave us?"

"What if we sabotaged the boat? You know, put sand in the intake, drain the gasoline, or tie the anchor around a rock," suggested Claude.

Captain Gregory smiled at Claude. "No, you forget my friend. We don't want them to stay. We want them to go."

"Oh, you are right, mon ami. My apologies."

Captain Gregory waved at Claude reassuringly. "That's all right, Claude. The same thought occurred to me."

"Then what do *you* suggest," asked Dr. Bellwether.

"We do nothing, except wait. And watch."

"This waiting game is driving me crazy," said Dr. Bellwether.

"Then go back to your lab and do something to take your mind off it," said Captain Gregory, calmly puffing on his pipe.

"I can't. All I can think about is that crazy fisherman and his bloodthirsty crew. Can't we do anything?"

"When the time comes to do something, you will know it, I assure you, Dr. Bellwether."

Dr. Bellwether wrinkled his nose. "Okay, you're the captain, but I think you're making a big mistake."

Captain Gregory stoked his pipe. "My dear Dr. Bellwether, I would be truly worried, if you didn't think so," he said, his eyes twinkling.

Dr. Bellwether turned up his nose and headed for the door. "Come on Claude, let's go *do* something down in the lab. I've had all I can take of this do-nothing attitude for one day."

Captain Gregory looked up at the display and saw that the red light was off, meaning that the boat had left. Sure enough, there was no boat showing on the overall map of the area, except the Coast Guard boat. "There is no need to *do* anything," said Captain Gregory.

"Why is that?" asked Dr. Bellwether as he stood at the door.

"Because the fishermen's boat just left."

THE SEA WAS GENTLE AND THE WIND WAS CALM as Richard Pearlman looked out toward the horizon, watching the sun setting in the western sky like a giant orange ball partially submerged in a cosmic ocean, and wondering where Cranston and crew had gone in such a hurry and when they would return.

His concentration was broken by several students who were pointing behind him. "Professor Pearlman, she's come back," said one. All of a sudden, two huge arms jutted out of the sea, then three more, twisting and turning until together they made the sign of peace just behind where some students were sitting. When they saw the sign, they let out a collective gasp.

The Queen slowly surfaced and Richard Pearlman literally beamed as he said, "Well, isn't this a pleasant surprise." The students sat on deck quietly, mesmerized by the tantalizingly long arms, the imposing head, and the large, gentle eyes. Not a sound could be heard, except the lapping of the waves, and the creaking of the boat. The students were amazed, mystified. Many exclaimed their surprise; others began to take notes. All were quiet as they watched, listened, and learned once again.

"Richard, I am here," were the bright yellow words emblazoned on her mantle.

Richard Pearlman smiled. It was Jane. "Ah, my darling, you came back."

"No, Richard, I never left. We have brought you something." The Queen lifted an arm and handed Richard Pearlman a large crab that had just been caught. He gave it to one of the students, who placed it into a pot on deck and brought it into the kitchen.

"I wish there was something that I could give you, but it seems that you have everything you need now that you are a woman of the sea."

"No you are wrong about that, my darling. I don't have you."

"Yes, I suppose you are right. It's really quite hopeless, isn't it?"

"No, never say that."

"But it is. You know that we can never be together. Not like before."

"We are together right now. There is a beautiful sunset. Let's enjoy that and not torture ourselves."

"Yes but I can't even touch you. I can't even hold your hand."

"Wait a second, dear, Isabelle is telling me something. There may be a way."

"Oh, come on," said Richard Pearlman, shaking his head.

"No, there is, and Isabelle is going to help us. She's really quite a wonderful woman."

"I'm sure she is."

"You must trust me on this. I will extend my hand, and then we can hold hands."

"Yes, but how?" asked Richard Pearlman, his forehead wrinkling. "You mean an arm. You'll extend an arm."

"You'll see. But you must realize that it will feel cold and slimy on the outside. But I can assure you that it is quite warm and dry on the inside."

The Queen puffed up her mantle until she looked to be as big as a house. She then projected the image of Jane upon her mantle.

"Amazing!" said Richard Pearlman. "You weren't kidding." Many of the students backed away, frightened, but he reassured them that there was nothing to fear. Jane smiled at him and winked at him with her left eye and then her right, as only she could do. As he looked at her, he was amazed that not a single mannerism was different about her. It was absolutely uncanny.

"Do you trust me."

"Yes, I am ready," he said, not knowing what would happen and not certain that he was ready. Slowly but surely Jane's arm, the one that was merely a projection, took three-dimensional shape and began to actually extend from the Queen's mantle! "Whoa, what's happening," exclaimed Richard Pearlman, putting his hands up to his cheeks.

"Do not be afraid, my darling. This is merely a granulation."

"You're joking."

"No, I am quite serious. You remember the granulations that we studied in the lab?"

"Yes, I know what a granulation is. A projection from the skin of a cephalopod used to complement a perfect system of camouflage. But I have never, ever, seen a granulation that was as large as this, as defined as this. It even seems to have rudimentary muscular control."

"Yes, it's great, isn't it?"

"But how can that be?"

"I don't know...Isabelle do you know?... She's not sure how she does it either. She only knows that she can do it. Now are you going to take my hand or not?"

"Oh, yes. It's just the total surprise, you understand," said Richard Pearlman, quickly recovering.

"Of course. But please don't be afraid."

"Afraid? Afraid?! Why should I be afraid of an eight-armed one-hundred foot long, multi-faceted woman like yourself," he said, laughing.

"Well, if you feel that way."

"No, I was only joking. You had a sense of humor, remember?"

"Oh, you're right. It's just that in my current state, you can understand me feeling somewhat vulnerable."

"Yes, of course, my dear. But don't you worry, we are here to help you, to protect you, and to..."

"Yes?"

"Well, to love you," said Richard Pearlman. He slowly took her "hand" and kissed it as the students watched in awe. The Queen came in closer so Jane's arms could reach over the gunwale of the Coast Guard boat. Turning around, Richard Pearlman wrapped them around his waist, and they both watched as the sun slowly dipped into the ocean.

For a moment, it seemed as if he and Jane were the only two on the planet. That feeling was soon shattered, however, when they saw a boat in the distance. "You must go soon," said Richard Pearlman. "There is a boat in the distance."

"We see it. I wish they would all go away, all except yours."

"I feel the same way."

"This has been a wonderful night."

"Yes it has. I thought I had lost you, and now I have found you again."

"Our first date together."

"I never in a hundred years would have thought it was possible."

"Yes, but Isabelle says that we should never give up hope."

"Why is that?"

"Because anything is possible."

As the sun set in the ocean, Richard Pearlman made a wish, took a deep breath, and said, "For the first time in a long time, I believe that you are right."

Twenty-Four

The Queen had not been able to go to sleep since the return of the fishermen's boat the night before. The baby queens were sleeping peacefully, two of their arms interlocked with each other. It was their way of holding hands, and it was the only way that they could get to sleep since the "bad man" had stuffed one of them into a bag. With the baby queens asleep, the Queen took advantage of her free time and rummaged around the cave looking for a hiding place for them, a place small enough and safe enough so that if her life was in danger, she could ensure that the colony would survive.

As she surveyed the cracks in the wall of the cave, she stole a glance at the lovely bouquet of flowers her troops had given her after the return of the baby queens. It was a matter of honor. They had not measured up to the confidence that the Queen had placed in them, and they had let her down. This was their way of saying that they were sorry, each and every one of them.

It was multicolored, composed of many varieties of sea flowers, and beautiful to behold and be held. The entire arrangement of flowers was thatched together, like an intricately woven needle stitch. In the center was a cylindrical, metallic object that looked vaguely familiar to her. But she could not quite put her tentacle on it. The entire piece looked like a colorful chandelier. She toyed with the idea of somehow hanging it from the ceiling of her home but decided instead that it looked more like the centerpiece to a fine dinner table. So she placed it on the large rock that had been her venerable place of fine dining these past few centuries.

The Queen turned away from the dinner table and continued the business of finding a suitable hole in the wall. She checked on the large holes filled with the exoskeletons of previous unsuspecting dinnertime visitors, but concluded that these, though quite comfortable and familiar, were too spacious. Too easy for the enemy to gain access.

She looked under a rock and thought about digging an underground hideaway, but she soon abandoned the idea after remembering that the sea floor was too silty to provide any kind of sturdy construction.

She had poured over every inch of every wall. She then moved up to the ceiling and began a thorough survey of it. As she scrutinized every inch, the rough lines of the ceiling reminded her of the rough lines on Captain Gregory's face. She turned somewhat red with embarrassment as she realized that everywhere she went, everything she did, everyone she met reminded her of him. It was at that moment that she realized that her better half, Isabelle, was utterly infatuated with him. No, Isabelle was utterly in love with him, as a woman to a man, and there was nothing that she could do about it.

She looked at the ceiling for a moment to inspect a loose piece of rubble wedged in a deeper crag surrounded by brush. With some effort, she was able to pull out the rubble, dig a little, and pull out some more until she had fashioned a small hole. She looked up at the rough lines on the ceiling, the mouth that she had just fashioned, and the sea brush that surrounded it like a beard. It definitely reminded her of Captain Gregory, and this made her feel more secure. She glowed bright yellow at the thought of Captain Gregory, so bright that the cave was considerably more light, and the baby queens began to stir. So as not to wake them just yet, the Queen toned it down a few shades and settled down for a few moments of relaxation.

"IT WAS TOO GOOD TO BE TRUE," SAID CAPTAIN Gregory, looking up at the display on the wall. Dr. Bellwether, Claude, and Jane nodded in agreement. The red light by Richard Pearlman's boat had been on all night. The good Professor and his men had caught sight of Cranston's boat long before the horn-rims had made visual confirmation. Once the boat arrived though, the horn-rims had tracked it as it patrolled the island, shining a light in the water. Exhausted from tracking the whereabouts of the boat, the horn-rims were somewhat relieved to confirm that the boat had finally put in anchor in the same location for the third straight day, and there had been little movement for a while.

"I don't like it," said Dr. Bellwether. "It's too quiet. They must be up to something."

"Most likely sleeping," said Captain Gregory. "But just in case, Claude, double the sentries at the boat, and have the horn-rims notify us immediately of any movement from Cranston or his men." He got up and headed for the door.

"Aye, aye," said Claude.

"Where are you going?" asked Dr. Bellwether.

"I'm going to the head," said Captain Gregory. "Do you mind?"

"No, Captain, you go where you want," said Dr. Bellwether, not understanding. "It's just that this waiting game has got me on edge."

"Don't worry, Dr. Bellwether. I'm putting you in charge until I come back," said Captain Gregory, chuckling as he left the room.

Dr. Bellwether smiled. He always relished the moments when Captain Gregory would take a break and put him in charge. He knew that Captain Gregory wasn't really relinquishing his authority. If there was any real trouble, they could summon the old war horse back to the war room at a moment's notice. It was really more a matter of throwing Dr. Bellwether a plum on occasion, and he appreciated the gesture. The two had managed an odd truce that allowed them to have the semblance of a working relationship, no matter how strained.

Dr. Bellwether took over the control console, happily punching a few buttons here and there, checking on the status of the fishing boat, the Coast Guard boat, and the positions of the horn-rims. He asked a few official-sounding questions of the console and it responded.

"How many troops are posted within fifty feet of the cave?" he asked. The number 70,555 flashed across the bottom of the console screen, which was a miniature of the large display on the wall.

"State of readiness?" he asked.

"Highest."

"How many are awake?"

"Two-thirds."

"Why?" asked Dr. Bellwether.

"Isn't it obvious," said Claude. "The Captain has no idea when an attack might occur. So at any given time, approximately two-thirds of the troops should be awake."

"How many are gathering food?" Dr. Bellwether asked the control console.

"2050."

"How many troops total?"

"80,015."

"What? I thought there was supposed to be 800,000."

"That was the number of hatchlings," said Jane. "Usually, only about one in ten make it to maturity."

"Is that enough to defend the colony?" Dr. Bellwether asked the control console.

"Unknown..."

Claude shook his head. "I think we're about to find out," he said pointing to the display, which had just updated to show ten divers approaching the cave. Each was wearing a different-colored stripe on his sleeve, for easy identification, Claude reasoned.

Dr. Bellwether stood up from his chair and pointed to the display. "Holy Toledo, how many of them are there?" He counted, mumbling the numbers. "One, two, three...four, five, six, seven...eight, nine, ten! Claude, get the captain, right away!"

"He's in the head."

"What are you talking about, Claude! We've got a crisis here. Would you please speak in standard English, not some colloquial Navy triple talk!! Where is he? They're getting closer!" he said, raising his voice, eyes glued to the display. They were under attack, and he was in charge. As the realization hit him, a bead of perspiration formed at the top of his forehead and rolled down between his eyes.

"He's in the bathroom," said Claude.

"What do you mean he's in the bathroom? What is he doing there at a time like this? It's all in his head. He doesn't need to do that. None of us do, really. Tell him to get back here immediately," said Dr. Bellwether as he unbuttoned the top button on his shirt.

"Should I get the captain on the com?" asked Claude.

"Yes, yes, do it, and get Isabelle while you're at it too."

Claude got on the com and announced, "We have a Code Red, Level 1, the console screen is Flashing. I repeat, Code Red, Level 1, the screen is Flashing. We are awaiting your orders, Captain."

Captain Gregory burst into the room at full speed, buttoning his shirt as he took the console. "Gentlemen, change of strategy. The moment has arrived where we must test our mettle. Claude, man the weapons bank. Dr. Bellwether, track enemy movements on the front display. Jane, see if you can identify the enemy. I want to know which is my friend Cranston." Captain Gregory rubbed his hands together, as if he was enjoying it. And he was. It was what he had trained for his whole life. To lead troops into battle. To prove himself. And to save a nation.

Captain Gregory was completely intense, yet the lines on his face belied the hint of a smile, something that made Dr. Bellwether absolutely incredulous. "What on earth are you smiling about?"

Captain Gregory punched up several views on the console screen. "The chance to put our training to the test. The opportunity to settle this thing once and for all. And the honor of serving our commander-in-chief, and a great lady."

"You must be nuts," said Dr. Bellwether. "I don't want to fight them. I want them to go away. Where is Isabelle?"

"I am sure that she is quite busy at this moment," said Jane.

"Don't you get it, Bellwether, she put us in charge, and she's relying on us to figure out what to do about the enemy, to outsmart him," said Captain Gregory. He stared ahead, intent on the display. "The moment has arrived ladies and gentleman when one must send the pail into the well deep within, and find out if there is any water down there."

The beads of perspiration were joining forces to form small rivulets of panic on Dr. Bellwether's forehead. "Yes, yes, enough with the speeches. What do you suggest we do?"

Captain Gregory turned to Claude. "Regiments 1-4. Position in a circular formation. Take cover on the sea floor. Full camouflage. Regiments 5-8, retreat to the base."

"To where, Captain?" asked Claude, who was busy punching buttons on his console.

"Send regiments 5-8 to the cave, to the cave," said Captain Gregory. "Do not attack until regiments 1-4 are positioned in front of and behind the enemy. Then and only then on my command. Understood?"

"Yes, Captain."

Just then Isabelle walked into the room and looked up at the display. The ten divers were about one hundred feet from the mouth of the cave, moving slowly toward it. "What are you waiting for?" she asked. "They are almost upon us."

"Not yet."

"But why are we just sitting there? Shouldn't we attack?"

"No, Isabelle, if we attack too soon, they will get away."

Isabelle looked up at the display and grew pale. "And if we don't, they will come in and kill us. I'm going to issue the order to attack, before it's too late."

Captain Gregory shook his head. "No, don't. You must trust me, and you must let me lead. I've given up fishing. I can't give up leading. If you take that away, you take away everything I've worked for, and you take away me. And then what would I have? You have to understand, Isabelle, this is something that I, and I alone, must do."

"Then do it already," said Dr. Bellwether, growing impatient.

Claude looked at Isabelle and then Captain Gregory, looking for direction. She took a deep breath and extended her hand toward Captain Gregory, reaffirming his command.

Captain Gregory smiled. "At last, a crew that is tried and true." He put his hand on his chin, intently watching the display, which showed the troops in a circular formation. The divers were well within the circular formation of the troops, about seventy-five feet from the cave. They had tightened ranks considerably, so much so that two of the divers became entangled. Before going any further, they paused for a moment to disentangle their equipment. The one with the red patch made several gestures to hurry up, but the other divers were having difficulty getting the divers unhooked from each other.

Captain Gregory stood up in front of the consoles. "Now is the time. We will launch a full-scale counter assault. Jane, take over command signals from Claude; I want his undivided attention on the weapons bank. Send these signals to the horn-rims: Prepare to assault. Full noose on targets one through ten. Full ascent. 100 degrees until even with the enemy. Then pull the cord. That's NOOSE formation, full ASCENT, PULL cord."

"Yes sir, Captain," said Jane. She scoured the console feverishly. "Where's the PULL button?"

"It's in the CONFIGURE array. We added it during training."

"Oh yes, I see it," she said as she pressed the buttons to relay the communications.

The horn-rims and their troops sprang into action. In rows many layers deep, they closed in on the enemy, who quickly drew their knives, shot their spear guns, and attempted to punch a "hole" through the ever-tightening noose formation, to no avail. The spears were quickly expended. Several of the troops were skewered but the hole in the formation was quickly closed. And they continued to close in...

Captain Gregory drummed his fingers on the console, as if he, himself, was itching to fire at the enemy. "Claude. Arm the ink torpedo banks and the poison cartridges."

"Yes sir, Captain," said Claude. "Should I acquire targets."

"Yes, acquire targets, by all means."

Several of the men broke ranks as if they were going to charge the troops, but instead they suddenly dove, while several others began to ascend...

"They're breaking ranks," said Captain Gregory. "Fire the ink torpedoes. NOW!!"

Claude was a near-blur of motion as he fired off all of the ink torpedoes, which resulted, moments later, in a large black cloud in the middle of the display.

"Now! POISON attack, and FIRE every round of poison available," Captain Gregory said, firing off orders faster than Claude could fire the buttons.

The horn-rims and their troops continued on the attack, closing in, spraying ink, tearing off face masks, removing mouthpieces, ripping hoses, biting, and injecting poison... Half of the divers, the lucky ones who dove below and above the cloud of ink and vast entanglement of arms and legs, got away. They had not been bitten and the horn-rims and their troops did not give chase. Instead, the troops fought with the remaining divers until the poison set in and they could no longer fight.

"Why aren't we going after the others?" asked Claude.

"Because the troops are trained to attack only as a countermeasure in defense of the realm," replied Captain Gregory. "They have not been trained in the art of offensive maneuvers and tactics."

They all watched on the display as one by one, the divers surfaced and disappeared into the boat. When all the divers had returned to their boat, the horn-rims returned to their posts. The fight was over for now, and it had been a decidedly one-sided battle.

Dr. Bellwether extended his hand to Captain Gregory. "You did it, Gregory. Didn't know if you had it in you, but you did. We won the battle, thanks to you."

"Yes, but the question is, will we win the war?" said Captain Gregory. He shook hands with Dr. Bellwether. "Just the same, I thank you for your vote of confidence. It's been a long time coming." Claude and Jane clapped and shouted their congratulations to Captain Gregory. The war room became the scene of a rather raucous party as Claude uncorked a bottle of champagne and poured glasses for everyone.

"A toast, to the finest captain in the Queen's Navy."

A tear welled up in Captain Gregory's eye as he raised his glass. "To the finest crew in the Queen's Navy." Before extending his glass to the others, he added, "And God save the Queen."

The sound of ringing glasses filled the room. They sipped champagne, laughed, and sipped some more. Then Isabelle stood in front of the group, facing Captain Gregory. "For your meritorious service to the Queen, the colony, and future generations, I extend my congratulations and heartfelt thanks." For all to see, she kissed him on the cheek. "You deserved that," she added, as the others clapped and cheered.

"I only wish, my dear lady, that I will be of greater service in the future, so that I might be deserving of much more," said Captain Gregory amidst the laughter and good cheer.

As he laughed aloud, Captain Gregory wondered privately how long it would be before Cranston and crew would be back. But he wouldn't think about that now. He wanted to enjoy the laughter while it lasted. He knew that though today's battle was over, the war had just begun.

Twenty-Five

On the morning of the fourth day, Cranston was angry...seething...livid. He was angry that his plan had not worked. He was seething that a bunch of eight-armed squid wannabees could ambush and repel their futile attack on the cave, a cave which was more like a fortress. And he was livid that he had not yet killed the beast. All of that would change.

Cranston assessed the damage. There was no damage to the boat of course, but there was plenty of damage to their crew. They had lost five men the day before, men he would need to corner his quarry. They would have to find another way. The cave was too heavily guarded, patrolled by several thousand small octopuses that seemed to understand his objective. Their movements were coordinated and disciplined, as if commanded by someone who understood tactical war maneuvers, someone like Captain Gregory, once a man, now a ghost of the sea.

Cranston had always believed in ghosts. In fact, he had wanted to be one himself someday—the bad kind of course—

but he wasn't quite sure how to do it other than the traditional way, turning the gun on himself. Killing others was fine—and good, wholesome entertainment—but killing himself had little appeal. The instinct for self-preservation was too great. Somehow, though, he had rediscovered his arch enemy, an invisible enemy, an enemy bent on his destruction; and he was sure that the enemy was commanding the octopuses to do things they had never been capable of doing before. The dirty old devilfish!

It was as if the giant beast was possessed by Captain Gregory! That was it! The giant beast *was* possessed by Captain Gregory and he'd ruin everything. Cranston kicked the side of the ship and pounded on the gunwale. He'd get Captain Gregory if it was the last thing he did.

As he twisted the nylon of an old seine shrimp net in his fingers, Cranston reviewed his options. With Manuel gone, there was only five divers left, plus the three worthless sushi chefs hand-picked by Mr. Oh, and Rhub. Another attack would be futile. They would surely lose more divers, not that he cared; but he did need enough manpower to accomplish the mission. The problem was, there were just too many ugly little pods. As he twirled the net in his fingers, it occurred to him that the solution was within his grasp. He would kill them all in one fell swoop.

This pleasant thought was rudely interrupted when Rhub emerged from the galley. "Everything okay up here, boss?" Cranston just stared ahead, hatching the details to his plan. "Breakfast is ready," Rhub added, hoping to draw his attention.

Cranston nodded. "You're an old shrimper, aren't you Rhub?"

"Yea, boss, did it all the time as a kid."

"Good, let's catch some shrimp today."

"What? I thought you wanted to catch the big red."

"I do, but we gotta kill those pesky pods guarding the cave," he said pointing down at the sea below. "These pods like shrimp. So we catch some shrimp, put 'em in an old net, cut some holes in it, and lower the bait. Then when they come out to feed, we circle the whole lot, net 'em, drown 'em, and dump 'em."

"Boss, you're a genius."

"Yea I know. But here's the best part of all," he said lighting a cigar and waving it wildly. "We take some underwater torches with us to the cave. Then if any of the little beasts get near us, we burn them to a crisp."

"That'll teach them a lesson they won't forget."

"Yea, that's the idea. Say, where are those other idiots?"

"The other idiots?" Rhub said, looking around the deck and back at himself. Then he smiled, pointing down below. "Oh, those idiots. They haven't gotten up yet."

One of them, a long-haired, wiry, weather-beaten man, stuck his head out of the galley. "We've been talking it over. We don't want any part of this. You said we'd catch a ton of octopus, not the other way around. We're taking the dinghy back."

Cranston smiled as he thought about the holes he had never repaired in the dinghy that was beside the ship. "Suit yourself, Reggie. If you don't want to go down in history as the greatest fisherman, fine. If you don't want a part of a million bucks, fine. I'm not sure I want to cut *you* in on the deal anyway."

Reggie scratched his head, completely surprised. "Well, that's the way we want it, I think."

"Well, nobody's stopping you. You want to leave, leave. Leave now. Get your lilly-livered candy asses off my boat. I don't want your help. I don't *need* your help."

"It's not that we don't want to help you. It's just that we don't want to get killed. And we don't want those kids in the

Coast Guard boat to turn us in. That's the difference between you and me. I'm not crazy."

Cranston grabbed him by the shirt. "No, the difference between you and me is: *You* want the catch of the day. *I* want the catch of the century. If you don't want any part of that, that's fine with me," he said, pushing him away. "I'll kill the beast myself. I'll ram the Coast Guard boat, too, just for good measure. Then I'll take the money and outfit this thing to catch humpback whales again. The Japs down in the galley, you know Sushi-yaki and the rest, they know about a black market in Tokyo where humpback and sperm fetch $500 a pound."

"We might be interested in that."

"You know, I gotta do this first. I gotta have the money to convert the ship over again. That's just plain business, you know? Building capital and equity on a foundation of sound business principles."

"What in tarnation are you talking about, Cranston?"

"What I mean is this: are you in or out? Cause there's no in between."

"We're in."

"Then round up the others. We've got work to do. We've got to kill us a giant devilfish!" said Cranston, smiling as he realized how easy it was to manipulate Reggie and his crew. It was almost as much fun as fishing, but not quite.

THE USUAL SPARKLING ARRAY OF bioluminescent colors had been replaced by somber colors and an ever-present pattern of triangles ever since he had been sent away. Archie had been unable to understand why. He had swam a great distance hoping to forget about the repudiation that had made him so unhappy that he was unable to stop eating, unable to sleep, and unable to think about anything else.

He had gone over the message over and over in his mind: *Please do not ask me why, only know that you go with the love and affection of a Queen, her subjects, her children, and her colony.*

She still loved him, yet she sent him away. It was a riddle, a riddle that had greatly troubled him ever since. Why would anyone who loved someone send him away without so much as an explanation? Archie couldn't figure it out, and he had thought about it many times until he was literally blue in the face, a condition which had left him deeply melancholy.

As he swam by some crabs, he saw them quickly retreat into their caves, and that gave him an idea. Perhaps he should turn the question around. Why would he send the Queen away? There was only one answer to that question. He wouldn't. He wouldn't dream of it unless...unless he knew that danger was imminent. That was it! She didn't send him away because she hated him. She sent him away because she loved him! With this realization, Archie immediately glowed warm yellow all over. The warm yellow was quickly partitioned and then intermixed with red, the most alarming red Archie could illuminate. The Queen was in danger! The Queen was in danger!! The QUEEN WAS IN DANGER!!! And he had swum away just when she needed him most.

Archie quickly turned and headed back at full speed, hoping that he wasn't too late.

CAPTAIN GREGORY AND THE OTHERS HAD had a good night's sleep after their victory the day before. They had all hoped that the fishermen's boat would leave during the night and that the sentries who manned the war room while they were asleep would have good news for them in the morning. They did not. So Captain Gregory and his crew were back in the war room, intently watching the displays, waiting for Cranston's next move.

Captain Gregory was the first to notice that a large congregation of troops had gathered about fifty yards from Cranston's boat. "What are they doing out there?"

"I don't know," said Dr. Bellwether. "It appears that they are eating."

"Well, I don't like it."

"Monsieur, the troops have to eat too, no?" asked Claude.

Captain Gregory turned to Claude. "Yes, of course. But they should wait for the red-rims to bring the food in piecemeal, and eat in shifts, same as always. There are too many of them, and where would they get that much food at once?"

Isabelle entered the war room and pulled up a chair. "It is my understanding that they are just eating. Many of them are hungry from the battle the night before. Perhaps they are feasting on several large lobsters."

Captain Gregory got up from his seat and walked closer to the display. "There's so many arms and so many of them that I can't see what they are eating. This is too strange. Perhaps it's not food. But what, then?"

"Look at them, they're swarming," said Jane.

"A regular feeding frenzy," agreed Dr. Bellwether.

Captain Gregory shook his head. "Well, I've never seen anything like it. Reminds me of how fishermen attract sharks... No, I don't like this at all."

Several of them reacted at once. "What? You don't like what?" asked Dr. Bellwether. "What do you mean, how fishermen attract sharks?" exclaimed Isabelle.

"Wait a second," said Captain Gregory holding up a finger. "Jane, send the command, RETREAT. Take COVER. I repeat, RETREAT and take COVER."

"Sending the commands right now, Captain."

"For the love of Mike, would you tell us what it is?" asked Dr. Bellwether.

"It's a bait trap, Dr. Bellwether."

"A bait trap!" they all exclaimed.

"Yes," replied Captain Gregory. He turned to Jane. "Jane, have you received an acknowledgment from the horn-rims?"

"No, we can't get through. There are so many infrasignals being sent there that all lines are jammed," said Jane, holding up her hands, as if there was nothing she could do.

"What? Who is jamming the lines?" asked Captain Gregory.

"The troops are," said Isabelle. "It's as if you had thousands of children in a playground and all of them are yelling at once. I am going out there."

"No, you're not. I mean, you can't, your highness. They'll be using a net no doubt and we can't have you get caught in one of those," said Captain Gregory. He turned to Jane. "Try again."

"Yes, try again," said Dr. Bellwether, avoiding Captain Gregory's reproachful eyes.

They all watched in horror as a large trawl net slowly swept through the area, like a giant spider web catching and entangling everything in its path.

"My children!" exclaimed Isabelle.

"Send out the signals to DIVE and SURFACE," shouted Captain Gregory.

Jane sent the signals again and, apparently, some got through. Some of the troops surfaced and were able to climb over the top of the nets. Others escaped by diving to the sea floor. Others were not so lucky. The vast majority either did not receive the signals, or it was just too late to react.

The giant death trap encircled them and pulled tighter and tighter, entangling the octopuses in the webbing, severing many limbs. Thousands were captured and they were drawn tight into a huge ball of cephalopod flesh and drowned.

"This is a catastrophe!" cried Jane.

"We're ruined!" exclaimed Dr. Bellwether, kicking the console.

Sitting in her chair, Isabelle stared at the wall and sobbed softly. "My children! My troops! What will we do? What will we do?"

"Do not worry your highness," said Claude. "Captain Gregory will think of something. He always does."

Captain Gregory put his arm around her. "When this is all over, we'll do the only thing we can do. We'll rebuild the colony, arm in arm, hand in hand."

Twenty-Six

After wiping out the small army of octopuses the day before, Cranston and crew had been eating them for breakfast, lunch, and dinner. That morning they were having them for a meal once again, and the gangly cephalopods tasted no better than the day before. Cranston spat out the rubbery arm of octopus he had been chewing. He could never get used to it, not in a million years. The others seemed only too happy to eat the stuff, so he left them and went on deck. Let them eat the salty white rubber if it made them happy.

The only thing that would make him truly happy was blood, the blood of the giant beast herself. He leaned over the rail and looked down into the water, anticipating her next move, and contemplating his own. It had been five days now, and it had been long enough. He was determined to kill the giant beast and to settle the score with the ghost of Captain Gregory once and for all. There were relatively few of the small army left, not enough to defend the cave, and certainly not enough to gather food, if that's what they did. She would be coming out for food soon enough and would end up in the tank onboard or at the end of a harpoon, whichever came first.

Cranston smiled and thought how funny it was that such an ugly, foul-tasting beast would be sought by so many. Although the Kashimoto Corporation would pay dearly for the entire beast, he would conceal—no, steal—part of an arm. After all, the three sushi chefs would be hip-deep in tentacles. With a two-ton beast to butcher, who would miss a couple of hundred pounds? The rare octopus flesh could be sold along with other delicacies in the black market in Tokyo. Lizards, snakes, reptiles. Ha! They were penny-ante stuff. A pound of rare octopus flesh would fetch $500. That's where the real money was to be made, in the trafficking of rare and endangered species.

Besides the money, there was another reason he did it, one that was perhaps more important to Cranston than any other. It was particularly gratifying to catch a rare and endangered species. To hold it. To admire it. And to kill it. Cranston could hardly believe that people would pay him money for something he really enjoyed doing. It was what he did best. First, though, he needed to catch the beast.

He scoured the waters, looking, feeling, sensing, when and where they should make their next move.

Plan A was to wait for the beast to be caught in the trap, but almost everyone on board was getting tired of waiting for that to happen. Rhub thought that she was too smart to get caught in the same trap twice. The Japanese had their opinions to be sure, but they most generally talked quietly among themselves, keeping a tight-knit circle of secrecy.

Then there was Plan B, which they had rehearsed and rehearsed. Five of them would attack the drones at the front entrance with torches, spear guns, concussion grenades, the usual, and drive the giant beast to the back of the cave. Cranston would sneak in through the back entrance and they would trap her. Of course, he would get the honor and pleasure of being the one to shoot her with the spear gun, one shot, right between the eyes. They had gone over Plan B many times, and Cranston had enjoyed thinking of the shot, killing her in his mind over and over again. There was only one problem with Plan B: They had not yet found the back door to the cave. But Cranston felt certain there was one. That afternoon, they would search until they found it. First, they would need to wait for Professor Pearlman and his gang of busybodies to return from their dive. Then perhaps they could go on their dive without any interference.

Cranston went below deck to spy on the Coast Guard boat. Once below, he slowly opened a porthole and cautiously looked out. Professor Pearlman and his gang of busybodies had just surfaced. Several had caught abalone and were bringing their catch on deck. Judging by the chain lines attached to the boat, they also had several cages in the water. The professor pulled them up one by one, each with a large crab inside. Cranston didn't see how anyone could eat the rubbery meat of crustaceans for lunch. He much preferred fish.

He was glad, though, that the professor would be having lunch soon. That would give him and his men a chance to scout around for the back door to the cave. The five remaining crewmen were busy getting on their wetsuits in the galley, and everyone would soon be ready.

But the good professor did not take his wetsuit off as did the others. Instead, he combined all three crabs into a single cage and surreptitiously dangled them over the other side of the boat, away from Cranston's old whaler. He then looked over at the vessel, checking to see if anyone was watching.

Satisfied, he went down the ladder, swam over to the other side, and submerged. At that moment, Cranston realized that those crabs weren't for their lunch. They were for *her* lunch! The beast!! "He's feeding her, the dirty bastard. Well I'll put a stop to that. No wait. Maybe this is just the break we've been looking for," Cranston said aloud to no one in particular. The professor was going to lead them right to her back doorstep, handing her on a silver platter. He couldn't have planned it better himself.

"Rhub, get me a tank, quick," Cranston called. With his red shirt-tail flapping in the wind, Rhub grabbed an oxygen tank out of the cupboard, checked the gages, and handed it to him.

Cranston put on his face mask and quickly assembled his men. It was time for Plan B. One by one, quickly, quietly, they hoisted themselves over the rail, grabbed hold of the ladder, and slowly lowered themselves into the water. Under water, Cranston motioned to his divers to start moving in at the front of the cave. He would follow Pearlman, who was about thirty yards ahead.

The divers swam toward the jutting rock guarding the entrance to the cave and were immediately met by a hundred or more octopuses, which attempted to encircle them, moving in closer and closer in a slowly tightening noose. But this time, the divers were ready. They immediately turned on bright, glow torches and continued their advance, waving them in front and behind them. Several octopuses attacked and were immediately burned by the torches, causing their arms to curl up, shrivel, and writhe in pain. As they broke through the circle, the divers cut, slashed, and burned their way toward the cave in a coordinated attack.

In response the troops mounted a counterattack. Led by one of the horn-rims, they came at the advancing divers in a "dense pack", hoping to gain protection in numbers, but they were quickly netted and killed by the divers. Others scattered and attempted kamikaze attacks on their adversaries, attempting to rip their mouthpieces away or bite at any exposed skin to administer poison, but this time the divers were better prepared. Every inch of skin was covered by wetsuits, hats, face masks, and gloves, and the glow torches were effective at keeping the horn-rims and their troops at bay. Unable to get close to them, the octopuses countered with ink, camouflage, and releases of poison into the water, but to no avail.

As the divers rounded the corner, past the jut of land protecting the entrance to the cave, a multitude of drones landed on three of them, furiously biting through their wetsuits. Using their torches, the two remaining divers were able to scorch the octopuses and pull them off of their comrades, but it was too late. Their bodies were full of poison.

Enraged, the two divers tracked down the other octopuses and killed them too. Then they turned up their torches and slowly moved toward the mouth of the cave where they met weaker resistance. Apparently most of the forces had been outside the cave. The few remaining soldiers fought valiantly, but the two men burned them with their torches, stabbed at them with their knives, and finally, for good measure, hacked off their arms, having fun while they were doing it.

THEY WERE ASSEMBLED IN THE WAR ROOM again, and this time everyone knew that the moment of truth had arrived. "I don't think I can hold them any longer, your highness," said Captain Gregory.

"You've got to," Isabelle answered.

"I can't. Extend your probe through the front and see what is happening. All of your sentry guards monitoring the entry have been knocked out. I think the divers are about to enter the cave."

"But what has happened to my men?"

"I hate to say this Isabelle, but I think they are all gone."

"No, that can't be."

"There's no time to argue. If you don't believe it, extend your probe and see for yourself."

"Please. For once, would you just do what he says?" pleaded Dr. Bellwether.

"Since when do you *ever* do what he says?" asked Jane.

"That's beside the point," said Dr. Bellwether.

"Please, ladies and gentlemen. Please stop arguing," said Claude.

"It's time you and the baby queens escape through the back door. You must leave this place at once," said Captain Gregory to Isabelle. "I'm afraid, my dear Isabelle, that it's sink or swim."

THE QUEEN EXTENDED A PROBE OUTSIDE OF THE cave just around the corner. She was shocked at what she saw. She knew of the devastation that the wars between the colonies had wrought, and she knew the devastation that the fishermen could leave in their wake. But none of this knowledge prepared her for the utter devastation that was just outside her cave. Her troops were laying wounded everywhere. Arms hacked off here and there, bodies scorched by the torch lights, and blood and ink everywhere.

The divers had penetrated the shield in front of the cave, and they would soon be inside. Before going in, though, they were checking the gages on their suits. The troops had attacked them, attempting to twist off their gages, rip out their mouthpieces, and dislodge their goggles.

The Queen quickly withdrew her probe. No need to survey the situation any longer. She knew what was next. They were coming in to kill her.

A wave of panic swept though her as quickly as a complete change of color. She glowed crimson red with fear and anger, and her blood raced through every inch of her body. She looked over in the corner of the cave where her children had been playing, and they were gone. My children! What have they done with my children! Then she felt a tap on her arm. She whirled around and felt both of them attach to her mantle, aware of the danger and very much afraid. She quickly grabbed her children and brought them up to the hiding place in the ceiling. Gently, but firmly she nudged them into the crack, but they resisted. She blared infrasignal alarms at them, and forced them into the crack. *Stay there and don't move! You'll be safe here. Mama will come back for you. I promise. Please, don't move. For once, mind your Mother!*

As fast as she could crawl, she headed toward the back of the cave. As she went by the dinner table, the shiny metallic tube in the middle of the centerpiece caught her eye. It would make the perfect memento in case she never returned. As she did, she had a revelation. It wasn't a metallic tube. It was a GUN!! She quickly grabbed the entire centerpiece arrangement. Suddenly, two divers came in the front of the cave and slowly approached her. The Queen blew herself up in the shape of a giant bell, startling the divers momentarily. That gave her just enough time to quickly pull herself through the back corridor as if she had been sucked in by some strong current. They quickly gave chase through the corridor and into the maze of interconnecting tunnels that comprised the way to the back door. She crept, inched, and poured herself through a maze of twists and turns, most of which were tall enough, but barely wide enough, for a man to get through. When she had gotten a safe distance away, she looked back and could see their torch lights as they doggedly followed her. At least they had left her children alone.

She continued to crawl through the tunnels, looking back every so often, hoping that they would reach an impasse. They did not, though it was slow going in several stretches. Up ahead, she could see the large, open chamber that was just fifty yards from the small unobtrusive back door. She did not want to go there. It would be too dangerous, according to the captain, and he was probably right.

The only thing left to do was to hide. There was not much vegetation in the tunnels but there were rocks and occasional formations behind which she might hide. She finally found a large crack that was well protected by rocky protuberances. She turned the color of the rocks, poured herself into the small space, and flattened herself out, allowing only rock-like granulations to protrude from her mantle, making her almost invisible in her surroundings.

If she waited long enough, perhaps they would get lost in the tunnels. Perhaps their oxygen tanks would run out. Or perhaps they would give up. She waited and hoped, hoped and waited, wondering when the moment of truth would arrive, thankful that she did not make bubbles as she breathed under water. Out of her narrowed eyes, she saw that the tunnel was becoming lighter. They were getting closer...

AFTER A WHILE, THE BABY QUEENS GOT UP their nerve and peeked out of the crack in the ceiling of the cave. Mother was gone. There was no food. And they were hungry. At first, they were too terrified to leave their hiding place, but little by little, their confidence increased in proportion to their appetite, particularly Victoria's. She was the first to venture out of the crack, probes first, to make sure that the coast was clear. Elizabeth reprimanded her for venturing out of the cave, annoyed that she had not been the first to do it.

Hey, come back here. What if the fishermen come?
There's nothing to be afraid of, they've left.
But Mom said to stay here.
We are here.
No, I mean in the hole. If you don't get back right now, I'm telling.
Oh no you're not, or I'll tell her about the time you snuck out in the middle of the night.
You wouldn't.

Of course I would. Now, keep your beak shut and come with me. We have to find out what's going on. Mom might be in trouble.

Do you really think so?

No, of course not. Mom can take care of herself. But if she asks, that's the story. You got it?

Okay. But the first sign of trouble, we head back.

Of course. Come on, let's get something to eat. I'm hungry.

Me too.

Slowly, carefully, surreptitiously, they crawled along the ceiling, headed toward the entrance to the cave, and peeked out. The coast was clear, and so they headed out to the jut of rock protecting the entrance to the cave. As they rounded the corner, Elizabeth stopped in her tracks and turned bright red. She pointed to the ocean floor to the right and to the left of them. There were the bodies of tens of hundreds of the troops strewn all over the landscape. Victoria turned red too, though not quite as bright.

Oh no, the boys!! Look at them, they're...they're dead! What do we do! What do we do!!

Uh-oh. Something bad happened here.

I told you we shouldn't have left the cave. I told you.

Now don't get all excited, sister. There's nothing we can do.

Don't get all excited? Don't get all excited? They're our brothers.

Of course they are. But you know what Mom taught us. Not to get too attached to them. They're soldiers, and soldiers fight, and soldiers get killed. Now don't look at them. Just look straight ahead.

Are you crazy? How can you say that? I'm going home. There's something wrong, something really bad.

Come on, there's three crabs straight ahead. Let's grab two of them, and then we'll go home.
Not me. I'm leaving now.
You wouldn't leave me. You can't leave me, we're sisters. I see you inching away. You come back here this instant. Hey, come back.

Elizabeth turned her head and jettisoned back toward the cave. Victoria hesitated for a moment, frightened, not knowing what to do without her sister there. If her sister reacted one way, she would always react the other way. In every situation, then, she knew exactly how to react, the opposite of her sister. Now that her sister had left, she didn't quite know what to do. Then it came to her. After all, her sister did leave. That meant she should stay, or at least that's what she told herself. It would be just a few more feet to get to those scrumptious-looking crabs. Maybe she could take two, one for now and one for later. Maybe she'd share the other one with her sister after she admitted what a scaredy-catfish she was. These thoughts helped her to take her mind off the terrible fate that had befallen her brothers. Whoever or whatever had done this was gone, and there was nothing to be afraid of, at least that's what she kept telling herself.

She crept up to the crabs, who had become very agitated. As she was just about to pounce on them, she wondered why they didn't try to crawl away. Instead, they seemed to be moving, but they weren't going anywhere. It was very strange. She grabbed one of them and quickly bit it. It moved a little and then quit moving as the poison settled in...

She was about to bite a second crab, when suddenly she felt a presence. She quickly whirled around and was most surprised to see that it was Uncle Archie!! He was swimming toward her from a distance, his colors quickly, clearly, and simply telling her... *No, no! Danger!! Get away from there...*

She looked at him, not understanding, and flashed her response... *Uncle Archie! You came back!! Look Uncle Archie, I caught my own crab, and there's one for you...*

The floor suddenly shifted and moved away, and it began to pull tight, surrounding her on all sides. *What's happening! Oh, no, it's a trap! It's a trap!! Oh, why didn't I listen to my sister?!* Victoria cried out. She sent out one infra-distress signal after another and tried in vain to climb the "walls" of the trap, which was being quickly pulled up to the surface. As the trap pulled shut, the daylight was suddenly gone, and she could see nothing, only darkness.

WITH A MIGHTY BURST OF SPEED ARCHIE bridged the distance to the trap, which was being raised by a large overhanging boom. As the trap reached the surface, he extended a long tentacle up and out of the water and wrapped it around the boom, jerking on it with great force, causing the bow of the giant boat to rock back and forth. Then with all of his might he began to pull on it and slowly swim deeper in an effort to capsize the boat. He pulled and pulled with all of his might. It would only take a few more feet, and he would sink the boat and free the precious baby queen inside the trap that was dangling above the water in a stalemate between the giant trap and the giant catch.

Just as Archie thought that he would either snap the mast in two or capsize the boat, he heard a loud noise and moments later a terrible pain as something ripped into him. After the initial confusion cleared, he knew what had happened. It was what he had dreaded all of his life. He had seen them rip through many a whale, causing them to writhe in pain and agony. Now it had happened to him. He had been hit by a harpoon. And it was terribly painful. But there was something else even stronger than the pain, and it was not fear. It was anger. It was rage! It was FURY!!

With the anger, the rage, and the fury of a volcano, he erupted, shooting up to the surface, sending out long tentacles in all directions, and fomenting a great splashing, churning, and bubbling of white salt water. With his huge, saucer-like eyes above sea level, he saw the filthy beasts for the first time. He attached two more arms to the mast and snapped it like a twig, causing the trap to fall into the water. Three of them came at him with knives, but he swung an arm over deck like a giant mast and knocked them onto their backs. When they got up, he wrapped three arms around their necks, and began to squeeze, tighter and tighter. As he did so, he heard men screaming and the red-shirted one barking orders to them. The red-shirt yelled "HARPOON", but he did not understand the language. The three men whose necks he was wringing were struggling to break free, but to no avail. He pulled the triple noose tighter and tighter until their eyes popped out of their heads. As the red-shirt was shouting and scurrying about, he pulled the three overboard and dumped them in the ocean, all the while keeping an eye on board.

The red-shirt had gotten up to the harpoon stand and was aiming another harpoon right at him. At that moment, he understood what the red-shirt had been trying to get the others to do. Archie dove straight down and straight under the boat as fast as he could, but he could not swim very fast. When he was a distance away, he found that he could not go any further. He had avoided the second shot, but the first harpoon was in him, and it was attached to the boat!

He knew that his only chance was to break free of it. So he backed up, and then with all of his might he swam forward at full speed, only to have the harpoon stop him abruptly, ripping deeper into his flesh. He shuddered with pain and was stunned for a moment. He backed up for a second time and then swam forward at full speed, only to be stopped again. This time, the harpoon caused further damage, and for a few minutes he barely moved. He was bent and twisted in pain, and he doubled back to look at the harpoon. It was lodged near his tentacles, impeding his locomotion. He was in such bad shape that there was not much hope, but he would have to try one last time.

He backed up slowly, summoning all of his strength, and then stopped. Suddenly, he realized that he had been going about it all wrong. Instead of swimming away from the boat, he should swim toward it! He abruptly turned around and swam straight toward the boat, then under the boat, and then to the other side, picking up more and more speed. With one last burst of speed, he reached the end of the rope... and the harpoon was yanked out, ripping him from the inside out.

The pain was intense, and he let out several calls of distress as he laid on his side, the blood pouring out of him. In a few moments, he shook off the pain and began to swim. He was free! The harpoon lay on the ocean floor, and he was free!! Without looking back, he swam away slowly, painfully, and carefully away. With each rhythmic movement of his long narrow body, he gained hope, the hope that he would live and the hope that he would one day make it back to the cave to find out if his precious baby queens had survived.

THE TWO DIVERS IN THE TUNNEL WERE ALMOST upon the Queen, and she was beginning to feel that she had made a mistake by hiding in the crack. It was too large, and there was room in the tunnel for them to maneuver their spear guns. If they were able to spot her, they could shoot her at point blank range.

She could see the two divers stop when they came to the spot where she was hiding. They went forward a few steps and then backed up. One examined the floor, searching for evidence that she had been there. The other looked in the crack. Suddenly he nudged his partner and pointed right at her. Then slowly, he started to take the spear gun off of his shoulder.

The Queen didn't know what to do. Luckily, Captain Gregory did. He ordered her to shoot and run. So she fired off a tremendous blast, filling that part of the tunnel with jet black ink. While the two divers fumbled around, she quickly exited her hiding place and crawled ahead through the tunnel, stopping after the next sharp bend. There she attached herself high upon the wall and waited, perfectly still, almost afraid to breathe for fear the small current it made would give her away. It didn't take long for them to regroup. Soon, she could see the tunnel get brighter and brighter as they came closer and closer once again.

As they rounded the corner, she sprung into action. Her huge arm encircled their heads, the large sucker disks effectively covering their faces, while another encircled their legs, and another encircled their arms, causing them both to drop their torch lights to the ground. More arms followed until the two divers were tightly wrapped. They struggled but they could barely move as she slowly drew them into her mantle, bit them, and administered a lethal dose. It only took a few moments for the poison to take effect. After it was all over, she released them and then stuffed them in the bend in such a way as to prevent any more divers from getting through.

She then headed for the back door to the tunnels for a quick escape. As she rounded a corner and entered a large chamber connected to the back door, she ran into another diver! Startled, she turned her head to jettison away and saw that it wasn't just any diver. It was Richard Pearlman!! He was carrying a cage full of crabs to feed her, returning the favor. She looked at him and wanted to laugh, to cry, and to smile, none of which she could do. Or could she? Suddenly, she turned yellow and then "drew" the symbol of peace on her mantle.

Richard Pearlman smiled and then opened the crab cage and handed the crabs to the Queen, who accepted the offer but quickly tucked it away. There was no time for eating now. It was time to go. Before she could go, though, he stroked her gently. It felt soothing, even reassuring, and the panic she was feeling subsided momentarily. As the colors of her mantle changed, she, too, changed her mind, sensing that it was safer in the chamber with Richard Pearlman.

After a while, the Queen had resummoned her courage to face the unknown, and Richard Pearlman had picked up his cage to go. As they were about to leave, they stopped, stunned by the sight of Cranston standing at the mouth of the cave, spear gun in hand! The Queen immediately headed back to the tunnel, but it was blocked by the two divers she had dispatched before. She was completely trapped.

Cranston raised his spear gun and pointed it at her. Richard Pearlman stepped in front of the Queen and waved at Cranston to leave. Cranston waved his spear gun for him to move away. Richard Pearlman refused. Cranston waved his spear gun one more time but he refused again. Then Cranston smiled and pulled the trigger. The spear shot through the water and struck Richard Pearlman in the chest, and a red cloud surrounded his upper torso. He clutched at the spear and then stumbled backwards, falling within inches of her.

The Queen's first instinct was to help Richard Pearlman, to cradle him in her arms and bring him under the protection of her mantle. But that would be useless. The spear had penetrated his chest clear through to the backside and the blood was oozing from his prone body, lying there on the floor of the cave, motionless, except for the motion of the currents that were causing feint movement in his arms and legs. There was nothing more that she could do, at least right now. There were no bubbles escaping from his mouth, no gestures for help, and so she concluded that he must be dead, or close to it. Jane would be devastated. She had grown very fond of Jane these past few months, and the sight of Jane's lifelong mate lying there on the floor of the cave stoked a passion deep within, one that she had only felt one time before in her entire life. It was rage. Pure rage. Focused on one man and one man only, the man who at this very moment was slowly, methodically, confidently removing the other spear gun from his shoulder...

THE ENTIRE CREW WAS SEATED IN THE WAR room, each at their designated stations, except Jane. She was touching the display on the wall of the war room, weeping. The others were preoccupied with Cranston who had the spear gun off of his shoulder and was checking the release mechanism. He only had one shot apparently, and he didn't want to miss.

"You've got to save him," Jane whimpered.

"I'm sorry, dear, but there's nothing I can do about that right now," said Isabelle.

"But you must."

"There's no time for that now, Jane. We've got to save the Queen first," said Captain Gregory sternly. He turned to Isabelle. "Are you sure that what you've got there is a gun?"

"Yes, I think so, but I can't get the flowers untangled from it, so I'm not sure."

"What are we going to do? This guy isn't going to wait for Isabelle to untangle the centerpiece from her dinner table. He's going to put her *on* the dinner table," cried Dr. Bellwether. "Where are our troops? Don't we have any more troops?"

"The troops have been dispatched, scattered, gone," said Claude.

By the glow of his torch light, they could see Cranston had just finished adjusting the spear gun and was slowly raising it to his shoulder.

"Fire a round of ink, now, before he shoots," shouted Captain Gregory to Claude.

"I am sorry to report, Captain, but we are out ink."

Dr. Bellwether wiped the sweat from his brow. "That does it. Our goose is cooked for sure. I told you that we should do something before. But no, no one listened to me. Well now we're trapped, trapped like a bunch of lobsters at the corner fish market!"

"WOULD YOU SHUT UP!!" shouted Captain Gregory. "I'm trying to think."

They all stared at the display as Cranston looked through the sights and slowly took aim, raising the tip of the spear, so that it was directly in their line of sight...

"You're missing the point, but he's not going to. He's going to send a spear right between her eyes! You've got to do something, and do it NOW!!" shouted Dr. Bellwether.

"Would you two stop it!! Stop it now!!" ordered Isabelle, pointing to the display.

Suddenly they saw the Queen put an arm in front of her so as to conceal the flower arrangement from Cranston's view. They could see her struggling to get the final part of the thatchwork untangled. Finally, she grabbed the barrel and shook the flowers loose from the handle.

"Would this help?" asked Isabelle, pointing to the display again.

"Who on earth gave you that gun?" asked Dr. Bellwether.

Captain Gregory was intense, his gaze transfixed to the display. "Never mind that now, Bellwether," he said.

"But what can we do? We don't have any controls for a gun," said Claude.

"Yes, what good is a gun, if you can't shoot it?" asked Dr. Bellwether.

They could see a smile come across Cranston's face as he moved the tip of the arrow up, then down, and then up again.

"What is he doing? Why doesn't he just shoot and get it over with?" asked Dr. Bellwether.

"He's toying with her. Making her sweat. Gloating. And he's finding the best location to make the perfect kill."

"Why doesn't she just grab him?" asked Dr. Bellwether.

"I am afraid, my friend, that if she makes one move, he will shoot her. Isn't that right, Captain?" asked Claude.

Deep in thought, Captain Gregory did not answer. "I've got it," he exclaimed. "I've got it!!" He turned to Isabelle. "Full-scale granulation, now!"

"Of what?" asked Isabelle.

"A full scale granulation—of me."

"You?! You're not serious?!! I don't know if I can do that."

"You've got to. DO IT NOW PLEASE!!!"

CRANSTON METHODICALLY MOVED HIS SPEAR gun around, while keeping a watchful eye on the movement of the yellow-eyed demon in the fiery red dress. I've got you now, and I'm not going to miss, he thought. I'd bite you between the eyes myself but I'll save that for later, after I've cut the arms off your rubbery carcass. You've caused me enough trouble already, you eight-armed monstrosity.

Cranston rubbed his finger along the contours of the trigger, savoring the moment. Just as he was about to pull the trigger, he saw something move out of the corner of his eye, something on the surface of her skin. Intrigued, he paused to look at it. He could hardly believe his eyes, mesmerized by the spectacle of spontaneous physical transformation unfolding. Her skin began to loosen and fill up slowly, appearing to inflate, like a giant balloon filled with helium, only it was not helium, but the lifeblood of an entire species. It was not a new appendage, but a complex granulation, a granulation with clothes painted on by a camouflage artist's hand. It was a granulation like none he had ever seen. As it developed, it was moving and changing, filling, lifting, shaping, coloring, and defining the essence of something, someone, it couldn't be...it was...Captain Gregory!!

Shaken, he lowered the spear gun and backed up a step, a step back in time. Somewhere between the ebb and flow of the underground tide pools, between the exhalation of bubbles, and between the flicker of his torch light, Captain Gregory had come back to haunt him. Cranston just stood there in a trance, seemingly terrified, unable to act...

"NOW'S OUR CHANCE," SAID CAPTAIN GREGORY. As the figure of Captain Gregory got larger and larger, Dr. Bellwether and Claude were awestruck.

"Now listen carefully," said Captain Gregory. "Slowly place the gun in my right hand." They watched as the Queen concealed the gun in her arms, and surreptitiously placed it in Captain Gregory's right hand...

"Unbelievable," said Claude.

"Unreal," said Dr. Bellwether.

Captain Gregory ignored Dr. Bellwether and Claude. "Good, now put my right finger in the round hole by the handle." Captain Gregory's right finger was placed in the trigger.

All of a sudden, they could see Cranston jerk his head and snap out of his trance. By the look on his face, they all knew that Cranston had seen the gun. Cranston quickly raised his spear gun to fire...pulled the trigger...and nothing happened. He quickly lowered the spear gun to adjust the trigger mechanism.

"Oh, I can't bear to watch," said Dr. Bellwether, who watched anyway.

"Raise my right arm, now, quickly, while we still have a chance," said Captain Gregory. The arm raised. "Aim it at him." The gun raised a bit...

Cranston hurriedly raised his spear gun...

"PULL THE TRIGGER."

"What's that?"

Amidst all the shouting and yelling, Captain Gregory yelled, "The trigger. The trigger!!" Isabelle looked at him perplexed. "THE RING IN THE ROUND HOLE!!"

"OH THAT!!" she exclaimed. In what seemed like an eternity but was really only a split-instant, the gun went off...

The bullet fired through the water and hit Cranston right between the eyes, causing him to fall backward and pull the trigger on the spear gun, causing it to fire...

For an agonizingly long moment, no one said anything. "Are you hit, Isabelle?" asked Captain Gregory.

They all leaned forward, waiting for Isabelle's response. A few moments later, she smiled. "I am happy to report to you, Captain Gregory, that the spear missed."

"Hooray," shouted Claude.

"This *is* cause for celebration," said Dr. Bellwether.

"You did it," said Captain Gregory. "We owe it all to you, Isabelle."

Everyone was celebrating, except Jane, who was still staring at the display. "He's gone," she said. "Now I will never see him again."

The cheers and the shouts for joy stopped for the moment. "I'm so sorry," said Claude.

"Maybe he is still alive. Let's have a look," said Dr. Bellwether. "After all, I am a doctor."

"Yes, my dear," said Captain Gregory. "Maybe there is something yet that we can do."

They all looked up at the display and watched as the Queen slowly inched over to Richard Pearlman.

THE QUEEN TOUCHED RICHARD PEARLMAN'S hands, but they were cold, very cold. Then she checked his eyes and they were glazed over. His lips were puffy and blue. She changed her color to blue, too, to reflect a mood which had in moments gone from ecstasy to melancholy. She picked him up, cradled him in her arms, and gently stroked his face. After a while, she resolutely turned him over, brought him under her mantle and bit him on the back of the neck...

For a moment, she thought about carrying him back to her cave, when she realized that she had a greater responsibility, one that she had completely forgotten about in the heat of battle. Her babies! Oh, her babies!! She was a terrible mother not to have come back for them by now. She would never forgive herself if anything had happened to them. The Queen turned her head forward, and with all of her might, she jettisoned out of the entrance to the cave.

On her way, she noticed that the fishermen and the fisherman's boat were gone. They had abandoned their efforts apparently, and she hoped that they would never come back. The only thing remaining was the jagged end of a mast floating in the water, and the remnants of the tarpaulin trap they had set. As she surveyed the damage, she could hardly believe how many of her children had been scorched by the torch light and how many others had drown in the fisherman's nets. She had lost many of them, including most of the horn-rims, her favorite of the male children.

When she arrived, she found the baby queens in the corner of the cave, sheet-white with fear, too terrified to move. She moved in and cradled them under her mantle, gently caressing them and calming them down. It's okay. Mother's here. The bad men are gone. With a rapid formulation of complex chromatophore configurations mixed in with a highly structured stream of infrasignals, she asked them why they had come out of their hiding place.

So they related their story, with Victoria doing most of the communicating. After the bad men had left, they had gone out to see what was happening. Then they saw the crabs. Elizabeth crawled home but Victoria was caught.

But I told you to stay away from that trap... Their mother interrupted them in mid-story.

We know, we know, and we're sorry. But that's not all. Uncle Archie rescued us, but the fisherman speared him with that big sharp thing.

A harpoon?

Yes, we think so. The harpoon, that's what it was.

Oh no, don't tell me. Is he dead?

No, we don't think so.

Good. Thank heavens you're all safe.

Then you're not going to punish us?

I didn't say that.

Oh.

You'll have to wait and see.

Please, take your time mommy.

Very funny. Now try to go to sleep. You've had a rough day dears.

Safely back in her cave, the Queen held her children until they went to sleep. She then took them to their favorite nests in the hole in the wall and placed them gently in it.

Her troops, or what was left of them, brought her some scraps to eat. Hungry, exhausted, and sad, she gently caressed them and gratefully accepted the food. As she ate, she reflected on the day. In many respects, it had been a glorious day. They had vanquished the enemy. They had saved the Queen, the baby queens, and the colony. They had won, at last, but she could not take comfort in it. As she surveyed all of the devastation, she cried about her troops, who had laid down their lives to ensure the survival of the colony, and worried about her good and heroic friend Archie, who had been more than a friend to her these many years. There would be plenty of time to rejoice tomorrow. For tonight at least, there would be no joy, only sorrow...

After eating, she turned her attention to her children. She left the cave escorted by the troops. Slowly and methodically, one by one, with the help of her troops, she tended the wounded, some of whom were clinging to the cliffside, others who had crawled into holes, and others who were laying in the sea grass. And she cried for those she couldn't help.

After she was done tending to her children, she turned her attention to Richard Pearlman and that nasty fiend, Cranston. They would need to be removed from the cave before they attracted the scavengers, or worse yet, the sharks. She swam around to the back door of the cave, went in, and found them as she had left them. Richard Pearlman did not look much different than before. There was a large bullet hole in Cranston's forehead, and the frontal skull bone had caved in from the impact. As she stared at him, she felt no remorse, just wonderment at the horrible weapons that man had devised.

She stopped for a moment to consider what she would do with each of them. She decided that she would return Richard Pearlman to the Coast Guard boat with spear intact, so that the people in the boat would know that she had not hurt him, and so that she could convey to his friend Nancy what had happened.

Cranston, on the other hand, was a different matter. She decided that the only place under God's blue ocean that would be fitting for him was the tarpaulin trap. She would carefully lay out the tarpaulin and hook him to it, leaving him there like a large chunk of shark bait, until there would be nothing left but table scraps not fit for an indiscriminate hermit crab, a desirable end to a most undesirable fisherman. How delicious, she thought, that a fisherman would end up on the end of his own hook.

Twenty-Seven

The fishermen were gone, at long last. It was a day of thanksgiving and celebration, the Queen's first day of freedom since her children had been born. As she ventured out of the cave that morning, she surveyed the beautiful landscape around her, a landscape that only hours earlier had been tarnished by the presence of the fishermen. There was, thankfully, no trace of them now or of the final battle that was fought; the troops that had survived had seen to that.

The colors around her were bright and vivid, but she chose not to reflect them. Instead she reflected her innermost feelings, a vast, emotional landscape, a mountain with many peaks and valleys and variegated colors. Each of these were illustrated in a complex mosaic of bright and somber colors in ever-changing patterns reflecting the emotions taking place below the surface. There were many feelings: She felt joy and sorrow, anger and inner calm, hatred and love; but mostly she felt love, love for her children, love for Archie and all he had done, and love for her guests.

Most of all, she felt thankful that her colony had survived and that her guests had been able to stake out some small piece of happiness in their new world. Jane had been able to see her gentleman friend once more, and though she didn't know it yet, would likely see him soon, for he had just shown up on the patient rosters at the hospital. Claude had saved an endangered species, proving himself worthy of the Queen's finest esteem. Dr. Bellwether had redeemed his father's work, making discoveries beyond his wildest imagination. And Captain Gregory had been given what he had been waiting for all of his life, the command of a ship and the adventure of a lifetime.

She was thankful for all of these things, and oh yes, one more—her relationship with Captain Gregory, who had made the great matron of the sea, the commander-in-chief, and the Queen of the Cephalopods into a woman for the first time in her life. He had lit a slow-burning fuse that set off a tremendous blast, an independence-day firecracker of exploding passion, sparkling love, and booming joy that would forever change the way she felt about everything. As she thought about the marvelous chain of events that had brought her to this wonderful realization, it made her want to laugh, to cry, and to do it all over again.

The Queen chuckled inwardly. It had all started with a little sympathy for Jane, a desire for communication with the enemy, and the hope that somehow she could become friends. In her wildest dreams, she never suspected that the life rope that she had extended to Jane would become a biosubmarine for man, a sanctuary of sorts, and a floating military base. She would look forward to the day when the baby queens would be old enough to be told. And the people inside were her family, her human family, to whom she had built a bridge, not a bridge over water but a bridge from land to water, where the conveyance was interspecies communication and understanding.

Twenty-Eight

---⊕---

At the same time that the Queen was celebrating with her children, Isabelle was celebrating with her guests. There were many festivities, but that afternoon, Isabelle had anticipated none more than her rendezvous with Captain Gregory.

As she freshened up in the bathroom in the Captain's Quarters, she wondered whether Captain Gregory would find her negligee pleasing. There was no telling with men, so she had asked Jane to help her pick it out. After blotting her ruby red lipstick on a tissue, she put the finishing touches on her flowing auburn hair. She took a deep breath, opened the door, and slinked over to the bed where Captain Gregory was waiting with great anticipation. As she sat upon the bed, she could tell by the enraptured look in his eyes that he had not been disappointed.

Captain Gregory moved slowly toward her and kissed her once, as gently as the sea laps against the shore. She literally glowed, and he wondered if she too were bioluminescent. It didn't really matter. All that he knew was that he had been looking for the catch of a lifetime, and he had finally found her. She had been worth the wait. He moved in to kiss her again, but she slowly backed away.

"Do you love me?" she asked, batting her eyes ever so slowly.

"What do you mean?"

"What do you mean, what do I mean? I *mean*, do you love me? After all, we come from two different worlds."

"That's true, we do come from two different worlds. I come from the land, and you come from the sea."

"Yes, but do you love me?"

Captain Gregory smiled, realizing that she wasn't going to let him off the hook that easily. "Well, let me explain. All my life I've been looking for a special place, a place where the land and the sea meet, a place where the land and sea are one. I've studied nautical maps. I've plotted longitudes and latitudes until my eyes grew weary. But you can't find such a place on a map, and you can't get to it from here or there. There's only one place where the land and the sea meet, and that place is you Isabelle. And I can't think of any place I would rather be."

"Then you're saying you love me."

"I'm saying it's always been you."

"Then you do love me."

"All right already, I...I love you. There, I said it. Are you happy?"

"Yes," she said dreamily, moving closer to him.

"Good. Permission to kiss you, my Queen."

"Permission granted, Captain," said Isabelle, smiling.

Isabelle crawled in under the sheets. Captain Gregory playfully pulled the sheets over their heads, and Isabelle giggled as they came together in a passionate embrace.

Twenty-Nine

---⊕---

In the early evening, the Queen lay there watching her children celebrate as the currents gently bathed her. She was no longer thinking about what had been or what was; she was thinking only of what might be, what could be, or what would be. As the sun filtered in through the depths of the sea, for the first time in a long time she could see the sea horses playing in the sea grass not more than a few yards away, clams opening their gaping jaws to reveal silvery pearls at the base of their mouths, and multitudinous fish scavenging among the sea brush. She could also see a future for her and her children and, perhaps, for her children's children, which she wanted very much to live to see. It was no longer a future of solitude but one filled with the richness of discovery with her guests, and the opportunity to build a new world together inside her mind. Her guests were like colonists, but in a sense she, too, was a colonist exploring the world of human beings up close. The collision of her world and theirs had allowed them a unique opportunity to enjoy three worlds at once: land, sea, and space, the vast expanse of cerebral space.

As the Queen looked out into the gathering twilight, she pondered whether she and her guests were really alone or whether there was yet another new world out there. It had been so long since she had communicated long-distance with her species that she wondered if she knew how after all these years, and if any of her kind were left.

As she moved to higher ground, she thought she received a feint call, perhaps a call for help or just a call to see if anyone was out there. She waited a few minutes to see if the call would be repeated, but it was not. Perhaps she was imagining it, perhaps not. Perhaps it was her long-lost sister, perhaps not. But one thing was for certain. Unless it was her sister, she would be wary of sharing her little secret. Her species had become so warlike over the centuries that such a secret would be dangerous in the wrong arms. Tonight at least, she would not let such thoughts spoil her celebration with her children.

They continued their celebration long after the sunlight faded from the ocean and was replaced with the more romantic moonlight, a light that shone not only on her home but also in her mind, shining into the porthole in the Captain's Quarters, where Isabelle and Captain Gregory were making love at long last in a way she had never dreamed possible, until now. Oh, if she ever got in touch with her sister again, there would be plenty to talk about.